THE
HANGING
MOUNTAINS

Other Pyr® Titles
by Sean Williams

THE RESURRECTED MAN

THE CROOKED LETTER
BOOKS OF THE CATACLYSM: ONE

THE BLOOD DEBT
BOOKS OF THE CATACLYSM: TWO

THE HANGING MOUNTAINS

BOOKS OF THE CATACLYSM **THREE**

Sean Williams

Published 2007 by Pyr®, an imprint of Prometheus Books

Inquiries should be addressed to
Pyr
59 John Glenn Drive
Amherst, New York 14228–2197
VOICE: 716–691–0133, ext. 207
FAX: 716–564–2711
WWW.PYRSF.COM

11 10 09 08 07   5 4 3 2 1

Library of Congress Cataloging-in-Publication Data

Williams, Sean, 1967–
    The hanging mountains / Sean Williams. — 1st American hardcover ed.
        p. cm.
    Originally published: Sydney, Australia : Voyager, an imprint of HarperCollins, 2005.
    ISBN 978–1–59102–544–3 (alk. paper)
    I. Title.

PR9619.3.W667H36 2007
823'.914—dc22

                                                                                    2007007858

Printed in the United States of America on acid-free paper

To STEPHANIE SMITH,
for reacquainting me with magic

". . . serpent   ". . . ice   ". . . hand

". . . serpent	". . . ice	". . . hand
mountain	homunculus	flood
truncation	ferryboat	spoon
factotum	wax	poison
eldest	summit	vindication
homunculus	wound	fire
crystal	exile	homunculus
tomb	obstruction	forest
road	pollen	severence
metropolis . . ."	darkness . . ."	snake . . ."

Keywords Isolated from Seer Transcripts,
Year Thirteen of the Alcaide Dragan Braham

Grey clouds hung low like damp sheets over worn stone buildings and streets that smelt faintly of shit. Habryn Kail wrinkled his nose. He'd never much liked cities, and Laure only reinforced that opinion. While he could forgive much on account of its recent flooding, his patience only extended so far.

"That's an exorbitant price," he told the stall owner, "for a compass that doesn't work."

"None of them are working as they ought." The dirty, pale-skinned man pulled a sour face at the wavering needle on the dial before him. "I assure you, sir, that if north could be measured reliably, this fine piece would do the job better than any other."

The stall owner came out from his tent to pursue the sale, but Kail waved him away. Kail wasn't interested in compasses; there were other, more reliable means of maintaining a course. Food, however, he did require, along with a large hooded cloak. And a camel, if he could find one in his price range likely to live out the week. Unfortunately, Laure wasn't Tintenbar, where traders from all over the Interior gathered to meet their counterparts on the far side of the Divide. No need went unfulfilled in those markets and, for an assiduous purchaser, obtaining anything of quality was not an issue. Laure's isolation, however, meant that quality cost money—money he didn't have. He would have to work hard at stretching what he did have to fully provide for the journey ahead.

At least, he thought wryly, water wasn't likely to be a problem. Within days of the flood that had filled the Divide from side to side, ominous clouds had swept in from the east, bringing with them rain unseen in those parts for generations. The Laureans had quickly familiarised themselves with the phenomenon; where once they might have

7

danced in the streets at every drop, now they muttered about flooding and cursed the threatening sky.

Atop their slender poles, the yadachi sat like crimson-plumaged, long-tailed birds, taking the measure of the weather in absolute silence. What they thought of it, Kail couldn't imagine. He didn't ask, either. His visit to Laure wasn't a social one. Once he had his supplies, he would be on his way.

A camel herder relented under heavy coercion and sold him a barely adequate old nag for more than half the money he had. Half of the remainder went on the cloak. By the time he had filled his new saddlebags with dried meat, flat bread, and salted plums—a guilty pleasure he always indulged on long overland trips—he had barely a coin left in his purse.

A pawnbroker occupied one corner of the market, his grubby stall cluttered with the detritus of failed dreams and addictions. Kail briefly considered divesting himself of the one truly valuable item remaining in his possession. In the course of asking after his former companions as he went about his business, he had learned that the Surveyor Abi Van Haasteren was organising an expedition back to the ruined city known as the Aad on the other side of the Divide, there to seek a marvellous, opalescent relic called the Caduceus. One piece of the Caduceus wasn't with the others, because it currently rested in a cloth bag suspended from a thong around Kail's neck. He knew Van Haasteren would want it, to complete the artefact, so it was bound to fetch a fair price.

A fear that he might regret too hasty a decision made him hold on to it. The Goddess only knew when he might need the money more than he did now, or if he might need something to barter with the Stone Mages—or how much attention he might draw to himself in the process of selling it . . .

"You've got a well-travelled face," called a withered old seer as Kail stood, with one hand on the camel's harness, running through a mental checklist to make sure he hadn't forgotten anything. Clad in a dusty shawl that might once have been brilliant blue and red, the seer clutched shaking hands in her lap and wore brass rings on hooked toes. "Why not let me tell you what lies on the road ahead?"

Kail almost didn't bother responding. Market seers were as likely to possess actual talent as the jewellery in the next stall actual gems.

"If you can tell me what lies behind me, old mother," he said, "then maybe you can tell me what's ahead."

"A test, eh?" The seer cackled heartily, exposing more gaps than teeth. "It doesn't work like that, son. It's as hard to look into the past as the future, and few people will pay me to do that. They usually don't like what they learn."

That was an odd comment. Intrigued, he led the camel closer. It snorted and resentfully butted his shoulder.

He ignored it. "Why wouldn't they like it?"

"Some say the future is a book we haven't read yet." The old woman appraised him with one eye as he approached, the other screwed shut as though dazzled by a bright light. "The past is a book too, but not one we've read. It's one we've *written*. That's why I don't like telling the past. People object to hearing that their book contains lies of their own devising—lies they tell themselves to make sense of things, to make it all bearable, to go on living. No one likes being caught out in a lie, do they?"

He smiled. Talented or not, she was no fool. "No, they don't."

"People lie about the future, too," she said, squinting even harder, "calling it hope or faith. I'm willing to bet I can't catch you out at that. A pragmatist like you lives in the moment. He knows that life is just a series of moments, one after the other. They come and go like beads on a string. If the string ever breaks you'll be lost, and—ah!" She leaned back with her mouth open in triumph. "Yes! Got you."

"What do you mean?" he asked, although he knew full well. He'd felt his face tighten at her comment about being lost, and she—trained charlatan and observer of faces—had spotted the slip.

"You're on a journey. A long one." Her expression sobered. "It may not be the one you originally set out on, and your destination might not be the one you hope for. But a journey it is, and you will be changed by it in ways you don't expect." She paused. "Pull up a seat, son. Let's talk."

A light rain had started outside the canvas covering of her stall. The weather didn't faze him, but it did unsettle the camel. His curiosity pricked, Kail tied the restless beast to a post and folded himself into the seat opposite the woman. Reaching into his purse, he produced a coin and put it on the table between them.

She waved it away. "Pay me afterwards. For now, just give me your left hand."

Kail did so, and she took it in both of hers. The skin of her fingers was rough with calluses as they explored his palm. Her eyes flickered shut.

He felt a tingle not dissimilar to pins and needles shoot up his arm. He almost pulled away, recognising the feeling—she was Taking from him!—but curiosity held him still. If she genuinely had some facility with the Change, perhaps her other claims weren't completely false.

"You said I was on a journey," he prompted, "a journey that would change me."

"No great revelation there. Anyone could tell that much from your clothes. And journeys always change us, otherwise there'd be no point going on them." Her attention wandered as though she was concentrating on something distant and hard to make out. "Your home lies far from here," she went on, and he felt the tingle again. "The sea calls you, but you don't hear it. The ones you serve have lost your respect. You follow them no longer. You're seeking your own path. You—" She stopped. A sudden, indrawn breath hissed between her teeth. "You have been touched by darkness. A darkness I cannot see through. Not death. Not the Void. The darkness of—of ending. The ending of all things. I cannot—"

A deep menacing hum rose up as though an invisible cloud of bees was swarming around them.

She pulled free of him and clutched her hands to her chest.

"What's wrong?" he asked, shaken by her reaction.

"I don't want to see," she said, shaking her head. Her voice quavered. "It's too close!"

"*What's* too close?"

"The darkness!" She took a deep, shaky breath. "I've seen it before, but never so near. Your shadow stretches before you, blacker than night. You're walking to the end of the world and do not know it."

"Where?" he asked. "How?"

She opened her eyes slowly, painfully. "That you'll have to find out for yourself. I can't see it. It is utterly beyond my ken."

Kail wanted to press her for more information, but he took pity on her. She seemed abruptly to be much older now than earlier, and weary with it. Her gaze wouldn't meet his.

"My apologies," he said, adding another coin to the one already sitting on the table. "I didn't mean to burden you."

"That is so often the way, son."

He stood. The rain hadn't eased. It had strengthened, if anything, falling in hot, heavy waves over the market stalls. People scurried for shelter and covered their wares. The drenched camel snorted and stamped its feet.

"Blood will run like water," the seer whispered, her voice so soft he could barely hear it over the downpour. "Blood will run like water ere the end comes."

Chilled despite the dense, humid air, Kail took his leave of her and made haste from the city.

Hungrily, in the distance, a wolf howled.

The twins shivered.

Do you think—? Hadrian started to say.

Best not to, his brother cut him off.

A clatter of stones made them jump. Their connection to the world was growing stronger every day, but details remained sketchy beyond a few metres of their unusual body. Their four legs spread wide, they scanned the area around the campsite for any sign of trouble. It seemed to them that the light had dimmed, but whether that was because of cloud cover or nightfall they couldn't tell. Far-off sounds might have been rain falling or wind sweeping across the barren earth outside their shelter. They were fairly certain it wasn't anything more sinister than that.

The wolf's call was a little closer this time.

Hadrian shivered and the Homunculus skin containing him and his brother rippled. Set up under a stone slab as large as a three-storey building, their campsite offered protection on just two sides. Despite this, Kail had assured them they would be safe, that no one would dare bother them, and they had accepted the Sky Warden's assurance readily enough. Nothing had prepared them for the sound of a wolf.

I don't feel secure here.

Seth agreed. *We could move, I suppose—but where to?*

Keep on going, Hadrian suggested. *Northeast. Kail would follow us. He knows how to.*

We'd be more vulnerable out there than we are here.

Do you really think if we stay still and don't move, it'll just go away?

Both Seth and Hadrian recovered the same memory at exactly the same moment. Their minds had been so intimately entangled in the Void that they had started thinking as one. Independently yet together, they reached for the words Pukje had spoken to them, a hundred lifetimes ago: *Wolves know how to wait.*

Neither of them knew how much credence to give that particular statement. But the fear was very real, and so was their ignorance; they understood too little about the world as it existed now. Talking to their guide only made the situation worse.

The sound of rattling rock grew louder. They pulled further into the shadows, instinctively raising their arms to present a more threatening figure. Their legs tensed to run.

"It's only me," called a familiar voice.

A large shape pressing out of the gloomy myopia surrounding them resolved into Habryn Kail leading a camel under the overhang.

"We weren't sure," said Hadrian, letting down his guard. "We didn't know *what* you were."

Seth remained as taut as a bowstring. "Did anyone follow you here?"

"If they did, they're a better tracker than I am."

"You were gone a long time," said Hadrian.

"I had a lot to do." The rangy, tall man settled the dripping camel and eased himself down to a squatting position. His dark skin blended almost perfectly with the shadows. "I found out that Marmion and the others have gone upriver along the Divide looking for the cause of the flood and the man'kin migration. And you, I presume. They'd be fools to presume you dead without evidence."

"Are they still hunting us?" asked Seth.

"Not actively. They have no trail, and no hope of finding one. The flood has proved a stroke of good fortune for you."

Seth finally began to relax, allowing the Homunculus's many-limbed shape to move. Together they sat and addressed the tracker face to face.

"How are they travelling?" asked Hadrian.

"That's the interesting thing. Our maps become increasingly unreliable the further east you head, so overland journeys can be dangerous and slow. Given the resources of the Strand, if I was still with them I would have suggested following the course of the Divide when the initial turbulence of the flood died down—but Laure doesn't have boats, and probably lacks the infrastructure to make one in a hurry. So I assumed that Marmion had taken the hard road and wouldn't be far ahead of us."

Kail's words came with an unfamiliar bafflement, as though for once the long-limbed tracker's instincts had led him astray.

"Tell us," said Seth.

"Three days after the flood, the Engineers in the expedition found the skeleton of a hullfish in the torrent. They hauled it ashore, cleaned it, and tested its fitness. Apart from a couple of minor breaches, it held water. They must have worked amazingly fast to get it ready, but that's how they're travelling; exactly how I least expected them to."

"Hullfish?" asked Hadrian.

"Sometimes called an ivory whale." The tracker adopted a cautious expression they had come to recognise. "You don't know what that is?"

The Homunculus's head shook as both twins indicated their ignorance.

"It's a beast normally found in the deep ocean. Ten, twenty metres long, and almost impossible to kill because of their thick, bony hide. The carcasses are airtight, so they occasionally drift ashore when they die. Five of the largest ever found became *Os*, the Alcaide's ship of bone. You've never heard of that, either? Well, you only need to know that one hullfish is enough to make a perfectly serviceable vessel. Especially with the Change strong in the Divide."

The twins struggled with the explanation. Kail obviously thought it made sense, and they supposed it did, in a way. There had been minds to talk with in the Void—desperate, dwindling things that had told stories among themselves in order to prolong existence before the endless hum ground them down. The twins had sometimes moved among them, and learned of the world outside through those stories. Their memories were confused, though; it was sometimes hard to disentangle the distant past from the stories of the Lost Minds after an eternity of sensory deprivation.

The twins remembered skyscrapers and a world overflowing with people. They remembered machines and power grids and television and ballpoint pens. Now the world's inhabitants had buggies and airships and the Change. The Lost Minds had told of empty ruins and depopulated wastes, and spoken of cities as fearful, haunted places.

It seemed utterly preposterous to the twins that the corpse of a fish as large as a whale could be fashioned into a ship, but Seth remembered an equally preposterous vessel called *Hantu Penyardin*—and Hadrian had used the Change to fashion a pencil into a spear in order to kill the energuman, Volker Lascowicz. They could accept strangeness as fact if they had to. As far as they knew, Kail had no reason to lie.

"Could we travel that way?" they asked. "Upriver?"

Kail shook his head. "Even if we could find another hullfish, I couldn't make a ship of it on my own, not in time. No, we're best sticking to the original plan: I ride the camel while you walk alongside, disguised under the cloak. That way, we'll be slow but steady. And we won't have to worry about what the flood's left in its wake."

"What do you mean?" asked Hadrian.

"Well, the Divide was home, or prison, to more than just man'kin. And sometimes a burial ground for creatures that might not be completely dead, even now. The water will stir all manner of things from their rest."

Kail stood and went to the camel. He opened a saddlebag and took out a handful of small, nutlike objects. He picked at them, flicking seeds out into the darkness, and paced as he talked.

"I worry about the others. They're rushing into a situation for which they're ill prepared. I know you've tried to explain what's growing up there in the mountains, but I still don't entirely understand what it is. It's dark and dangerous, you say, and it eats people. It comes from before the Cataclysm and isn't really part of our world. If I called Marmion with this information, he'd think me mad—and then he *would* be hunting you again, because he would have good reason to. So I can't tell him that he's putting himself and the others in danger—and I don't like that."

The twins let him think aloud. Their thoughts were full of dying cities and worlds rent asunder, of billions dead and more to come.

"They're too far ahead for us to catch up, even if we walk our mount into the ground," the tracker said. "We can't steal a buggy because it won't work with you aboard. There's no point in calling Shilly or Sal, since Marmion won't believe them either, not without evidence. We don't have any other options that I can see, but to walk. Do you have any suggestions?"

Features blurred in the Homunculus's face as the twins shook their heads.

Kail nodded. "I've promised to get you to the mountains so you can deal with this thing, whatever it is. My path and my conscience are clear. I just wish there was more I could do to help the others. There has been, as you said, enough death already."

The howl of a wolf cut the air like a knife.

"What?" asked Kail, head snapping around as the twins jumped in fright. "What is it?"

"Didn't you hear it?" asked Hadrian.

"Hear what?" The tracker's brows crinkled.

Kail didn't hear it, said Seth, his internal voice brittle. *We're not imagining it, are we?*

Perhaps he can't *hear it.*

It's just for us, then? A warning?

Or a threat, said Hadrian. Another thought struck him. *Perhaps the time isn't quite right yet.*

For what?

For the gloves to come off.

"We think we should get moving," they told Kail. "Standing still for too long probably isn't a good idea."

"Want to explain why?"

Hadrian tried to explain. "There might be people out there—"

"Things," Seth added.

"—who remember us and the way the world used to be. Some of them good, some of them . . . less so. I'm not sure they count as evil, but they don't always want the same thing as us. And we hurt them, a long time ago."

Kail studied their strange black features for a long moment. "You're not talking about this Yod creature. This is something else entirely."

"Yes."

"An ally of Yod's?"

"No." Hadrian's memories of Volker Lascowicz's brutal death and the snarling of Upuaut, the demonlike creature that had inhabited him, were painfully clear to both of them. "Not an ally, but just as deadly."

Kail nodded wearily. "Then I guess we need to get moving—and talking. The more you tell me, the more I'm going to understand. And the more I understand, the better I'm going to be able to keep us out of trouble."

"We're trying," the twins said. "We really are trying."

"I know," said the tracker, pulling a thick cotton cloak out of a pack and holding it up for them to slip into, two arms into each sleeve. "Believe me, so am I."

THE SERPENT

"Things in nature change of their own accord. There is no mind in the flow of a river or the grasping of a tree. There is, simply, the Change. Yet minds as sharp as ours once believed in gods of nature, seeing the need for design where nature alone is sufficient. They could not grasp that mind can ride the crest of the wave of nature without itself driving the wave. A single breaking wave is the summation of an entire ocean and all the wind that blows across it; in one moment, it is more than a mind will ever be throughout a lifetime."
THE BOOK OF TOWERS, EXEGESIS 1:7

S kender saw it first, for no other reason than his face happened to be closest to the water. With his body bent over the boneship's rough milky-white side and a rope firmly tied around his waist, he had little opportunity to look at anything other than the choppy, foaming water, relatively clear of debris since the flood eleven days earlier, but still an impenetrable muddy brown. He had no idea how deep it was, and preferred not to think too hard about that. He had no knowledge of sailing, let alone of large bodies of water in general. All he knew was that with every wave the boneship lurched from side to side and sent his stomach surging with it. His face burned when he thought of Chu, whose sense of balance had in no way rebelled at this mistreatment and whose sympathy had, to date, consisted of slapping him on the back and telling him, unhelpfully, that he couldn't puke forever. He wasn't so sure about that. The nausea showed no sign of abating. He wondered if he would ever eat again.

His only consolation was the memory of Gwil Flintham taking one look at the vessel bobbing precariously on more water than he had seen in his entire life, and swearing that he would never, ever set foot on it. If Skender had thought like that, he wouldn't have been feeling so miserable, but at the same time he would have never seen anything, never met Sal and Shilly, and never *flown*.

Far above, riding the turbulent thermals rising from the surface of the flooded Divide, Chu glided as freely as a bird under the warm afternoon sun. Dark, crumbling cliffs loomed on either side of the surging water and there were few places for the ship to dock. The boneship's crew had no way to see what was ahead, so Chu had volunteered to reconnoitre the shorelines upriver. Only her word, and the shadow of the Hanging Mountains growing ever-larger, reassured them that they were actually getting anywhere.

Skender tried his best to focus on the distant peaks—vast, immoveable, and shrouded in permanent cloud—rather than the rocking, rolling boneship and the water beneath.

Goddess, he thought, feeling as though he might throw up yet again. *If you're going to kill me, do it now!*

At that moment, something glassy slid through the water not a metre from his nose. It resembled ice but moved with a sinuous muscularity that made him think of a lizard or a snake. Its surface was carved with scales as perfectly hexagonal as honeycomb and worn with age. He froze in shock. One metre glided by, then two, before Skender thought to sound the alarm.

He hauled himself back into the boat, unable to take his eyes off the thing in the water below. It was still uncoiling. How long *was* it? He turned to shout a warning to where Marmion stood at the bow, bandaged arm held protectively to his chest, but the boneship shifted violently under him and he found himself dumped hard on his backside instead.

Everything went crazy. The boneship shook and rattled. "Whirlpool!" the cry went up; a warden ran by, leather-bound boot narrowly missing Skender's face; spray flew over the bows. Skender skidded from side to side across the slippery deck, unable to find purchase long enough to stand. Bilge water soaked him from head to foot.

Distantly, he felt a thunderhead of the Change building as the wardens concentrated on steadying the ship. Sal was in that blend of wills, and Highson Sparre, bolstering the reservoir stored in the hull of the boneship itself. Skender cursed himself, told himself to get his shit together and *stand up*. The rope around his waist tangled in his legs and he went down again.

A large hand grabbed the neck of his robes and hauled him to his feet. Startled, he windmilled and kicked frantically until his feet found something approaching a grip on the deck. The hand let go, and he clutched the tunic of the person who had rescued him. Kemp's broad, pale face beamed down at him, entirely too amused.

"Here." The albino pressed the rope into his hands. "Hold this and try to stay out of trouble."

Kemp went to move off, but Skender pulled him back. "Tell Marmion. This isn't just a current. There's something else. It—"

The boneship tipped under them, throwing more people than just Skender off his feet. Kemp went sprawling, and so did half the wardens.

"Hold tight!" bellowed Marmion from his position at the prow. "Concentrate! We'll ride it out!"

Skender couldn't blame him for thinking it would be that simple. This wasn't the first patch of restless water they had encountered on their journey; nor was it likely to be their last. The Divide was a nightmare of capricious currents and barely navigable hazards.

Gripping the rope tightly with both hands, Skender managed to bring himself vaguely upright again. He didn't stop to wonder at the disappearance of his nausea. In the face of a concrete threat, he didn't have time to be sick.

Another powerful jolt sent people flying in all directions. A cry of pain testified that someone had gashed themselves on a bony protuberance. The bilge took on a reddish tinge.

"Listen to me," shouted Skender over the cries of alarm. "Something in the water is trying to capsize us!"

Marmion, poised at the front of the boneship, glanced at him, then at the churning water ahead. Skender couldn't tell what he saw, but he raised his bandaged arm above his head and waved for attention.

"Sal! Up here!"

Wardens parted for Sal as he left the tiller and moved forward. Skender couldn't make out the words he and Marmion exchanged. The boneship shook again, and Skender hoped the crunching sound he heard wasn't bone breaking. Hullfish owed their buoyancy to bubbles of air trapped in their featherweight bones. If the attacker shattered enough of them, the boneship would sink.

Skender broke out in goosebumps, chilled by more than just the water. Water-sickness and giant snakes were bad enough; not being able to swim capped off the situation beautifully.

Marmion and Sal finished their hasty consultation. Nodding, they drew apart. Marmion called for his wardens to cluster around him. They made furious plans as the boat shook beneath them. Skender felt the flow of Change begin to shift into a new configuration.

Wind alone was insufficient to propel the boneship against the incessant current pouring down from the mountains. They relied on the efforts of the wardens to move anywhere but backwards. Following Marmion's instructions, the steady acceleration that had carried them from Laure suddenly ebbed. Skender felt the boat give itself completely to the current and begin to float downstream.

The mental effort made by the wardens didn't ease off, however. It was in fact redoubled. Skender looked around, saw their eyes closed in concentration. Some muttered words under their breath; some leaned with palms spread flat against the yellowish bone; others traced complex geometric shapes in the air with their fingers—employing whatever means suited them best to focus on their common purpose.

A handful of the shapes Skender recognised; he had glimpsed them in books and, once seen, never forgotten them. A sign for *mastery over water* came and went, followed by one controlling the flow of heat. A cloud of steam rose up from the surface of the boneship when Sal lent his wild talent to the charm, giving Skender a hot flush.

A new crunching sound arose from outside the boat. Not bone this time, but ice. The boat spun through a slurry of half-frozen water that cooled even further as the charm stole its warmth and sent it billowing in clouds to the sky. The bone deck shuddered underfoot, and Skender clutched the rope, wide-eyed.

Suddenly all was quiet. The boneship sat with its prow slightly upraised in a miniature iceberg that bobbed and spun gently on the surface of the Divide. The snake had been locked in the ice, trapped in midsqueeze.

"Good work," said Marmion into the uncanny quiet. Apart from the sound of water lapping against the ice and people regaining their footing, the silence was complete. "Now, let's take a look at what we're dealing with."

Wardens spread out around the edge of the boneship and peered carefully over. Kemp joined them, and so did Shilly, emerging from the hollow cavity at the heart of the bony hull, leaning heavily on her walking stick. She looked as startled as Skender felt. He had no intention of going any closer to the edge than he absolutely had to.

"Can you see it?" called one of the wardens.

"There's something over here," someone else replied.

"And here," said another from the far side of the boneship.

Skender pictured long, pythonlike coils entwined around the ship, frozen solid in the act of crushing it.

"What *is* this thing?" he asked.

"I've never seen anything like it before," said Highson, standing at the tiller Sal had earlier abandoned.

"Want me to cut off a piece?" suggested Kemp, raising one leg to hop over the side of the boat.

Ice cracked and the boneship lurched. Kemp almost tipped out as one coil of the frozen serpent, then another, broke free of the ice. Hands clutched at Kemp and strained to pull his bulk back to safety. More cracking sounds came from all around the boat. Icy, translucent coils whipped and writhed. Cold splinters and cries of alarm filled the air.

The head of the snake appeared over the bows, a conelike, tapering affair boasting numerous writhing whiskers that shook itself free of the last of the ice with an uncannily doglike motion. Skender could see no eyes or nostrils—not even a mouth—but he had no doubt that it could see *them*. The whiskered head stabbed down at the boneship, narrowly missing Marmion. It emitted a keening, hissing noise more piercing than a whistle as it pulled back into the air.

The boat lurched free of the short-lived iceberg. Kemp had almost made it aboard, but slipped back as the boat tipped under him. Wardens pulled at his arms. A glassy coil flailed over Skender's head, and he ducked barely in time. Remembering his despairing death wish, he hastily retracted it. The last thing he wanted was to be killed by a monster.

The head rose up to strike. Sal pushed forward, mouth set in a determined line. The air crackled around him, ripe with wild talent. Shards of ice flashed into vapour where he stepped.

The snake sensed him and its screeching grew louder. It swayed to triangulate on its intended victim then lunged downwards.

Sal blocked the strike with his arms crossed in front of his face. The snakehead ricocheted away and, with a piercing snarl, struck at Kemp instead, impaling him on its whiskers as though they were the spikes of a mace. Kemp roared with pain and would have been thrown from the boneship entirely but for the wardens holding him fast.

The snakehead pulled free, dripping blood from its deadly whiskers. Kemp fell limp. Sal leapt over him and caught the snake about its throat. Although unable to get his fingers completely around the slippery body, the Change made up for what he physically lacked. With a loud cry, he wrenched it down and smashed its head against the boat's bony bulwarks.

A silent concussion pushed Skender off his feet and turned the day momentarily dark. The boneship skidded sideways, missing the cliff on the starboard side by the smallest of margins. With one startled squawk, the snake shattered into a cloud of fine sand and blew away on the wind.

Skender blinked dust from his eyes and hurried with Shilly to where Kemp lay on the rocking deck. The albino bled profusely from two wounds: one to his abdomen and the other to his thigh. Sal had dropped like a stone after killing the snake and lay next to him, unmoving. Shilly brushed long, mousy hair out of her lover's eyes and made sure he was breathing.

"Is he—?" Skender didn't know how to finish the question.

"He's still with us," she said. Her brown eyes brimmed over with concern. "He'd never go that far again."

Skender didn't hide his relief. Every Change-worker knew that the Void Beneath awaited those who took too much of the Change at once. That Sal had drawn so deeply as to knock himself out was worrying, but Skender believed Shilly when she indicated that Sal would recover. She knew Sal better than anyone, even Sal himself.

Kemp was a different question. The healer among the wardens, Rosevear, had stooped to examine him. A young man with dark skin and thick, curly hair, he was already sweating from exertion. "The wounds are very deep," he said. "We need to stop him bleeding before I can do anything else."

Rosevear Took from three of his colleagues to staunch the flow of crimson from Kemp's side. Afterwards, the albino looked even paler than usual. Skender sat by him, wishing there was something constructive he could do. Remembering the albino coming to his aid during the attack of the snake, a new sickness filled Skender's stomach.

Rosevear's will moved deep in Kemp's wound. A glassy shard as long and sharp as a toothpick emerged from his side and fell to the deck with a faint, almost musical sound. Marmion, closely watching the healer's ministrations, ground the fragment underfoot.

"Please, give me space," Rosevear requested, leaning back on his heels and breathing heavily. His hands were bloody. "A steady surface to work on would help, too."

"Understood." Marmion stepped back and waved at the wing circling anxiously above. "I'll see what I can do about that."

At his signal, Chu dropped like a stone, tilting her wing and alighting at the last minute on the broad deck. A breath of air rippled across the boneship. Wardens took the weight of the wing from Chu's back as she unclipped her harness and hurried forward, brow wrinkled with concern.

"Skender, what happened? I couldn't see clearly from the air."

"It's Kemp," Skender explained. "He's been injured."

"Kemp? Goddess." For the first time, she seemed to notice the albino splayed on the deck. A complicated range of emotions played across her face. "Will he be all right? What can I do to help?"

"Tell us there's somewhere to dock not far ahead of here," said Marmion, "or at least somewhere to shelter from the current."

She nodded. "There's a subsidence just around the bend. I don't know how stable it is, but it could give you what you need."

"Good. Thank you." Marmion snapped orders to those wardens not assisting Rosevear. They moved off to rebuild the charm that propelled the boneship upstream while Rosevear worked on Kemp.

"*You're* okay, then?" Chu asked Skender, her deep, half-moon eyes studying his face closely. "When Marmion called me down, I thought—" She hesitated, seemed to gather herself. "Well, I didn't know what to think. That you'd puked your guts right out in all the excitement, maybe. I mean, this is the longest I've seen you upright in days. Could you *finally* be empty?"

She clapped him on the back, and went off to collapse her wing.

All right, Goddess, he thought with a wince. *I've changed my mind— but this time I'm sure of it. You forget one little thing, and you pay and pay and pay. Spare me this torture!*

If anyone heard him, Goddess or otherwise, no answer came.

Shilly barely noticed the exchange between Skender and Chu as she tended to Sal. Everything had happened so quickly: the turbulence, which she had learned to endure by staying well out of the way, then Skender's cry that there was more to it than simply crosscurrents. By the time she had emerged, Marmion had frozen the snake and solved the problem—or so it had seemed.

She had been too slow to help Sal when he'd rushed forward to save Kemp. Frightened, she hadn't been able to show him how to refine the charm he'd used against the snake. What he lacked in subtlety he had made up for with sheer grunt, turning a simple rock-crushing mnemonic into a powerful weapon. As a result, he lay unconscious before her, and there was nothing she could do about it.

His reservoir of the Change was empty. There was no strength left in him on which she could call to help him return. She would just have to be patient, to let him come back to her in his own time.

Make it soon, Sayed, my love, she whispered in her mind, using his heart-name. *Make it soon.*

The warmth of the afternoon sun was fading. The days became colder the deeper the boneship travelled in the foothills of the Hanging Mountains, but the nights weren't as bitter as they could be in the desert. Shilly liked the crisp, moist air in the mornings. It helped her wake up, when she had to.

Beside her, Rosevear worked hard to save Kemp's life. He moved quickly, assuredly, binding the less-serious gash in Kemp's massive thigh with thick cloth bandages and concentrating primarily on the stomach wound. His expression was grim.

"He's going to be okay, isn't he?" she asked.

"I'm not sure." Rosevear glanced at her midministration. "I'll need to watch him closely. If the poison spreads, there might be nothing I can do."

Poison? she wanted to echo, numbly. The sides of her mouth turned down at the thought that Kemp might die. She had known him since her childhood in Fundelry. Just moments ago he had been strong and lively. That he could be so suddenly lost to them cast everything around her in a new light. She felt as though the bottom had dropped out of the boneship and they were falling free.

Beneath her, the vessel surged ahead, seeking the shelter Chu had promised. The sun swung in the sky as Marmion ordered the course changed. Highson, Sal's natural father, still recovering from his pursuit of the Homunculus but determined to contribute in any way he could, swung the tiller hard to port. The rudder acted more on the Change contained within the boat than the water surrounding it, glowing a faint pearly white at night and leaving behind a trail of tiny bubbles during the day. She had watched the tiller's attachment to the boneship in Laure, and wondered how so delicate a filigree of threads and filaments could possibly help the ship stay on course. Wardens used an entirely different watercraft than the fishers she had known in Fundelry.

Voices called. She leaned over the bulwarks to look at the river below. The Divide wall closest to the boneship had subsided under the raging torrent of the flood, spilling boulders into the water. Some had been carried away in the initial rush; enough remained to form a bulky spit that even now, days later, the water continued to shape. The relatively calm space behind its jagged leading edge gathered sediments and debris in growing mounds. Scrapes and bumps on the underside of the boneship made Shilly nervous, thinking that perhaps creatures worse than the snake were trying to get in. Nothing else happened, however, and her fear abated.

"There." Marmion pointed with his one remaining hand at a suitable mooring spot, and Highson guided them in. Two wardens leapt the closing gap and tied ropes to secure-looking stones, anchoring the boneship in place. Sheltered from the relentless current the boneship became, for once, mercifully still. While not as sensitive to water-sickness as Skender, Shilly had no love for the endless rolling of the deck underfoot. Sleep usually came with difficulty, even in the dark rounded cavities of the boat's hollow interior which reminded her of the underground workshop she and Sal called home, far away. She would be glad when they returned to dry land.

"Wh—" Sal stirred on her lap. His eyes fluttered. "What—?"

"Easy." She stroked his face to soothe him. "Everything's all right. The snake is gone. You don't have to worry about that any more."

"But . . ." He tried to sit up. She helped him turn and lean into her, so that his head rested heavily on her breast. He took in the boulders and the sundered yellow cliff face looming over them. "Where are we? How long was I out?"

"An hour or less. We're stopping so Rosevear can work on Kemp."

Finally he took in what he hadn't, perhaps, wanted to see. Shilly felt him trying to reach out to take the measure of Kemp's injury through the Change, but he was still too weak. She explained what she knew: that the injury was deep but not fatal, depending on how far the poison from the snake's crystal barbs had travelled. Much would hinge on the coming moments, as Rosevear worked hard to secure what advantage he could over the spreading sickness.

They had a clear view of Kemp's face and upper chest as the wardens worked on him. His rib cage rose and fell reassuringly with every breath, but the skin of his face, so pale it bordered on transparent, hung loosely from his cheeks. Half-open eyelids showed only white. What little colour he had had was utterly drained away.

Skender came to check on Kemp's progress, leaning with a worried expression over Rosevear's shoulder.

"It's my fault," he said. "If I'd sounded the alarm sooner—"

"Don't," said Sal. "If I'd killed the snake sooner, or the wardens had frozen the snake more tightly, or Kemp hadn't tried to take a piece off it, then maybe things would've been different. Or they might have been exactly the same. There's no point blaming anyone, including yourself."

Skender nodded, but didn't seem reassured. When Rosevear irritably brushed him away, he swung over the edge of the boneship to explore the rocky spit against which the boat had moored. Several of the wardens were already climbing the uneven slope up to the top of the cliff, there to take the mission's bearings and estimate the distance they had travelled. Shilly wondered what they would see.

When the Divide and the Hanging Mountains were perfectly in line, she made out a glimpse of green below the ever-present pall of clouds ahead. Chu's talk of fog forests and balloon cities smacked of fable, not fact—yet the hint of verdancy remained, suggestive and alluring. In all Shilly's life she had never seen vegetation thicker than low saltbush.

She wasn't about to leave Sal's side to explore with the others. Even when he stirred and successfully managed to stand up on his own, she didn't suggest they move far. He needed to recuperate.

"What were you doing when the snake hit?" he asked her as she led him by the arm into the boat's central cavities. Smooth bubbles of bone opened up around them, providing a cabin large enough for six people to lie comfortably beside the supplies purchased in Laure. "Were you asleep?"

Shilly shook her head. She had been awake since midmorning. He lay down on the thin mattress at the rear of the space and she showed him what she had been working on, distracting herself from thinking about Kemp.

"The dream again, Carah?" he asked, examining the sketches she had made. Page after page of intricate scribbling; vain attempts to capture the complexity of the patterns she saw in her mind.

"It won't let me go," she said. "Always the same things: sand and something buried; a pattern I'm supposed to transcribe; being outside my body, looking at myself. I think it's important, if I could only work out why."

"Have you talked to Tom about it?"

She shook her head. Since the flood, she had avoided the young seer for fear of what he might tell her. Already, the dream that he had revealed to her in Fundelry was beginning to come true: *You and I were riding a ship of bone up the side of a mountain . . .* The rest, about frozen caves and the end of the world, didn't bear thinking about any sooner than she had to.

"This doesn't feel like prophecy," she said. "I'm not seeing what's going to happen, but something that *needs* to happen, I think."

"Could it be a message?"

"Who from?" She frowned. "The only person I can think of is Habryn Kail, if he's still alive—but if he had something important he needed me to know, he could just tell me outright."

"*Could,* yes."

She dropped her chin to her chest. Thoughts of Kail provoked equal parts sadness and anger in her. The nephew of Lodo, her first teacher and guardian, the tracker would have been the closest thing to family she might have had, had he only revealed himself to her before being swept away by the flood.

"You saw through his eyes, at the end," she said to Sal. "If you'd learned something through him, or felt something, you wouldn't keep me in the dark. Would you?"

"Of course not," he said instantly.

And she could tell that he wasn't telling her the whole truth.

She sighed. What was it about Sal and Kail? Ever since Marmion had told her the truth about him, Sal had been on edge. Whenever the tracker's name came up, he did his best to change the subject. She didn't want to believe that Sal was keeping something from her, and she had no real reason to believe he was—apart from a gut feeling.

That feeling wasn't going away in a hurry, and she had learned to trust her instincts.

She opened her mouth to ask him outright.

"How are we doing in here?" Highson Sparre's stocky frame filled the circular entranceway, casting them into shadow. "Need a hand?"

"No, we're fine," said Sal. "Thanks."

Sal's father didn't take the hint. Light returned as he came to join them. Sal's wiriness had no origin in Highson, whose broad shoulders looked as though they carried more than their fair share of worries; deep lines around his eyes and mouth and dark hair running rapidly to grey completed the impression.

"I actually came to ask you—" He stopped when he saw Shilly's drawings. "What are these?"

"I don't know," Shilly said quite honestly. "Have you ever seen anything like them before?"

"I don't think so. You should run them by Skender. If they're in the Keep library somewhere, he'll have seen them."

Shilly had thought of that, but Skender hadn't been capable of intelligent conversation since leaving Laure.

"You were going to ask . . . ?" she prompted.

"Oh, yes." Highson turned to Sal and lowered his voice. "When you were holding the tiller, did you feel any trace of the Homunculus?"

"No," said Sal.

"Are you sure?"

"Why? Did you?"

"I don't think so." Highson's broad forehead creased. "But I'm not a water-worker—none of us are, and why would we be? The Alcaide would hardly send someone like that inland." He laughed softly at the irony that a river now flowed where just a week ago, and for centuries beforehand, only dust devils and man'kin had roamed.

Sal and Shilly exchanged a glance. She was glad to know that she wasn't the only one obsessed with their own personal mysteries.

"Perhaps you should talk to Marmion," Sal suggested. "He might've felt it."

Highson shook his head emphatically. "Not until I'm sure he's come around to our way of thinking. We don't want the twins dead. He's tried to kill them once already and would've left them to the flood without second thoughts. I want to know why they saved me before I'll hand them over to him."

Sal nodded but had nothing to add. He lay back on the bed and closed his eyes.

"This isn't the best time," said Shilly, trying not to be harsh. At least father and son were talking.

"Of course. I'm sorry." Highson backed away until he was blocking the light from the entranceway once more. There he hesitated long enough to say, "That was a powerful move, and bravely done. On the deck before, I mean. You've grown so much since the Haunted City."

With that, he was finally gone.

Shilly felt the coolness of Sal's scalp and whispered softly when he went to speak. "No, my love. Sleep. You've done all you need to for one day."

"Kemp?"

"I'll check on him later. He'll be okay. I promise."

Her gut niggled at her, telling her not to be so sure of that. The serious nature of the wound and the poison spreading through Kemp's body made any prognosis uncertain. As Sal's breathing deepened and became gradually slower, she wished she had been less nervous of Tom. He rarely offered his visions unasked. If he'd seen the attack on the boneship ahead of time and told her about it, she might have found a way to avert the situation they now found themselves in.

Sal woke to the sound of arguing.

"I'm telling you he could die!"

"That's a risk we have to take."

"Is it? I don't understand how you can be so cavalier about this."

"I'm not being cavalier. I'm being practical. Kemp's life means as much to me as it does to you. I simply have other concerns to weigh against it. Kemp may not die. There may be resources ahead that we can use to save him. On the strength of those possibilities, I say that we will forge ahead."

Sal recognised the voices. The second, arguing for the mission to continue, belonged to Marmion. The first was Rosevear. Such was the concern in the young healer's voice that Sal feared gravely for his friend. Alive, yes, but for how long?

He sat up. His ears still rang from the effort of bringing down the snake that had attacked the boneship, but he could live with that. Ringing was better than the hum that always rose up when he dipped too deeply into his wild talent, a deadly, droning warning that if he went any further the Void Beneath would take him.

Swinging his legs off the thin mattress, he stood and took a moment to recover his balance. His head no longer felt as though it might shatter at the slightest touch, so that was an improvement. Kemp lay in one of the other cots, haggard and labouring under his injuries. Shilly had gone out onto the deck, presumably to observe the confrontation. He followed in her footsteps, weaving only slightly.

"If he dies," Rosevear said, "it'll be on your conscience as well as mine."

The sun had moved during his recuperative nap and now hung far to the west over the cliffs of the Divide. Even so, its light was still bright enough to dazzle Sal as he stepped out of the bone enclosure. The entire crew had gathered: Marmion and his wardens, standing in ones and twos across the long deck; Chu and Skender sitting side by side on a coil of rope, their thighs not quite touching; Highson and Shilly near the entrance to the boneship's interior, just to Sal's left. Even Mawson, the animated stone bust of a man with high temples and brooding expression, watched from the sidelines, propped up against one of the bulwarks and surrounded by knees. He, out of everyone, arguably had the most to lose if Kemp succumbed. The immensely strong albino frequently acted as his arms and legs.

"If Kemp dies," Sal said, speaking loudly so all could hear, "there's only one proper place to lay the blame."

Heads turned to face him. Marmion's eyes narrowed. "And where might that be?"

"On the snake, of course. That's not to say we shouldn't do our best to care for him—he deserves no less than that—but we can go only so far in providing that help. Our mission was always going to be a dangerous one, and he knew that. He wouldn't want us to turn back just for him. I'm sure of it."

Marmion looked relieved, and perhaps a little surprised that Sal had sprung so readily to his defence. "Thank you."

Rosevear wasn't to be mollified. "You don't know the full situation, Sal. I can't treat Kemp with the limited resources I brought with me."

"We've been over this," Marmion said. "There are forests ahead, less than a day's journey from our present location. There will be all manner of herbs and fresh water at your disposal. Kemp will be better off there than here, or perhaps even in Laure."

"And if he dies before we get there?"

"Tell me honestly: how likely is that?"

Rosevear looked crestfallen. "I don't know. The poison has spread throughout his body. There was nothing I could do to halt its progress. He has a fever and the wound will not close: either of these factors could lead to complications." He sighed and examined his hands, front and back. "A day might make all the difference in the world, or none in the slightest. To be utterly truthful, I'm not sure that anything I can do will help. No matter where we are."

The news was sobering. Sal felt for the young healer. He had tasted impotence, and found it bitter and lingering.

"We will make all haste," said Marmion soothingly. "You are

absolved of any blame should your worst fears be realised. I will take that responsibility."

Rosevear nodded, but clearly took little comfort from the warden's words.

"Right." Marmion put the matter behind him with a brisk round of instructions. The wardens set to work, preparing to cast off from the rugged shore by tightening cables, building charms, and stowing the remains of a hasty meal. By the look of things, Sal had missed dinner. His stomach rumbled at the thought, and he was heartily glad when Shilly joined him, pressing a sandwich of flat bread and salted meat into his hands.

Wary of getting in the way, they retreated into the heart of the boneship where Rosevear had returned to sit with Kemp. The healer looked tired. Sal's sensitivity to the Change hadn't recovered, but he could imagine the toll saving Kemp had taken. Rosevear glanced up as they entered, then away.

"I'm sorry that didn't go the way you wanted it to," said Sal. "If it helps, remember that agreeing with Marmion doesn't come naturally to me."

Rosevear managed a wan smile. "The worst thing is that he would expect no different if it was him here, not Kemp. He may look as though he's recovered from losing his hand, but I can assure you he hasn't."

"No," said Shilly, rubbing absently at her stiff leg. "You don't lose something like that easily."

"It just pains me to be so helpless. Look." Rosevear peeled back the bandages covering Kemp's stomach. Bluntly geometric black tattoos stood out against the albino's pale skin, one of them only half finished. "Have you ever seen anything like this?"

Sal winced at the sight of the wound. Ragged and round, its lips were inflamed and red. A clear, thin liquid trickled freely from it. Rosevear dabbed at the ghastly puncture with a clean white cloth, and held it up for Sal and Shilly to examine. The fluid possessed no colour at all.

"This could be anything," said the healer. "I can tell you what it *isn't*, though. It's not blood or bile, which you'd expect from a wound of this sort."

"What about the other wound?" asked Shilly. Her dark skin had paled, but she didn't look away. "Is that the same?"

Rosevear nodded. "I've never seen an infection like this. Even with access to a greater range of herbs, I'm not sure what I should do to treat it."

"Then we'll keep our fingers crossed that someone else will," said Chu from the entranceway. The flyer moved to join them, her patched leather uniform creaking stiffly. "There must be people in the forest. Where else could my ancestors have come from? And the snake too, if you think about it. There's a good chance it was swept downstream, so whoever's *up*stream might have seen its like before."

"That's true." Rosevear seemed slightly reassured as he bound Kemp's wound. "I was talking to Warden Banner this morning. She's been trying to work out where the hullfish came from. They're not river creatures, and they've never been found inland before. It's possible that someone brought it all the way from the coast . . . perhaps traders intending to sell it."

"Who would they sell it to?" asked Shilly. "The best market for something like this is right back where it started."

"Exactly. And the carcass was fresh, when the meat should have rotted completely from the bones before it reached anywhere near the Divide. Maybe your mysterious forest people can tell us about that, too," Rosevear said to Chu, "when we find them."

The deck moved beneath them, not enough to signal casting-off, but a sure sign it wasn't far away.

"Excuse me," said Chu. "I'd better get back to work, while the light lasts."

"Good flying," said the healer. "Keep your eyes peeled."

"I will." She hurried off. The wing needed a degree of elevation for her to make it safely into the air, so she would have to climb the Divide wall until she found a suitable launching point. Sal had watched her take off on a number of occasions. Each time brought back giddying memories of his one brief flight with Skender, and the near-crash his friend had called a landing.

"How are *you* feeling now?" Rosevear asked him.

"On the mend." He had no physical symptoms of overusing the Change, beyond exhaustion and a mild headache. His major discomfort lay in his disconnection from the rest of the world: until his full potential returned, he would remain cut off from the usual ebb and flow of life around him. "But Marmion had better keep us well away from monsters for a while, or he'll be on his own."

"Have you seen Tom anywhere?" asked Warden Banner, sticking her curly head through the entrance and looking around.

"No," said Shilly. "Why?"

"He's gone missing."

Only then did Sal realise that the young seer hadn't been on deck during the argument. Everyone *but* him.

"We can't leave until we've found him. Come and help me look. Everyone else is busy getting us under way."

What the unnamed boneship lacked in sophistication, it more than made up for in size. The main cabin area was just one of several bulbous spaces nestled inside the bony hull. Most had been filled with gear the wardens had brought with them, including collapsible tents, food stores, and all manner of cross-country equipment. Few such spaces were large enough for a person to stand upright; some measured barely a metre across.

"We're actually sailing the boat backwards, you know," Banner said as they moved aft, where the bony chambers joined to form cramped tunnels and dead-ended tubes. Sal was too big for most of them. "These used to be the hullfish's sinus cavities."

"Great," said Shilly, her voice muffled. She had just wriggled head-first into one of the smaller spaces. "I suppose it could be worse."

"*Much* worse," agreed Sal, thinking of the prow where Marmion perched. He didn't want to know what part of the hullfish's anatomy that corresponded to. "Tom?" he called. "Are you about?"

A faint movement came from deep within a tunnel too narrow for him to squeeze into. He craned as far as he could and saw the hem of a blue robe peeking out from around a corner. "Tom? What are you doing down here? There's no reason to hide."

The hem pulled out of sight.

"Come on. What are you frightened of? Is it something you've seen?"

The reply came in a tiny whisper. "I know he's dead. I saw it."

"Who?"

"Kemp."

"Is that what you're worried about? Well, it's okay now. I killed the snake. And Kemp is just injured."

"I could've warned him, but I didn't. He died because of me."

Sal retreated to tell Banner to go back and inform Marmion that Tom had been found. While the boneship's journey resumed, Sal and Shilly would sort out what was bothering him.

"Listen to me, Tom. No matter what you saw, Kemp isn't dead. He's sick, but he is still with us."

"No, he can't be. He has to be dead. That's the only way it'll work."

"The only way *what* will work, Tom?"

No answer. Shilly elbowed Sal out of the way to wriggle into the opening and have a go.

"Why don't you come and see Kemp for yourself, if you don't believe us?"

"I know what I've seen."

"But so do we, Tom. And you can't stay here forever. We're casting off any second."

The boneship moved beneath them at that moment, and Sal felt the slight hollowing in his stomach that came whenever they moved on the open water. The shouts of wardens came distantly through the bone walls.

"We're going forward," said Tom. It wasn't a question.

"Yes."

"Into the ice."

"If you say so. The mountains, anyway."

Shilly pulled backwards out of the opening so suddenly that Sal couldn't avoid being poked by her walking stick. She unfolded from the cramped space to reveal that Tom had decided to emerge as well. Long and thin—so long it amazed Sal that he had fitted into such a small space—with a shock of black hair and worried eyes, Tom shepherded them ahead of him until there was room in the hullfish's sinus cavities for the three of them to crouch together.

"Kemp is really alive?" he asked, looking from Sal to Shilly and back again.

"We wouldn't lie to you about that," Sal said.

"Will you tell us what you saw?" Shilly asked him.

Tom sat heavily and put his head in his hands. "I saw the thing under the ice again," he said. "The dark, ancient thing. It's stirring, getting stronger. The creature that attacked Kemp is frightened of it, like the man'kin and the golems—like everything in the world. I'm frightened of it too." He looked up and took Sal's arm in a strong grip. "Kemp is important. He helps. But he has to die first. It has to be that way."

"Why? Help how?" Sal retreated from Tom's sudden intensity, but couldn't pull free.

"Kemp is the only one who stands between you and Shilly when the end comes."

Tom spoke with such conviction that a chill went up Sal's spine.

"Between us?" echoed Shilly.

Tom turned to her, and nodded.

"You mean physically, or like in an argument?"

"Both."

"What's the argument going to be about?"

The seer let go, looking like he wanted to crawl back into his hole. "Whoever wins gets to choose the way the world ends."

"The *world?*" Again Sal felt something creep through him that was more than physical. "Do you know who wins?"

He shook his head. "I can't see. There's nothing."

"It's hidden from you?"

"There's nothing," Tom repeated.

Sal remembered something Marmion had told Shilly about the Haunted City's seers failing to see beyond a certain point in time.

"I don't like the sound of that," said Shilly, undoubtedly thinking the same thought. "I *knew* we should've christened the boat before we left. It's unlucky to sail in a ship with no name."

"But it's not as if we never argue," said Sal in a weak attempt to rob the moment of its gravitas. "And Kemp really didn't die. We know that."

"He's not out of the rip just yet."

"But what if he *doesn't* die? And how could either of us possibly choose how the world will end, anyway?"

"How can two people live in the same body at once?" she shot back. "How could the twins cause the Cataclysm and still be alive today? How could the Divide have come to be flooded?"

He took her point. "I think we should talk to someone about this."

"I agree." But instead of moving off, she turned to Tom. "Why didn't *you* tell Kemp what you'd seen? Or Marmion, or us?"

"I wanted to. Honest." Tom's voice had reverted to the singsong tone he had used as a child. "But I had to let it happen. It's all connected: the snake and Kemp; the Cataclysm and the Homunculus; the two of you and the rest of us. The whole world is connected. Sometimes I can see the pattern. Other times it's just one great big tangle. When it's clear, I don't have any choice."

"We know the pattern changes," said Sal, thinking of Shilly's dream. "I've changed it, once, in the Haunted City."

Tom looked more miserable than ever. "I don't understand how that works. I can only see inside this pattern at this time, and then only occasionally. It's like . . ." He fumbled for a way to explain. "Like trying to walk backwards while looking in a mirror. Maybe there's a different path to follow, but I can't see it."

Shilly touched his arm. "That's okay. You're doing your best. Why don't you go forward and reassure Warden Banner while Sal and I talk for a moment? Then check on Kemp. We'll be there soon."

Tom nodded, but didn't immediately move off through the bony cavities. "It does have a name, you know."

"What?" asked Sal.

"The boat. It's called the *Eda*."

"Really? Where does that come from?"

"I don't know, but that's what it's called."

Tom crawled away, leaving Sal and Shilly to untie the knot of information he had wound around them. Giant snakes; strange visions; grim prophecies; mysterious names. Things were getting weirder the further up the Divide they went. What awaited them at its terminus, in the foothills of the Hanging Mountains, Sal was afraid to contemplate.

THE FALLS

**"What is today but yesterday's tomorrow?
What is memory but a dream of the past?"**
THE BOOK OF TOWERS, EXEGESIS 19:2

From the air, the Divide looked nothing like a river. Skender had seen maps and he knew how tributaries snaked across the land, curving and winding in search of the Earth's lowest points, eventually meeting at the Strand where sea took over from stone. He had a rough idea that rivers started off fierce and furious in the mountains, then became languorous and lazy in their old age. He had read of rivers slow and wide-backed, choked by silt; of rivers crossing their own path and pinching off stagnant lakes; of rivers full of fish and reptiles, lined with overhanging trees and vines.

The Divide was none of these. A jagged split in the world, it zig-zagged like a lightning bolt without respect for highlands or lowlands, or for human habitation. Skender knew that the city of Laure had been struck in two during the Divide's formation centuries ago, causing massive subsidence and loss of life. People lived there still, against all odds, although the city was haunted by the Divide's reputation as a home of horror and mischief, as well as its physical hardships.

From desert to mountain, and possibly beyond, the Divide stretched without pause or deflection. For all Skender knew, it stretched right across the face of the world.

In the last week it had become a course for water originating some-where high in the Hanging Mountains. That didn't make it a river. The water was held in the channel created by the sheer, rugged walls. It might bite into the wall here, or make sandbanks there, but the flow of water couldn't radically alter the path given to it. That would take centuries or more. Perhaps, Skender thought, if the water kept flowing, future Van Haasterens might look at the old maps and wonder what became of the sharp-cornered Divide, where now flowed smooth-banked, sinuous tributaries instead.

If there ever are any future Van Haasterens, he thought.

On the night Kemp was injured, Skender and Chu rode updraughts billowing from the hot Earth with the fading sun behind them. The charm she used to see the wind guided her truly through a scattering of dirty clouds that scudded ahead of them, forming and dissolving ragged limbs as though aspiring to but never quite achieving particular shapes. Some resembled animals real and fantastic, while others reminded Skender of faces he had seen in old books or paintings. Chu ascended in a gentle spiral between the clouds, always keeping the shrinking dot of the boneship below within sight.

He was glad she had let him come with her. All grudges and hostilities stayed on the ground when they flew together. She hung behind him, which enabled her arms and legs to maintain the greatest control over the wing above them. Her warm presence comforted him. He felt her shifting her balance from side to side, smooth muscles stretching and compressing with limber ease. At times he found himself instinctively helping her, swaying with the wing as it rode the endless currents of the air.

Officially they were watching the boneship's progress for any sign of obstruction. Unofficially, Skender sensed Chu's restlessness with the task they had been given. Always the nose of the wing turned to point forward and upward, at the line of clouds that marked the beginning of the fog forests—a shelf of white that stuck out from the buttressed flanks of mountains. The land hidden by those clouds was supposedly fertile, perhaps even fecund. A hint of green at the base of the shelf was enough to convince him of that.

But the details were utterly obscured, and that ate at Chu. Given her freedom, she would have flown steadily eastwards—of that he was certain—into the cloud and in search of the wonders beyond.

"Now I see why they're called the Hanging Mountains," Chu said into his right ear, face held close to be heard over the sound of the wind. "Look. Magnificent!"

He did look, but could see nothing to solve that particular mystery. All he saw were clouds, really. The fading sun painted them all manner of oranges and reds and yellows, and he imagined fleetingly that he could see the shadow of the wing and its passengers writ large on those distant, ever-changing ramparts.

"Yes, but—what?"

"The name isn't referring to the mountains behind the clouds, but the *actual* clouds. *They're* the Hanging Mountains. Get it?"

And suddenly he did. Instead of trying to look through the clouds or at colours or shadows painted across them, he saw the clouds themselves. They did resemble mountains cut free from the land below and set dangling in the sky. Incredible, flat-bottomed, weightless mountains of whiteness.

"I get it," he said, "but I'd maintain that poets shouldn't be cartographers."

She laughed and sent the wing tilting to his right. "You're no fun."

"So what do we call the real mountains, then? Don't they have a name?"

"I don't know. Do they need one?"

"Everything has a name, even if you only ever see it on a map. Otherwise we'd get lost."

"Names don't always matter, not in the real world. I can find my way back to Laure perfectly well without knowing the names of any of the places we've flown over."

"But what if you had to ask for directions?"

"I'd take a pointed finger over a name any day. Anyway, we're not likely to get lost out here with the Divide to follow."

"True enough." He sought out the boneship in the fading light, and found it taking a sharp turn to port around one of the Divide's sudden corners. He wondered what was happening down there. A twinge of guilt reminded him of the responsibilities he still had, no matter how far above them he flew.

"Look," he said, pointing. "What's that?"

The wing tipped as Chu peered in the direction he indicated. "Where?"

"There . . ." Close to the base of the clouds, something broke the Divide's regular lines. A smooth, circular patch bulged from one side, while the edge facing away from the mountains vanished in haze. "It looks like a lake."

"There must be a blockage," she thought aloud. "Still several hours away, at the rate they're travelling."

"We should let them know anyway."

"Go ahead."

Skender reached under his robes and produced the shuttered mirror Warden Banner had made for them. His memory recalled the details of the code with perfect acuity, enabling him to construct a brief message. *Obstruction ahead*, he flashed through the medium of stored starlight. *Lake. Three hours.*

He waited for the flash of acknowledgment before putting the mirror away. Duty done, he was able to concentrate on the obstruction itself while the light lasted. It wasn't the first they had encountered along the way. The worst had been a section of the Divide not far from Laure where a tight turn had become choked with debris and rapids, necessitating the building of a channel deep enough to allow the boneship to pass in safety. That had held them up for half a day, with Chu and Marmion chafing impatiently for very different reasons.

The dusk deepened. Red-tinged clouds formed an impenetrable wall ahead of them, while behind them the last glimpse of the sun faded into the haze of distance. The wind grew colder, and Skender hugged his windswept robes tighter about him.

"What are you hoping for from the people in the forest?" he asked. "Your family left them generations back, and you've never known why. What if they moved on for a very good reason?"

"There might well have been a dozen good reasons, all forgotten now. But no one ever told me I shouldn't go back. I take that as a good sign."

"People have a way of forgetting things they don't want to remember."

"Do they?" she asked with a hint of sharpness.

"Not me, of course," he amended, kicking himself. Whatever had happened between the two of them that night in Laure, he desperately wanted to remember, but no amount of mental persuasion or cursing himself could shake the details free. He had barely touched araq since then, for fear of a repeat performance.

"I just worry," he said, "that you might be disappointed."

"I bet you say that to all the girls."

They flew on in silence over the darkening land.

The wardens slept in shifts as the boneship sailed onward through the night. Tom and Highson occupied the camp beds next to Kemp and Sal. Shilly stayed up, watching with a feeling of apprehension as blackness slid across the sky, stealing away the stars. She couldn't see the clouds, but she could feel them creeping over her, their mass increasingly oppressive and ominous. Ever since Skender's warning of an obstruction ahead, she had been unable to sleep. When Sal had returned to oblivion, still drained from the encounter with the snake earlier that day, she had come forward to meditate on the boat's deck, her thoughts as dark as the sky above.

Whoever wins gets to choose the way the world ends . . .

Water rushed by the boneship's charmed bows with a sound of heavy wind. Marmion sat on the prow, as unmoving and solid as a figurehead, the stump of his right hand cradled protectively in his lap.

Almost she moved to join him, but in the end decided against it. The night was quiet; she wasn't going to push her luck.

The Divide walls drew steadily closer together as the boneship continued eastward. That, combined with the spreading roof of clouds above, gave her the feeling of a trap closing around them. Periodically, one of the wardens keeping watch would play a powerful beam of mirrorlight across the way ahead, checking for obstacles not seen in the dark. Each time the light flashed, she swore the cliffs were nearer and taller, rising like black wings to sweep them away.

Two tight turns came and went. The water grew choppier, more restless, whispering like people engaged in a furtive argument. Shilly felt the boneship straining forward, rushing headlong to their unknown destination.

Gradually, over the muttering of the river, a new sound became audible: a roaring that put her in mind of the flood itself, all bass and treble mixed up into one growing cacophony.

Shivering, she did eventually move forward, exchanging her wariness for the desire not to be alone.

"What is it?"

Marmion looked at her with dark-rimmed eyes, then turned his attention forward again. Although she could make out very little in the darkness, she knew that wardens had ways of negotiating water not available to ordinary people. They could see well even under faint starlight. The Change made many such things possible, for those with the knack of tapping into it.

"Waterfall," he said.

"How far away?"

"Around the next bend, I think."

"That must be the obstruction Chu saw."

Marmion nodded. "All complications are unwelcome, but this one particularly so. We'll have to stop until dawn, then survey the ground ahead. If we can't raise the boat over the falls, we'll be forced to continue on foot." He looked at her. "Walking long distances will be difficult for you, I know. Don't doubt that I'll do everything I can to spare you that chore. And Kemp."

She studied him as best she could in the darkness. Was he trying to be nice to her? It seemed so. But his choice of words was unfortunate. Irrespective of her own feelings, she was sure Kemp wouldn't like to be lumped in with a *complication* like a waterfall.

Instead of berating him, however, she tried a small joke. "Here's hoping it doesn't come to full-on mountain climbing, or we'll both be in the shit."

One corner of his mouth curled upwards, then both went down. His eyes turned forward. "I still feel it," he said, shifting his bandaged stump a little. "The fingers . . . They itch. I long to scratch them."

"I still dream I'm running, sometimes." She wanted to tell him it would get easier, but there was no way she could promise him that. Her leg had healed to the point where at least she could walk again. Marmion didn't have that hope to cling to.

"We're an odd lot," he said. "Cripples, fugitives, wild talents, failures. Does it seem fitting to you that we're the ones racing to meet doom head-on, not some brawny band of adventurers?"

"Perhaps it's fate."

"*Fate is for fools*," said a familiar voice from below them, barely audible over the rising sound of the waterfall.

Shilly turned to look at Mawson where he sat on the deck behind her. The dome of his stony skull was barely visible. "Can't sleep either, huh?"

"*I do not ever sleep.*"

"Tell us, then," said Marmion. "What does Tom see, if not the workings of fate?"

"*He sees history in reverse. You look back and see connections between events; he looks forward and does the same. You both see an illusion. The connections are transitory. From moment to moment, all things are separate.*"

"To you, maybe," said Marmion, "but not to us. Our lives are entirely about connections. Without them, we are no better than animals, devoid of conscience, morality, hopes, and dreams."

"*I am not without such qualities.*"

"How can you dream if you don't sleep?" Shilly meant the question facetiously. She knew better than to get into an argument about time and destiny with a man'kin. The stone intelligences saw all things at once, and more besides: some things that didn't happen Mawson claimed also to know about.

The man'kin didn't grace her comment with a reply, as she'd expected. Marmion called over his shoulder to indicate the last turn before the waterfall. Shadows shifted around them. Looming limestone cliffs slid smoothly by. A faint gleam of green light caught her eye, and she squinted to make out where it came from. It couldn't be a star, since the dense cloud cover obscured everything in that direction, and it was too low to be a signalling flash from Skender and Chu.

She was about to point it out to Marmion when the boneship rounded the corner and she had her answer.

Shilly gasped, and heard Marmion's indrawn breath at the same time.

Before her, the Divide narrowed in fits and starts to a jagged bottleneck. One of the canyon's steep slopes had collapsed into the water flow below. The tops of massive boulders poked out of the turbulent water like the heads of submerged giants; rounded natural steps led to the top of the Divide on the southern side where the earthfall had originated. Between that side and the other, through a gap in the top of the landslide, the water had forced a way.

The sight was magnificent. Shilly knew that the sea at night glowed sometimes. As waves rolled in and out at the beach near Fundelry, tiny sparkles of green glittered in the foam; the short-lived trickling gleams had captivated her as a child. In the waterfall at the base of the Hanging Mountains she witnessed the same phenomenon, only magnified a thousandfold. A great sheet of water, divided into three unequal sections by protruding spars of dark stone, jetted over the lip of the rock shelf six metres above them and plunged in a glorious green rush to the canyon below. The splash it formed was an explosion in viridescence. Shimmering concentric ripples of light expanded in vivid waves across the river. What caused it, she didn't know. Some happenstance confluence of the Change at this particular location, perhaps, or an ancient charm long-buried in the Divide, awakened by the flood. Either way, it was beautiful and eerie at the same time.

She glanced at Marmion, and saw that he was looking down into the water ahead of them, not up at the falls. The water's glow, although quickly diluted, still cast enough light to see by. Squinting down, she could make out what lay at the bottom of the river amongst the rubble tumbled too recently to be covered with silt.

There she saw faces: a multitude of upturned eyes and mouths gazing back at her with mute appeal, the bodies they belonged to pinned between stone slabs heavier than houses. Hands clenched and unclenched as though trying to reach her; legs kicked futilely for freedom. The boneship sailed implacably over their resting places, mute witness to the fate that had befallen them.

"Man'kin," she breathed.

"Yes," Mawson replied. "The Angel told them to run, but still they didn't escape the flood."

Shilly thought of all the man'kin swept away from the walls of Laure when the flood had come. Those obviously weren't the only ones caught in the raging torrent.

She shuddered. The man'kin weren't dead, but they were trapped. If silt ever buried them, they would remain in darkness forever.

What sort of fate was that? Couldn't the Angel have warned them to run faster?

Shilly thought of Tom and his own dire warnings. She had had quite enough talk of end times and the failure of prophecy for one day.

"Do you still want to wait until dawn?" she asked Marmion, indicating the phosphorescent waterfall. Its light was bright enough to cast a shadow.

The warden considered the alternatives for a moment, green gleaming off his balding pate. "Perhaps not. We'll wake the others and consult the Engineers. I trust their opinion on such matters better than my own."

He turned to move from his perch, and Shilly went to follow him.

An arrow flashed out of the darkness and thudded fast into the bone between them. So violent was her recoil from the vibrating shaft that she would have fallen over the bow but for Marmion's good hand pulling her back.

"Ware!" the warden cried, rousing the crew. "Archers!"

He pulled Shilly after him to the relative safety of the boneship's central cavities. The Sky Wardens hauled the ship around, presenting a smaller target to the Divide walls. Shilly peered out at where the arrow still protruded from the boat's bony flank. It had come from the south side of the Divide. Green light glittered off it as though from glass.

Marmion's dark eyes took in more than hers, darting from the cliff face to the shimmering veil of the waterfall and back again. Other wardens crouched on the deck, in positions of relative safety, doing the same. Shilly saw no obvious weapons, but she didn't doubt they had some at hand. Not without good reason did Sky Wardens rule half the known world.

The boneship kept turning until it was facing back the way it had come. Nothing moved in the surrounding darkness. The only sound was the river's steady gurgle. Shilly tensed, struck by the thought that the archer might be in the water, not firing from the shore. However, she could see no sign of anyone swimming in the luminescent current.

They completed one full rotation without incident. Marmion raised a hand and the boneship steadied, began to move forward again. Light flashed as one of the wardens signalled Chu and Skender, high above.

Shilly felt a familiar, warm presence join her. Sal's hand slipped into hers.

"What's going on?"

She pointed out the arrow. "We're not alone."

"A warning shot?"

"I think so," said Marmion, "but I won't assume it to be so. A hand's-length to the left and Shilly would've been hit."

Sal looked at her in horror. She brushed off his concern. "Either of us could have been targets. They're just trying to get our attention, whoever they are."

"They certainly got that," Sal breathed. "If they were trying to warn us off, though, the message obviously didn't sink in."

Marmion raised a hand for silence as the warden signalling the lookouts overhead reported what he had learned. "Chu has spotted movement along the edge of the Divide, but she's finding it hard to see through the vegetation up there. If she flies closer, she risks crashing or being fired at herself. The base of the cloud cover is limiting her movements as well."

"Tell her to keep well away," said Marmion, "until we find out who shot that arrow and why. If anything changes, tell her to use her judgment but not to land until we signal her."

The warden moved off to relay the order. During the brief conversation Shilly's gaze, frustrated by the lack of light elsewhere, had alighted on the glowing waterfall. Its magnificence only increased as the boneship drew nearer. The ceaseless flow of water and the roaring it made had a faintly hypnotic effect. She hadn't blinked for at least a minute.

When she did so, she realised that the oddly shaped twist of water that had snagged her gaze wasn't water at all, but a person bathed in green, standing with one foot higher than the other on a stone. Willowy and tall, possessing a slightness that hinted at femininity, the figure stared calmly back at her, making no gesture or sign of recognition. Even across the distance between them, Shilly felt that patient gaze meet hers.

Before she could open her mouth to raise the alarm, the mysterious glowing woman stepped back into the water and disappeared.

"Hail!" cried a man's voice across the water. A dozen dark shapes swarmed down the sides of the waterfall: men and women in dark uniforms with weapons upraised. Blades mainly, but two bows among them. They took up position on the stone steps at the base of the waterfall, waving for attention.

"Hail, travellers!"

Marmion stood. "Hail!" he called back. "Is it your custom to fire on innocent people?"

"Not us," shouted the leader of the band through cupped hands. "Pull to, and I'll explain." He gestured and the men and women with him sheathed their weapons. The two archers placed their bows carefully on the ground and held their hands in the air. Shilly couldn't make out their faces. By the unnatural green glow of the waterfall, their uniforms looked black.

"Let's do as he says," Marmion told his crew, "but keep a sharp eye out. That arrow didn't come from ahead of us, where these people are standing. It came from the side. There could be any number of archers waiting for us to sail between them."

Shilly tried in vain to see the tops of the Divide walls. The last of the stars had disappeared in the west, leaving the night utterly dark beyond the reach of the waterfall's eerie glow. The boneship could have been plying subterranean waters, for all she could see of the sky.

Enough hallucinations, she told herself. *This night is already complicated without making stuff up.* She kept her eyes fixed on the waterfall as the boneship steadily approached.

No one else appeared to have noticed the glowing woman—if she had been there at all.

"This is a strange vessel."

"It's not one we'd ordinarily choose," Marmion responded, pacing the deck from port to starboard with his injured hand tucked protectively under his robes. Sal watched from the sidelines as the two leaders sized each other up. Lidia Delfine was the extraordinarily deep-voiced woman—not man—who had hailed them from the edge of the waterfall. The boneship had taken Lidia and one of her lieutenants aboard, then moved out of range of the spray and the waves to parley. By mirrorlight her thick cloth uniform was a reddish brown in colour and decorated with two black circles stitched into each shoulder. Her black hair was pulled back into a practical bun. She stood no taller than Marmion, but radiated strength and confidence from every gesture.

Her eyes and skin were matches for Chu's, as were those of her companion, a very large man with an edgy demeanour. The rest of her party remained on the bank by the waterfall, similarly dressed and featured.

"We come from the Haunted City in the service of the Alcaide," said Marmion. "Whom do you represent?"

"The Guardian of the forest. Here." She took a quiver her companion carried and held it outstretched. "Inspect these arrows. You'll see they're of quite different manufacture to the one sticking out of your ship."

Marmion plucked an arrow from the quiver and rotated it, holding it up to take in its features. Even from a distance, Sal could see that one was distinct from the other: the arrow Marmion held was long and skinny and clearly made of wood, while the one protruding from the bow of the boneship was short and glassy, more a dart than the sort of fletched arrow he was used to seeing.

"This proves nothing," Marmion commented, tossing the arrow back to Delfine, who caught it lightly with her free hand and inserted it back into the quiver. "But I am prepared to take you at your word, for the moment. If you didn't fire this arrow at us, who did?"

"The Panic," she said, with a slight tightening of her eyes.

"Who are they?" asked Shilly. "What do they want?"

Delfine looked at her, assessing her with one sharp glance. "Who

knows what they want, beyond banditry and murder? My orders aren't
to understand them but to stop them."

"Are your orders to stop us, too?"

"That depends." Delfine looked at Marmion again. "It depends on
what you're doing in the Pass, and why the Panic fired on you. Your
being human might explain the latter, but there could be more to it
than that."

The Pass was the Divide, Sal assumed. "What does being human
have to do with anything?"

"Yes," said Marmion. "Tell us more about the Panic. Did you drive
them away?"

"Unintentionally. I suspect they saw us coming and retreated to
size us up. Were our forces smaller, they might have taken us both on."

"Why?"

That, however, was all they were going to learn about the Panic for
the moment. Delfine laid down her ultimatum calmly and with only a
hint of challenge: "What brings you here, so far from the Alcaide's seat?"

Marmion outlined their mission in the briefest possible terms, referring only to the flood and the man'kin migration. He mentioned neither
the Homunculus nor the odd readings of the seers. With the glowing
waterfall as a surreal backdrop, he introduced Wardens Banner and Rosevear, Highson Sparre, and Sal and Shilly. This gesture of Marmion's
pleased Sal—the two of them had been routinely ignored, or worse, by
Marmion after a bad beginning to their relationship with him.

Delfine took in everything with a sharp nod. "And what about
your friends above? Tell us about them."

"Chu and Skender are our forward scouts. I wasn't aware you'd seen
them."

She looked smug at that. "If both hands hold a dagger, keep one
behind your back. So my martial instructor used to say."

Marmion nodded. Almost too casually, he produced his injured
arm from where it nestled under his robes and let it hang at his side.

"I don't like it," growled the lieutenant to her left, a tall, solidly built man, with chiselled features and a sparse black beard. "First the flood. Now wardens with wings. Send them back where they came from and be done with it. The forest has suffered enough."

"Suffered from what, exactly?"

The lieutenant ignored Shilly's question. "They have the stink of the bloodworkers on them."

"What *exactly* is it you don't like about us?" snapped Marmion. "That we aren't from here? That we don't look like you? That our dress isn't the same as yours? Get it off your chest now, man, so we can talk in earnest."

The lieutenant loomed over Marmion. "What's important is the forest. We are sworn to protect it. Threaten it, and you will die."

"No one's threatening anything, Heuve, so put your pride back in your pocket." Lidia Delfine waved her lieutenant back. He retreated, albeit reluctantly. "Is there anything else we should know?" she asked Marmion.

He nodded. "One of our number was injured during the journey here. We lack the facilities and the knowledge to treat him. Perhaps you can help us with that."

"Let me see him," she told Marmion. "Then I will decide. Heuve, stay here."

Marmion led her into the cabin, followed by Rosevear. They were gone only a moment, during which time Heuve looked at everyone in the ring surrounding him, one after the other, openly measuring them up.

"You've no reason to be frightened of us," said Warden Banner soothingly.

"He has every reason," Highson disagreed with a wicked smile. "He's just one versus ten. I'd be nervous too, if I were him."

"If any harm befalls me—"

"Oh, be quiet," said Shilly, tired of posturing by self-important men.

Delfine and Marmion returned. The woman's expression was grim. "We'll have to take him to Milang," she told the gathering in general.

"Who's that?" asked Sal, recognising Chu's surname with some surprise.

"It's not a 'who.' It's a place. It's where we live."

"And where is that, exactly?" asked Marmion.

She pointed at the waterfall, then upward and along the Divide.

"I urge you to reconsider, Eminence," said Heuve.

Delfine cast him a look as sharp as a needle. "That's enough. Warden Marmion, take us b ack to the shore. There's a path past the falls. You'll want to explore the way if you intend to bring your ship of bone with you."

"I'd like to, yes. Is the Divide clear beyond this point?"

"For a fair distance."

Marmion nodded. "Banner, Eitzen, I'll want you with me. The rest of you stay here. There's nothing you can do for now, and we'll need all our strength to move the boneship." Marmion looked at Sal when he said this, and Sal nodded his understanding. "Good. Someone flash Chu and Skender and tell them it's safe to come down. Highson?"

Sal's father had taken his familiar position by the tiller. He guided the ship smoothly towards the base of the falls. A cool, luminescent spray drifted across the boneship, making Sal's face wet.

Delfine and Heuve jumped ashore, followed by Marmion and the two wardens he had asked to accompany him. They immediately began climbing from stone to stone up the side of the falls, where the rest of Delfine's people waited.

"How old do you think she is?" asked Shilly, tapping Sal's leg with her cane.

"I've no idea. Why?"

"Just wondering why a big guy like Heuve is taking orders from someone as young as her. He doesn't look the sort who'd do that without a reason."

Sal watched the pair with keener attention as they climbed. Heuve's expression was determinedly disapproving, but couldn't hide genuine concern. He stayed as close to Delfine as she would let him, and his hand never strayed more than a few centimetres from the pommel of his sword. His gaze moved constantly, taking in everything and everyone around them.

Bodyguard, he thought, *not just a lieutenant*—then he carried that thought to its logical conclusion. Delfine hadn't truly explained who she was or what she had been doing by the waterfall. *Just who are you, Lidia Delfine?*

Knowing sleep wouldn't be easy to come by until this and other mysteries were resolved, he wished he hadn't agreed so readily to stay behind.

THE OUTCAST

Skender felt Chu's nervousness as the wing spiralled down to land. The two of them watched the people moving up and down the side of the ghostly waterfall. They were little more than dots, but he knew who they had to be. Chu's people. The ones she had come from Laure to find.

"When Sal finally met his grandmother," he said, "I thought he was going to wet himself. It didn't go very well. And that's okay. You don't *have* to like your family. There's no rule that says you must. I just—" He felt himself beginning to babble, and tried to slow down. "They're no reflection on you, if they're not who you want them to be. That's all I'm trying to say."

She was silent for a long moment as she guided the wing down into the close confines of the Divide. "I don't have any family," she said. "My parents are dead. I've never known anyone else. These people— well, I don't know who they are to me, but I do want the chance to find out. Don't worry," she added with her usual bravado, "I can look after myself. How bad could it be, anyway?"

His stomach tried to jump out of his mouth as the ground suddenly rushed up at them. Cliff faces and roiling water blurred into one.

"Is this your way of telling me to change the subject?"

The wing twisted to one side, rose slightly.

"The Divide is too narrow and turbulent where the boat is," she explained, tugging vigorously at the frame. "I'm going to have to land further up. It's wider there, and therefore safer."

Skender nodded, understanding that he played no part in the decision-making process. The wing swooped downward again, this time aiming further uphill from where the boneship floated, docked at the base of the glowing waterfall. The source of the water lay in a small lake, where the Divide had been dammed. Cupped into a stone niche formed by the collapse of the cliff face, and given space to grow by further collapses, the lake stretched perhaps thirty metres across, with a flat space to the east where the canyon resumed its normal zigzagging progress into the mountains. Not far beyond that point, the cloud cover became impenetrable. Even as the wing came in to land, wisps cut across its flight path, momentarily blocking their view. Cold shivers ran down his neck and spine.

Snatches of voices reached them as they descended. Hands waved. He hoped it was in welcome.

"I'm starving," said Chu, taking aim for the smooth shoulder of land she had picked as their landing spot. "And dying for a drink."

Skender would've been just as happy to curl up somewhere for a quiet snooze, but figured there was little chance of that any time soon.

He braced himself for landing. His legs would be the first to make contact with the ground, so the one responsibility he did have was to hit it cleanly. Too early and he would never be able to run fast enough to keep up with the wing, thereby driving its nose downwards into the ground; too late and they would land on their backsides. He was gradually improving at it, but he had plenty of bruises to prove that he had learned the hard way.

He ignored a renewed shouting and waving as the ground came up at them. Whatever they wanted, it would have to wait. Chu tipped the nose up, slowing them. The ground hung just a metre out of his reach. It gleamed slightly. A smell came off it that reminded him of his home's ancient latrines.

Only then did he feel the slightest misgiving.

"Wait, Chu. I'm not sure—"

Too late. Chu brought the wing down and he splashed feet-first into thick, cloying mud. He tried in vain to run, but all that did was drag him down more quickly. The wing tipped and wobbled and barely remained horizontal as, first, his legs then Chu's were sucked in. Eventually, all airworthiness evaporated and they fell face-forward into foulness.

For a terrifying moment, all was brown and muffled. A hideous taste crept down his throat. He gagged. Then his kicking legs hit something solid, and he managed to force himself—and Chu, strapped to him, along with the wing—above the surface of the mud.

He choked and spat and wiped at his face. Chu did the same, with a healthy dose of cursing, as her slippery fingers fumbled with the latches. The wing fell away, and he found himself able to stand upright, still submerged up to his waist but at least well clear of the noisome surface. Chu slipped and splashed back in, making a dense *glop* sound as she vanished under the wing. He tugged it aside and helped her back to her feet.

"Nice landing," called a man's voice. Skender blinked mud out of his eyes and made out a dark figure standing on solid ground some metres away. "Are you all right in there?"

"We'll be fine," Chu snapped, pulling away from Skender. She looked barely human. The stink nearly overpowered Skender, who was trying to breathe through his mouth as much as possible.

"Come this way." The man beckoned with both hands. "The ground is firmer."

Skender heard footsteps and a smattering of laughter as others came to watch. "Chu, are you okay?"

"Give me a hand with this," she said, fumbling the wing in her haste to collapse it. "How was I supposed to know there'd be mud here?"

Skender did his best to help, but it only seemed to worsen her mood. He didn't blame her for the unfortunate landing. Until the flood, she had never seen a body of water larger than a bathtub, so the existence of mud-banks wouldn't have occurred to her. They looked flat from the air, and flat was *good* for a Laurean miner seeking somewhere to land.

By the time they had bundled the wing into a cocoonlike shape for easy carrying, she was fuming so thoroughly he thought it a miracle the mud on her hadn't baked into clay.

"This way. That's it. Keep coming." The man who had called to them continued to offer words of encouragement as they splashed through the thick sludge. When they were within reach of the spectators, he helped them out of the mud and onto blessedly solid rock.

"I can manage," Chu said, brushing away hands at her elbows and back. "Be careful with that!" The people who had taken the wing from her put it down on the ground between them. "What are *you* laughing at?"

The last she directed at a smirking young woman with a long black ponytail and eyes as exotic as Chu's. They all had the same eyes, Skender realised, and hair in shades of black. Their skins were neither black nor white, but something in between, and their uniforms rust-brown. There were six of them. Two carried wooden brands that cast a bright orange light, like glowing coals.

"Yes, Navi," chided the man who had helped them. Older, with splashes of grey at his temples and several gold circles of varying sizes stitched into the breast of his uniform, he kept any amusement he might have felt carefully contained. "Don't add mockery to their list of misfortunes."

The woman called Navi saluted with a fist over her heart, and stepped forward to help Chu with the wing.

"I'm Schuet," said the older man. "You must be Skender and Chu. Her Eminence told us to keep an eye out for you."

"Her what?" Chu asked.

"The Eminent Delfine. She's down there now, talking with your man Marmion."

Schuet pointed at a huddle of people on the far side of the lake, where a cloud of glowing mist rose from the waterfall.

"Not *our* man," growled Chu.

Skender spat in a vain attempt to get rid of the taste in his mouth. One of the uniformed men handed him a flask of water, which he gratefully accepted.

"Who are you people?" he asked after gargling and spitting again.

"Foresters," said Navi, saluting again, "and servants of the Guardian, at your service."

"We'll give you space to clean up in a moment," said Schuet. "I know you're eager to. Just let me ask you something first. During your descent, or earlier, did you see anything unusual?"

"Unusual how?" asked Chu.

"I'm not sure, exactly. I've never seen it properly myself. People talk of a wraith or phantasm, but I'll keep my mind open until it stands before me and I can give it a name of my own."

The members of the uniformed band had lost their amused demeanour. For all its oddness, Skender could tell that the question was seriously meant.

"We saw nothing but those who met the boneship," said Skender, "and they're your people, I suppose."

Schuet nodded, although he didn't seem entirely pleased by the answer. "Well and good. It's only newly night, and I expected no more. Still . . ."

A uniformed man jogged up to the gathering. "Seneschal, Her Eminence calls for you."

Schuet nodded. "I'm on my way. Chu, Skender—Navi will show you where to bathe. We'll find some clean clothes for you while yours dry. I'll talk to you again later."

With that, he hurried off in the direction of the waterfall. Navi gestured at two uniformed men, who picked up the wing between them and followed Schuet at a more measured pace.

"Be *careful* with that," warned Chu again.

"Don't worry," Navi reassured her. "We're not going far. Just there, where the bank slopes down to the water." She pointed. "The lake is shallow there, the water clean."

"Not an *actual* bath, then?" muttered Skender, longing for the warm water and brass tubs of the Keep. Even the tepid sinks of the Black Galah in Laure would have done.

Navi's teeth flashed white in the gloom. "The nearest is a day's walk from here. Think you could bear your stink that long?"

He grimaced. "Pass." Feeling mud squelching between his toes, he followed Navi around the shoreline to the place she had indicated. Chu's expression was completely masked by the drying mud, but he could tell she was embarrassed and annoyed at herself, and perhaps dreading the thought of having to wash in front of a bunch of strangers as well. She said nothing, however, and he imitated her stoic silence.

"There you go," said Navi when they arrived. She turned her back to give them privacy, and indicated that the others should do so too. "Sing out when you're done. If your new clothes aren't here by then, put your old ones back on for the time being."

Skender splashed into the water with a startled cry. It was much colder than he had expected. Chu gulped a deep breath and dived completely under. She emerged a moment later, shivering and rubbing at her muddy hair, her licence removed and tucked into a pocket, and her skin returning to normal. He resigned himself to doing the same, and dunked himself with his eyes shut and nostrils pinched tightly closed. His robe billowed around him, tangling his arms. When he stood up, the water had turned brown around him, and Chu was unlacing her leather top.

He concentrated furiously on what he was doing. Tugging his robe over his head, he wrung it out under water and draped it over his bare shoulder. A quick scrub sluiced the last of the mud from his upper body and face. He had no intention of removing his underwear in front of anyone—especially in such frigid circumstances—so he did his best and left it at that.

When he turned back to the shore, he found that Navi had broken her promise. She stood facing them with her hands on her hips. Her friendly expression had quite disappeared.

"You!" she exclaimed, pointing directly at Chu.

He turned to look at Chu who, dressed in sopping singlet and shorts, was occupied with flushing the last of the mud from the delicate folds of the wing.

She looked up, puzzled. "What?"

"Step out of the water."

"I don't understand."

"Do as you're told, or we'll come in there and get you."

Skender stepped closer to Chu, whose shocked look perfectly matched his own. Navi's harsh commanding tone was at complete odds to her earlier manner. "Hey, now," he said to the uniformed woman. "You should think carefully before trying that."

"Be quiet, Skender. This isn't your problem. It's hers." To Chu she said: "I see you clearly now. Put down the wing, Outcast, and come out now. I won't ask again."

"Outcast?" Chu repeated in a soft voice.

Navi snapped her fingers, and two of the uniformed men splashed into the water. Skender put himself between them, and called on his memory in desperation.

Stone Mages were rarely challenged on their side of the Divide. Even in Laure—ruled by isolationist bloodworkers—Skender's status had earned him a certain amount of authority. That had been in part due to Chu's insistence on introducing him as a full-fledged mage, not the nearly graduated student he actually was, but the fact remained that mages were respected and sometimes feared, with good reason.

He would never be a strong mage, his talent being for minor things like lighting stones and starting fires, but he knew more than his fair share of tricks. A lifetime of scanning through books and an eidetic memory had to be worth something.

Calling forth a little-used mnemonic from the depths of his mind, he raised his hands to point at the men closing in on him and Chu.

With a soundless flash, every one of his tattoos changed from black to bright red. Running in parallel lines down his arms, crossed every ten centimetres with a symbol culled from the deepest recesses of the Keep's library, they burned as brightly as the wooden brands two of Navi's companions still held. That small effort almost drained him, but the foresters weren't to know that. Using the last of his reserves, he coaxed an impressive rumble from the stones along the shore. Pebbles tinkled in tiny avalanches down the side of the Divide.

"Stop right there," he said.

To his amazement, they did just that.

Shilly was the only one on the boneship who didn't hear the commotion. She was with Rosevear, helping the warden prepare Kemp for moving. The albino's skin was hot to the touch and flushed pink all over his abdomen and chest. She didn't need to see under the bandage to know that he was getting worse.

Sal, fidgeting restlessly on the bunk behind her, suddenly sat up. "There's a problem," he said.

Rosevear had frozen in the act of trickling water between Kemp's slack lips. His dark curls shook as he looked at the entrance to the cabin. "You'd better hurry."

"What?" asked Shilly. "What am I missing?"

"Skender's in trouble."

Sal was on his feet and out of the door before she could ask him more.

She clambered awkwardly to her feet and put her good leg forward. Cursing her lameness—not for the first time, and hating the word in the act of thinking it—she did her best to catch up to Sal.

The deck of the boneship had become a riot of movement. Wardens ran everywhere, stirred up by the same call that Sal had picked up. Tom

caught Shilly's elbow and helped her over the side of the boat, onto the
gangplank leading to shore. Only then did Shilly stop to think through
her automatic impulse to help. How was she to climb the rocky rise up
the side of the waterfall? With stones slick underfoot and a weak leg as
well, hurrying was only going to lead to further mishaps.

Besides, she thought, she might already have missed her chance.
Brown-clad figures were clambering down to join the two left behind
to watch the boneship. Sal made it past them, perhaps because he was
one of the few aboard the ship not wearing the blue robe of a Sky
Warden. Highson, who had also rushed to Skender's aid, wasn't so
lucky. He turned back towards her with his hands in the air.

"Do you have any idea what's going on?" she asked Tom. He stood
beside her on the bank, watching events unfold with a worried expression.

"Skender is drained. We'll have to wait until Sal gets there."

"I meant from your dreams."

"Just the waterfall," he said, "and something about an old woman
with sharp teeth. I don't know what that is."

Shilly shook her head, shivering at a sudden chill. She looked
behind her, at the boat, and noticed that the mist rising off the water
appeared to be thickening. The wind tugged it into strange, tortured
shapes that danced and writhed in the ghostly green light.

"Maybe nothing," she said, remembering Tom saying once, *Sometimes a dream is just a dream.*

Six of the forest people arrived with Highson and one of the wardens in tow. An older man at their head assessed her and Tom with a
quick glance. With a wave of one broad gloved hand, he indicated that
they should board the boat.

"There's nothing you can do out here," he said. "Don't make my
life more difficult than it already is."

"Tell us what's happening first," she said, not moving a centimetre.

"Just a misunderstanding." He made a placating gesture. "It'll be
sorted out in a moment, I assure you."

"Why should I believe you?"

"Because I ask you to."

"I'm going to need a better reason than that."

"And who exactly am I talking to?"

She smiled tightly. "Someone who'll make your life much more difficult if you don't do as I say."

To her surprise, he laughed, tipping his head back and barking loudly at the sky. "A good answer, I suppose, to a blunt request." He held out his right hand. "Ordinarily I'd much rather talk than make demands of people. In the heat of the moment, that's sometimes easy to forget. I am Seneschal Schuet. Could we move back to your ship of bone and discuss what's happening above? There are already enough axes chopping at that particular tree."

She warily took the proffered hand and shook it. "Shilly of Gooron." She looked past Schuet to where Sal had disappeared over the top of the waterfall.

"All right," she said, waving Schuet forward. "You'd better come aboard."

Schuet nodded and went first, leading Highson, the warden, and the rest of his uniformed men and women. Shilly and Tom came last.

"So, tell me," she said.

"There are two things you need to know about us, Shilly. The first is that we have an instinctive distrust of things that fly. The second is that we are a proud people. Of all things, we are most proud of our home. It is fragile and precious. We shield it with our lives."

"The forest?" Shilly interrupted.

"Yes. You have heard of it?"

"Not until a week ago, in Laure, and then only as a distant legend."

That pained him: she could see it in the lines around his eyes. "Not so distant, Shilly. You stand on its very borders. An hour further up the Pass, and you would be within its boundaries. Nowhere else will you find such richness, such vibrancy. When the sun sets through the boughs and the mist turns orange and the birds call to each other—ah! I would rather die than turn my back on it."

He sobered. "When people *do* turn their backs on our home, we find it hard to forgive."

"What's that got to do with us?"

"Your friend, the flyer."

"Chu?"

"Yes. She is of us." He indicated his hair, his eyes, his face. "Or she was. Whatever she is now, she's no friend of the forest."

"But she's never been here. Her family left generations ago."

"Exactly. They turned their backs on us. They have no love for us, or we for them."

"That's a stupid thing to say when you know nothing about her. What if she loves the forest when she sees it? What if her family had perfectly good reasons for leaving?"

"Are *your* people never stupid?"

"Frequently, I'm sorry to say." Shilly folded her arms. "That doesn't make them right, and I would fight them as determinedly as I'd fight you over this."

"Then you're fighting a war you can't win. People like to be stupid. It saves them from having to think."

"And that benefits the forest how, exactly?"

He smiled grimly, and didn't answer.

"Bloodworkers, man'kin, *and* Outcasts." Lidia Delfine's bearded bodyguard looked darkly vindicated. "*Now* will you listen to me, Eminence?"

Sal could barely restrain his frustration. The ludicrousness of the situation was appalling. He didn't know whether to laugh or scream.

Skender and Chu remained up to their ankles in water, shivering and defiant. Sal had never seen Skender so angry; the flickering red glow of his tattoos testified to that. A crowd had gathered before them, spread out along the shore, and didn't dare come any closer.

By the time Sal had arrived, the argument had barely begun. Lidia Delfine had explained the situation, the end of which he had just caught. Chu didn't know why her family had left the forest, but that didn't seem to matter in the slightest. She had inherited the stain of leaving, and nothing Marmion said seemed to make a difference.

"Your counsel, Heuve, is always in my ears." Lidia Delfine looked torn. With hands on hips and face tilted dangerously forward, she regarded the wardens and their companions from under stormy brows. To Marmion, she said, "It is possible that you people do not know our customs. I am inclined to forgive you that. But there are some things foresters cannot forgive. If you would proceed, *she* must turn back."

"Ridiculous." Marmion argued for all he was worth. "I will not submit to this decision without appealing to a higher authority. To whom do you answer? Let me raise this matter with them."

"I answer to myself and the people of the forest," Delfine said coldly. "You will find no higher authority here."

"Then I will simply not recognise it."

Her chin came up. "Are you challenging me?"

Marmion didn't back down. "I will defend my right and the right of my companions to travel freely into the mountains. If defending my freedom constitutes a challenge to you, so be it, but I will not willingly break the peace between us. The first blow will be yours."

"That is acceptable," said the bodyguard, stepping forward with his blade drawn.

"Wait," called Chu as Marmion raised his one remaining hand and the Change gathered tightly around him. "I *could* turn back," she said. "If they hate me that much—"

"No." Although Skender spoke softly, his tattoos flared anew. "You wanted to come to the forest. You've dreamed of it your entire life. They're not going to deny you that."

"But it's their forest. They have the right to say who comes in and out." Her voice was level despite tears glistening in her eyes.

"We mean them no harm," said Marmion, glaring at the body-guard with his hand still upraised. "Individually, or as a group, or as official representatives of the Alcaide, we have come here in peace and in search of aid for our injured companion. In return we have been greeted with hostility and suspicion. Attacking us is tantamount to a declaration of war. Retribution will be swift. Is that what you want, Delfine? Do you want to see your precious forest put to the torch?"

"You have no concept of what you're saying," spat the bodyguard, face turning purple with anger. "I curse you and all your family. Your line will wither on the branch and rot forgotten in the dirt. Your air will dry and crumble you to dust. You—"

"Heuve." Delfine's hand came down on his shoulder. To both men she said, "Let us not speak too hastily of curses and war. We each have responsibilities and, yes, they conflict, but that doesn't make us enemies." She included the wardens and Skender and Chu when she said, "We have laws, just as you do. You intend to break one and ignorance is not a defence. It is my duty to stop you."

"Do you answer to laws," asked Sal, "or to the people of the forest?"

Delfine's cool brown eyes turned on him. "The former protects the latter."

"But the forest has suffered, and we have suffered too. Isn't that fact more important than some forgotten wrong?"

"We know who caused the deluge," said Heuve. "The Panic Heptarchy has long been a thorn in our side. How are we to know you don't work for them? What will be destroyed next if we allow you into the forest?"

Conversation stopped as a rush of cold air swept across the lake. Sal looked up the Divide. The light from the gleaming water was just strong enough for him to see as far as the next bend. It seemed to him that something dark and nebulous was rushing downriver towards them, riding that icy wind.

All turned towards it, including Skender and Chu, standing in the lake and beginning to turn blue.

Heuve put down his sword and moved closer to Delfine. She grew pale and her eyes widened.

"What is it?" asked Marmion. "What approaches?"

"We don't know," said Delfine, "but it killed my brother two nights ago, and I will see it dead. To me!" she cried to her people. "To me! We meet it here, on the flat!"

"Let us help you," Marmion insisted.

"Just stay out of our way," growled Heuve. "Fight if you wish, to save your own lives, but come between me and my mark and I will not hesitate to strike."

With that he backed away, keeping Delfine behind him, to form a defensive circle against the wall of the Divide with his back facing the stone.

Marmion didn't waste time being offended. He waved Banner and Eitzen to him. "Skender, Chu, out of the water. It seems we have bigger things to worry about."

Sal felt the wind turning colder with every second. "Come here." He put his hands on Skender's and Chu's shoulders and called on an old charm for drying laundry on wet days. The mnemonic was simple. The problem, as always, lay in keeping it from getting out of control. He wanted to dry his friends' clothes so they wouldn't catch a chill, not set them on fire.

Chu puffed up her cheeks and rose on tiptoes. Her short hair stood on end. "Wow! You could make a fortune doing that."

There wasn't time to joke. Sal could feel the darkness bearing down on them, and a flash of Tom's prophecy went through his mind. "Quickly. Get behind us. Skender, you too. You need to ride this one out."

Skender didn't argue. His tattoos were lifeless and black now the crisis with the foresters had passed. He stood next to Chu with his hand on her arm, and Sal couldn't tell whether he was supporting her or drawing comfort from her, or both at once.

"Don't do anything sudden," said Marmion. "Let's see what we're dealing with first."

Sal's guts tightened. Ignorance was dangerous. In his life he'd faced golems, ghosts, ice creatures, man'kin, and the snake he had smashed less than a day earlier, but that knowledge didn't reassure him. He was still not at peak strength and nature knew many ways to kill.

Tendrils of mist were branching across the faintly glowing water as if sliding on ice; they groped blindly towards them, probing the air and finding it empty. A dense wall of fog followed. This, Sal realised, was the source of the intense cold.

The temperature dropped further still. A blast of frigid air assailed them, forcing him back a step. The wind made a sound like glass being ground underfoot. His scalp crept. Marmion reached out and put a hand on Sal's shoulder. The Change surged through him. For the first time Sal felt the strength in the man, and he was impressed. Marmion wasn't as strong as Sal, but what reserves the warden possessed were carefully structured and focused. A lifetime of discipline had honed him into a keen Change-worker.

That's what I could have been, Sal thought, *had I been given the opportunity. . .*

Then the clouds rushed forward in a wave of bitterness and hate, and he gagged on the taste of spite.

"*Concentrate!*" Marmion's voice came through the Change. Sal forced himself to lean into the wind and stand upright with his eyes open, ready to face whatever might emerge from the whipping cloud. Feathery tendrils slid by, lashing at his face.

A geometric pattern slid into his mind, a jagged tangle of triangles and many-pointed stars. He clutched at it, knowing it came from Marmion, and wrapped his thoughts around it. The vicious fog recoiled, and he thought he heard a hiss of anger from its heart.

Then a dark shape rushed at them. Black on grey—he couldn't tell if it was a gap in the mist or something solid. Two long arms opened wide to snatch at him, and the hiss grew into a shriek.

Marmion thrust himself forward, ruined arm out-thrown like a spear. The dark shape recoiled with a scream and shot skyward, trailing a vortex of loathing and fear powerful enough to throw Sal and Marmion to the ground.

Then it was gone. Hands clutched at Sal, pulling him to his feet. His ears were numb; he couldn't hear what Skender was saying. His friend's face was pale and Chu's eyes were as round as he had ever seen them. Marmion huddled over the stump of his missing arm, and Sal pushed forward to see if he had been harmed.

Marmion looked up, dark skin grey with shock. The bandage covering his blunt wrist seemed undamaged to Sal's untrained eye, but Marmion held it in front of him as though it was on fire. The warden's one remaining hand shook as he took Sal's and let himself be hauled to his feet.

Lidia Delfine pushed forward. He could faintly hear her asking what had happened. Had Marmion killed it? Was it gone? The warden shook his head, words seeming to come from a great distance away. Sal looked around, feeling the small of his back a-twitch. The mist was breaking up and the ghostly dark shape wasn't immediately visible. But there were other dark shapes streaming down the walls of the Divide and arrows raining out of the darkness.

Sal's ears slowly recovered to bring him the sound of Sky Wardens and foresters, Stone Mage and Outcast, all turning to face this new threat, shouting orders and, for the moment at least, putting aside their differences.

Then from the boneship at the base of the waterfall came the sound of screaming, and he forgot everything else.

THE PANIC

"The Panic are monstrous beings who track wanderers through the forest, catch them with hooks at the end of long wires, and drag them up into the sky. So parents tell their children to stop them straying from the well-known paths. When these children grow up, they naturally believe that the Panic Heptarchy is responsible for crop failure, disease, internal unrest, and any other misfortune the forest should suffer. If the King should ever return, the foresters say, peace will end and the sky will fall. This is their simple but earnest belief."

STONE MAGE ALDO KELLOMAN: ON A PRIMITIVE CULTURE

Skender had no idea how much information lay in the recesses of his memory. Certainly everything he had ever read—but how much was that? How many books had he scanned in the Keep's enormous library and his father's private collection?

Associations surprised him, sometimes. Years ago a strange glyph carved on a milestone on the road across the Long Sleep Plains had reminded him of one described in an ancient tome as the lost cenotaph of an ancient ruler—and such it had turned out to be when Surveyors had followed up the connection. A line of verse from a children's song overheard in Millingen matched one transcribed in Boliva thousands of kilometres away and five hundred years earlier. He never knew when something would leap out at him to say, *You've seen me before. Can you tell where?*

It could be distracting at times—and was almost fatally so when a half-dozen strange creatures suddenly dropped from the walls of the

Divide in front of him. Luckily, dropping and firing arrows didn't marry well, so he and Chu were spared while darts hit people behind him. Skender and Chu dived under an overhang to let those with skill and power battle it out. Seeing the two of them defenceless, Heuve immediately took a knife from one of his fallen comrades and tossed it to Skender.

Then the creatures—quite different from the deathly cold shadow that had knocked Sal and Marmion to the ground—were among them, long-limbed and agile, and not quite human in shape. Their silhouettes seemed familiar to him, although he couldn't imagine why. At close quarters they slashed with curved hooks and ducked under sword strokes. White teeth gleamed in the mirrorlight; wide eyes flashed in the light from the foresters' glowing brands. Hooting calls and shrieks matched the cries of anger and surprise from their human adversaries.

Only when one dropped on all fours in order to dodge a knife-thrust from Heuve did recognition fall into place. The *Book of Towers*, yes—but the Fragments or Exegesis? The former, perhaps. A snippet of words, and a drawing. *Definitely* a drawing . . .

The creature didn't move fast enough. Lidia Delfine caught its throat in an upswing. The slash was powerful enough to send it spinning sideways to land at Chu's feet, spraying blood and thrashing as it died.

Chu turned her face away. Skender barely noticed. He was thinking: *"Pan troglodytes sapiens?"* That was the handwritten note scribbled on the side of the drawing he remembered—a drawing which captured the same posture, the same wide mouth and teeth, the same outstretched arm as the creature prostrate before him, gurgling its last.

He felt as shocked as he would have if the mountains themselves had suddenly sat up and walked off. These things were legends. Stone Mage scholars had debated their existence for hundreds of years. Kept deep in the heart of the desert lands were memoirs written by men and women who had devoted their entire lives to dividing and classifying imaginary beasts such as these—and here was one of them dying at his feet, still hot from the exertion of trying to kill him!

Chu pulled him back as the outflung arm twitched one final time, swinging its smoke-blackened hook towards him. It missed by more than a metre. He stared in fascination at the creature's hairless body and sinuous limbs; the leather harness and apron it wore; its long fingers and toes; its mouth set in a permanent pout; its pale pinkish skin. Each hand bore curved nails painted a deep green, the colour of leaves. Stitching in black thread traced a pattern of branches and roots across its chest covering. A cap of densely woven black thread protected its domed skull, but left the protruding ears exposed. One lobe was pierced with a single ebony stud.

For a timeless awestruck moment one single thought utterly consumed him: *What had been its name?*

Then chaos returned as Lidia Delfine's foresters fell back, shouting and arguing. Blood-spattered blue robes jostled alongside them, forming a defensive ring within which a hurried conversation took place.

"There are too many of them!" Delfine said, favouring her left arm.

Heuve nodded tightly. "We must retreat back up the Pass."

"But we can't! The boneship!" Only then did Skender realise that their number wasn't complete. He looked around, growing increasingly frantic. One of the wardens was missing, and so was . . . "Sal! Where is he?"

Marmion pressed closer, thinning hair in disarray. "He went back alone. I couldn't stop him."

Of course, Skender thought. *Shilly*. "We can't leave him behind. We can't leave *them*."

"We must," Heuve insisted. "The Panic lie between you and the boneship. You'll die if you try."

"So we run?"

"We survive," Delfine's bodyguard snarled. "Our duty is to Her Eminence."

"Not mine!"

Skender lunged forward, his intention only the Goddess knew what. A slight but strong hand pulled him back.

"No," said Delfine, lips twisted as though every word pained her. "Heuve is right, although I hate to admit it. I have loved ones down there, too. They are strong; they may prevail. We can regroup later, or not at all."

Skender looked at Chu in despair. She nodded. He let his muscles go limp.

"The Panic?" he asked, querying her earlier use of the word.

Delfine answered his question by pointing at the body at his feet. "We leave now."

"What about the Outcast?" asked Heuve.

Chu gripped Skender so tight she hurt him.

Delfine looked at Chu, then at her bodyguard. "I place her in your charge, Heuve. It's up to you to keep the forest safe."

"No, Eminence, you can't—" He could say no more. She had moved into the fray and begun telling her people to fall back.

Chu stood taller and let go of Skender's arm. "Well, then. Shall we go?"

The big man's beard twitched, but he said nothing.

"Down!"

Seneschal Schuet pushed Shilly's head below the top of the gunwales. Something dark rushed over them with a deafening shriek. The tide of fog which, just moments before, had crested the top of the glowing waterfall now swept over them in a wind so cold it pained her.

A human scream joined the shriek. Shilly turned in time to see one of Schuet's brown-clad companions—one of the few who hadn't left in response to Lidia Delfine's call to arms—snatched off the deck by invisible hands and whipped upwards into the mist. He disappeared, but his scream continued.

Shilly stared in open-mouthed horror.

"What—?"

"Stay still," Schuet hissed. "Where it flies, the Panic are sure to follow."

She jumped as a glass dart thwocked into the bulkhead by her leg. "How do you know? *What's going on?*"

"Quickly!" He took her hand and pulled her to her feet. Hunched over to keep his profile low, he dragged her across the deck to the cabin entrance. She was half-limping, half-hopping, her walking stick useless. Thick mist wreathed the boneship, making even nearby objects hazy.

They stumbled through the door. Rosevear stared up at them, eyes full of questions they didn't have time to answer.

The scream of the taken man ceased with an agonised choking sound. A second later, something crashed onto the roof of the boneship. Arrows staccatoed sharp impacts all around her.

Two dark shapes loomed in the doorway. She raised her stick automatically until she recognised one as Tom and the other as Highson. A forester woman followed, holding a scrap of cloth to her forehead. Blood trickled around her fingers.

"How many?" asked Schuet as Rosevear tended to the woman's wound.

She shook her head, breathless. "All around us. Couldn't count."

"Too many to break through?"

The woman nodded. "There's only two of us on the boat."

Schuet cursed. "Why here? Why now?"

"I hate to be a wet blanket," Shilly pointed out, "but we won't be running anywhere. Look behind you."

Schuet did and saw Kemp, inhumanly flushed and motionless.

"Yes," the Seneschal said. "Of course. But what other hope is there?"

Something splashed outside. The boneship swayed beneath them.

"The ship," Shilly said, waving to attract Highson's attention. "It's a reservoir. How much potential is left?"

"Not enough to sail it away," he said. "Not on our own."

"I wasn't thinking of that. We can channel the potential somewhere else, use it to keep them at a distance—whatever they are."

"Just the Panic now," said the injured woman. "The wraith is gone."

"Thanks, but I'm none the wiser about either of them. Highson, can you do it?"

"We can only try. What do you have in mind?"

She thought furiously. Footsteps were audible on the deck outside. With the mist still thick, she couldn't see what was going on, but she presumed it wasn't rescue. The only voices she heard were unfamiliar inhuman ones.

"The man'kin," she said. "In the water beneath us. We're going to raise them."

Highson hesitated. "We don't know whose side they're on."

"That doesn't matter. At least they'll be a distraction."

"All right." He nodded, and closed his eyes. With one hand, he reached for her. "Guide me. You too, Tom."

The three of them joined, with Highson as the focus. Shilly had no natural talent, but she could help others to use theirs. Designing a charm was akin to drawing, but much more powerful. Instead of drawing from life, a Change-worker drew from *within* life, tapping into the deeper layers of existence where life made the leap from the abstract to the real, from thought to action. It was, she sometimes thought, the ultimate art. Tom's Engineering knowledge helped her refine the mnemonic she came up with even further, until the mental schema spinning in Highson's mind was one of the most elegant she had ever seen.

All that remained was to tap into the ship's stored reserves, which Highson did by leaning forward and placing his forehead against the bone deck. The Change thrilled through him, pure and unalloyed. Shilly's mind lit up like the sun in response, and she cried out for the joy of it.

She barely heard the explosion outside as two stony forms erupted from the surface of the water, limbs waving and tumbling through the air. They landed heavily on the shore with a distant clatter, like the echo of a stone tossed down a dry well. The bellowing they made as they shook off water and walked again struck her as little more than a murmur.

"There's something out there," whispered Schuet, who had inched forward to peer through the entranceway.

Yes, Shilly wanted to say, seeing through the Change the ferocious confusion of horns and claws that she and Highson had raised from the deep.

A stooped, vaguely humanoid figure loomed out of the mist and stood framed in the doorway. Schuet backed away, blade upraised.

"Yield, human."

Shilly returned to reality with a jolt at the sound of the voice. It wasn't a man'kin's voice. A crisp tenor, it reminded her of wood splitting. The face it belonged to was no less remarkable.

Small eyes peered from beneath low brows and around a broad nose with nostrils flared wide. Thick, freckled lips barely concealed the sharp teeth within. The creature's protruding chin was tufted with white hair that had been plaited and beaded with gold. It wore a leather uniform decorated with brown-and-black ribbed straps down its sides. The arms it held in readiness at its sides were prodigiously long and wiry, but muscled, perfect for a warrior. It smelt musky, of exertion and exhaustion, of flesh, not stone.

In its right hand it held a wicked, curved hook pointed directly at Schuet.

"Did you hear me?"

"I heard you," said Schuet. Over his shoulder, he asked Shilly, "What happened to the man'kin we raised?"

"I don't know." She was as surprised as he was. The charm had evaporated in her shock at seeing the creature before her.

"They ran away." The creature's eyes shifted to her. "Why would they do that, if you summoned them?"

"I don't know that either," she admitted, cursing the failure of their one and only chance. The boneship's reserves were now drained. She had no more surprises up her sleeves. "They're fickle."

"They are indeed."

"What do you want with us?" asked Schuet.

"We hunt the winged old one. We assumed it came at your bidding, until we saw it take one of your own."

"We thought it yours." Schuet stood poised for a moment, then lowered his blade. "If we are not to be harmed, I will yield to you."

"Seneschal!" the other soldier exclaimed.

"Quiet, Mikia. I have little choice."

"Indeed. We outnumber you three to one." The creature took Schuet's blade from him. "Your safety is assured, if you do as you're told."

"Wait." Shilly was confused. Did that mean Schuet had surren-dered? Where did that leave her and the others? "Who are you? *What* are you? Where did you come from?"

"I am Griel," said the creature, frowning. "Do you not know my kind?"

She shook her head.

He—given a lack of obvious breasts and hips, Shilly settled on that pronoun—looked around the chamber at the wardens, then back to her. "His kind—" Griel pointed a long index finger at Schuet "—the foresters, call my kind 'the Panic.' We call ourselves kingsfolk. We live in the forest."

"I thought *they* lived in the forest," she said, pointing at Schuet.

"We both do," said Schuet. "Therein lies the problem."

She understood, and so did the wardens captured with her. Highson raised his eyes to the ceiling. Tom sat heavily on a bale of sup-plies. Rosevear stayed carefully between Griel and his patient.

They were caught in the middle of a territorial war.

Two more long-limbed Panic appeared in the entranceway. One said something to Griel in a whisper too soft for her to overhear. Griel nodded.

"We're leaving," he announced. "All of you, including the sick one. You're coming with me to stand before the Quorum. Pack everything you need, quickly."

With a hollow feeling in her stomach, Shilly thought of Sal, last seen on his way to help Skender. "What about the others?"

"They fought well. The survivors are retreating up the Pass as we speak."

Who? Shilly wanted to ask. *Who are the survivors?* But Griel was unlikely to know names. To him, they were probably indistinguishable: flat-faced, short-armed, in various shades of brown.

"How long will we be gone?" asked Rosevear, rummaging among his supplies.

"Assume forever," said Griel, turning and walking out onto the deck. He clicked his fingers before disappearing into the mist, and two guards came to take his place.

"This is just great," Shilly muttered, fighting tears of frustration and anger. "*Now* what do we do?"

"As we're told," said Schuet. A significant glance added more clearly than words, *for now.* It was little comfort. In the time it took them to think of a plan and escape, they might be marched kilometres away. Where would Sal be by then? Would he think her dead?

Deep inside her burned the spark connecting them. While that lived, she would never give up hope—and neither would he, she knew. But hope was a tenuous thing, just like life itself. It could be snuffed out in a moment. She dreaded that day more than she dreaded her own death.

Putting the thought from her mind, she set about packing on the assumption that Sal would join her at some point, stuffing as many of their belongings into one bag as she could carry, then helping Rosevear prepare Kemp to be moved.

Sal stopped by one of the human bodies to pick its pocket. Seeing the narrow hilt of a pocketknife protruding from its belt, an idea occurred to him—one both unpalatable and necessary at the same time. He needed something more permanent than the muddy concealment charms he had drawn on his forehead and chest while descending. Already the waterfall was beginning to undo the protection they provided.

Ducking into a small recess near the base of the waterfall, he set to work. The sound of fighting from both quarters had died down, but he was aware that he might be spotted at any moment. Charms to confuse the eye and ear were second nature to him, but he had never been in such concentrated combat before. He preferred not to test them against a sword-wielding warrior whose senses were heightened from adrenalin.

The blade was clean and sharp. Its tip tugged neatly across his skin, leaving bloody lines in its wake. Quickly, calmly, he redrew charms that wouldn't fade in a hurry. Just as long as his concentration remained intact, so too would the illusion that he wasn't there. The pain helped keep his mind focused.

When he was finished, he folded the blade closed with a snap and put it into a pocket. Blood trickled down his cheeks and neck, but he ignored it. Stepping out of the recess, he headed off through the fading fog to where the boneship still floated, tied firmly to the shore. Shilly was in there; he could feel her anxiety, her nervousness. He wanted to call her, to put her mind at ease, but feared alerting the Panic. If there were Change-workers or sensitives among them, he would immediately reveal himself by doing so.

Two slope-shouldered Panic stood on guard by the gangplank. These creatures had the same physical arrangement as a human of two arms, two legs, trunk, and head, but the way they walked and moved was very different. When they attacked the humans on the beach, he had seen that they loped with smooth grace across flat and stony ground and that their long arms had the extra strength that better leverage would allow. When they stood erect, their heads jutted forward in a profoundly threatening manner. Sal had no intention of taking anyone on face-to-face if he could avoid it.

Slipping into the water under cover of water-hugging mist, he waded out, then swam when the bottom dropped out beneath him. He wasn't a strong swimmer, but he managed the distance to the ship. Getting aboard was more problematic, and it took him several attempts to get a hand up onto the bulwark and pull himself over.

He crouched on the deck for a moment, catching his breath and dripping red-tinged water. He could hear footsteps all around him. The Panic were ransacking the ship's supplies, rummaging through everything, and obviously taking what they thought valuable. That fitted their reputation for "banditry and murder," as Delfine had put it. He only hoped their need for the former had put the latter on hold for the moment.

One of their number ran towards him. He shrank back into a niche, putting his trust in the charms to keep him hidden. The Panic ran by, but it had been a close call. It wouldn't be long before one of them tripped over him. He needed to get off the deck and find somewhere to think.

Up. When the way was clear, he climbed onto a barrel and then raised himself up onto the boneship's sloping roof. The piscine shape of the hullfish skeleton was most apparent from that vantage point: a ridged crest ran along the top, where dorsal fins had once been attached; various holes and indentations, all now carefully caulked or turned into exhaust vents, marked where eyes, ears, and other organs had reached from the protected interior to the world outside. Sal slipped off his sandals and clambered on the balls of his feet towards the front of the ship.

What he saw there chilled him even further than the water had. A man's body was splayed on the bony surface, unnaturally still. His russet uniform had been torn open in several places and Sal saw deep gashes in sickly white flesh. Blood—surprisingly little—lay in a spreading pool around him. Not a large man in life, he now looked like a broken doll discarded by a giant child.

Sal remembered the dark shape that had swooped on Marmion and him above the waterfall. He had no evidence to connect that shape with the dead man before him, but it seemed to fit.

It killed my brother two nights ago, Delfine had said with hatred in her voice, *and I will see it dead*.

Sal carefully skirted the body, hearing voices faintly through the boneship's roof. Shilly and Rosevear were down there, along with Tom and Highson and another man whose voice he didn't recognise. When he reached the forward edge of the roof, he peered carefully over. Another two Panic guards watched the doorway, making sure the prisoners couldn't escape. He considered dropping down on them, but didn't feel confident of taking on two at once. If only Kail had been there . . .

He killed that thought immediately. The missing tracker had surprised Sal with his ruthlessness. Kail would probably have slit the throats of the unsuspecting guards without a second thought, and gone on to kill anyone or anything who happened to cross his path.

There had to be a better way.

A Panic soldier strode across the deck, scattering the last shreds of mist, and walked through the doorway. His voice, commanding and confident, told the prisoners they would be leaving soon. Shilly asked how Kemp was expected to travel, and she was told not to worry about it; that wouldn't be a problem. She demanded greater assurance than that, no doubt thinking of the stress that carrying a stretcher would have on the other prisoners, and probably worrying about her leg as well. Neither she nor Kemp were up to climbing the cliff faces around them, down which the Panic had so easily descended.

A deep droning sound from above distracted Sal from the conversation. Fearing the return of the ghostly creature, he rolled over and reached for the pocketknife. A large shape was descending from the clouds. Not a ghost, but a floating craft of similar shape to the boneship and a quarter its size. Suspended from two spherical balloons—each held at a constant distance from each other by a complex system of wires and cables—the gondola reminded him of the Laurean heavy lifter in which he had briefly travelled from the city of Laure over the Divide. That, though, had been a crude machine in comparison. This vessel possessed a baroque beauty that spoke of superior Engineering and maintenance, not just aesthetics. It looked more like a deep-sea fish than a bird.

The humming grew louder as it descended. This, he realised, was the means by which the Panic would take their prisoners away.

He had to get aboard.

Voices called. The crew of the balloon threw ropes when they arrived within range of the boneship. For a moment he feared that the flying ship might land on him, but it dropped to hover level with the boneship's deck about a metre away from its edge. Perhaps its bottom touched water, but he couldn't tell. Either way, a gangway soon connected the two craft, and stolen goods began to flow from one to the other.

Panic voices barked commands. The captives filed out of the boneship's cabin, Kemp suspended on a makeshift stretcher between Rosevear and a broad-shouldered man with greying hair who Sal had passed while climbing up the waterfall. There were only two foresters among them. Shilly came last, leaning heavily on her cane. She groaned when she saw the balloon, and muttered, "Here we go again."

Sal smiled and slithered across the roof to the side closest the balloon. Chu's talk of balloons and forests came back to him as he thought about what to do next. What else had she said? Something about cities in the trees and constant fog. Nothing about a nonhuman species of creature wielding thoroughly sharpened hooks.

The boneship rapidly emptied. There was no sign of Marmion and the others. Sal didn't have long to consider what to do. Somewhere, on the other side of the mountains and through the permanent cloud cover above, dawn was on its way. His camouflage charms wouldn't hold forever.

Two Panic soldiers carried Mawson like a sack of flour between them, and dumped him heavily out of sight. As the last of the bounty was loaded onto the balloon—which sagged ponderously under all the extra weight—and the last of the Panic straggled aboard, Sal decided. He would jump across as the balloon ascended and grab hold of either the edge of the gondola or one of the many ropes holding it secure. He would hang there, unseen, while the Panic carried their prisoners away. When they landed, he would drop away and hope to avoid being spotted by whoever waited on the ground. And then, depending on where he found himself, he would work out how to free Shilly and escape.

The gangplank retracted. Knots slipped and ropes fell away. The humming noise returned and slowly, steadily, the balloon began to rise.

Sal stood and backed up several steps. He tensed, waiting for the right moment. When the balloon was higher than his head, he ran forward three paces and threw himself into open air.

The gondola rushed at him. He clutched its side, scrabbling for a handhold even as the air whooshed out of his lungs from the impact. His momentum sent the whole thing rocking. Cries of alarm went up from the Panic flyers. The ascent ceased. He slid downwards, caught a cable in a desperate one-handed grip. The thin wire bit into his fingers and he knew he couldn't hold on. With a cry he slipped free.

Strong hands grabbed his wrist and arrested his fall. He jerked like a puppet in midair. His shoulder felt as though it had been dislocated.

"Here's the problem," called a voice from above. Sal looked up into the dark eyes of the Panic soldier who had ordered Shilly and the others to get ready to leave. Other long arms reached over the edge of the gondola to help haul Sal aboard. He didn't fight them. His attempt to rescue Shilly might have been unsuccessful, but at least they would soon be together.

He tumbled gracelessly over the edge and sprawled to the deck, surrounded by leather sandals. Abandoning the camouflage charms, he clambered upright to take stock, blinking blood out of his eyes. Two soldiers searched him, took away the knife he had found but let him keep *yadeh-tash* on the thong around his neck.

"Are you hurt?" Shilly pressed through the Panic with concern and relief mingled in her eyes.

The leader kept her at arm's length. "You know this one?"

"Yes. He's with me. Can I—?"

"Not until I know what he wants."

Sal stood, flexing his stinging hands in a manner he hoped wasn't threatening. "She already told you. I'm with her. That's all."

The leader of the Panic assessed them quickly, then nodded. "All right. Sit down, both of you. If you cause any more problems, I'll tip you out."

Sal nodded and went to join Shilly. She put an arm around him and led him to where Highson sat on one side of the gondola. Tom sat on the other side, watching him with a worried expression. Rosevear reached into a satchel and offered him ointment for his cuts.

"You took your time," Shilly whispered. "I was beginning to worry."

"You didn't honestly think I'd let you go without me, did you?" He tried to smile reassuringly, but it didn't sit well.

"What about the others?" she asked. "Are they all right?"

Instead of answering, he cast his mind out into the night.

"*Skender, can you hear me?*" The balloon's humming engines grew louder and they ascended rapidly into the mist. "*You don't have to say anything. Just let me know you're listening.*"

The faintest hint of recognition came from an unknown distance away.

"*We're okay,*" he broadcast, hoping the message was getting through. "*The Panic have us. No one's been harmed. I'll keep you informed if things change.*"

Feeling Highson's eyes on him, Sal added, "*Tell Marmion to keep on going without us. We'll catch up later. Okay?*"

Again the barest hint of affirmation.

"They'll be all right," he told Shilly, squeezing her hand and trying not to think about what might happen next.

On the fifth day from Laure, the twins collapsed in midstep and fell unconscious to the ground. Kail, taken by surprise, was momentarily unsure what to do. He had assumed the twins' body to be indefatigable. Although it had bled a strange silver gas after being stabbed by Pirelius during the siege of Laure, the wound had closed over within hours and left no visible scar. He had had no occasion since to believe that Highson Sparre's strange creation might not last forever.

Here, though, was evidence of its fallibility. He immediately stopped and managed—with no small amount of difficulty—to get it onto the back of the camel, where it lay splayed like a giant drugged spider. The body was warm to the touch. Neither Seth nor Hadrian Castillo stirred at his rough treatment of them. They rode insensate while he looked for shelter.

He found it in a sprawling copse halfway up the shoulder of the Hanging Mountains. They had travelled an appreciable distance since buying the camel in Laure. Every night he slept in the saddle, lulled by the regular swaying of the broad back beneath him, while the twins loped steadily alongside, as black as the deepest night and engaged in what manner of internal conversation he couldn't tell. It was peculiar to say the least to see individual faces moving beneath the unnatural skin of the creature's head, faces which moved at odds but also in perfect unison, creating strange, ever-shifting expressions he found impossible to interpret. Only practice enabled him to distinguish one from the other in a head that at first glance looked like nothing more than a monstrous amalgam of features.

During the day they kept to old roads where they could. As the ground slowly rose beneath them to meet the mountains ahead, the trees and grasses grew taller, denser, and greener, and the going became increasingly difficult. In situations where there was no obvious track to follow, they shadowed the edge of the Divide itself, although Kail felt exposed in the wasted, crumbling terrain. He didn't want to be seen by Marmion or anyone else before time.

When the time to be seen would come, he didn't know. He kept moving in the hope that it would announce itself in due course.

Untying the Homunculus and letting it collapse to the Earth in the shade of a wide-branched tree not common along the Strand, he set up a temporary camp for the three of them, treating the camel with the same respect he would himself or his odd companion. Night wasn't far away, so he prepared a fire and went off in search of game. With two rabbits in hand, he returned to find the twins sitting up and hand-feeding the irascible camel grain from one of the saddlebags.

"What happened back there?" he asked, placing the rabbits on the ground and skinning them with long practised strokes of his knife.

"I think . . ." The twins hesitated, and their form dissolved for a moment as each individual within moved at odds with the other. "I think we fell asleep."

Kail nodded, having wondered if that might have been the case. "You've been in that body for two weeks or so. It's about time it needed a rest."

"We didn't see it coming," said one of the twins—the more strident of the two, with whom Kail had learned to associate the name *Seth*. "We just dropped in midstep. What sort of body *is* this? When's it going to fail on us again?"

"All good questions." Kail didn't offer any false reassurances. "I've been asking them myself. Highson Sparre made that body and put you in it. It's still working, even though everything around you is dead of the Change. That seems contradictory to me."

"I have a theory," said the more thoughtful of the two: *Hadrian*. "It goes back to where we came from, what we are. I belong to the First Realm, Seth to the Second. In this body we're existing side by side just as we did in Bardo, the place you call the Void Beneath, between our two Realms. But we're not in Bardo any longer; we're in your world. And whatever sort of Realm this is, it's still adjusting to us being here."

Kail nodded, even though he didn't entirely understand the twins' talk of Realms and other worlds. Only the existence of the Void Beneath encouraged him to keep an open mind. That *was* another world, of a sort. There might be more no one else had ever suspected.

"This world doesn't like us," Hadrian went on, his half of the Homunculus moving inside Seth's like a tarry ghost. "We don't work like it does, we don't fit in, but we're not completely alien. We made it, after all. It's modelled on us. It might try to reject us by cutting us off from the Change, but we have our own powers. We're the source of everything."

"And the end of everything," added Seth in a more baleful tone.

"We could be," Hadrian agreed.

Kail tugged the skin off the second rabbit and tossed it aside. "Your body, the Homunculus, is quickened by the Change like every other living thing. Is that what you're saying?"

"It has to be," the twins said.

"But if you're cut off from the rest of the world, that means the Homunculus is drawing directly from you, and I don't care how old you are or how powerful you might be, that's got to cost you in the long run. You have to learn to feel the symptoms and rest when you need to."

They offered him no argument to that. "Do you think we should try to eat?" Hadrian asked.

"It certainly won't hurt."

The twins watched him gut the rabbits with quiet fascination. He couldn't tell what they were thinking.

"I remember being a vegetarian," said Hadrian after a while.

"When you were twelve," Seth countered in a mocking tone. "You did it to get attention."

"That's what you thought I was doing, but I really meant it. At least, I think I did."

Both heads lifted at a sound Kail couldn't hear. He waited a moment, watching them closely. This happened regularly, at least once every day.

"Want to talk about it yet?" he asked.

The twins didn't reply immediately. They turned away to resume feeding the camel. It snorted at them and moved off to crouch on bony knees, resting.

"I killed a man, once." Hadrian, surprisingly, said that, over the Homunculus's shoulder. Kail would have thought Seth the more likely to commit murder. "He wasn't just a man; there was something else inside him, controlling him."

"A golem," said Kail.

The Homunculus's head came up. "I thought they were made of clay, a bit like robots."

"You can indeed house a golem in a clay body, but they don't last long. Flesh is better. What are robots?"

"Never mind. Back then, this thing was a creature of the Second Realm, but it could join with people in the First Realm, as it did with this man, in order to act on both sides of Bardo. We called such alliances *energumen*. They had their own agenda, their own plans. The creature inside the man I killed was Upuaut, the Wolf. It hunted and tried to kill me. When I killed its host, it disappeared. Ordinarily, I guess, it would've gone back to the Second Realm, but the Realms merged so it was free to stay. It has probably been looking for me all the time since."

"And now it's found you," said Kail, even as he wondered why anyone would willingly let a golem into their body. "Is that what you think?"

"Maybe. *Something* out there is howling at us."

"Well, a golem can only take over a Change-worker if they've over-extended themselves and entered the Void Beneath first. When they do that, their bodies are left empty, easy to take over. If you've no talent in the Change, you're not in any risk from this thing."

"Except from someone else," Seth said, "someone who *has* been taken over."

"Conceivably, yes, but your body is still strong. You have no need to be frightened."

He could tell that his words offered little comfort. "You don't know Upuaut," said Hadrian. "If there's a way to hurt us, it'll find it."

"Were there only forces for evil in your world?" asked Kail. "Per-haps some good has survived as well."

"Perhaps." The twins returned to introspective contemplation, and he couldn't rouse them until the rabbits were cooked and cooling. Even then, they did little more than pick at the roasted meat he served them, clearly feeling no hunger at all.

What had they seen? What had they done? Not for the first time, Kail turned over what little he knew about the Cataclysm, fruitlessly searching for clues. That he was talking to the only living eyewitnesses to the event and was barely able to wring sense from them seemed a terrible tragedy for all concerned.

The day grew old. Kail was in no hurry to move, and the twins were loath to press him. Their collapse had profoundly frightened them. What might their Homunculus body do next that they hadn't expected? What if it were to just *stop* one day, reach an expiration date built into its strange flesh, unknown to them, and bring their mission to an inglorious end?

"I don't understand," Hadrian said to Kail as the sky flooded with reds and oranges. "I don't understand how the sun sets."

He had been watching it ever since the sky had become clearer to them. At first, the world had been little more than a blur. Gradually, pieces of it were resolving into focus. The sun and moon were two such pieces, although they made less sense the more Hadrian could see. The moon appeared to have phases like the ones he remembered, but those phases followed no obvious pattern. The sun didn't so much set each night as shrink into a hazy dot on the western horizon and vanish.

"'Sets'?" echoed Kail, not understanding the question.

Hadrian didn't pursue it.

What does it matter, little brother? asked Seth, feeling his frustration. *We don't need to know how the world works. We just need to save it.*

What if we can't do the one without the other?

Seth had no good answer to that.

"Who's the Goddess, then?" he asked instead. "I've heard people mention her, but I don't know if she's a myth or a legend, or someone real."

"You're asking the wrong person," said the tracker. "I'm neither theologian nor historian. I studied just enough to get through the Novitiate, and no more."

"You must have *some* idea."

"Well . . . They say she shaped the world after the Cataclysm, gave it form and laws and set all its peoples in their places. There are a lot of stories about her: that she was haunted by ghosts who whispered constantly to her; that she lived in the sky and will return again, one day. Whether she actually existed, I don't know. She might have been modelled on a leader who saved her people from the chaos you left in your wake."

"Not us," protested Seth. "Yod."

"It was our plan to bind the Realms together," Hadrian reminded him. "There's no point hiding from what we've done. The world must've been in a terrible state when we went into the Void. All the old rules broken, no new rules to take their place. Things must've been in one hell of a mess."

"That's what we hear," said Kail. "All the folk tales about the Cataclysm, all the stories in the *Book of Towers*, are concerned with strange deaths and the world shifting underfoot. Unreliable, dangerous—that's what it was like back then. Whoever the Goddess was, it's a fair bet we wouldn't be here at all but for her."

Who could it have been? asked Seth within the private space of the Homunculus. *Kybele and Agatha are dead. Sheol is destroyed.* A memory came to him, communicated to Hadrian as clearly as if it had been his own. *Could it be Horva or another of the Holy Immortals?*

It could be anyone, Hadrian said, not wanting to entertain too many outlandish possibilities. He had enough in his head as it was.

"How big is the world?" he asked Kail. "You're a tracker. You must know *that* much about it."

The big man's lips curled up on one side. Not quite a smile. "You'd think so. I can walk from Kittle to Muombin blindfolded, and draw the Strand from memory for three thousand kilometres. I can tell you a species of grass from a single straw, and identify a beast from one glimpse of its spoor. There are patches of the Broken Lands no person alive has seen but me—so yes, I know a lot about the Strand, but little outside that area. That's the truth of it. Could you tell me how big *your* world was?"

That, the twins had to admit, they couldn't.

"But what shape is it?" Hadrian pressed, sensing he was on the brink of something important. "Is there ice to the south and tropics to the north? Or the other way around? It would help to know which hemisphere we're in."

"Hemisphere?" Kail repeated.

"You know . . . north or south."

"There's talk of ice in the mountains and you know which direction they lie in: northeast, where this shadow of yours is growing."

"That's not what I mean. Every big mountain has ice and snow. Are there poles where there's snow and ice all the time?"

The tracker shook his head, genuinely failing to understand.

Hadrian gave up. That line of investigation was going to get them nowhere, like the others. So it went: every time he probed at the nature of the world, they hit a fundamental failure of comprehension. It was like trying to explain the finer points of Beethoven's Fifth to someone completely tone deaf. Either the twins weren't asking the right questions, or Kail was failing to grasp their meaning.

"Tell me this, then," he said in desperation. "What would happen if you walked in a straight line forever? If you just started walking one day and didn't stop, where would you end up?"

"Where I started," said Kail without hesitation.

"So the world is round. We've worked out that much, at least."

Kail was shaking his head before Hadrian had finished the sentence. "It's not round. There's no edge to it."

"Not round like a plate. Round like a ball."

"Why would it be like that?"

"Because . . ." The twins were momentarily lost for a deeper explanation than *because that's the way it has always been*. Things changed; they knew that with certainty. There was no *always*.

"We don't know," said Seth. "We're just trying to make sense of the sky."

"Sounds to me like you need an empyricist, not a tracker."

"What's that?"

"Someone who studies the sky."

"Like an astrologer?" Seth asked.

"Astronomer," Hadrian corrected him.

Kail was unfamiliar with either of those words. "There's an empyricist in the Haunted City. Never had much to do with him, though, since our fields were so different. A strange man with strange thoughts. No idea where you'll find one like him out here."

Astrologer, oastronomer, empyricist: the three words had a kind of rhythm to them, Hadrian thought—philosophically speaking, anyway. Astrologers had plied a very real trade prior to the Cataclysm-before-last, when the First and Second Realms had been one. After the sundering, astronomers had come into their own, for the world no longer operated under "magical" rules and instead had succumbed to descriptions that didn't take into account the will and desire of observing humanity. Now the two Realms were closely interacting, if not actually joined, and a new science was required.

"I'm tired," he said. "I'm tired of feeling confused all the time and it being our fault doesn't help at all. It was either that or let the world end."

"Some choice," agreed Seth.

"How did you know you had a choice?" Kail asked. "Were there creatures like man'kin in your world who could see the future?"

"No. There were the Sisters, though. And Sheol and the Third Realm."

Kail looked momentarily nonplussed. "There were *three* Realms?"

"Still are, I guess," said Seth. "But this Goddess of yours only knows what has happened to the Third."

Kail shook his head. "I'm as lost and tired as you, I'm afraid. Unlike you, though, I need to sleep on a regular basis, and I relish the thought of doing so flat on my back for a change, rather than in the saddle. Do you mind?"

"No," the twins said. "Go ahead. We'll keep watch."

"Wake me if you hear anything. Anything at all."

They nodded, and the big man lay on his side with his head on a sack of camel food. Within a minute, he was breathing heavily.

Hadrian envied him that ability. Even in life, he'd been a light and restless sleeper. He remembered that clearly. Too many thoughts going around in his head, over and over into the small hours of the morning. He found it no easier with two-heads-in-one.

The fire crackled. Its heat dispelled Hadrian's fear of Upuaut, but only slightly. He wondered what the wolf-spirit was doing at that moment. Lurking just outside the campfire circle, peering in at the people warming themselves and talking about things they barely understood, or prowling the landscape of the new world, tearing throats and cracking bones in endless frustration?

Maybe we're going in the wrong direction, Seth said. *Maybe we should go to this Haunted City of theirs to talk to the empyricist before blundering into something we can't get out of.*

No. We have to keep going. There isn't time to screw around with other stuff. Yod is waking. I can feel it, and so can you. If we're not there when that happens . . .

What?

I don't know. Something bad. It'll eat everyone, like it tried to do before.

Just because it's awake doesn't mean it's free.

We freed ourselves eventually. It will, too.

That was a chilling thought, one that made the twins shiver in rare synchrony. Seth's memories of the Second Realm were vivid: Yod, the giant black pyramid growing fat on the dead, surrounded by monsters who thought nothing of sacrificing every creature they could find to their master's insatiable appetite.

The world is changed, Hadrian thought, *but it's still a food chain. Eat or be eaten; kill or be killed. Will it never end?*

Only when everything is dead. Seth's words were blunt. *Is that how you'd rather things were?*

Hadrian thought about it. *No,* he said. But part of him wondered.

The fire burned on. At midnight, with the moon riding high among the strange gleaming stars, Kail woke and they resumed their journey into darkness.

THE FOREST

**"Where there's a way, life will take it.
When a way can't be found, mind will make it."**
MASTER WARDEN RISA ATILDE:
NOTES TOWARD A UNIFIED CURRICULUM

The mist grew thicker as Skender fled with the others up the Divide. There was a path along the constricted water channel, one built up over the previous days from debris and made smooth by settling mud. Still holding Chu's hand tightly in his, he blindly followed those ahead, fearing an arrow in the neck at any moment. All he could hear was the squelching of feet and the grunting of breath. Winded, frightened, and shocked by everything he had seen, it was all he could do to keep his mind on not falling over on his face.

Finally they paused to catch their breath under an overhang large enough to hold all of them at once. Chu let go of him and bent over double, wheezing. The two foresters who had been carrying her wing dumped it unceremoniously at her feet. The message was clear: he and Chu would be carrying it the rest of the way. Skender acknowledged them with a breathless nod.

There were six foresters—Delfine, Heuve, Navi, and three others —plus three wardens—Marmion, Banner, and Eitzen. With Skender and Chu, that made a party of eleven. It wasn't much of an army if the Panic followed. Heuve stood, powerfully poised, all bearded chin and muscles, at the edge of the overhang watching the way they had come. Periodically, he scanned the cliff faces too, no doubt wary of another vertical ambush. How Heuve saw through the thickening fog, Skender didn't know. He could barely see as far as the river's edge.

"I can still taste," Chu said, "that fucking mud."

He relished the opportunity to clap her between the shoulders in mock sympathy. "There, there."

She looked up at him with a baleful gleam in her eye. "Don't push your luck."

"You call *this* luck?" He indicated the chaotic scene around them. Cut off from the boneship; chased by legendary half-humans; threatened with expulsion if he hung around Chu; and, yes, he could taste the mud too, cloying and foul at the back of his nose. "I'm sorry, but nothing you could do will make this any worse."

She laughed at that, perhaps a touch too loudly, then straightened. Grabbing his face in both hands, she kissed him hard on the lips. Caught totally by surprise, it was over before he could decide whether to recoil or kiss her back.

"There," she said, as though in satisfaction. "We're alive and we're together. Things could be a lot worse. Eh, Heuve?"

The bodyguard didn't demean himself by so much as looking at her. "The Outcast will not speak unless spoken to."

"Or what? You'll spank me?"

A muscle in Heuve's left cheek twitched. Instead of responding, he took back the knife he had given Skender and turned to address Lidia Delfine, who had been checking the well-being of the others. "Eminence, we appear to have left the enemy behind."

"They let us go," said Marmion, grey-faced and holding his injured arm close to his chest.

"I agree." Delfine tugged off her cap and scratched at the tightly bound hair beneath. "Furthermore, I think they were keeping us busy while the rest of them dealt with that ship of yours."

"You think that was the real object of their attack?" Marmion looked at her askance.

"You tell us," said Heuve in a low rumble. "You've yet to be entirely clear on why you're here in the first place."

Delfine silenced him with a wave of her hand. "The moment for accusations and recriminations is not now, Heuve. There'll be plenty of time for that in Milang."

Chu's attention pricked at the mention of her surname. "Milang?"

Delfine looked at her. "You've heard of it?"

"It's my surname."

"Unlikely." Delfine dismissed the matter by turning pointedly to Marmion. "It's not safe here. We'll keep moving, deeper into the forest. Are you coming?"

"I believe we have no alternative," the warden said, glancing at Chu and Skender, "for the moment."

Skender bit his lip on another protest about Sal and the others. If Delfine and her band of soldiers were still wary of going back, what could he and a trio of drained Sky Wardens do in their place? He didn't think being a Stone Mage would count for much among the Panic.

At that moment, Sal's voice came to him through the Change.

"Skender, can you hear me? You don't have to say anything. Just let me know you're listening."

He turned his back on Marmion and the others as they argued about where to go and how long it would take. His reserves were low, but he tried to signal that he had heard as best he could.

"We're okay," Sal continued after a moment, as though he had received Skender's faint call. *"The Panic have us. No one's been harmed. I'll keep you informed if things change. Tell Marmion to keep on going without us. We'll catch up later. Okay?"*

Skender resisted the impulse to try to send *No, it bloody well isn't okay. We're in unknown territory at the mercy of strangers! What else could possibly go wrong?*

Then the memory of Chu's kiss returned to him, and he flushed. His lips still tingled. *We're alive and we're together. Things could be a lot worse.*

He sent a weak affirmation. It was the best he could do.

"Can I ask you something?" He broke into the huddle to address

Lidia Delfine. "You just said 'deeper into the forest.' Does that mean we're officially in it now?"

"Of course. It's all around us." She looked at him as though he was mad for asking.

Chu and the wardens peered out as one from under the overhang. With the glowing brands close at hand, the misty night was impenetrable. Even so, they had seen no sign of vegetation during their mad flight up the Divide. From the bottom of the mighty canyon, they could have been anywhere on the arid plains to the west of the mountains.

"You'll see," Lidia Delfine said, glancing at Chu and frowning, "but for now, we press on. Dawn is an hour away. We must be well out of danger by then."

"Is sleep an option at any point?" asked Chu, barely smothering a yawn.

"No," Heuve stated flatly. "The Pass is no place for the soft."

"Or for people with a sense of humour, obviously."

"This is no laughing matter."

"No, and I can see why her so-called Eminence brings you on these trips. Life must seem pretty good back home compared to being with you."

The bodyguard stiffened. For a horrible moment, Skender fully expected him to pick her up by the throat and strangle her on the spot.

Instead, he turned his narrowed gaze out into the mist. His jaw muscles clenched and unclenched. If a dozen Panic had chosen that moment to appear, Skender wouldn't have liked the chances of any of them walking away intact.

The Eminent Delfine put a calming hand on his shoulder, an unexpectedly intimate gesture. "We leave now," she said. No one argued. Skender offered Chu his hand again, but her mood had soured. She strode off ahead of him, head down and concentrating on not slipping in the mud.

The way became increasingly difficult as the night wore on, not least because the path was treacherous and visibility poor. The constant roar of water rushing by made conversation difficult. Constrained to a relatively narrow channel, the flood foamed and fought just metres away, dowsing them all with spray. Exhaustion and sensory overload soon took their toll, reducing Skender's world to that directly in front of him.

It came as a complete surprise, then, when the party suddenly slowed and began climbing the cliff wall to his left, heading for the top of the Divide wall. Cut into the stone was a series of deep notches, providing a means of getting to the top. He forced his aching muscles to keep moving up in the hope that it would all be over soon. When they were out of the Divide, there was a chance they could sleep. That was what Heuve had implied, and he didn't seem the sort to lie about anything, on principle.

Skender crawled over the top of the Divide. The edge was as bare as the edge at Laure or Tintenbar or the Lookout, but as his gaze rose from the ground immediately ahead of him and penetrated the swirling fog all around—beginning, even then, to glow with sunlight creeping around the mountains to the east—he saw the first low bushes and vines of a mat of vegetation that rose and thickened into a wall of fern and branch not five metres from him, hugging the sides of the steepening foothills. Trees rose up like statues within the undergrowth, supporting a canopy that looked well-nigh impenetrable. It extended upward as far as he could see, vanishing into the impenetrable fog, utterly fecund and utterly unbelievable for someone raised in a desert.

So much life! He couldn't see over or through the overlapping boughs. For the first time, he could appreciate how it might be possible to lose oneself in such a profligacy of plants.

Still, he thought, *how deep can it go? A dozen metres or so? Perhaps twenty? Not much more, surely.*

Delfine and Marmion stood to one side, conferring as the last of the foresters and Banner climbed up from below. Marmion looked pale and drawn after the long, one-handed ascent. Chu stared at the wall of forest with an unreadable expression. She said nothing, and Skender was wary of approaching her.

Heuve ascended last. Taking one long look down the stone ladder he declared with confidence that they had not been pursued.

"Good," said Delfine, flexing her left arm and wincing. "That's one thing to be thankful for." Her cool façade broke, just for a moment, and Skender glimpsed the grief she felt at leaving her friends behind. She had already lost a brother. He considered telling her about the message from Sal, but he didn't want to give her any false hope.

"The path is clear," Heuve stated, inspecting a patch of the forest wall that looked no different from the rest. "We should keep moving."

"How far is Milang?" Skender asked.

"Half a day's march," said Delfine.

On the other side of the forest, Skender assumed. Once they were through the trees and out in the open again, the only thing they would have to worry about was the increasing gradient.

"I need to rest," said Marmion. "You can go on without me if you like—"

"Of course we won't. You're injured." Delfine dismissed the suggestion out of hand. "There's an arbour along the path. We'll pause there to regain our strength. Will two hours be long enough?"

"It will suffice." Marmion accepted the offer with a nod. "Thank you."

"I'll lead the way. Please, all of you, do not leave the path—for the safety of the forest, as well as your own—no matter what you might see or hear."

That puzzled Skender until they had broached the outer fringes of the forest and plunged inside. It was dark in there, and full of life. Everywhere he looked, plants crowded, blocking out the first glimmerings of dawn and choking any possible attempt at passage. The path beneath his feet was little more than a rut wide enough for one small person; roots snaked across it, always ready to snag an unwary foot.

He preceded Chu through the wild growth, holding one end of the wing behind his back with patient familiarity. Getting it up the cliff face had been a chore, but one he shouldered as his due. Leaving it behind for the Panic to claim as booty wasn't an option. Although it had been Chu's decision to come along on Marmion's expedition, he would still blame himself if anything happened to the wing or to her.

They didn't walk far. Delfine called a rest break when they reached a human-made clearing ten paces from the track. It was barely large enough for the eleven of them, even with the wing standing on one end, propped up between Skender and Chu as they sat and caught their breath. Skender leaned back and listened to the noises of the forest. Animals called constantly, hooting and hollering from unknown distances. Birds chattered among themselves, either ignorant of, or just plain ignoring, the humans in their midst. Smaller creatures rustled through the undergrowth. None of them were visible. All he could see when he looked into the forest were plants, some of which he recognised from books, but others he found strange and almost threatening in their weirdness: fungi clinging to rough-barked pines; ferns crowding every available space; brightly coloured flowers nodding sleepily in darkened recesses, heavy with nectar. Life thrived all around him, perhaps a little too vigorously for his liking.

His eyes closed in the moist air. He slept without knowing he had fallen asleep, and drifted into a strange state wherein he seemed to be awake but suspected he wasn't. Events followed no obvious logic. People and things came and went without warning. He wandered among them, lost and confused and unsure how to make it stop. If he was asleep, why not give in and stop worrying about it? If he was awake, things had become very odd indeed.

"It's the way of things," said a sinister, insidious voice from the bushes. "Don't you know that, rabbit?"

Skender stiffened, looking around him in a guilty panic. "*You*— here?"

A wall of fronds parted to his right, revealing the twisted, scarred face of the jailer he had left behind in the Aad, horribly injured by the

Homunculus and abandoned to die in the dirt. "Yes. It's me. You'll never be rid of me. Ever."

Clawed, black-nailed hands reached out of the forest, clutching at Skender's face, and he jerked awake with a cry and leapt to his feet.

"Easy," said Navi, leaning over him. "It's just a bad dream."

"He has them all the time," said Chu blearily from the other side of the wing.

"He was here, *right here* . . ." Skender pointed vaguely at the ferns, aware that the foresters were watching him with a mixture of weariness and alarm. He scoured the undergrowth, afraid of what he might detect in there, and of course he saw nothing.

"It's gone now." Navi leaned away from him, staring at him as though he had gone quite mad. "There's nothing to be frightened of."

"I'm sorry," he said, genuinely embarrassed at what, to her, must have seemed a total overreaction.

"Sit down, Skender," said Chu, reaching around the wing to tug at his robe.

He resisted, still rattled by the dream and an uneasy feeling about what the undergrowth might be hiding.

"*Sit.*" She pulled him so hard he almost fell on her. "There's nothing you can do about it," she said, not very helpfully. "Instead, look at that tree over there and tell me why it's so weird."

He did as she indicated, knowing she was only trying to distract him and perversely reluctant to go along with it. The tree was by far the largest abutting the clearing, with a broad, rippling trunk from which extended branches heavy with glossy dark leaves. He had glanced at it on arriving in the arbour but given it no more than a single thought. A tree was a tree was a tree.

He chastised himself for being so lazy. Rocks weren't just rocks, just as deserts weren't just deserts and people weren't just people; everything in nature came in many different shapes, sizes, and qualities. To a forester, each tree was probably unique, with its own strengths and character. He wouldn't get very far if he assumed everything was the same.

Looking at the tree more closely, he realised that there *was* something odd about it, on two levels. Superficially, strange whorls and lines marred the relative smoothness of its bark. The patterns didn't look entirely natural, as though they had been carved there as a sapling and left to heal over. Like scars, in other words, or tattoos.

And like the tattoos he had earned during his training, these marks appeared to follow flows of the Change. With senses more subtle than sight alone, he traced powerful energies moving up and down the trunk, from its roots to its branches and back again. The tree glowed like an enormous candle, rich with life—and more than that. The whole forest was full of life, but most of it was without direction. This tree took that life and did something with it.

But what *was* that?

"Well?" Chu nudged him, waiting for an answer.

"I don't know." The dream was quite forgotten as he contemplated the problem. "It doesn't seem to be alive—"

"You mean someone killed it?"

"No. Just not alive like we are. It's not about to uproot and go for a walk, or start talking to us."

"Well, that's a relief."

He thought about it some more. "I wonder if this is why we're here, in this particular spot. The tree could be a signpost."

"Or a guard?"

"How do you mean?"

"To stop enemies from coming up the path—out of the Divide and into the forest. Maybe it'll fall on anyone who is unauthorised."

"Interesting." And it was. The Keep's library contained nothing like this.

"Keep it down, you two," said Heuve. "People are trying to rest."

"Sorry." Skender was genuinely repentant. His own fatigue had begun to return after his shocked awakening. He would have been quite happy to let the matter of the tree drop forever, but for the bodyguard's next words.

"The forest is none of your business. Keep your nose well out of it."

"Kind of hard to do that *now*," said Chu testily, "don't you think?"

Heuve ignored her, and Skender ignored him in turn. His attention drifted back to the tree. He sensed more than just innocent exhaustion in Heuve's irritation. Was there something about this particular tree he didn't want them to see or understand?

Tracing the trunk up into the canopy, Skender tried to follow and count the branches through the tangle above him. Even with the help of the Change, he couldn't do it. The tree was intimately bound up in the fabric of the forest, so whatever capacity it possessed, the forest possessed it too.

Bringing his gaze back to the clearing, he found Marmion watching him. The warden inclined his head in something that might have been a nod, then closed his eyes and went to sleep.

By midmorning, the forest was raucous and stifling. Mist curled through the trunks like ghostly fingers, making the air heavier and warmer than it had been in the Divide. Skender rolled up the sleeves of his robe, but that didn't stop him sweating. The rumbling of his stomach as they resumed their journey only made him more uncomfortable still.

"What, no breakfast?" Chu had commented on Delfine's call to rise and resume their journey.

"Did you bring any food with you?" asked Navi, brushing down her uniform and adjusting her boots.

"There wasn't time."

"No breakfast then, I guess."

"What about fruit? There's plenty on the trees."

"Can you tell the safe from the poisonous?"

"No, but I presume *you* can."

"The Outcast will not take from the forest," grated Heuve, even grumpier after a couple of hours sleep than he had been before. "If she does—"

"Yeah, yeah. I get it. I'll just starve, then."

"We eat in Milang," said Delfine, more reasonably but with a warning edge. "We lost our supplies in the attack, too."

Chu had turned away and busied herself with getting the wing ready to travel. This time she went first, leaving Skender with nothing better to do while he walked than contemplate his empty stomach and her behind.

The sun, diffused by fog and leaves, cast no shadow, but he could follow its steady progress across the sky through breaks in the canopy. He reckoned by its position that they were heading due north. By the time the sun reached directly overhead, he felt ready to take his chances with the local produce and Heuve both. The wing seemed to weigh a ton or more, and his fingers were getting cramp. But he didn't complain. The thick moist air left him panting like a dog. He had barely enough energy for walking. The others, Chu included, seemed to be in much the same state, as no one spoke at all, except to curse.

The forest towered over them, seeming more impenetrable than before, not less. His eyes were becoming desensitised to green. Remembering his expectation that the forest would soon peter out, he began to wonder just how far it might extend. They had walked at least two kilometres through the dense vegetation, their path rising and falling and taking sudden turns to avoid sheer rock faces that couldn't be crossed, but in general their altitude rose. He watched for paths leading elsewhere; they either didn't exist or were as well hidden as the entrance to the forest had been. Soon the fog was so dense that he could barely see as far as Lidia Delfine, leading the way at the head of the group.

Finally the foliage parted before them. Chu stumbled as she stepped from thick undergrowth onto solid stone, and he did the same two paces later. When he had recovered, his gaze lifted up to find nothing but fog ahead and above him, its hazy white brilliance blinding after the mottled shadows of the forest.

Chu put down the wing to look around. Those ahead of them had stopped on the edge of a cliff and were peering along an insubstantial-looking rope bridge which vanished into fog barely halfway across its span. The far side was invisible, except as a very faint shadow. There could have been anything there.

Skender regarded the bridge with a sceptical eye. It appeared to be well maintained, but the planks were thin and the way narrow. Ropes at his waist height provided the only handholds.

"Looks safe enough to me," pronounced Warden Banner, the Engineer of the group.

"Of course it's safe," said Navi. "Unless you're Panic soldiers, in which case . . ." She mimed cutting one of the ropes securing it to the cliff wall.

"How would you know if we were Panic or not?" asked Chu. "Who can see through this murk?"

"There are lookouts stationed at every bridge," said Delfine with the air of someone determined not to reveal any secrets. "We call this the Versegi Chasm, after the man who built the first bridge across it. People used to think it bottomless; if you drop a stone anywhere along the bridge's length, you'll never hear it hit the bottom."

"What is down there?" asked Skender, hoping it was soft, just in case.

"A riverbed, and plants growing from seeds that fall from above. It's very dark and very quiet. The people who live there are said to be mad or mystics, depending on who you ask."

Marmion acknowledged this with a nod. "Very good, but shall we keep moving?"

"I thought you'd like the chance to rest for a moment."

"That will not be required."

Skender was about to protest that it was indeed required when he realised that Marmion's revived testiness came from a desire to put the bridge behind him. The crossing would be especially difficult for him with only one hand to balance himself. No wonder he was acting with such impatience.

Then Skender remembered the wing, and groaned. He too would be crossing the bridge without both hands on the guide ropes. If he dropped the wing, he might as well follow it over the edge. Chu wouldn't suffer him to live after a mistake like that.

"All right, then." Delfine nodded. "Let's keep moving."

"How much longer?" Skender blurted.

"Not far. I'd suggest keeping your eyes up as you go across, but I don't want you to slip either."

With that, she headed out onto the bridge and strode confidently over the chasm. The bridge swayed alarmingly with every step she took. Skender tried not to pay too much attention to that.

Marmion waved Eitzen after her, then followed when Eitzen had vanished into the mist and the bridge ceased dancing. He walked slowly and carefully, making no attempt to be as quick as Delfine or young Eitzen. Hunched like an old man, he made it across in twice their time.

"We'll go last," Skender told Heuve as the other foresters went ahead.

"No. You'll go next."

"Do you think we'll run away?" Chu asked him. "We have no idea where we are, and just one path to follow. It wouldn't be a very smart move."

"No," Heuve repeated, cracking his knuckles. "It would not."

Chu rolled her eyes and turned to Skender. "Want to go first?"

"Sure." He swapped places with her and picked up his end of the wing. The truth was, heights didn't bother him. He had spent much of his early life scaling the cliffs into which the Keep had been built centuries ago. It was slipping and falling to his death he didn't like the thought of.

"If I said I was nervous," he asked Chu, "would you kiss me again?"

"Nice try, but I want you concentrating firmly on your feet, nothing else." The wing poked him in the back. "Get going, mage, or you'll let the crowd down."

Skender took a deep breath and stepped out onto the bridge. It wobbled underfoot, but not as badly as he had feared it might.

"Keep going." The wing poked him again. "The faster you go, the easier it'll be."

He had no choice, the way she was shoving him. With his left hand alternating between the guide ropes and steadying the wing, he moved forward one step at a time, eyes fixed firmly on where his next footfall would be.

The fog swallowed the two of them, tugging at their clothes and the wing with insubstantial fingers. Wind moaned eerily along the canyon, growing louder with every step he took. In his peripheral vision he noticed the cliff face behind him fade to grey long before their destination appeared.

Even when it did, he kept his eyes down and his pace unchanging. He resisted the urge to hurry as the last metres swept by. The last thing he wanted to do was become overconfident and trip on the verge of safety. Only when hands reached out for him and the world stopped rocking did he breathe easily again.

"Well done," said Marmion.

Delfine nodded in approval at the warden's side. "You can look up now," she said.

"What? Oh, right." He put down the wing—thinking for the first time how much easier it would have been just to fly over, if only the foresters would have let them—and tilted his head back.

What he glimpsed through the fog made him gape in awe—and when Chu softly exclaimed "Goddess," he could think of no better word.

THE QUORUM

"Jade is stone like any other, and as such it possesses distinct chimerical properties. The angels of jade who carried the Goddess aloft might be nothing more than metaphorical creations, but they might also be very real beings we have simply failed to encounter in our exploration of the world thus far."
THE BOOK OF TOWERS, EXEGESIS 25:11

The balloon swayed and rocked as it travelled through the fog. Shilly shivered, feeling cold and damp. She shuffled closer to Sal for warmth, and he snorted awake, having nodded off without her noticing. She apologised and encouraged him to lean on her. The cuts and scratches on his face and hands had turned brown and stopped bleeding long ago, thanks to Rosevear's ministrations. They might not even scar. That took some of the edge off her apprehension. The camouflage charms had been part of their life for years, since their return to Fundelry from the Haunted City, but she had never wanted them to be permanently etched on him.

That raised a whole series of thoughts she was reluctant to pursue at that moment: how *did* she view their future, if hiding forever wasn't an option? She and Sal had no intention of starting a family any time soon; they were too young, for a start, and their existence on the outer fringe of Fundelry didn't allow easy access to schooling. At some point, kids or not, they would have to reconnect permanently with the world around them. But how, and when, and where? Perhaps, she thought, they had already done so by joining the expedition hunting for the Homunculus. Perhaps it was already too late to turn back . . .

Too edgy to sleep, she tried to focus her attention on the world around her rather than on her thoughts.

It was impossible to tell how high they were flying, since the cloud —even with the dawn slowly lightening it from behind—was impenetrable, but they had to be well above the treetops that she had glimpsed while taking off from the boneship. The Panic crew swarmed all over the balloon and its gondola, adjusting vanes and tightening stays with assurance, gripping wherever they needed to with strong hands and feet and sometimes using the hooks they carried at their sides as well.

Their long-armed grace was prodigious and sure; they moved as though gravity barely mattered to them. One even scurried up and over the forward airsac, dropping with quiet grace in front of her when his job was done. Their leader, Griel, watched from the rear by the pilot. Behind goatee beard, ebony eyes, protruding jaw and brow, his mood was unreadable.

Shilly's fellow passengers maintained a subdued silence. Rosevear tended Kemp with weary diligence. She was afraid to ask how her old friend was coping, fearing the worst. Tom, like Sal, had fallen asleep and slumped open-mouthed against Highson, who watched the world as she did, with a frown.

How long they travelled she couldn't tell. She felt cut off from the world, as though the balloon was hanging motionless in a grey void.

"This isn't the first time you've flown," said Schuet, sitting opposite her with hands clutching the rail.

"No," she admitted. "You? Oh, yes, that's right. You said your people don't trust things that fly."

"It's dangerous and disrespectful." One of the Panic soldiers issued a noise that might have been a snort of amusement, but Schuet ignored it. "Our place is among the trees, not above them."

Shilly wondered how that fitted in with Chu's image of balloon cities in the forest. "Do you worship the trees, then," she asked bluntly, "or just like them a lot?"

"Something in between. We protect them and they shelter us. We tend them and they provide for us."

"How? By letting you build houses and fires out of them? Doesn't sound like much of a deal for the trees to me."

The response came from Griel, not Schuet. Reaching down between his feet, he produced one of the brands the foresters had been carrying and tossed it to her. She caught it with both hands, too surprised to wonder whether it might still be hot. She had glimpsed such brands glowing red with heat earlier, as if recently pulled from a fire.

The brand was cool and surprisingly heavy. As long as her forearm and slightly thicker at one end, it looked at first as though it had been carved. Closer inspection revealed that the patterns were the work of boring insects, weaving and digging under the protection of the bark outer skin which had since been stripped away. She turned it over in her hands, feeling the faint but unmistakeable tingle of the Change.

"It's a reservoir," she said, understanding now that the glow hadn't come from heat, but from the release of more subtle energies. Her walking stick had been imbued with such potential by Sal, although she wasn't about to admit that to anyone else lest it be taken from her.

The brand was almost empty, containing barely enough for the flicker of light that danced across the faces of those around her, making them momentarily brighter than the filtered light of dawn.

"Houses *and* reservoirs, then," she said, amending her earlier pronouncement.

Schuet shook his head. "We didn't make that brand," he said. "We grew it. The *forest* grew it."

"Sure, and you chopped it off and filled it with the Change. The end result is the same."

"We don't chop anything, Shilly. We encourage particular plants to tap into the forest's root system and draw out the potential we need. The wood is grown to be rich in the Change, and grown to be harvested, too, like seeds. It's a partner in the process."

Before Shilly could ask for more details, Griel barked a command to his crew and reached for the brand. Shilly handed it over as the balloon began to sink. She could sense no change in the misty haze around her, but her stomach felt light and the stays holding the airsacs in place thrummed as though plucked.

"Are we landing?" she asked.

Griel shook his head, an ambiguous gesture that could have been a simple *no* or a warning to keep quiet. Shilly opted for the latter, telling herself to wait and see what happened next.

She wasn't kept waiting long. Dark shadows loomed out of the fog on either side—nebulous, elongated shapes that could have been towers or branches, or even the fingers of a giant hand—reaching up to enfold them.

In looking around to see better, she woke Sal again, who blinked blearily at the view. "Where are we?"

"Home," Griel rumbled.

One hand tugged at a stay, adjusting the balloon's trim. The dark shapes grew slowly clearer, resolving into the trunks of giant trees, dozens of them stripped of their branches and covered with cascading vines. They reminded Shilly of the poles of a rotting jetty protruding from a dried-up sea. The balloon and its crew navigated between them with long-practised ease.

A larger shadow coalesced ahead of them—a shadow composed of many shadows, like that cast by the leaves of a tree. Shilly narrowed her eyes, trying to make out what lay behind the mist. The larger mass resembled an upside-down triangle, or a mountain turned on its head. The smaller components had no common size or shape. It was difficult to tell how far away these objects lay, and therefore how large they were. They could have been just off the balloon's forward bow in dense fog, or kilometres away in relatively clear air. Only the unmoving, stately trunks that glided slowly by suggested that the objects were neither small nor near.

A gust of cool wind rattled the gondola. Shilly clutched Sal's hand, reminded of the vast drop below them. Even though they must have risen far up the side of the mountain to be so deep in the clouds, she had seen no sign of solid ground.

When she looked ahead again, the shadow had resolved into a city of balloons—or rather, when she took it in properly, a city suspended by wires beneath hundreds of balloons untethered to the ground below. The structure as a whole was too large to absorb at once. Her gaze skated over its complexity during their approach. Teardrop shapes were most common among the balloons, but there were also spheres or fat ovals or discs made from gold and silver fabric. The structures beneath ranged from simple platforms to long cylinders with windows and curving walkways leading between them. Balloons swooped and glided around it, trailing white wakes. Light gleamed off occasional highlights of metal and glass, but wood and canvas predominated, dyed or painted every imaginable colour. Shilly estimated the city's size to be about half of Laure's—which made it all the more impressive for something hanging unsupported in the air.

A Panic soldier raised a compact curved horn to her lips and blew a loud call, rising in pitch as if questioning, which was immediately answered from the city. A yellow light began to flash on the underside of one of the larger structures, a bulbous quarter-moon canted slightly so its horns pointed downward. The balloon changed direction to head for the space between the horns. As it drew closer, Shilly made out several large hooks hanging from ropes. Another balloon—this one a complicated arrangement with five bladders of various sizes bundled up in netting like a bunch of grapes—had been snagged on the hooks and tugged upward into some sort of dock. Panic swarmed back and forth, carrying sacks and boxes deeper into the structure.

The balloon fell under the shadow of the city, and even the feeble light of dawn dropped away. Shilly felt a chill pass over her. She could sense Sal's mood beside her, and it was as wearily sombre as her own.

"What's that up there?" asked the forester called Mikia, pointing.

Shilly followed the direction indicated by Mikia's finger and saw a much larger shape nestled in the underside of the city's many structures. It resembled an oval brass vase tipped on its side, dozens of metres long, with a round opening at one end and a long spike at the other. A curved metal keel protruded at an odd angle, tapering to a stubby point and lending the structure a boatlike shape. What a boat was doing floating in the sky over a forest of fog, Shilly couldn't guess.

Griel stroked his gold-beaded chin and didn't answer Mikia's question. As they drew nearer, Shilly made out patches of corrosion in the metal hull. Whatever it was, age had taken its toll. A line of boltholes suggested that another keel, equal in size to the one she could see, had once graced the far side. Cannibalised, perhaps?

The balloon came level with the dangling hooks, distracting her from that particular mystery. Two members of the Panic crew reached out the starboard side and caught one, and swung it closer to attach it to the gondola. Two on the port side did the same. Shilly's stomach lurched as the hooks tugged the balloon upwards to where a spindly looking gantry awaited them, sticking out of the side of the half-moon structure like an insectile tongue.

"Stay where you are until I tell you to stand," said Griel. "Then I want you to file off one at a time and wait until we've all disembarked. There's no point trying to escape—"

"Why would we?" said Schuet. "We've nowhere to run, and no way to fly."

"Exactly." Griel stood on strong legs and leapt to the gantry as it approached. The thought of the drop below them didn't seem to bother him—or any of the Panic, as they tied stays and carried stolen goods out of the gondola. The balloon creaked and swayed, and Shilly hung onto Sal with a sweaty grip.

Opposite her, Tom came awake with a slight start, and looked around him with wide eyes. "We've landed," he said.

"No, just stopped." *Land* was definitely the wrong word.

Griel came back to help them off the gondola, one after the other. Shilly refused to look down, even though she knew all she would see was clouds. That was worse, in a way, than seeing clear to the ground. She felt she might fall forever.

Mist-filled glass globes dangling from bulkheads above glowed with a pale light, illuminating the scene. Curved wooden walls awaited them, decorated with dots, parallel lines, and spirals that snaked in waves around corners, across ceilings, and along passageways. They might have been navigational markers or just ornamentation. Dock workers crowded around the gondola, ensuring it was safely secured. Everywhere Shilly looked she saw inhuman faces: big ears, shadowed eyes, mouths that stretched too wide when they opened. The air was full of harsh shrieks and cries. She forced herself to breathe evenly, calmly.

The Panic carried Kemp out of the gondola and rested him on a stretcher. He looked deathly pale and didn't seem to be breathing. Rosevear went to check on him, but was held carefully back. A dozen Panic in black-and-brown uniforms had hurried up to join them on the gantry and stood in two lines before Griel, waiting for orders.

"Anix, see to the cargo. I want it catalogued and assessed within the hour. Erged, call the Quorum to order; we'll be coming before them shortly." The soldiers Griel addressed bowed briskly and hurried off. "Ramal, take this one to Vehofnehu and tell him to do what he can." Griel indicated Kemp, then pointed at Rosevear, Tom, and Shilly in turn. "Take these three with you. I don't think they'll give you any trouble, but be careful anyway. I don't want them wandering about on their own."

The Panic called Ramal—a burly female with bushy eyebrows set in a permanent glower and two short, metal-bound ponytails suspended from the back of her domed head—bowed crisply.

"Wait," said Shilly, feeling an instinctive alarm at the thought of being separated from Sal again. "Where are you taking us? Why can't we all go?"

"Because the rest of you are needed here," came the simple answer.

"Why? What is the Quorum? Who is this Vef—Vehofen—?"

"Vehofnehu." Griel came to stand before her. He was only slightly taller than her, but seemed enormously broad. "He's many things; a healer is just one of them. You can trust him, just like you can trust me. I give you my word: if we have no reason to fear you, then you have no reason to fear us."

Torn, Shilly looked at Sal for support. Should she fight or give in? Did she have any real choice? He seemed as uncertain as her.

"Go with Kemp," Highson said to her. "Look after him. He'll want a familiar face by him when he wakes up."

Can't Tom do that? she wanted to retort. *He's known Kemp as long as I have.*

All resistance left her when she realised how petty that would sound. Kemp did need her, and she and Sal had survived separation before. Griel hadn't hurt them yet. She could only hope that he—and the Quorum, whatever they were—would see that she and her companions were innocent bystanders in the Panic's squabble with the other foresters.

She kissed Sal's warm lips and hugged him, then went to stand with Tom and Rosevear, the bag slung over her shoulder. Beside the two young wardens, she felt very vulnerable.

Griel nodded his satisfaction. "Thank you for cooperating. If only all humans were so reasonable."

"Not just humans," said Schuet.

Griel snapped his long fingers and headed off along the gantry, drawing Sal, Highson, Seneschal Schuet, and Mikia—plus the two Panic bearing Mawson—in his wake.

Sal glanced over his shoulder at Shilly looking miserable, and wished there had been some way to avoid being separated. The sad fact was that they were severely outnumbered and a long way from help. It would be best to ride out what was coming in the hope that reason or compassion would ultimately prevail.

Still, the Change crackled through him like static electricity, wanting to earth itself in Griel's exposed back.

"Gently does it," whispered Highson into his mind. *"They know you have some talent, but they don't know how much. That knowledge could make all the difference, later."*

Sal nodded, seeing the sense in that. Although they had yet to meet any Panic with obvious sensitivity to the Change, he didn't doubt that they existed. *What would they be like?* he wondered. *If Schuet and the foresters used wood as reservoirs, what did the Panic use?*

The question distracted him only briefly. A more pressing issue—that of negotiating the ways of the floating city—soon demanded all his attention.

He had noticed the way the Panic crew used feet as well as hands to clamber over the balloon during the early stages of its journey through the mist, before he had fallen asleep. Their toes were shorter than their fingers but much more flexible than human toes, and the shoes they wore were open at the front, allowing them full mobility. He had thought the antics on the balloon a matter of expediency, but learned how wrong that assumption was on encountering his first ladder, inside the moon-shaped dock.

Griel waved two of his troop ahead of him with arms that seemed too long to be real. The soldiers scurried up the near-vertical incline with smooth grace, as easily as though walking. Schuet and Mikia went next, with considerably less ability. The ladder consisted of a series of cylindrical wooden rungs roughly half a metre apart, polished smooth by time and regular use. When it was Sal's turn, he concentrated on each rung as it passed, and didn't look down.

He clambered onto level ground at the top, feeling winded. Highson was flushed and breathing heavily behind him. The two Panic carrying Mawson didn't appear inconvenienced in the slightest.

Griel didn't give them a chance to rest. He wound his way through the dock and beyond, leading them up and down ladders and across bridges that swayed unnervingly beneath them. They passed Panic everywhere they went, following even more dangerous-looking routes up ropes and across gaps that made Sal ill just thinking about them. Wire cables reached upward from every flat surface, some just to the structure above, but others stretching right up out of sight to anchor points under balloons much higher. Because of its haphazard nature, the city possessed few vertical or horizontal surfaces. Sal constantly felt as though he might slip and fall if he stepped wrongly.

The deeper into the city's heart they went, the more Panic they saw. Even though it was the middle of the night, the city was alive with motion and life. He didn't know how many people lived there, but they were crammed in tight. Every vertical surface was studded with windows, pipes, drains, exhaust vents, and the like. Washing lines and mist globes hung suspended from every available anchor point. Voices called across the gaps between buildings, creating a constant backdrop that he doubted would ever ebb completely. Big-mouthed, big-eared faces stared back at him from windows, doorways, and in passing. With Panic moving in all directions around him he felt under intense scrutiny, and once again had to resist the urge to use the Change, albeit for hiding rather than fighting.

They obviously weren't the first humans to come to the city, but it was just as clearly not an everyday occurrence. Some of the Panic exposed their teeth in frightening sneers at Schuet and Mikia, recognising from their uniforms that they were captured enemies. Highson and Sal were obviously guilty by association. Mawson drew stares of open curiosity.

Sal didn't know how long he could stand it. The smile he maintained, trying to deflect hostility, was soon aching with strain. He tried to keep his eyes on the ladders and ramps he had to follow, in a vain attempt to move as easily as Griel.

"Where are you taking us?" pressed Highson. "Who are the Quorum? Why do we need to see them?"

Griel wouldn't answer, and soon they had no breath left for questions.

After an hour of climbing, they slowed. At the entrance to a bell-bottomed structure hanging from three giant golden balloons, a Panic female draped in flowing green fabrics anchored at shoulders, wrists, and ankles ran up to Griel. Although smaller and as slender as a rope compared to him, she stopped him in his tracks.

"Are you insane?" Her expression was furious. Beaded hair that hung to her waist rattled with every movement of her head. Brass rings on her fingers and toes gleamed in the misty light. "Do you pursue this course because you're mad, or do you have a genuine desire to ruin us all?"

"Jao, listen—"

"No, *you* listen for once." She poked at the stitching on Griel's massive chestplate hard enough to force him back a step. "While you've been hunting that accursed wraith of yours, Tzartak and Sensenya have been ousted, allowing Oriel to fill their seats with his goons. Still, the Heptarchs might have listened to reason from you, had you not turned up with these—these *groundlings* in tow." The look she cast Schuet and the others was one of pure contempt. "What game are you playing? Do you have any conception of what might be at stake?"

Griel's spine was as stiff as a board, recoiling so far away from her that he was almost standing completely straight. "I'm trying to do what's right."

"I know, fog take you." In complete defiance of the anger and betrayal displayed by her expression, she stepped closer to kiss Griel on the lips. "Good luck, you mad fool. They're waiting for you."

Griel ran a hand over Jao's beaded scalp with surprising tenderness, and nodded. He brushed by her and waved for the others to follow.

Sal ignored the hot stare of the Panic female as he had ignored other Panic during his journey with Griel. Two high, arched doors opened in the side of the structure ahead. Griel led them once more with an unhurried but distance-eating lope through the doors and along a grand corridor that followed a spiralling path into the interior of the structure.

"Who are the Heptarchs?" asked Highson, who had taken advantage of the brief respite to get his wind back.

Griel glanced at him, and to Sal's surprise relented: "The caretakers of the Panic. Our rulers."

"I assume that's who we are going to meet."

"No. The Quorum advise the Heptarchs on certain matters."

"What matters?"

"I'll explain later. For now, know only that we must move quickly, before this opportunity is taken from us." Griel's tone, more than his words, told Highson he should obey.

Sal reviewed what little they had learned in recent moments. Someone had been ousted from the Heptarchs, allowing someone else called Oriel to gain more influence over the Panic's ruling body. Without knowing who stood for what, it was impossible to tell whether that would be a good thing for the "groundlings" or not. Griel and Jao obviously thought it was a bad thing, though.

The turning of the corridor tightened. Alcoves lined the interior wall, deep niches containing odd-looking objects identified by nameplates that made no sense to Sal: *Main Logic Board—Atlanta. Reverse Gate—NL320-U*. He had seen displays like this in the Haunted City, where spaces had been set aside to exhibit unusual artefacts recovered from Ruins all over the Strand. A faint tingling of the Change radiated from the niches. He noted each one as he traversed the long corridor, his biological father close at his side.

The motley group came to another set of double doors. No guards inspected them or asked what they were doing. After a dozen breaths, the doors swung ajar. Flickering green light spilled from the room beyond, painting their faces in sickly tones. A strange smell, not unlike the sparking of a chimerical engine, made Sal wince.

Griel straightened his broad shoulders and walked forward through the doors. Sal followed, not knowing what to expect.

Beyond the doors lay an octagonal room with black walls lined with bookshelves. Each wall reached high above their heads and curved inwards to a point, forming an eight-pointed star overhead. Its rays gleamed in the green light that came from a wide font resting waist-high on three attenuated legs in the centre of the room. Thirteen dark-robed shapes stood at varying distances around the glowing pool, their faces hidden by hoods. The one closest to the font, and therefore more brightly lit, looked up as they entered.

To Sal's surprise a human face greeted him from beneath the hood. Not one of the Panic. A man with rounded features and glowing skin, he regarded each of them in turn, then moved to speak to his companions.

The words that emerged from his lips were unlike any Sal had heard before. Although he strained to understand them, their meaning eluded him completely.

"Bahman acknowledges you," boomed a voice from behind them. Sal turned to see a female Panic also dressed in robes. Hers, however, were silver and her hood hung limply down her back. Her hair was grey and straight and her face deeply lined; with stately, measured paces she stepped out of the shadows to confront them. "Bahman recognises you."

Griel genuflected before the Panic female. "Tarnava." The name rolled respectfully off his tongue. "Forgive this interruption."

"It is of no consequence," declared a second female on the far side of the room. Dressed like the first, whom she distinctly resembled, she stepped into the green glow and smiled as though at a massive, secret joke. Her full lips stretched impossibly wide. "The Quorum was expecting you."

"They told you we were coming?" Griel stood and glanced from one figure to the other.

"They *remembered*," Tarnava corrected him.

Both Panic females turned to listen as a conversation broke out between the robed human figures. Incomprehensible words flashed between three in particular: the man who had first spoken, Bahman, and two women. Sal found it difficult to judge the tone of the exchange; it could have been angry or simply impatient. Their gestures were odd, as impossible to interpret as their words.

"Who are they?" Sal asked. "What are they saying?"

"Elomia, explain."

The second Panic female came around the font in response to Tarnava's request. The conversation among the strange figures ceased for the moment. Their eyes gleamed in the green light, watching her.

"The Quorum is unique in this world," Elomia said. "Its members may look human to your eyes, but patently they are not. You can hear their speech for yourselves. Their words are obscured to all bar those with the gift, such as I and my cousin possess." Tarnava bowed slightly; Elomia acknowledged her with a nod. "This is not the full extent of the mysteries surrounding them. They, like the stone ones you call man'kin, see time in a way very different from us. They have knowledge of the future—as full as we have of the past. However, the past is as obscure to them as the future is to us, and the difficulty lies in interpreting what they tell us."

"And asking the right questions."

"Indeed. Only those of royal lineage possess the ability required," said Tarnava proudly. "We were raised in this very room so our talents would achieve their full maturity. As adults we now serve as interpreters and guardians, teaching those who follow us to do as we do."

Elomia whispered to one of the Quorum, who responded with a stream of babbling speech. This triggered another rapid-fire discussion that Sal couldn't follow.

This was an entirely new sort of frustration for him. He had travelled from the Strand to the Interior and back again; he had argued with bloodworkers and grappled with man'kin on the bottom of the

Divide. Not once had he encountered a language barrier like this. When people talked, he understood their words, at least.

He glanced at Highson, whose expression perfectly matched his own state. Not even the twins, the sole survivors of the world before the Cataclysm, had seemed so alien as these incomprehensible beings.

"What are they saying now?" asked Schuet, watching the strange assembly with ill-disguised unease. At his side, Mikia clutched her arms protectively across her chest and seemed to have forgotten how to close her mouth.

"They are talking about your man'kin."

"He doesn't belong to us," said Sal automatically. "He's his own person."

As if to prove the point, Mawson chose that moment to address the members of the Quorum in their own strange speech.

The reaction was sudden and dramatic. Elomia and Tarnava furiously closed ranks and descended on the man'kin. Their lips stretched wide in sharp-toothed growls. The Panic holding him upright almost dropped him in the face of their anger.

"Silence, stone man," Tarnava snarled. "It is not your place to speak."

"Not here, not ever!" Elomia removed a black cloth from beneath her robes and tied it tightly around the stone bust's mouth, as though to gag him.

"What did you do that for?" asked Sal, wondering how much more of this strangeness he could endure.

"Because his kind are not to be trusted," Tarnava said, turning to Sal. A long thick nail stabbed at him and a thin ring of white flashed around each deep black iris. "His words sound innocent enough, but they will charm your mind into knots."

"He's a friend," Sal insisted. "He has earned my trust."

"You might think so," Elomia said with a sad shake of her head, "but you would be wrong. Man'kin do not know the meaning of the word 'friendship.'"

"He spoke to the Quorum," said Schuet from the sidelines. "Are you sure it's not *that* that you find most upsetting?"

The cousins hissed and moved away to stand among the hooded humanoid figures. "Such rudeness. Such ill-mannered guests. What are we to do with them, Elomia?"

"Throw them overboard?"

"No. We shan't do that just yet."

"Imprison them?"

"Perhaps, perhaps."

"Shouldn't you at least ask who we are and what we want?"

Both Panic females turned to face Sal, grinning as though they found the question hilarious.

"Why should we?" Elomia retorted. "We either know the answers already or don't care what they are."

"Interrogating you is my job," said Griel in gruff tones. "If I may . . . ?" He genuflected again, inclining his head low before the two women.

"Yes, of course." Tarnava waved a hand dismissively. "The Quorum will not detain—"

A sharp utterance from one of the robed figures cut her off in mid-sentence. An angular woman stepped forward to pluck at Tarnava's sleeve, her movements jerky and oddly uncoordinated, as though her limbs weren't quite working properly. She whispered something too low to hear into Tarnava's ear, then stepped back. Sal glimpsed the face of the woman beneath the hood, and found her to be surprisingly young.

Tarnava frowned. "I am instructed to ask about the Homunculus. Specifically, has it arrived yet?"

At Sal's side, Highson's posture became suddenly rigid. "Arrived? So it *is* alive."

"How would they know that?" Sal asked Tarnava. "How do they know anything about the Homunculus?"

"Their sight is not as ours. I told you that." The Panic female's demeanour became irritable again. "Well? Answer the question."

"We haven't seen it," said Highson, addressing the hooded woman directly, not her interpreter, "but if you say it's alive, then it's almost certainly travelling in this direction as we speak."

Elomia relayed the information. The robed humanoid woman didn't respond in any visible way.

Goosebumps shivered down Sal's arms as he realised that, almost as one, the members of the Quorum had looked up to stare at him. Their eyes glittered beneath their hoods.

"Time to go," said Griel, turning and ushering his captives towards the door with sudden haste. "Our thanks," he said, bowing to Tarnava and Elomia as he left. The Panic females didn't acknowledge him at all.

The doors boomed shut behind them, cutting off the piercing green glow. Normal colour returned in a welcome rush.

"What was that all about?" Sal asked.

"The Quorum advise the Heptarchs and they see things we don't. They can tell what is important. I needed to know how they would react to you before proceeding." Griel kept talking while he retraced their steps along the corridor. Sal had to hurry to keep up. "Now I have, and the Quorum acknowledges you. That means you have a part to play in what's to come. No one can say, now, that you're to be lightly disposed of. Not Oriel, not the Heptarchs, not Jao—not even me."

"How likely was that before?" asked Schuet, his expression sober.

"In the current climate, it's best you don't know." They came to the outer door, where the female called Jao awaited them with relief naked on her unusual features. Her prominent brows unbunched; her thick lips relaxed.

"Where to from here?" she asked, joining the party hastily following Griel's lead. "Take on Oriel single-handedly?"

"Yes," he said. Griel stopped suddenly at a ladder and spoke to a soldier. "Ardif, take these five to the holding cells. I'll deal with them later. No, don't argue," he said to Sal, who had opened his mouth to do just that. "It's for your own safety. I won't be long. You have my word."

Twice now Griel had promised to deal with them fairly and thus far the Panic soldier had been as trustworthy as Sal could reasonably expect. His prisoners remained unharmed. Sal was certain Elomia and Tarnava were only trying to frighten them when they had threatened to throw them over the side of the city. Fairly certain, anyway.

"All right," he said. Had Shilly been there she might have pushed the point harder, he thought, but Griel looked harried and distracted and Sal didn't want to give the soldier any reason to deal with them more harshly.

Griel inclined his head and hurried up the ladder with Jao not far behind him. They moved much faster now they weren't burdened by clumsy humans. The sound of their arguing faded into the distance.

"Wait," said Sal as the Panic soldier left in charge raised a hand to hurry them away. Sal crossed to where Mawson sat cradled in the arms of his bearers. With a short tug, he pulled the gag off the bust's mouth. What real effect it had had—if any—he didn't know, but the man'kin seemed to have a less indignant appearance when it was removed.

"What did you tell the Quorum?" he asked.

"*I simply answered their question about the Homunculus.*"

"But they hadn't asked it yet."

"*To their minds, they had, and the answer given was insufficient.*"

"What do you mean? If the twins are still alive, they must be on their way here. We know that from their past behaviour."

"*That isn't what the Quorum asked. They wanted to know how long the Homunculus had been in the world. How long, in other words, the Void Beneath had been open.*"

Understanding dawned. Elomia had said that the Quorum could see the future, but had no knowledge of the past. "And you told them."

"*Yes. Twenty-three days.*"

"Why is that important?"

"*It marks the beginning of the end for us, and the end of the beginning for them.*"

That didn't make any sense, on the face of it. "So how did you know how to talk to them?"

"*I talk to them the same way I talk to you,*" said the man'kin, "*only backwards.*"

Before Sal could ask what Mawson meant, their Panic guards decided that the time had come to move on. A firm hand on his shoulder propelled Sal along the corridor and he didn't resist.

"*I don't understand,*" said Highson through the Change. "*Does that mean the Homunculus is alive or not?*"

Sal could only shake his head, and swear that he would try to unravel the mystery later.

THE MOAI

**"'If wood is no more than stone,' the people
of the forest say, 'build me a fire out of rocks
and set the hills ablaze.'
Sometimes I am tempted to do as they ask,
just to see the looks on their faces."**
STONE MAGE ALDO KELLOMAN: ON A PRIMITIVE CULTURE

The city of Milang occupied both sides of a steep ridge-face that
jutted precipitously out of the rising mountainside and up into
impenetrable cloud. Its sides were nearly vertical in places but densely
covered with trees regardless, and in the trees, almost smothered by
the sheer canopy, was a teeming city. Ordinary stonework would have
utterly failed to cling to such a slope, not without heavy-duty charms
similar to those that held Skender's home together. He quickly learned
that the foresters who inhabited the city had much more powerful
tools at their disposal: the trees themselves. The massive trunks and
boughs he saw before him dwarfed any they had passed so far. While
his knowledge of plant biology was limited to the desert species most
Stone Mages wrote about, he understood the root systems of such trees
had to be extensive and very strong to hold their weight against
gravity. These were what enabled the trees to cling to and thrive on the
edge of a mountain with a small city in their arms.

At the end of the rope bridge he and Chu crossed, his gaze was
drawn upwards, along an avenue of trunks strung with vines and exotic
flowering plants. Branches crisscrossed overhead, forming a dense mat
across which walkways and floors had been laid. The deeper into the

forest he looked, the more such levels he discerned, and the more people he saw moving back and forth.

His gaze didn't know where to settle. Even as Heuve urged them onwards, along the path leading from the bridge to the city, he swung his head from side to side taking in the details. Only the sight of an enormous stone face staring back at him through the trees gave him reason to pause.

At least four metres tall and bodiless, the head leaned out of the side of the mountain between two thick tree trunks with its mouth half open. Its solemn, slitted eyes were blank, but they seemed to see him. He stared back at it, frozen by its odd appearance and wondering what it was doing among the trees.

Chu had noticed his sudden distraction and had pinpointed the source. "There's another one up there. Look."

He followed the nod of her head, up and to his right. Sure enough, a second stone face peered out at him, partially obscured by a wild spray of ferns. As he took that knowledge on board, he noticed a third, and then a fourth at the limit of his vision, barely visible through the mist.

"They're everywhere," he breathed.

Only then did he realise that the deep moaning he had become aware of while crossing the bridge wasn't the wind blowing along the canyon. The mournful sound originated from ahead of him, not behind.

"It's *them*."

"Yes, it is," said Heuve. "Now get moving. We don't have all day."

Skender forced himself to concentrate on putting one foot ahead of the other, even as his mind remained fixed on the enigmatic statues and their unearthly calls. Were they man'kin or something else entirely? Was this handful the total sum of them or were they scattered through the entire mountain range?

The party of mixed foresters and captives entered the city of Milang at its base, past a steep wall of foliage between two giant trees that looked old enough to have been around since the Cataclysm.

Skender had never seen such trees before. Their branches were angular and evenly spaced, tracing out—he realised with a shock—the shape of two giant charms, one for security and one for hospitality. The path between them was wide and well travelled, thickly coated with pine needles so their footfalls were almost silent.

Sentries watched them from the branches above, holding bows at the ready. Delfine saluted them briskly but didn't stop. The way gradually steepened until it reached the level of the first platform, Delfine leading them across a walkway onto a level surface woven from branches, all carved with whorls and swirls like the one Skender had seen in the forest, and secured every square metre or so by winding, living vines. That was the last time in their journey that they touched the ground.

From there, they followed ramps and stairways up through the trees, rising ever higher into the city. There were few traditional buildings, as Skender knew them; individual dwellings blended into one another, overlapping as organically as did the trees themselves, linked by walkways that ranged from simple planks to broad thoroughfares covered with thatch. The cliff face and the plants that inhabited it were always visible, thickest in shadowy nooks and on miniature plateaus. The sounds of foraging animals and birds came clearly through gaps in the floors and walls. They made the trees their home, just as the foresters had. Skender wondered how well the many species coexisted, and thought uneasily about bugs and spiders getting into everything.

Within the canopy, it was hard to see very far. To make up for that, a complex system of bells, sirens, and whistles sounded constantly, enabling the citizens of the city to communicate across distances greater than a few metres.

Skender kept an eye out for such details as he went. If he ever made it back to the Keep, his father would want to know all about the cultures of the forest and the various homes they had made there. Every beam was unique in shape and size, and great care had been taken in making the joints and stays that kept the greater structure whole, and yet flexible too, to allow for different rates of growth. Wooden limbs entwined around each other, adding sinuous strength and liquid beauty; floors and walls merged seamlessly into trunks and branches, giving Skender cause to wonder how much was fashioned and how much grown that way. Occasional tingles of the Change suggested that there was more to the city than met the eye. Some trees fairly throbbed with potential, like the one in the clearing where they had stopped to rest the previous night. He could feel powerful currents running beneath his feet, through branches and along entangled roots, spreading naturally into the city all around him.

The foresters had made it like that, he reasoned. They had come to the forest bringing Change-workers and other artisans, and from dumb static trees they had fashioned a city that could change both with its environment and with the people inhabiting it. It could expand in size, or contract, if needed. It possessed all the flexibility that a stone city didn't have, and had the added advantage of growing itself. Stone-masons would be in very short supply in a city like this.

But what about ironmongers, Skender wondered. How would the foresters cook, or fashion their tools? They might be able to pluck food from the branches around them or tend stepped farms on the ridge's broad flanks, but he doubted that growing swords or arrowheads would ever be practical.

They walked all morning, ascending steadily by switching back and forth across the steep cliff face. The cloud grew ever more dense and cool on his skin, making him feel clammy all over. Skender's arm muscles burned from carrying the wing, and his knees protested with every step upwards he took. His head swam with hunger and the need for food.

Finally, Delfine called a rest break. On a circular platform surrounded by five muscular tree trunks, the party stretched out on flat brown cushions and rubbed aching muscles. Attendants appeared as if from nowhere, bringing food and water in sufficient quantity to feed twenty people. The foresters broke warm bread and dipped it in pastes and honeys of different hues, sampling from each bowl in sequence. Skender ate and drank without restraint, not worrying about the strange tastes greeting his greedy tastebuds. Only when the gaping void in his stomach was filled did he become slightly more discriminating.

The pastes satisfied him less than the array of meats available in delicate white wooden bowls. He discovered at least three different sorts of flesh, marinated and cooked to the point of dissolving in his mouth, barely needing to be chewed.

When he asked Chu what she thought they were, she shrugged as she took a swig of purple fruit juice. "How would I know?"

"That one," said the woman called Navi, indicating a morsel Skender had just raised to his lips, "is frog."

"Frog?" he echoed, feeling instantly less hungry.

"Ghost frog, specifically. They live on fungus at the bottom of the city. The one you just ate is roast crabbler flesh. Do you know what a crabbler is?"

He nodded, blanching. Crabblers were a species of giant spider that lived in the Divide walls.

"The third—"

"I don't want to know," he said, putting the morsel of meat back on the plate and holding up both hands. "Really I don't."

The first inkling that Navi might be teasing him came when Chu laughed. "Nice one," she said. "Crabbler meat is black and bitter. What are we eating, really?"

Navi maintained a blank expression for a second, then broke into a wide smile. Skender felt himself flush deep red as she explained: "Game hen, possum, and fig bat."

The last sounded only marginally more acceptable than frog to Skender's suddenly restless stomach. Then a worse thought occurred to him.

"Have you really tasted crabbler?" he asked Chu.

She shrugged. "You've seen where I live. If you're hungry enough, you'll eat anything."

Skender sincerely doubted that he would ever be *that* hungry.

"Where *do* you come from?" asked Delfine, perhaps realising only then that Chu and Skender shared different origins.

"Laure," Chu replied. "It's literally a hole in the ground. The Divide cut it in half a thousand years ago. Things went downhill from there."

Delfine looked from Chu to Skender, then to Marmion, Banner, and Eitzen eating in silence to one side. "Such an odd mixture of people. I understand how recent events might have affected someone from Laure, but what difference do they make to the Haunted City? To the Nine Stars?"

Marmion avoided the question. "How has the flood affected you? May I ask that?"

She nodded, her face very serious. "You've come upstream, along the great fissure we call the Pass. For all you know, the flood follows its length right to its source. I tell you now that it does not. The flood joins the Pass in a valley not far from here. A community called Chiappin once thrived on the flanks of that valley, home to one thousand people, young and old. Chiappin is now gone, swept away by the terrible waters. Everyone who lived there is dead."

"And the trees, too," said Warden Banner, nodding. "If the flood was strong enough to threaten Laure, far downstream, here the effects must have been truly devastating."

Delfine's eyes shone. "Yes, they were. Where trees two centuries old once stood now lies nothing but dead earth and stone. The naked mountainside is scarred and hideous. I can't bear to look at it."

She pushed her plate away.

Skender reined in an automatic complaint at the description of exposed stone as "hideous." Had it undoubtedly not been ghoulish to ask just then, he would have been curious to know more about the backbone of the mountain.

"Let's keep moving," said Delfine, standing smoothly. "We're only an hour from the summit. There we'll talk properly and consider what's to be done with you."

Skender resigned himself to more walking as the party gathered itself together and headed off. The promise of rest faded in the face of fear of the foresters deciding that Chu wasn't welcome or that Marmion's quest could not be tolerated. Their rest might be all too brief and conducted in a cell, followed by an enforced march back the way they had come.

He wondered if Sal and Shilly and the others were faring any better. That he was, at least, a captive of members of his own species was small comfort, but one to cling to during their long march.

As the day wore on, the fog thinned slightly, allowing Skender to see further through. It became clear that Milang spread as far across the ridge's face as it did upwards, woven through the trees as inseparably as the mist. From a great distance, the telltale signs of its presence—unnaturally straight lines and sharp angles; gleams of glazed ceramic or glass; moving shapes that couldn't possibly belong to birds or ordinary tree creatures—would be effectively invisible, even without the fog to hide them. He wondered if that was deliberate, and then wondered what the foresters had to fear from the forest around them.

Without the fog, the arboreal city's existence would have been decidedly uncertain. Everywhere he went, he saw sheets of charmed cloth artfully arrayed to catch the moisture in the air. Stately pyramids condensed mist in their cool hearts, channelling steady drips into containers or channels designed to collect every skerrick. In some places, the trickle of water was so loud it reminded him of rain.

Their upward climb couldn't last forever. The summit Delfine spoke of wasn't the top of the mountain range itself, but the uppermost and westernmost point of the ridge the city clung to, hidden deep in the permanent cloud cover. The trees continued to grow over it, but the ground fell away beneath them. Skender noticed a change in ambience long before he worked out what had happened. The sound of creatures in the undergrowth faded as the trunks surrounding them grew steadily narrower.

The summit consisted of a broad structure built around the trees' uppermost reaches, like a crown resting on spiky hair, not touching the head beneath. A vast wooden citadel with a tall belltower in one corner, surrounded by an immense skirtlike shelf that formed an approach on all sides, it would be the only building visible from outside the forest, although who could possibly see it through the fog and at such a great altitude, Skender couldn't imagine. Inside the outer walls, a row of broad wooden steps led up to a boxy central building with a single square entrance and no apparent windows. Guards in ochre uniforms lined either side of the stairwell; six more stood at the entrance. Dark eyes watched them closely as they approached.

Here we go, thought Skender, remembering the Magister of Laure and her cabal of sinister bloodworkers. *Why can't the locals ever be friendly?*

The guards at the entrance to the central building bowed as Lidia Delfine approached and opened the doors for her. She led the party inside through a series of skinny trunks that formed cloisters around the building's heart. Skender looked up as they entered, startled by the lack of a roof. The cloud-swathed sky seemed brighter to his eyes simply because of the frame around it.

The walls were not painted or carved, but covered in a series of elegant mosaics. Artisans had fashioned many different shades of wood into slivers and placed them in patterns evoking images of wind and fog. The sunlight, even filtered through the clouds and fog, cast them into bright relief.

A sudden softness beneath his feet made him look down. The floor wasn't wood, as he had expected. It was grass—real grass, growing in real dirt, high above the bases of the trees holding the citadel aloft.

"Daughter."

A deep woman's voice echoed from the cloisters and the chamber's delicate mosaics. In the centre of the chamber stood a woman of middle years wearing a long, many-folded robe in green and brown. Short-cropped silver hair matched the sky above so perfectly that for a moment Skender mistakenly assumed it to be a cap of some kind. Her features were broad and lined with care. Her arms opened to embrace Lidia Delfine as she approached.

"Mother." Delfine returned the brief clasp of the older woman then knelt respectfully at her feet. "Forgive me. My quest was not successful."

"That I am given to understand." The woman nodded, not unkindly, and looked up at Marmion and the others, waiting uncertainly on the edge of the grassed area. Grief cut deep lines in the corners of her eyes. "Success comes in many guises, however. Sometimes we know it not, though it stands openly before us."

Lidia Delfine glanced over her shoulder. "You believe these people are meant to be here?"

"I don't know, yet, what they are meant to be." The woman gestured that her daughter should stand. "You, Sky Warden," she said to Marmion. "My youngest child is dead. Can you tell me what killed him?"

Marmion stepped forward and executed a deep bow. "I fear that I cannot." His expression recounted the horror of their brief encounter with the wraith more eloquently than words. Skender would never forget the viciousness of that unprovoked attack. "I am an emissary of the Alcaide Braham of the Strand. Our mission has brought us here for very different reasons."

"Really? My people have been hunted every night for the past two weeks. Moai vanish from places they have rested for hundreds of years.

And now you arrive on our doorstep, asking for help. All things are connected in the forest, whether you see the roots or not."

Marmion bowed again. "Perhaps that is the case."

"Tell on. Why are you here?"

Skender couldn't hide his restlessness as Marmion commenced another explanation of the Sky Warden's quest. This time, though, the warden didn't stop with just the flood and the man'kin migration. He touched on the odd readings of the seers, but still kept the runaway Homunculus and the twins to himself.

"You didn't mention this prophecy before," Lidia Delfine accused him, coming around her mother to confront him directly. Heuve scowled to one side, as though all his worst suspicions had been confirmed. "What else are you hiding?"

Marmion opened his arms, a picture of wounded innocence. "I didn't lie to you. Before, you were a potential obstacle. Now, your mother believes our problems to be connected. You are quite correct in pointing out that we are in your territory now. We cannot proceed on our own. By the same token you need us just as much. The flood affects us all. We must work together to strike at its source."

Delfine fumed on, but her mother seemed mollified. "Your name, warden?"

"Eisak Marmion. May we have yours?"

"Caroi Delfine, Guardian of the Forest. Is this one your guide?" She raised a hand to point at Chu.

"No. She is one of our party, a citizen of Laure."

The Guardian's expression turned sour. "An Outcast, then."

Marmion didn't argue the point. "We came here in innocence, knowing nothing of your laws."

"*She* should know."

Skender felt Chu fairly vibrating with the need to defend herself. The wing lay at her feet and her hands hung clenched tightly at her sides. She, like him, was looking filthy and worn after their dunking in mud, dousing in freezing water, and long trek up a mountainside. The bags under her eyes were as dark as her pupils.

"She *didn't* know," she said through gritted teeth. "*She* was raised by a mother who didn't once tell her about the place her ancestors came from. *She* came here hoping to find out what sort of people they might have been. And *she*, she's got to say, is not very impressed so far."

Heuve showed his teeth in warning. Lidia Delfine looked pained and, in that moment, much younger than she ever had before. "Mother—Guardian . . . I didn't desire to bring her here, but we were attacked by the Panic and there seemed no alternative. I am aware that by doing so I too have broken the law. That seemed better than leaving her to die."

"I see." Her mother's expression became less stony. "It's clear I need to hear the full story before leaping to any conclusions. You and you—" one long, elegant finger stabbed at Marmion and Chu "—stay here. The others may rest."

"Hey—" Skender began to protest, but was cut off when the finger pointed at him.

"Not you, young mage. There is someone else who needs to make your acquaintance." The Guardian's lips tightened. To a silver-clad aide within the cloisters, she said, "Tell the observer to attend at his earliest convenience in a subchamber of your choice." The aide bowed and moved off. "Heuve?" Lidia Delfine's bodyguard looked surprised to be addressed directly. He bowed and moved forward. "What is that mark on my daughter's arm?"

The big man remained bowed before her, every muscle frozen. "Forgive me, Guardian. I take full responsibility."

"No." Lidia Delfine stepped in front of him, hiding the cut with one hand as though ashamed of it. "It's not his fault. The Panic attacked when my guard was down. Heuve did his best to protect me. I—"

She fell silent. Her mother had raised her hand with a swish of fabric and indicated that she should move aside.

"I thank you, Heuve, for bringing my daughter back to me alive. I would not lose two of my children in one week."

Heuve dared raise his eyes and saw the Guardian smiling at him with tears in her eyes. He flushed from hairline to beard, and backed away.

Skender felt a hand tug at the sleeve of his robe. Aides had stepped from the shadows to take him away. He went reluctantly, looking over his shoulder at Chu. She stood defiantly on her own. As he slipped into the thicket of pillars, her gaze met his, and she shrugged.

"Who do you think you're going to meet?" asked Eitzen as the aides guided them back down the stairs, the rows of blank-faced guards as stony as man'kin.

Skender shrugged.

"Call us if you need help," said Warden Banner, touching his arm. Her warm round face and curly hair combined in a picture of maternal concern, and his thoughts turned automatically to his parents, so far away. What were they doing? Were they worried about him? Would he ever see his father again, high in the cavelike warrens of the Keep?

At the base of the stairs, the aide guided him in a different direction from the others.

"Don't you worry about that," he told Banner. "If anything happens, you'll hear me hollering up and down the mountain."

Banner smiled and waved, and then he was on his own.

THE OBSERVATORY

"Imagining the future is no great feat. Seers do it every day. Imagining a future without us in it is the greater challenge."
THE BOOK OF TOWERS, EXEGESIS 19:8

Shilly and Tom trailed Ramal closely enough to make it clear they were keeping up, but not so close as to breathe down her neck. The female soldier radiated a low-level hostility that discouraged any attempt at familiarity or conversation. Rosevear walked beside Kemp, still slung between two solid guards whose creaking leather uniforms made a counterpoint to the steady slapping of their sandals. Ramal led them along a confusing route through the Panic city, grunting with annoyance when the humans failed to keep up. Shilly doubted she could have retraced their steps. She wasn't seriously considering making a break for it, but if she had been, that alone would have made her think twice.

Tom didn't appear at all worried that they were captives of strange creatures in a city far from home. He seemed perfectly happy, craning his head to glimpse the sweeping curves of the structures around them. Every time they turned a corner, something new came into view. Surprises constantly loomed at them out of the mist. Panic children suspended upside-down by ropes above a net strung between two buildings, tossing a ball backwards and forwards in some kind of game; a low-pitched elegy sung by a deep-voiced male with a throaty flute accompaniment; a curling, tenuous sculpture of mist formed by three gold-clad Panic females waving large fans back and forth; rows and rows of thin wooden planks suspended from parallel cables that rocked faintly in the night air, purpose unknown. It was enough to make Shilly feel dizzy.

"Is Sal going to be all right?" she asked Tom, unable to stop worrying about the others, as well as herself.

The young seer nodded. His hair had sprung up into vigorous waves thanks to all the moisture in the air. It bobbed like a living thing. "I see you two together, at the end."

Of course, she thought. *Arguing about how the world will end.* "Would you tell me if you knew otherwise? If you'd dreamed that he was going to die?"

He turned to look at her, frowning. "Would you want me to tell you?"

"Of course, so I could do something about it."

"But what if I said you couldn't? How would you feel then?"

Shilly couldn't imagine what that would be like. She didn't *want* to imagine. "I think I'd want to know anyway."

"I've dreamed all our deaths," he said, as calmly as though talking about the weather.

"What?" Her stomach felt suddenly hollow. "Are you serious?"

"Of course. Yours. Mine. Sal's. Kemp's." He looked away, following with his gaze the curvaceous sweep into cloud of a tethered building. "But they're not necessarily real. You know how dreams— real dreams, not a seer's dreams—are about everyday stuff? Things we forgot to do, or should have done, or wish we could do?" She nodded. "Well, being a seer is part of who I am, so I dream about it. I dream about seeing things. Those sorts of dreams sometimes aren't about knowing what's going to happen, but how it *feels* to know." He shrugged. "It's very complicated."

So she was beginning to appreciate. "You dream about seeing the people you know die—and then what? You try to help them?"

"No. I know I can't. There's nothing I can do. I'm trapped."

"Goddess. That sounds awful."

Tom nodded.

Ramal guided them across a broad walkway to a giddyingly high beanstalk of a tower, its base steadied by cables tied to five neighbouring structures. Its top disappeared into the clouds that were growing lighter with approaching dawn. Shilly pictured a lighthouse taken between two gigantic hands, stretched, and given a slight twist. They stepped through a gaping circular door into a round room with a caged platform in its centre and the base of a spiralling ladder-staircase to the left. There was no ceiling. Windows dotted the tubular interior, letting in shafts of pure white light. High above, the top of the tower faded into a blur.

"The injured ones go in there," Ramal said, pointing at the cage. Her voice was rough and matter-of-fact. "The rest of us will climb."

Shilly and Rosevear watched anxiously as Kemp's two guards lifted him from the stretcher and arranged him on the floor of the cage.

"Now you," said Ramal, pointing at Shilly.

"*Me?* I'm not injured. A long time ago, yes, but—"

"The ascent is steep and exhausting, even for those whole of body," said the Panic soldier, glancing upwards. Her dark recessed eyes glinted. "Your pride is not my concern."

She indicated the cage again, and Shilly climbed aboard. One of Ramal's fellow soldiers shut and locked the door behind her. He untied a cord fixed to one side of the cage and gave it an almighty tug. Seconds later, the cage lifted off the ground and began its smooth ascent to the top of the tower.

"Uh." Shilly shifted awkwardly, unable to stand fully upright. The cage was wider than it was tall, and wasn't built with human comfort in mind. Its floor consisted of nothing but wire netting. After waving nervously to Tom and Rosevear, she swore not to look down for any reason.

The cage rose at walking pace, powered, she assumed, by a chimerical engine at the top of the tower. If she moved, it swayed slightly, so she stopped doing that too. All in all, it struck her as a rather strange contrivance. Why have stairs *and* an elevator? Perhaps to ferry supplies to whatever lay at the top.

Kemp stirred at her feet. His waxen forehead crinkled.

"Don't you worry about a thing," she told him. "It's all under control. Probably."

She tilted her head upwards, hoping to gain a glimpse of their destination. The lines of windows converged impossibly far up—so far that she was soon heartily glad not to be climbing, despite the awkwardness of the cage.

A strange feeling overcame her. She squatted down on her haunches, feeling suddenly dizzy. The thin wire seemed to twinkle under her fingers.

The Change, Shilly thought. Some kind of charm, and a powerful one at that, was at work in the tower. She couldn't fight it, but she did her best to study its effects.

The swaying of the cage slowed; her limbs grew heavy; time dragged to a halt.

Then she blinked and the effects of the charm had vanished. She looked around her, then up, and saw the top of the tower's shaft finally coming into view.

She stood up as the cage creaked to a halt, suspended from the complicated-looking system of pulleys and wheels that had lifted it so high. The cage had risen into the centre of a broad, disc-shaped room with windows all around the outer wall. She had an unobstructed view of the entire space. Bookshelves, workbenches, chairs, cushions—all demonstrated that this was an inhabited space. But where was its inhabitant? There was no sign of the mysterious Vehofnehu.

"Hello?" she called. Bright yellow light poured through the windows, casting golden glints off instruments and ornaments. It was difficult to tell which was which. "Is anybody here?"

Something occurred to her as she waited for a response: *yellow* light, not white. The only way that could be was if the tower poked straight out the top of the forest's permanent cloud cover.

"Do I hear someone calling?" An unusual head popped up from behind a workbench. What hair remained—in a narrow tuft around the ears—was frizzy and grey. His distinctive Panic brow and mouth were heavily wrinkled and age-spotted. "Is that a visitor on my stoop? Ah!" On seeing Shilly and Kemp, the speaker stood up and smoothed down a faded aqua robe. Angular joints stood out beneath the fabric. "I'm not ready. No. Had no warning. No warning in the slightest. This won't do, won't do at all." The grizzled Panic male bustled about, muttering and looking for something. Beyond that quick initial glance, he seemed happy to ignore Shilly completely.

"Are you Vehofnehu?" she asked him, swivelling to keep him in her line of sight as he overturned cushions and upended piles of notes.

"Eh? Oh, that's just one of my names. I've had several. Ha!" From beneath a ceramic plant pot that contained nothing but a bare stick the strange figure produced an ornate key, which he held up in triumph. "Knew it was here somewhere. Hold still, young human girl. I won't keep you dangling much longer."

The cage hung in a hole surrounded by gleaming brass rails. All the furniture in the room pointed away from the hole—bookcases, desks, chairs—except at one point where a small gangplank rested, hinged away for storage. A tube dangled over the rail near that point, terminating in an ornate nozzle. The other end of the tube disappeared into the floor. Vehofnehu picked up the tube and blew into it, then recoiled when a cloud of dust blew back at him.

"I told you to give me notice when you send me visitors," he barked into the nozzle. "It's discourteous and improper. What if I'd been working on something important? What if you'd distracted me?"

A tinny voice, too low for Shilly to decipher, squeaked back at him, and he held the nozzle to his ear for a moment.

"That's as may be," he said, "but the fact remains. I—"

More squeaking. Vehofnehu nodded, then rolled his eyes at Shilly. "I'd better not keep her waiting then, had I? We don't want to add insult to injury." He draped the tube over the rail, ignoring the ongoing squawk from the far end. "Now," he said, tugging a section of railing out of the way and unfolding the gangplank, "let's take a look at your sick friend."

He shuffled out to the cage, unconcerned by the height, and worked the key in the lock. His hands were sure and steady, despite his age. The cage door sprang open, but Shilly was prevented from exiting by a hand held palm outwards at her. She didn't move, more startled by the odd symmetries of his thumb and fingers than by the gesture itself.

"Not so fast, young lady. I can look quite well from here, but I can't watch both of you at once."

She resigned herself to spending longer in her half-crouch and leaned heavily on her stick as the elderly Panic male knelt down to examine Kemp.

"Hmmm." Vehofnehu peeled back the dressing on Kemp's stomach wound and tested the clear liquid issuing from it with one long finger. The same hand cupped the albino's cheek and lifted one eyelid. Shilly gasped before she could stop herself at what lay beneath. Instead of Kemp's pale blue iris and black pupil, she saw nothing at all. Not even the white of his eyeball. What lay behind was the same colour as his skin, which was itself looking very strange indeed.

"All right," Vehofnehu said, backing up. "We'll need to get him out of the cage. Can you help me with that?"

"I can try."

"And do *you* have a name? Just one will do."

"Shilly," she said. "He's Kemp."

"Not any more, I fear. You take his legs and I'll carry his head."

Awkwardly, and leaving her no energy for conversation, Shilly and Vehofnehu carried Kemp out of the cage, across the gangplank, and away from the elevator shaft. She glimpsed blue sky as she neared the windows. She blinked, dazzled, and almost tripped over a brass telescope lying on the floor.

"Careful! That's very valuable. Lay him down—here on this couch will do. I can see him much better now. Yes."

Shilly let go of Kemp's feet with relief, and staggered back on her good leg. Her injured thighbone ached from the exertion. She clutched her stick and waited impatiently for her eyes to adjust.

"Where are you from, Shilly?" Vehofnehu asked her. She could hear him rustling and fiddling as he examined Kemp, but she couldn't quite make him out. Again, the feeling that a powerful charm was at work nearby thrilled through her.

"The Strand," she said, fighting the dizziness by concentrating on his words. "Kemp and I used to live in the same town, but he lives in the Interior now."

"And now you're both here. That's odd, isn't it?"

She blinked the last of the glare from her eyes, and saw Vehofnehu hunched over Kemp's broad, hairless chest. For a moment, she saw someone quite different: a younger version of him, perhaps, with straighter back and thick dark hair, his strong, straight fingers outspread as though feeling the warmth of a fire, not bent and arthritic. A faint red spark burned in the centre of each of his pupils.

Then she blinked, and he was old again. From somewhere—a pocket, maybe—he had produced a pair of wire-framed glass spectacles and placed them over his eyes.

"I can think of odder things," she said.

He laughed and turned to face her. "I'm sure you can. You've seen a thing or two in your time, judging by the look of you."

She glanced down at her dusty dress and plain leather sandals, all fraying around the edges. "Well, I wasn't expecting to be kidnapped when I got up yesterday morning—"

"No, Shilly. That's not what I meant. Your eyes. Your face. Everything about you tells me you've experienced more of the world than most people. You've seen a glast, at the very least."

This confused her. "A what?"

"A glast." Vehofnehu indicated Kemp. "The thing afflicting your friend here."

"That's what it was called?" It was a relief to have a name for the creature, finally. "It came out of the water in the Divide and took us by surprise. Kemp was hit. The venom spread before we could stop it. Rosevear tried—"

Vehofnehu held up a hand for silence; again, the reminder of his nonhuman nature stopped her in her tracks. When he talked and moved, she could easily pretend that he was nothing but an old man, hunched and scrawny with age. But those long fingers, the oddly foreshortened thumbs, the lined, pink palms . . .

"Let me make something clear," he said. "The shape it possessed when you encountered it—that's not the glast. That was just one of its victims. Where did you say it came from? From the water?"

She nodded. "A giant snake, eyeless, with whiskers."

"I've heard of such things. They live high in the mountains, in glacial lakes where the prey is plentiful and the competition light. They don't usually come down to the plains. Was that where you encountered it?"

"A short way into the foothills," she said. "A day or so from the forest's edge."

He clucked his tongue, making a surprisingly loud noise. "Very much out of their range. Not that it would have made much difference. Your snake wasn't a snake any more. It was a glast, possibly infected during the flood, or before, or after. Am I making sense to you? Something poisoned the snake and turned it into a monster. Not a physical poison, but a chimerical poison. The snake in turn poisoned Kemp, and now he's turning into a glast too."

A feeling of foreboding was growing in her belly. "Is there anything you can do for him?"

"No." Vehofnehu straightened. "Shilly, your friend is already dead. It's best you accept that. He will never return to you, as you knew him. Our only concern now is what to do with the glast. This is one occasion on which all my skills as a healer will be of no use whatsoever."

Shilly backed away, every last hope for Kemp settling into dust. She didn't doubt for a moment that Vehofnehu was telling the truth. The pallor of Kemp's skin grew worse with every hour. The weeping of his wound continued unchecked. Either his hair had begun falling out, or it was losing even the little colour it had once possessed.

The brightness of the sky brought tears to her eyes. Kemp would never see the sun again.

Then something Vehofnehu had said came back to haunt her.

"What do you mean: *as I knew him?*"

Ramal and the others took longer than an hour to climb the stairs. By the time they reached the top, Tom was red in the face, and Rosevear looked set to become one of his own patients. Even the Panic soldiers accompanying them seemed winded, stretching gratefully on reaching the summit and accepting Vehofnehu's offer of a drink.

"This is all terribly inconvenient," the empyricist muttered while bustling about, pumping water from a large brass tap near the elevator shaft and shifting rolls of charts and diagrams off seats. His mood had turned from friendly to irritable again, and he treated the soldiers with exaggerated, almost sarcastic deference. The soldiers in return maintained a bored distance from the observatory and empyricist both. Only Ramal watched closely as Vehofnehu repeated the explanation he had given Shilly to Rosevear and the others.

"Glasts, you see, don't reproduce like other creatures. They don't breed and have children. They don't mate like us, or like other animals." The empyricist rummaged behind a stack of dusty books until he found an elaborate family tree, which he unrolled and placed on the ground. "Here is the lineage of the kingsfolk. At the top, the Handsome King. His children married and had children of their own; his grandchildren did the same, merging and mixing the bloodlines until they were inseparable. That's the way the Panic work—and humans too, although they place more store in who begat whom than we do. A glast, now—" He pointed at the top of the family tree "—a glast starts off alone in the world, a creature that is neither body nor mind but something else entirely. How did it come into existence? What was the first begetting from which all glasts arise? I can't answer that question. I *can* tell you, however, where *more* glasts come from. Not by finding another glast, oh no. By infecting an innocent host—a host with which the essence of the glast merges to create an entirely new glast. Not the old glast in a new shape, but a new being, one with the nature of a glast and something of the donor, too. Thus the lineage progresses. Water snake is infected, becomes a glast-snake. Glast-snake infects Kemp, and he becomes a glast-Kemp. The lineage could continue forever that way, if unchecked."

Vehofnehu let the parchment roll shut with a snap.

"Is that clear?"

Tom nodded. Rosevear looked slightly stunned. "But he still lives."

"Only after a fashion. Look." Vehofnehu stunned everyone by crossing to Kemp, removing the thick bandage placed over his weeping stomach wound, squeezing the moisture it contained into a small glass, and knocking back the thimbleful of clear liquid in one gulp. "Pure water, nothing more. What did you think it was?"

"I—I wasn't sure. That is—" Rosevear had trouble finding words. "I didn't know—"

"You couldn't have known unless you'd seen a glast in action before."

"And you have, I suppose?" asked Ramal.

"Not me personally, but someone I know well." Vehofnehu hurried to fill the guard's pitcher with water from the tap, and managed to spill a small amount on Ramal's armour.

"I *knew* he was dead," said Tom.

That brought Shilly out of her daze. She had sunk into a seat, half-listening as she processed the information herself. "And that makes you happy?" she snapped. "He was your friend. You coached him through School and the Novitiate. You knew him even longer than I, you—" She stopped, seeing Tom recoil and turn away from her. He didn't know why she was so angry at him, and she wasn't entirely certain, either. Kemp hadn't been her best friend in the whole world. She had actively hated him during his years of bullying in Fundelry. He had put that behind him, though; he had begun to make a life for himself in the Interior. The tattoos that Stone Mages placed such value in had begun to take shape across his skin. In time, perhaps, he might have become a Surveyor, like Skender's mother, and unearthed all manner of mystery from Ruins across the world.

But Tom had condemned him to death, or something even worse than that, by not warning him of the glast's attack. Shilly didn't care if the glast was important; she didn't see the future as Tom did. She just knew that someone she cared about was gone, and Tom had allowed it to happen.

Her chain of thought suddenly skipped a link. Something had moved on Kemp's strange skin. She stood up, pointing through a hot rush of tears.

"His tattoos! Look!"

Vehofnehu bent over Kemp's body. The black marks that had once stood out so strongly against the albino's paleness were shimmering, shifting like reflections on milky water.

"Fascinating. Truly fascinating."

Shilly resisted an impulse to whack Vehofnehu across the bony shoulders. "Is there *nothing* we can do?"

"Well, we can remember that to the glast this wasn't an evil act. You might see it that way. Your friend undoubtedly would. But the glast is a creature in its own right, with the right to fight for its survival."

"The right to kill?"

Vehofnehu shrugged. "Do you eat meat?"

"Yes, but that's all I do with it. I don't take it over and parade around in it."

"What about leather, soap, glue, perfume, wool, oil—?"

"All right, all right." She conceded the point ungraciously. "I get it."

"And glasts only use one body at a time, so arguably this one here will kill less than you in your lifetime."

"Okay! So what will it be like? The glast-Kemp?"

"There's only one way to find out. Wait until it wakes up."

Shilly turned away, not sure what she thought of this plan. If Kemp was truly dead, then perhaps it would be better to kill the glast that had killed him, to stop it infecting anyone else. But what if enough of him survived the transition and the glast remained recognisably Kemp? Would destroying it dishonour who he had been? Or would it just prevent the birth of a hideous, perhaps even dangerous, hybrid?

"Can we stay here?" Rosevear asked Ramal. "To wait it out?"

"Here?" spluttered Vehofnehu. "Impossible. I have work to do."

"What work?" Ramal snorted derisively. "I've got better things to do than babysit all day."

"Such as?"

The soldier's upper lip curled into a sneer. "You may not have noticed, old fool, but there's a war brewing. Better out there in the thick of it than cowering in here, I say." The rest of the soldiers uttered an approving rumble. "You may stay," Ramal said to Shilly and the others. "Food and sleeping mats will be provided."

"And the others?" Shilly pressed, thinking of Sal and Highson, and how she might need both of them to stop the glast-Kemp if it went on a rampage like the snake.

"They will be brought to you in due course."

Vehofnehu raised his hands in exasperation and muttered furiously under his breath. His ears turned red in the wild thickets of his hair as he wandered away to bang and clank in the depths of a wooden chest.

"Thank you," said Shilly, although she was far from sure she was grateful. Sticking around to make sure that Kemp was, in fact, truly dead would be a grim and thankless task.

Vehofnehu rattled about in irritation, muttering with undisguised discourtesy. "Well, if that's the way it has to be, go fight your stupid war. The sooner you win or lose it, the sooner I can be left in peace."

Ramal sniffed through flared nostrils. "There will be guards at the bottom of the tower. Any attempt to escape will be harshly dealt with."

"I'm sure they understand." Vehofnehu shooed her and the soldiers toward the stairs, not letting them even suggest using the cage to descend. "I'll explain it to them again, should they harbour any illusions as to their status."

The sound of the Panic descending echoed through Vehofnehu's chamber. He stood at the top of the stairs, waving every now and again, until the sound had faded very much into the background.

"At last," he said, turning back to face Shilly, Tom, and Rosevear. "I thought they'd never leave."

"I'm sorry," Rosevear began, obviously feeling it was his duty as eldest to apologise. "We don't mean to be an inconvenience, but—"

"It's no trouble." Vehofnehu breezily waved away his concerns in a complete reversal of mood. "Now I know you're not friends with *them*, I can relax. But I couldn't let them know that, or they would've refused your request to stay here. Now, would you like some tea?"

"Tea?" Shilly echoed inanely.

"Yes, tea. You did have tea in that village of yours, didn't you? I can't imagine a civilised place without it."

Fundelry hadn't felt remotely civilised while she'd lived there, but she didn't argue the point. "Tea would be good," she said. Tom and Rosevear echoed her.

"Good." He fussed and bothered over a chimerical water heater. A moment's rummaging up to his shoulders in a cupboard produced five green ceramic mugs. "You'll have to excuse my kin. They have no manners, and no taste for subtlety. Few of the so-called kingsmen do, so I prefer to stay out of their way. They're spiteful as well as ill-mannered. Did you hear them questioning my work? Appalling behaviour." He poured hot water from a kettle and added a pinch of dried leaves to each cup.

"One for your friend," Vehofnehu said, placing the extra cup near Kemp's head. "The scent may soothe his journey."

"There really is no hope for him, then?" Rosevear asked.

"None," he said, with sympathy. "I am most dreadfully sorry. But look on the bright side. You'll be here tonight, and the skies are clear. We'll keep a vigil for your friend, and much more besides."

In the face of the puzzlement of his guests, Vehofnehu simply grinned and pulled a lever.

With a clanking groan, the ceiling of his circular room folded back, revealing a glass dome filled with arcane equipment: great tubes and clockwork and crackling chimerical reservoirs, drawing in the energy of the sun and the wind.

"The stars, my friends," he crowed. "We're going to watch the stars."

THE MAGE

"The Change is truly a wonderful thing, but one can have too much of a wonderful thing. That the mind exists in a world of change readily demonstrates the necessity for balance between order and chaos, rigidity and flux. The Change needs Sky Wardens just as much as Sky Wardens need the Change."
MASTER WARDEN RISA ATILDE: NOTES TOWARD A UNIFIED CURRICULUM

*T*hwack.

"Thoroughly unacceptable."

Thwack.

Skender flinched as a spray of petals fell across his face. He brushed them away and followed the Stone Mage Aldo Kelloman along the narrow path.

"Don't you think so, boy?"

An awkward second played out, during which Skender tried to think of something noncommittal to say. Kelloman spoke and acted with the aggrieved boredom of a civil servant, but inhabited the body of a young forest woman not much older than Skender. He had had her head shaved, and he dressed her in voluminous robes that more or less approximated a mage's formal regalia. He walked with the aid of a fragile-looking bowed cane carved from ivory. His voice never rose out of her lower registers, and his irritation with everything seemed unappeasable.

"What exactly do you mean, Mage Kelloman?"

"Everything! All these ridiculous trees and the *things* that live in them. The foresters and the farce they call a meal. And the mist—oh, bless my socks, the mist! Stifles during the day; chills at night. Puts rot and mildew in everything. How one is supposed to find one's way in it, I'll never know. And yet it never rains—ever. Unbearable!"

Skender cleared his throat. He agreed on some points, but he wouldn't go so far as to damn everything he had seen. The foresters had a right to live any way they wanted. As long as they didn't hurt him and his friends, they really could eat spiders for all he cared.

"I'm sure they're not always like this," he ventured. "I mean, after the flood—"

"After the flood? Not always?" Kelloman fired his words back at him with outraged venom. "I tell you, boy, their barbarism is untempered by the slightest degree of civilisation. Not even when word came from the Synod itself, instructing me to determine the source of the flood and giving me Special Powers to do so—" Skender heard the capital letters clearly in the mage's pronunciation "—even then, they continue to ignore my requests and relegate me to the shadows. I am ignored, boy. Treated as a second-class citizen. The irony, that one such as I should be so maligned, is unimaginable!"

The mage had stopped on the path to pepper his words with pokes at Skender's chest, as though trying to physically batter him into agreement.

"And the circumstances in which I'm expected to live . . ." Kelloman rolled his eyes and shuddered. With the sigh of one very much put upon, he turned and resumed his journey along the path. "Simply intolerable."

Thwack.

The man's long ivory cane whipped out and knocked the head off another flower. More petals flew and Skender winced. On the one hand, flowers were just flowers, so what did it matter if Kelloman wilfully cut them back? On the other hand, they were part of a forest revered by the people who lived in it. The foresters definitely wouldn't like it if they saw what he was doing.

Then Skender wondered if they knew full well what he did, and that was why they treated him with disdain. They might not go so far as to expel a representative of a distant, powerful country, but they could make life unpleasant for such a person.

Eventually they came to a small treehouse jutting out of Milang's upper levels. The position gave a clear view over the treetops—which meant a clear view of mist only—and it should have had a spacious feel. However, Kelloman's quarters were cramped and messy, filled with dirty dishes, discarded clothes, and thick with webs that Skender eyed with suspicion. The mage cleared two spaces for them to sit, pulled a bottle of something dark and pungent-looking from under a chair, and poured himself a drink. When offered one, Skender rapidly shook his head. The glass Kelloman took for himself was brown around the lip and fluffy where it had lain on its side in the dust. Skender had no doubt the one he received would be in even worse condition.

"If you haven't been sent to replace me, what are you doing here?" Kelloman asked, settling into a well-worn rut of immobility and dissatisfaction. He was sweating heavily after the brief walk, and Skender wondered why he didn't just take off, or loosen, some of his robes.

Skender opened his mouth to give the standard explanation: that they were seeking the source of the flood, the Angel, the reason for the failure of the seers to see beyond a certain point in the future, and the Homunculus, too, if it was still alive. But as he went to say it, he knew it wasn't the truth. Not the entire truth, anyway. His mission had ended on the rescuing of his mother from the Aad. He could have gone home to the Keep with a clear conscience, confident that Sal and Shilly would do what needed to be done next, wherever and however that might be. As much as he enjoyed their friendship and felt honour-bound to help them, that wasn't the complete answer.

He couldn't talk about it with Kelloman, of all people, but the thought of lying once more didn't appeal either.

"I'm looking for something," he said. "Or hoping to find something. Perhaps that's a better way of putting it."

"Something," asked Kelloman with a shrewdness Skender hadn't expected, "or some*one*?" He winked. "Perhaps the Guardian simply threw you to me as a distraction. A sop to keep me off her back for a day or two. Despite my best efforts to educate these people, they refuse to listen, but I persist, exercising patience beyond reasonable expectation. I will endure this indignity, as I endure others. Do you see, boy, how they disrespect us? How they wilfully turn their backs on civilisation? One can't be too judgmental—they are, after all, little more than savages—but one can be wounded on behalf of one's betters."

"How long have you been here?" Skender asked, relieved that the matter of his motives had been forgotten so quickly.

"Two years. And a long two years it has been, let me tell you, without proper spices or educated company, without the arid gravity of the desert, and without even a decent roof over my head. You know, these people have no use for stone. Can you credit that? None at all! It might as well be gravel to them, fit to crush underfoot. It's all leaf and vine, bough and trunk—endlessly fecund and feckless. Splinters and sap, I call it, and good for nothing. A breeding place for bugs and worse! You hear that buzzing sound? It's made by insects as big as your thumb, all whining at the same time. And—ah!" The mage jumped as something small and lithe dropped from the ceiling onto the back of his chair. "Speak of ill and ill comes. Look at this filthy rat, will you? An infestation in my very home. Appalling!"

Kelloman pushed the creature off the chair and to the floor, where it pounced on his feet. He kicked and sent it skidding into Skender's chair. There it rolled over with a skittering of claws and righted itself, and Skender received a proper look at it.

Not a rat, not quite. It was smaller than a possum, with disproportionately large, fanlike ears, tiny fingers and toes, and a long thin tail. Its hind legs were longer than its front, and its face tapered down to a pointed nose that sniffed curiously at his ankles. Its colouring struck him as distinctly unusual: bluish-brown on its body and black around

the eyes, its tail dark for half its length, fading to white at its brush-
like tip.

"Is that a bilby?" he asked, dredging the name from his voluminous memory.

"How should I know?" Kelloman shuddered, making an elaborate
display of wiping away imaginary germs. "Filthy thing keeps following me around. The locals won't do anything to get rid of it—yet
another example of their vile temperament. Disease-carrying rodents
don't worry them, but some tiny avalanche that destroys a bit of their
forest gets them all in a tizzy."

Some tiny avalanche, Skender wanted to say. That *bit of the forest* had
contained a village of one thousand people, all of whom had died. He
perfectly understood the concern it had caused, and felt no wonder at
all that they dismissed Kelloman's relatively minor complaints about
creatures living in his home.

Unable for a moment to think of anything to say that wasn't disrespectful or downright rude, Skender bent to touch the bilby. It didn't
pull away. If anything, it craned up to sniff at his finger, as though
hoping he had food in his hand. Tiny whiskers tickled him. Reassured
by its reaction, he stroked the rough fur of its neck and back.

"Don't encourage it," spluttered Kelloman.

Too late. The bilby leapt onto skender's lap and nuzzled into a ball.

"Perhaps I could take it outside," he suggested, although he was
quite touched by the way the creature had adopted him.

The mage dismissed the suggestion with a scandalised sneer. "Just
don't blame me if you get fleas."

"I won't."

Kelloman drank deeply from his glass. "So, to home. What news
of the Synod? Of Ulum?"

"Well . . ." Skender struggled to think of anything that might be
of interest. Interior gossip and politics had been effectively quashed by
more recent events.

"Come on. You're a Van Haasteren. I know that Keep of yours is a long way from anywhere, but you must have something to report."

Skender struggled through an anecdote about a councillor caught fiddling the books in one of Ulum's many underground halls. Kelloman soaked up the tale with relish, begging every detail Skender had overheard. Skender did as he was told, even as a strange sense of dislocation crept over him. Kelloman's manner and appearance were completely at odds, as were the circumstances of their meeting and their conversation. Not two weeks after the greatest flood the world had ever known, and on the brink of an even greater catastrophe, they discussed a minor scandal that most people had already forgotten.

Are you faring any better, Chu? he wondered. *Are your distant relatives still hung up on the actions of your parents?*

If the world ended, he thought, it would be because little things like this got in the way of doing what was right, not because of the actions of any one man or woman.

"So the Synod asked you to find out about the flood," he said, when an opportunity to change the subject presented itself. "What have you learned?"

"I told you," Kelloman sniffed. "The foresters won't tell me anything."

"But you *have* asked?"

"Of course! What do you think I am? They think the Panic did it, just as they blame the Panic Heptarchy for *everything* that goes wrong: floods, plagues, famines, even leaf-rot. You name it."

"Why would the Panic do something like this?"

"A good question, boy. To drive the Guardian and her cronies out of the forest is the accepted answer. Seems the Panic don't so much live *in* the forest as *over* it, and there are those who assume that the Panic would want it the other way around. Maybe that's so; maybe it's not. You'd have to ask the Panic and they don't talk to humans much these days."

"Have you ever spoken to them?"

"Stone the bards, no. That rowdy bunch is even worse than this lot."

"What about the wraith thing, then? Do you know anything about that?"

"Well, now. That *is* interesting." Kelloman leaned forward, fingers steepled in front of him. "Rumour has it something's been picking off the foresters one by one over the past two or three weeks—and the Panic too, apparently—but I have my doubts. The Guardian's fool son got himself killed during a patrol three nights ago and all manner of fuss erupted. They're so full of pride, these Delfines, that rather than admit he made a mistake—slipped off a cliff, perhaps, or shot himself with his own arrow—they've co-opted some ridiculous creature to explain the accident away."

"It's not ridiculous," said Skender stonily. "I've seen it myself."

"Have you really? Are you sure it wasn't the Panic? They're adept flyers, you know."

"I'd know the difference."

"You who have only just arrived and don't know one thing from another?" Kelloman laughed as resoundingly as his small frame would allow. "Dear boy, you overestimate the Guardian and underestimate the Panic. But at the end of the day, they're all savages. We could teach them a thing or two, if only they'd listen."

Skender fumed for a moment, then asked, "What about the Angel, then?"

"Ah, the Angel. No. Another topic the locals don't wish to discuss. They're a tight-lipped lot. Have you noticed that?" Kelloman leaned back in his chair and pressed the splayed fingers of his right hand against his temple. "You know, I once asked the Guardian if she talked to the trees. I mean, you must have seen how they go on about them. The trees are this. The trees say that. Well, I confronted her and she tried to fob me off. Embarrassed, of course, by the truth—which is that they *worship* the trees, and they know it to be wrong. Just by being here and being ourselves, we expose the ridiculousness of their stance."

"What exactly did the Guardian say?"

"Say? Let me see, now." Kelloman rummaged in a haphazard pile of notebooks and flicked through one in particular. "Yes, here. I remember noting it down because it seemed a particularly artless response. 'Does the sea need to talk to tell the tides?' she said. 'Does stone announce itself before falling in an avalanche?'" He rolled his eyes. "I mean, *really*. What utter rot! If they spent less time doting on the trees and more exploring the bedrock beneath, they wouldn't be tucked away in this bug-ridden corner of the Earth."

Kelloman indicated the bilby with a wave of one hand, then nodded smugly as though that proved his point completely. Skender hadn't the energy to argue.

"Have you got anything to eat?" he asked instead.

"Roots and berries," came the unhappy reply. "And the odd nut."

Skender's stomach rumbled. "Sounds wonderful."

"You might think so now, but try eating it for two years." Kelloman gave him directions, clearly not intending to move from his chair for anyone but himself. "Have they tried the ghost frog trick on you yet?"

Skender grinned. Yes, they had, and it would be a long time before he believed anything the foresters told him about food, but that didn't mean he disliked them. He might have done the same thing in their shoes.

The bilby ran up his left arm and onto his shoulder when he tried to put it on the ground.

"Don't feed it, whatever you do." Kelloman watched him sourly as he tried to coax it with an offering of dried fruit. "I'll never get rid of it."

The bilby snatched the morsel from Skender's fingers before he could withdraw it, and he hid a smile.

This wasn't the first time Skender had come face to face with the advanced Stone Mage practice that allowed Kelloman to inhabit the body of another while his body rested in an inert state far away. The Mage Erentaite, an elderly woman who lived in Ulum, could only attend the monthly Synod in the ruined city of the Nine Stars by occupying the body of an empty-minded girl. There were many other mages in similar circumstances. Such transactions were considered mutually beneficial by most, since the recipients of the minds of travelling mages were often unable to care for themselves on their own.

Skender found such a mismatch as Kelloman's between host and visitor spooky, though. Kelloman's presence seemed to strain at the seams of the body he had been given. When Skender looked away from the mage and pictured him in his mind's eye he was large of frame, overweight, and with hanging jowls—very different from his host's slight appearance.

Maintaining conversation wasn't a problem, despite this. Kelloman was much more interested in talking than listening. As long as Skender stayed awake and occasionally feigned agreement, the man was happy. Among the many things the man complained about were his reasons for being in the forest. It transpired that such a remote outpost hadn't come his way by accident. As Kelloman put it, he was the innocent victim of professional rivalry. An expert in transcorporeal studies, he had locked horns with a senior mage over a matter of theory and found himself posted somewhere well out of the way quick smart. Despite protests and pleas for clemency—and "no small amount of first-rate research under incredibly difficult circumstances"—there he remained.

Skender imagined the true story was more complex than the account he heard, but he didn't challenge Kelloman on its veracity. Best just to nod and pat the bilby—which had fallen asleep on his lap—and hope he hadn't been completely forgotten by those in charge.

They came for him at sunset. Three brown-clad guards appeared at the door and entered without knocking.

"You are to return with us."

Kelloman's face—already flushed red from pungent liquor—turned as dark as thunderclouds. "Now see here. My young friend has barely had a moment to—"

The lead guard raised a hand. "*Both* of you, if you please. The Guardian wishes to see you."

"What if I don't want to see her?"

Skender was disinclined to argue. He'd spent long enough in the company of Mage Kelloman and would accept any offer of a change.

"We'll come," he said, standing. The bilby started awake and scrabbled up his stomach and chest with tiny, sharp-tipped claws. He felt it tense for a moment, as though it might leap off, but it relaxed as Kelloman stood with a heavy sigh and smoothed down the front of his robe.

"Very well," he grumbled. "If I must. Do you see the sort of indignities I suffer, day after day? Come here; go away; come back again— without so much as a thank you or a by-your-leave. A lesser man wouldn't tolerate it."

He grabbed Skender by the arm and breezed haughtily past the guards, picking up his cane as he walked out the door. Skender readied himself for a furious row when the mage started thwacking at flowers, but fortunately Kelloman restrained himself. Conserving energy, perhaps, for the uphill climb. Despite the youthful body he inhabited, the trip soon took its toll. Kelloman was very much out of shape, and his clothes were completely inappropriate for the humid weather.

Skender looked back on his visits to the Haunted City and Laure and hoped he had never been so gauche.

They walked and climbed in silence, followed closely by the guards. The light of the fading sun deepened to pink through the clouds, casting the forest in peculiar hues: green leaves turned to black, while red flowers seemed to shine; wisps of fog resembled crimson streamers as they snaked through the branches. Bird calls echoed from the surrounding canopy as raucous daytime species settled in for the night and their nocturnal counterparts stirred. The bilby clung tight to Skender's shoulder, wide eyes watching for predators; each time a branch moved, twenty tiny pinpricks in four groups of five made Skender shiver.

"Ghastly place," panted Kelloman as they passed the halfway point.

Before Skender could answer, a chill wind rushed down the pathway, bringing the smell of blood with it. He stopped dead in his tracks, recognising that terrible spoor.

"Goddess! *Here?*"

"What, boy?"

"We need to get away. Now." Skender looked around for a hiding place, while Kelloman and the guards milled in confusion.

"It's just a breeze," said one of them.

"Believe me, it's not. It's the thing that killed Lidia Delfine's brother." He couldn't help yelling at them as the cold deepened and the fog grew tight around them. "The wraith!"

Comprehension dawned, but still they dragged their feet. Skender grabbed Kelloman's arm and tugged him off the wooden path. The mage had frozen in his tracks, staring wide-eyed uphill as though he could see what was coming and had been struck dumb by it.

"Come *on!*" The bilby scampered in fright from shoulder to shoulder across Skender's back. Kelloman weighed less than he had expected—fooled once again by the man's manner. Under the robes, the physical form of Kelloman's host body was as light as deadwood. "Down here!"

Skender had spotted a gap in the platform's boughs that led to the level below. Skender pushed Kelloman ahead of him. The mage dropped with a flutter and tearing of robes but surprisingly little complaint. Skender followed barely in time. The three guards had drawn their weapons and braced themselves against the rising wind. He glanced back at them and saw an icy blackness sweep down the path, snapping branches in its wake, and snatch one of them off her feet.

Skender dropped, hearing the beginning of a scream whip overhead. The cries of the other guards rose in fright and horror.

"What is it?" hissed Kelloman, clutching Skender's robe and pulling him close. "What's it doing to them?"

Skender furiously shushed him. A sound much like tearing wind came from above. Icy dust and leaf fragments rained down through the boards. A clash of weapons suggested that the guards were putting up a fierce fight, but then something hard clattered away from where the footsteps thumped and shuffled, and a dark rain began to fall.

Skender backed away, filled with revulsion. Blood poured through the cracks in the boards.

"What's going *on*?"

Skender dragged Kelloman further downhill, away from the slaughter. He could hear only one guard now as she fought for her life. Although his cowardice sickened and dismayed him, the thought of death was worse. He couldn't defend himself against such things. He wasn't nearly strong enough. Running was his only option. Or dying.

"No." Kelloman gripped him tightly, and not only out of fear. With a surprising turn of strength, the mage brought Skender to a halt. "Wait. Feel it."

Skender tried to pull himself free, then felt cold air coming upwards from below.

Another one.

Ice blossomed in his gut, radiating through veins and nerves like fractures in a pane of glass. Every sense became powerfully acute —but he might as well have been deaf, dumb, and blind for all the good it did him. The slightest tap would shatter him into a million pieces.

"Don't just stand there, boy." Kelloman's voice came from the other side of the world. "Give me a hand!"

The mage was clambering over the guide rail of the path and forcing his way through the canopy. Blood-spattered and out of shape as well as out of place, he made a ludicrous figure. Skender felt like screaming with laughter. *What's the point? It's going to find us in there just as easily as out here.*

With a squeak, the bilby jumped off his shoulders and scrambled into the canopy after Kelloman.

The hairs on Skender's arms stood on end as the shadowy, sharp-clawed fiend rushed up the mountain towards them. He could hear it shrieking, made hungry and urgent by the crying of the guards above. Perhaps it could smell the blood and honed in on its primitive power. The yadachi bloodworkers of Laure used the power of blood to bring life to their desiccated city, but it could just as easily be turned towards bringing death. The more the wraiths killed, the more power they would have, and so it would go until blood-soaked vampires ruled the night, and every living thing huddled in fear.

Blood. Trees. Power.

In a flash, Skender knew what Kelloman was trying to do. Skender vaulted the guide rail with a single movement and landed on a branch. It didn't move even slightly beneath him. Kelloman was up to his waist in a tangle of vines, flowers, and leaves, emitting a steady stream of cursing. Soft fungus broke and gave way beneath Skender's fingers as he dived in after the mage, tearing the foliage apart in his desperation to get deeper. The bilby ran back and forth, guiding him. He lunged with his right hand, felt it break through a tangle of roots and fibres. Something cool and hard and familiar greeted his questing fingers.

Stone.

With his other hand he gripped Kelloman's shoulder as tightly as he could.

"*Through me,*" he said via the Change. "*Whatever it takes.*"

Kelloman didn't grace his offer with a reply. Instead, the mage turned to face the creature that menaced them and channelled the Change contained in the mountain's backbone directly to his will.

The world whited out for a moment and a roaring noise drowned any sound Skender might have heard from either the second wraith or its intended victim. The smell of the forest, the feel of stone under his hands and wood beneath his feet, the taste of coppery fear on his tongue—all vanished. All he had left were his thoughts.

Granted, Skender told himself—even as the full force of the

bedrock flowed through him and into Kelloman's body—granted, the man was a fool. But he was also a trained mage, one powerful enough to throw his mind from one side of the world to the other for two entire years without suffering any ill effects. That said something. A person didn't need to have good manners or refined communication skills to use the Change, just as a blacksmith didn't need them to hammer iron or a mechanic to tighten a bolt. The world didn't care about such things. Only people did.

When people were being *eaten*, Skender would cheerfully put aside all his prejudices to avoid being one of them.

The roaring faded. Sight returned. Skender felt as though the world had aged several days, but his position in the canopy hadn't changed in the slightest. A shocked silence echoed through the tree-tops; even the moaning moai were silent. There was no remnant of chill in the air. In fact, it was dry-hot like an oven and smelled of ash. He took that as a good sign, and twisted to see what had happened.

Kelloman stood beside him, still connected to him by the hand touching his shoulder. The last dregs of the Change flickered through them both, and the mage's tattoos writhed into golden life over his host body's face and fingers: fine swirls and circular patterns that crossed and recrossed in ways that made Skender's eyes swim. Then they were gone, and the mage sagged. Skender caught the slight body just in time. The mat of vines and branches crackled and groaned beneath them, and he became acutely conscious of just how exposed they were. If the lot collapsed, they could skid down the side of the cliff face all the way to the bottom.

He had no choice but to try to get Kelloman back to the relative safety of the platform they had so hastily left. When he turned to judge the distance, however, grunting and struggling with his awkward burden, he saw that this option was no longer open to him.

The platform was gone. Where it had been there was a hole in the canopy, open to the sky. Tendrils of smoke and fog wreathed the charred remains of whatever had stood between Kelloman and the wraith: grey-black sticks marked the skeletal framework of supports, load-bearing beams, walls, ceilings, and floors. Nothing else had survived the power of the charm Kelloman had used.

Voices echoed from above, exclaiming, calling, inquiring. The burned canopy shifted beneath him again, and he struggled to maintain his grip on the limp mage.

"Over here!" he yelled at the top of his lungs. "I don't know how much longer I can hold on!"

The bilby leapt from his shoulder and scampered away through the canopy. He wished he could do the same, even as he cursed its sudden cowardice. He hollered until the ash in the air made him choke. Coughing violently, he felt his feet begin to lose traction and scrabbled for a new handhold.

"Help us!"

"Hang in there, Skender," yelled a familiar voice from above. "We're coming."

Blinking ashen tears from his eyes, he looked up into Chu's face.

Beside her, Heuve fastened a rope to a beam two levels up, allowing one of the guards to clamber down to his level. The bilby jumped off the guard's back as he drew nearer, and scampered up Skender's outstretched arm.

"Guess I shouldn't have been so hasty," he told it, as the guard took the mage's weight from him.

"I'll come back for you in a second," the guard told Skender as he and Kelloman were pulled away by those above.

Relief at being rescued faded as memories of the thing that had attacked them flooded back. He peered down through the blasted branches, searching for its body. All he saw was a blackened hole, smoking.

"Don't take too long," he called up at the others, and clung tighter to his awkward perch.

THE STARS

**"The sky is a mirror to the world.
Stare at it long enough and you will see yourself."**
THE BOOK OF TOWERS, EXEGESIS 5:33

A murmur goaded Sal onwards and upwards through the darkness. Every muscle burned and his spine felt like an overstressed mast. His head ached from the repetition of taking one rung at a time, over and over, without slipping. He kept climbing, safe in the knowledge that he was faring much better than his father, two rungs behind and breathing in rapid, ragged gasps.

The voice wasn't one he recognised. A curious mixture of excited and querulous, it followed long, lilting trajectories from topic to topic, not deflected by the occasional question or comment from those listening to it, but striking out along newly syncopated pathways leading the Goddess only knew where at its own whims. No matter how he strained, Sal couldn't quite make out the words. For what felt like a small eternity, he was caught in the darkness, reaching for some anchor of comprehension just as he reached for the next thin rung in sequence, one after the other, trying hard to ignore the gaps between them. Each time he thought he was getting a grip on the words, they slipped out of reach again. He found it maddening.

What would happen if he ever reached for a rung and it wasn't there? His body was so trapped in the repetitious rhythm of its ascent Sal was sure he would climb through one of the gaps in the ladder and fall down the way he had come, to a pointless and messy death.

Finally—inevitably, perhaps—burbled consonants and vowels coalesced into words, and words strung themselves into sentences. Sentences

175

tied knots of conversation and argument around concepts he had never heard discussed in so much detail before—not even in the Haunted City or the Keep, where such things, he supposed, *should* be discussed.

"I watch the stars every night," said the voice, "and I am no closer to knowing them than I ever was. Understanding? Yes, I aspire to that. But knowing them, no. That I will never achieve. How could I? It would be like watching a busy market, day after day, with the expectation of knowing every face in the crowd. I can imagine coming to recognise a number of individuals out of such a crowd, because some have distinctive features that recur every now and again, but would that mean I *knew* them? I fear not."

"There are maps," said a male voice. It sounded like Rosevear. "In the *Book of Towers*. I've seen them. Maps of the sky, with names."

"Yes, and great constellations marked too, I bet." The owner of the voice sniffed contemptuously. "A map is not the thing, my friend. I too could draw a map, right here and now; it might even be accurate one day in a thousand. Would that please you, make you feel you were closer to some deep understanding of the world we live in? Would it reassure you to have that piece of paper in your hand, even as you tried to find the stars you sought, and failed?" A balled-up piece of vellum fluttered past Sal, taking him by surprise. He forced himself to resume his steady rhythm. "A map is worth less than the paper it's printed on unless the person who drew it knew what they were doing. And even then, you need to know how it works. Maps are like machines, you see: only as good as the thought that goes into them, and liable to be a danger to those who *don't* think."

"What use, then, is studying the sky? If the stars are unknowable and their names are meaningless, what's the point?"

"The point is, of course, that although as individuals they cannot be known or even counted with any great precision, as a whole they are immensely interesting. Their ebb and flow reflects what happens beneath with more precision than you would credit, I'm sure."

"The Void Beneath?"

"No, here. On the ground. Well, you know what I mean. Do you?"

"You're saying that motions of the stars are influenced by what *we* do, how *we* move." A new voice, one Sal knew instantly. *Shilly's*.

"Yes, yes. And why shouldn't that be so? Everything else in the world is influenced by us. The Change flows through us from all corners of the sea, the stone, the sand—and the sky, too. It's all connected. *All* of it."

"Why?"

"What do you mean, *why*?"

"Well, just that. What makes us so special?"

"Oh, we're not special. No more so than the trees or the ground or the air. We're just part of it. And by *it*—because I know you'll ask—I mean nothing more than just that. *It*. Everything. Does there need to be more of an explanation than that? When a cup is full, do you wonder why it has to be full? What it means to be full? How it got to be full? The cup is simply full, and that's all we need to know about it."

Sal welcomed the argument. It was a fine distraction from the climb, and a sign that he was getting somewhere. Far above, at the very limits of his vision, a faint yellow patch had appeared, as of a light burning somewhere impossibly distant.

"Let me put it another way. Step on an ant and you don't even notice. But the ant notices, without a doubt, and so too do those around him. Was it special in some way to have been trodden on by you? Did you choose him specifically from the many you could have trodden on? Of course not. It just happened that way. We and the world are like that too. Are humans special to be living in this one, in this fashion? No. Are the man'kin, or the golems, or the kingsmen, or the glasts? No. We just are, and looking for higher meaning or a greater purpose is pointless.

"Patterns and processes, on the other hand—they are what we must seek. Learn the way things work and you can work them to your

will. Learn the way things will, and you can make them work for you."
The voice cackled gleefully. "Do you see? Mages and wardens understand some of this. The ones you call the Weavers understand more."

"You know of them?" Shilly sounded startled, with good reason.

Sal hadn't heard that word for a long time either, outside of him
and Shilly. The Weavers were a shadowy group that claimed responsibility for the Divide, and for maintaining a dynamic equilibrium
between the Interior and the Strand. Highson Sparre had once been
one of them, as had the Alcaide Dragan Braham.

"Of course I know of them. I see many things from up here—and
much that you ground-folk assume is well hidden, I assure you."

A wave of strangeness rolled over Sal between one rung and the
next. He froze in midclimb, fearing what such disorientation might do
to him at this point in the ascent. His head swam so badly that he
could hardly tell which way was up any more. There was no handrail
on the spiral staircase. If he put one limb wrong and slipped—

"Keep moving, Sal," called Griel from below. "I told you not to
stop, no matter what. Do as I tell you and it'll be all right."

Sal forced himself to obey the Panic soldier's gruff words. With a
tremendous effort of will, he brought his right hand out and forward,
to where body memory told him the next rung should be. It was
indeed there, and he gripped it tight, and forced himself onward, rung
by rung, until the effect faded.

The voice had stopped too. So he realised when his senses cleared.
The interior of the tower was silent, and the light above had become
abruptly brighter.

"Hello?" came a cry from the summit. "Is that more visitors I hear?"

Sal peered up and saw a stocky figure silhouetted against the warm
yellow glow, looking down at him. He managed a wave with one
cramped hand. "Are you the empyricist?"

"I'm many things. That will do for now."

Relief lent Sal new strength. Not only was Shilly at the top, but

Griel had led them truly. After their meeting with the Quorum, Griel had come for him, Mawson, and Highson in the holding cells as promised, leaving Schuet and Mikia behind, but he had been less than communicative during their crossing of the balloon city. When pressed, he had said only that Vehofnehu was an empyricist who could help them work out what to do next.

Sal knew what an empyricist was but had never met one before, not in the Haunted City or anywhere in the Interior—his stay in both places had been too short and tumultuous. He imagined charts and strange instruments, and the faint aura of instability that so often accompanied exploration into the arcane.

That he was proved right on all three counts didn't necessarily reassure him.

When the top of the spiral ladder-staircase finally came into view, he saw an ancient Panic male waiting for him—grey-cheeked, wild-haired, and dressed in a worn robe that might once have been green. A wiry but strong grip helped him up the last two rungs to where Shilly was waiting for him with arms wide and eyes relieved. The pressure of her cheek against his felt like coming home.

"When Mawson came up in the cage," she said, helping him to a seat, "we knew you wouldn't be far behind."

For the moment, Sal was too winded to speak. He let gravity take him and folded gratefully onto a dusty cushioned surface. Distantly, he acknowledged the space around him: a circular room with a roof and many windows granting access to the night sky. A handful of clear yellow mist globes provided dim illumination. Tom lay curled in a shadowy corner, sound asleep with a worried look on his face. Rosevear helped Sal's father out of the stairwell and into another chair.

Griel came last. Even with the Panic's natural stoop, he stood a full head higher than the empyricist. Despite that they gripped each other's hands as equals.

"You are welcome here, my friend. Always welcome."

"Thank you. I'm sorry I can't come more often."

"Pfft." Vehofnehu waved away Griel's apologies and went about pumping water for the new arrivals. "You have much to do below, I know, so I forgive you for sending that buffoon Ramal instead. How's Jao?"

Griel's protruding brow became even more thunderous, but with concern, not anger. "She fears for us. Fears where we're heading and what we might become."

"As should you."

Sal accepted a tall glass of water from Vehofnehu and drank it in one gulp.

"Where's Kemp?" he asked. "Were you able to help him?"

"No one can help your friend now," said the empyricist, turning his back and moving away.

"He's dead?"

The look in Shilly's eyes told Sal that Kemp's fate wasn't so simple. She explained the situation to Sal and Highson while Mawson watched stonily from the pedestal he had been placed upon.

Sal felt equal parts dismay and concern at what he heard and saw as he wearily stood by the couch studying the way Kemp's tattoos appeared to float over skin turned glassy and grey. That Sal had known nothing about glasts before now didn't concern him: strange things lived in strange corners of the world, and the Hanging Mountains were very strange indeed, judging by what he had seen thus far. He only wished he had been able to act more quickly on the boneship to save his friend, and wondered what needed to be done to prevent the glast-Kemp from endangering anyone else.

It was then his turn to bring the others up to date. His recollections of the audience with the Quorum possessed a dreamlike quality, as though it hadn't really happened, or not quite in the way he remembered it. Highson backed him up, however, supporting his description of the encounter with the cousins Tarnava and Elomia, who acted as guardians and translators for the Quorum itself.

"Glowing green, you say?" Shilly's brow crinkled at the description. "I saw someone like that at the base of the waterfall, just before the Panic fired on the boneship."

"Really? You didn't mention it before."

"There wasn't exactly time to, and I couldn't be sure I didn't imagine it. Now, though . . ."

"Why would one of the Quorum leave the city?" Griel asked Vehofnehu.

"They're not prisoners." The empyricist had listened to their conversation with one ear as he fiddled with glass lenses mounted in several strange instruments. "They come and go as they will."

"They never have before."

"That you're aware of." Vehofnehu winked. "They visit me here, sometimes. We talk as best we can."

"How?"

"There are ways. They pass through time in the opposite direction to us, that's all. To them, everything is reversed. We come, and they think we are going. They leave, and we see them arriving. That's why the man'kin can talk to them. Our stony brethren exist outside of time as both we *and* the Quorum know it."

Sal nodded in understanding, remembering the strange speech of the glowing figures and Mawson responding to them in kind. *I talk to them the same way I talk to you*, the man'kin had said. *Only backwards.*

"Where do you fit into all this?" he asked the empyricist.

"I?" The elderly Panic male raised his eyebrows as though Sal had accused him of a crime. "I don't fit into anything. I am merely an observer."

"How is that possible? Earlier, you said everything is connected. So did Tom. If that's true, you must be connected too."

Vehofnehu barked in amusement. "Indeed I did say that, young human. And indeed it is true. I am connected in ways you couldn't imagine. So are we all, in our unique ways. Who can say what effect our actions will have on the world? What changes we might wreak with a single word, the slightest gesture? Even a lack of action can make a difference. Mere observation, my friends, is a powerful tool."

As he spoke, the mist globes dimmed and darkness fell in the circular room. Sal reached out and found Shilly's hand. He clutched it tightly, feeling the night outside creep through the clear glass windows, bringing with it a chill of the mind rather than the body. He shivered.

Vehofnehu's observatory rose above the all-encompassing cloud cover. No wonder, Sal thought, the climb to its summit had taken so long. The sky was visible in all directions except to the northeast, where the shoulder of the mountains loomed. Apart from the mountains, under the cool, hard light of the stars Sal saw nothing but clouds.

Even after a lifetime spent in the borderlands or on the far fringes of the Strand, he felt that he had never seen the stars so clearly and in such quantities. Uncountable, unchartable, they reminded him of glowing grains of sand scattered across the surface of an icy black sea. They gleamed and glittered; they held his eye and threatened to hypnotise him. In the sky he saw nothing familiar, only alien forms.

He didn't see shapes, as some people claimed to. Stars weren't clouds in which one could see camels, fish, buggies, even faces, as high-altitude winds moulded them. He didn't possess the visual knack needed to connect all the disparate dots into a whole picture, although he suspected Shilly probably did. He saw the broader brush strokes instead, the patches of relative light and dark. The metaphors and similes he called on to describe them came from his knowledge of the world below: reefs and rivers where sprays of stars clumped together; barren fields where few congregated. In the former he glimpsed wonder, and a mystery he doubted he would ever fathom. Through the latter he felt as though he could see forever, to the emptiness at the edge of creation.

The moon rode low and dark over the horizon. Skulking, Sal thought, as though afraid of coming out into full view. He was glad for that. Had it been full, the spectacle of the stars would have been much reduced.

"As below," announced Vehofnehu, "so above. In recent times, the sky has been highly active. Instead of the usual tides, I have witnessed ruptures representing dramatic events in the world around us: significant births and deaths; disasters natural and unnatural; happenstance and circumstance that will affect many, in ways even I cannot always see. Your blossoming, Sal, was visible in the stars, as is the awakening to power of all wild talents. The making and waking of your Homunculus, Highson Sparre: that, too, I have seen reflected in the sky above me. Reflected, I say; not *directed*. The stars control us no more than sea or stone. But it is possible, I believe, to see in their movements a glimpse of what might be—just as the close examination of people enables one to guess what they will do next. Tides, yes. And tidings. The two are connected."

"You mentioned natural disasters," said Sal. "Does that mean you saw the flood?"

"Of course. It came to me as a mighty concatenation." The empyricist was in silhouette beside him, one long arm gesticulating in a vain attempt to convey what he had seen. "A juncture I have never witnessed before, and did not see coming. The sky shuddered, and shudders still, for those with eyes to see it. It quakes for what has been, and what might yet come."

"Oriel and the other Heptarchs believe the end times are here," said Griel.

"They aren't alone in believing that. Am I right, Highson Sparre, when I say that your leaders suspect the same?"

Highson acknowledged the guess as true, even though he knew as little about it as Shilly. If the Weavers had told him more, he wasn't letting on.

"They are correct in thinking so," said the empyricist. "The stars and the Quorum deliver the same message. We would be fools to ignore them."

"So we sit back and let it happen?" Sal heard the frustration in

Shilly's voice, but was too exhausted to be sympathetic. "We watch the world end without doing anything at all?"

"For me, in this age and place, doing nothing suits me. Sooner rather than later, perhaps, I will play more of a role."

"So there *will be* a later?" Sal asked. "I thought that wasn't guaranteed. Tom can't see anything beyond a certain point. Neither can the man'kin."

"There will always be a later," said Vehofnehu. "Not all of us will be in it, however."

"That's just splitting hairs," said Shilly with an irritable snap.

"Not to some. To golems, say. Or glasts."

"Who'd want to live in a world full of golems and glasts?" asked Rosevear.

"Golems and glasts, of course. And probably ghosts too, for all we know."

Shilly sighed and rubbed at her eyes with one hand. Sal could tell that she was tired. It had been a long day for all of them. "So what do you advocate for *us*?"

The empyricist waved his right hand and the mist lights came back up—not as brightly as they had previously been, but seeming so to Sal's eyes.

"Forces from before your time are stirring," Vehofnehu said. "Ancient, dark things that do not belong here and now. You have met one of them."

"The twins." Shilly stood and leaned on her cane.

"Yes, and others. One rises from the depths of stone: this one must be stopped, lest a fate worse than any Cataclysm befalls all of us. The three-in-one sleeps in an icy tomb, awaiting only the call to awake. Nine hunt the trees beneath us, killing all who cross their path. Ah . . ." The empyricist put shaking fingers over his eyes. "I see too much. Beings I had thought best forgotten are in motion again, just as the Quorum said they would one day be. I didn't believe them, and now it will cost us all."

"Peace." Griel came to the empyricist's side and steadied him with both broad hands. "You have done all you could. It's not your fault Oriel and the Heptarchs won't listen."

"Fools," the empyricist said in a softer tone, letting himself be guided into a comfortable chair. "We were fools. We should've killed it when we had the chance, and hang the consequences."

Sal glanced at Shilly, who shrugged. Griel handed Vehofnehu a glass of water and stood protectively over him as he recovered.

"Perhaps we should leave," said Highson, looking to Griel for guidance.

"You will soon enough," said the empyricist, straightening. "But not tonight. Tomorrow you hunt the hunters. To do that, you will need all your strength."

"Hunt who?" asked Shilly, frowning. "What hunters are you talking about?"

"The creatures that have been preying on both kingsfolk and humans of the forest in recent times. They must be stopped. With each blood meal they grow stronger and more daring, and hungrier still. If unchecked, they will sweep all life from the forest. You, Griel, will lead the expedition to rid us of them. The Heptarchs need not know."

Griel hesitated, then nodded. "You're talking about the wraith, aren't you?"

A brisk nod. "Not just one wraith. These are the nine I spoke of."

"I have authorisation to pursue that end." If Griel seemed at all perturbed by the thought of hunting *nine* of the things that had attacked the Sky Wardens at the base of the forest, he showed no sign of it. "Am I to go alone?"

"No. You will take the others. You're all connected, yes indeed. Fail in this instance and all will fall. I will remain here with the glast, so none but me will be infected should it break free."

"And who will stop *you*, when you become a glast?" asked Rosevear.

"If that looks likely, I will sever the way you came up here. You may have noticed," said the empyricist, beginning to regain his former garrulousness, "that it is much more than an ordinary stairwell."

Among the nods of agreement, Highson said, "Yes. It's a Way."

"And Ways can be sealed."

Sal understood, then, why he had felt a moment of disorientation while climbing the endless stairs. Ways connected widely separated points by means of a much shorter tunnel—such as the one connecting his and Shilly's underground home to the beach near Fundelry. Although that tunnel was scarcely three metres long, the workshop was in fact a hundred kilometres west, near a town called Tumberi. So, if the empyricist cut the Way connecting the top of the tower to its base, he would effectively isolate himself from the rest of the Panic.

Shilly looked unhappy. Sal couldn't tell which part of the plan upset her the most: leaving Kemp and Vehofnehu behind, or going out into the forest to hunt the wraiths while the issue of the Homunculus remained unsolved. He wasn't certain himself.

Before anyone could object, an ear-splitting cry came from a forgotten corner of the observatory. Sal jumped to his feet, picturing wraiths and glasts, the Change already stirring at his command. Highson did the same, moving spryly despite his age. The hook at Griel's side came out of its sheath with the sound of an indrawn breath.

All they saw was Tom, eyes wide with fright and one hand pointing up at the stars.

"Tom!" Shilly hurried to him. "What's wrong? What can you see?"

The young seer blinked furiously, noticed her at his side, and lowered his hand. It shook like that of an old man.

"Blood and fire," he whispered. "Death in our midst. In *the mist*." He shuddered all over. "I've seen them. So has Skender. It's already happened, will happen again. Fire. And blood!"

"Easy," she soothed him, warning the others away. Sal forced himself to back off. A nightmarish vision, not an actual attack, but no less alarming for all that.

"Do you have a name, Tom?" asked Vehofnehu softly. "Can you tell us the names of the things we face? The nine?"

Tom squirmed as though the dream still had him in its grip. "Hard names. Cold names. The strangler, the blood-red, the screecher, the black-hearted—" He drew a sharp breath. *"The Swarm."*

Vehofnehu nodded as though all his worst fears had been confirmed.

"Yes," he said. "Yes, I remember now. That was what they were called . . ."

"Are you going to lie there all day or do you have something in mind?"

Kail took his time answering. He wasn't just weighing all the options one by one. He was absorbing everything his senses told him. One of the first rules of tracking was to look everywhere a trail *shouldn't* be as well as where it should. Much could be learned from the periphery. Before considering a particular decision, he would examine every possibility once, and then again on the assumption that he had missed something the first time. Then if the decision he made turned out to be wrong, at least he would know that he had done his best with the information at hand.

From the lip of the cliff where he lay stretched flat on the ground, the Homunculus likewise beside him, he could see down to where white water churned and roiled, stirred up by the waterfall to the north. At the base of the falls, rocking sluggishly from side to side, was the boneship, apparently abandoned to the elements. A splash of blood surrounded the body of a man splayed across its roof. Despite the wounds he had suffered, visible through Kail's spyglass as dark rents in blackening skin, there didn't seem to be enough blood by half. That worried him.

Looking further afield, he saw signs of fighting: more blood scuffed earth, a broken arrow, even a gleaming knife left behind by mistake. A night fight, then, and one conducted on several fronts. Above the falls, where a broad lake lapped against a muddy shore, he saw more signs of recent disturbance. How long ago, precisely, he couldn't tell, but judging by the condition of the body on the roof of the boneship, no more than a day, maybe less.

Closer at hand, literally within arm's reach, he had already noted footprints and handprints along the Divide's edge, which meant that whoever had attacked the boneship had done so from above. Tree trunks some metres back from the edge bore marks of ropes and pulleys from which the attackers had descended. That they weren't quite human tracks also worried him.

Above, looming like the clenched brows of an angry god, the clouds of the Hanging Mountains utterly obscured the noonday sun and cast a grim pall over the scene.

"I'm going to take a closer look," he said eventually.

"What if you're seen?" asked the twins—and he could understand their reluctance. The three of them had gone to some lengths to avoid encountering anyone, especially the Sky Wardens whose path they followed.

"There's no one down there. No one living, anyway." He stood and dusted himself off, telling himself that he was as certain of that as he could be. The camel stood patiently as he removed a coil of rope from one of its saddlebags.

"We want to come too," said the twins.

"I won't stop you, but wait until I reach the bottom before using the rope. It won't hold both our weights at the same time."

The Homunculus's strange head nodded understanding, and he _ed backwards over the edge. Abseiling was an old skill from his riding days near Iron Knob, one never entirely forgotten. He moments of controlled freefall between each bounce, but ng able to see exactly where he was going. Given wings, he would rather have descended slowly and carefully, with bola spinning in readiness.

He landed on a rock by the side of the river and signalled for the twins to follow. They scurried down the rope like a giant spider, black limbs standing out against the limestone cliff. By the time they reached the bottom, he had picked his way across tumbled stones to the base of the waterfall, on the far side of which the boneship had been securely tied by persons unknown. Still nothing moved apart from water, but he proceeded warily, nervous of a trap.

Blood will run like water, the seer in Laure had told him. *Blood will run like water ere the end comes.*

What have you got yourself into this time, Eisak Marmion? he wanted to know.

Even from a distance Kail could tell that the body on the roof of the boneship didn't belong to anyone he knew. That came as something of a relief, but only relatively speaking. Whatever had killed the man had been vigorous and strong. The leather uniform he wore had been rent in numerous places, and by the look of it his throat had been torn out. Kail had seen a lot in his time, but this was one thing he had no desire to see at closer range.

He crept across the gangplank onto the boneship, noting signs of hasty craftwork as he went. The massive exoskeleton had been prepared with maximum speed and efficiency, with little opportunity for art, but he noted flourishes in odd places: a spiral motif, perhaps the signature of a Laurean carpenter pressed into unfamiliar shipbuilding service, repeated on gunwales, rails, and lintels; an impractical fineness to the handle of the tiller; a perfect symmetry to the anchor where none was required. Such examples contrasted with the roughness of bone underfoot, and the asymmetrical curves of the doors. *Os*, the Alcaide's ship of bone, was carved and polished across every surface, a seaworthy ornament big enough for thirty crew plus passengers. It made Marmion's boneship look like a toy in comparison.

Still, Kail thought, *full marks for effort and for taking an opportunity as it came*. Marmion's initiative hadn't impressed him much prior to that point.

The boneship's central cabin was empty, except for some ransacked crates and discarded goods. He hadn't really expected a pile of bodies stacked up for the scavengers to take, but he'd had to check before he could move on. Wherever Marmion and the others had got to, they weren't anywhere nearby.

The ship rocked as the Homunculus boarded.

"Any sign?"

"None," Kail said, stepping out of the cabin. "The boneship is drained. My guess is that someone used up the reservoir to fight off their attackers, failed, and was taken prisoner. Or they fled, and their attackers went in pursuit. Either way, someone took the trouble of removing the ship's supplies before leaving, and they did it in a hurry."

"The *Marie Celeste*," said one of the twins. Seth, perhaps, with a tone of wonderment in his voice, as though surprised by the memory.

"The what?"

"A ship found drifting in the ocean, empty, with meals half-eaten still sitting at the tables. No one ever learned what happened to the crew."

"I don't think there's much ambiguity here," he said. "There's an arrow sticking out of the starboard bow."

"Is this what boats are like now?" asked Hadrian, peering at the rough bony surface.

"A few. Not many." Kail had learned everything he could from the boneship and was already losing interest. "Take a look around if you like. Maybe you'll find something I missed."

Leaving the twins to explore the empty cavities of the massive ~~on~~, Kail walked to the front of the ship and stood with his ~~nst~~ the rails. He leaned there for a long moment, looking ~~h~~ the white-flecked water, apparently deep in thought.

~~t~~ masquerade, his sharp eyes peered out from under his

brows at the stark line cut against the clouds by the cliff face to his left, down which he and the Homunculus had recently scaled. He waited, not obviously but patiently, and was soon rewarded.

Something moved up there, exposed only by the silhouette it cast against the grey sky. Kail might not have seen it had he not been looking, made wary by small signs in the previous days—signs he had detected on the periphery of his senses, rather than on the trail itself.

Someone was following them. He didn't know who or what, but he had proof of it now. That was something.

"Find anything?" he called, turning from the rail.

The twins emerged from a nook at the rear of the boneship. "No notes to say where everyone went, unfortunately."

"They're a long way from here. That's my guess. And it's not our job to find them." Kail's shoulder blades itched, but he refused to look up. "Have you heard from that creature, Upuaut, lately?"

"No." The Homunculus's features took on a worried cast. "That's sort of worse than if we had . . . you know?"

"I think so." Kail was concerned. The twins described Upuaut as a being without flesh, much like a golem, but the figure he had seen silhouetted against the sky was definitely solid. "We'd better keep moving. We're exposed here."

That wasn't the worst of it, he thought, as they retraced their steps past the waterfall to where they had descended the cliff face and would now go back up. Someone at the top could cut the rope when they were halfway; or have poisoned their supplies already to do them harm later. Camels didn't make good watchdogs.

But if he didn't climb the rope, their pursuer would know that he, she, or it had been discovered.

"You go first," he told the twins, trusting in the resilience of their artificial body. They had survived one fall already, down the side of the Divide; one more wouldn't kill them. "Toss me the waterbags when you get to the top and I'll fill them while we have the chance."

If the twins suspected his ulterior motive, they didn't hesitate to be the first to climb the rope. Kail watched from the bottom as they scaled it with ease, four arms and four legs working independently but with an instinctive synchrony to raise them at a much faster rate than any ordinary human could manage. They did it silently, too, which only added to their alienness.

Kail had had a week and a half now to study the pair, and he was no closer to understanding them. Anything or anyone that could emerge from the Void Beneath with any memories intact was a miracle in itself; they had lived in that place for hundreds of years, trapped with each other in a state of nearly complete sensory deprivation, and emerged in a state at least approximating sanity—something he could barely credit. Yet there they were, undoubtedly present, and uniquely so, giving him little reason to doubt their story. He did know that they were not overtly malicious by nature, since they could have harmed him many times during their journey and had not done so even once.

They seemed calmest when moving, plodding faithfully to their goal, whatever that was, far to the northeast. When they had to stop, inner tensions emerged, bubbling up from the core of them to manifest in the Homunculus's black skin. Kail was used to silence, but the silence during such times was often riddled with tension. He imagined the twins arguing with each other inside their strange skull, perpetuating disagreements that might have raged for a millennium. What that would be like he could barely conceive.

He remembered the days when Lodo, his uncle and Shilly's former teacher, had caused an upset in his family: selected to join the Novitiate, Lodo had run away to the Interior midway through his studies, there to become a Stone Mage. For a family proud of their high standing in the Strand and delighted that one of their number might become a Sky Warden, the betrayal was unbearable.

Although open conflict no longer marred relations between the Haunted City and the Nine Stars, enmity remained in some circles. By leaving, Lodo had turned his back not only on the country of his birth but his family also. They had instantly closed ranks against him. Upon his return from the Interior, having learned that being a Stone Mage wasn't right for him either, and hoping to seek inspiration somewhere else, he must have thought the family front completely united.

But Kail had known the truth. On the inside, arguments had raged for days, forming cracks in previously close relationships, some of which turned sour overnight; others festered over the years until every word became poison. While Lodo had calmly gone into the west in search of his dream, his family had descended into rage and bitterness.

He tried to imagine his mother and her brother, Lodo, coping with confinement such as the twins endured. Or himself and his younger brother, an ironworker in Samimi. They hadn't spoken for two years, which suited both of them fine. Their mother had never acknowledged Lodo after his departure for the Interior. Not even on her deathbed.

Kail smelled the tension between the twins sometimes, like the vapour from an overcharged chimerical reservoir. When they were quietest, the smell was strongest. Sometimes he feared what might happen if their filial enmity reached a crisis point that could not be resolved.

The distant, spiderlike shape of the Homunculus crawled safely over the edge of the Divide. Kail chewed his lip, waiting for a sign that they had been attacked. He nodded with relief when the black shape reappeared, waving two pairs of arms. Moments later, a bundle of empty waterbags sailed down inside a sack. Kail did as he said he would and filled them from the clear water at the base of the falls. Then he slung them over his shoulder and began the slow, careful climb to the top.

Why are we doing this? Seth asked. *Remind me again. And keep reminding me. Maybe one day it'll start to make sense.*

You know why. Hadrian sounded as exhausted as his brother felt. The closer they came to Yod, to the shadow looming over the land, the harder each step became. *We have to finish things once and for all.*

But how exactly are we going to do that? What's your grand plan to kill a creature big and mean enough to eat everyone alive? Are you keeping something from me, or are you as much in the dark as I am?

We'll think of something.

I fucking hope so, or we're going to end up as dead as everyone else.

Do you have to be so negative? It's not just up to us, you know. There's Kail, now, and we know Pukje's out there somewhere.

You think this Pukje of yours is out there. You don't know anything of the sort. And what use will he be, anyway, wherever he is? That mutant dwarf could be on the other side, for all we know. He might not want us to succeed.

No, said Hadrian, stubborn as ever in the face of the evidence. *I saw him, flying. He's not just a dwarf. And he wants Yod to lose as much as we do. I couldn't be wrong about that.*

Yod losing doesn't necessarily mean we win. You should remember that, little brother. Kail has his own agenda too. Do you think he's helping us out of the goodness of his heart? Fat chance. He's doing it to save his own arse, and the arses of his friends.

Hadrian said nothing as they saddled up the camel. No doubt fuming over the "little brother" remark, Seth thought, wondering why they couldn't help needling each other. It didn't matter what they argued about; they always ended up in the same place.

Not everyone's like you, Seth.

If you want to win, you have to be.

Who wants to live that way? You're always fighting, always on guard even when you win, because there's another battle looming ahead. Where's the joy in that?

Life isn't about joy.

It's about more than fighting.

I don't know. We seem to do plenty of it.

An uneasy truce fell when Kail returned, heavily laden with the waterbags. They helped him load up the camel and prepare to resume their journey. The tracker seemed ill-at-ease, but that struck them as reasonable, given what they had found by the waterfall below. His friends had vanished, leaving a bloody corpse behind. That would worry anyone.

They resumed their lonely journey, following the Divide up into the mountains. Every day they had travelled, the cloud level came closer; the vegetation rose up to meet it, progressing from low desert shrubs to scrub, to patchy forest, and finally, judging by what the Homunculus's sharp eyes made out ahead, full-blown forest. Despite the clouds, it never seemed to rain, which struck Seth as odd, but the air was becoming cooler—and more humid without direct sun baking it dry. That was something to be grateful for.

Kail didn't talk about the boneship, and the twins didn't prompt him on the matter. They had learned that the tracker's silences could be long and productive. If he had something to say, he would say it. They were feeling talked out, anyway. Every conversation seemed to end in a tangle of unspoken assumptions. Clearly, the world didn't work they way it had when they'd last been in it. They were over that startling realisation, but they hadn't yet got their common head around what it had become. Flat but not-flat. Round but not-round. It seemed to have the properties of both, like an electron that was both a wave and a particle.

There were too many mysteries. It had been bad enough previously, in the First and Second Realms, with secret histories and unknown characters retaking centre stage during the Cataclysm. Part of Seth had hoped that things would have settled down after the global conflagration, but he now knew that thought to be naive. Nature always bounced back, filling empty niches with new creatures, some stranger and more dangerous than the ones before.

They walked until dusk, tending uphill at increasingly steep angles, then found a camping spot well back from the Divide in a clearing surrounded by trees. Seth didn't know their names, or if they had existed in the old world, but their trunks were broad and smooth-barked, and their branches formed a dense canopy overhead in which birds and possums nested. The Homunculus's ears detected all their movements with inhuman precision. Sometimes the twins imagined that they could even hear ants crawling in the grass, if they listened closely enough.

Seth felt Hadrian's relief as they gradually reconnected with the physical world, but he wasn't so certain it was a good thing. Could it be possible to become *too* connected? What might that mean to them and their quest?

Kail lit no fire that night. The tracker dined on dried meat, and scavenged berries from the surrounding trees. The twins sat restlessly against the trunk of a tree, wondering if they would be able to sleep; they could assume nothing with this magical new body. The silence was too deep. Upuaut's howling had put them on edge, but at least they had known the creature wasn't creeping up on them at that moment, tensing to pounce.

When full darkness fell, it was absolute. No stars—strange or otherwise—penetrated the cloud cover. Even the Homunculus's eyes were defeated. They lay awake listening to the sounds of creatures in the undergrowth, lulled into peace by the tracker's steady, somnolent breaths . . .

They woke with a start at the sound of a commotion nearby. Twigs crackled; branches whipped and snapped; flesh thudded against flesh, and more than one throat grunted in pain. The twins leapt to their feet, Seth the quickest to react, as always, slowed down by his sluggish brother. They braced their four legs firmly in the dirt and spread their arms wide. The sounds were coming some distance from the campsite.

"Kail? Is that you?"

"Over here! I've got him!" The tracker's voice was strained with effort.

"Got who?" They followed the sound through the trees, wishing for even the slightest trace of light. Leaves slapped their face as they ran; roots clutched at their ankles. "Kail, who is it?"

A low growling almost stopped them in their tracks. They had heard that sound before. It didn't come from a human throat.

"Seth, Hadrian—hurry!"

They found Kail and his captive in a taut tangle half in, half out of a bush. The snarling rose in volume as they approached and the air seemed to freeze at the sound of it. Seth forced himself to keep moving. It was Hadrian's fear he felt, not his own. He had never met Upuaut before. What did he have to be afraid of?

The captive wriggled and kicked but was no match for the Homunculus's inhuman strength. Seth and Hadrian soon had him securely pinned in all four of their hands, overlapping left with left and right with right so their individual hands wouldn't slide right through his real flesh, as they had in the Aad.

Kail was able to roll away and catch his breath.

"Thank you," he grated. Seth heard the scrape of a tinderbox. "Now, let's see who we have here."

Light flared. The first thing Seth saw was Kail's face, long and bloody from a wound to his temple. His eyes gleamed furiously.

They narrowed. "I know you," he said to their captive. "You were in the Aad, with Pirelius."

The man in Seth's arms struggled and spat but said nothing intelligible in reply. Seth twisted him in order to get a good look at his face. The man was indeed one of Pirelius's cronies. The smallest and meanest of them all, he had been chief jailer of the twins, of Skender's mother's party, and briefly of Skender too. Long, thin moustaches dangled on either side of his mouth. Networks of thick, ugly scars stretched down his chest and arms. He wore leather breeches and nothing else. The hair on his body was black and thick.

"His name is Izzi," Seth told Kail, remembering the feel of the man's spine beneath his fingers and the awful shriek that had torn from his throat. "We thought we'd killed him."

"Not so easy," the man growled, snapping with chipped teeth at the Homunculus's throat. "Is it?"

Seth kept him at arm's length. Izzi's flesh was hot, as though burning from fever—even through hair and dirt and blood it looked inflamed. His expression was as agonised as the last time they had seen him.

"What are you doing here?" Kail asked, holding up the flame. "Why are you following us?"

"Watching. Waiting." The man panted like a dog. His eyes were simultaneously cunning and mad. "A wolf knows how to wait."

Hadrian physically shook at the words, and Seth felt their grip on the man weaken.

Easy, brother! Don't lose it now.

"Where is Upuaut?" Hadrian asked.

"Where is death? All around you, everywhere. You can't escape it. Nothing you can do will stop it. It'll come for you eventually."

"We could kill you." Seth's fingers tightened on the man's skinny arms.

The man laughed at him, open mouthed, fearlessly, without looking away.

"Don't," said Kail. "Not yet. We need to find out what Upuaut wants. Is it aligned with Yod? Are there more of its kind out there? His host will tell us, even though it tries to hide inside."

The laughter turned to sneers. "A wolf doesn't hide. It conserves its strength. It waits in the shadows until the time is right. It *pounces.*"

"How's it going to pounce if we have you trussed up like a turkey?" Kail turned away, and spat contemptuously in the dirt. The spittle was blood red.

A cold wind rushed through the trees, making them shiver as though the Earth itself was quaking. The man in the twins' hands stiffened. His expression became suddenly intense and alert, all mockery forgotten.

"Here?" he breathed.

Dense fog descended on them, swirling down like a miniature hurricane from uphill and threatening to blow out Kail's flame. He cupped it protectively and looked around. Seth felt moisture condense on the Homunculus's ebony skin. That chilled him even more than the thought of Upuaut.

Three tenuous figures, blacker than the night itself, rushed out of the mist and stopped bare metres away, as though surprised. Feetless, they floated like ghosts on legs that terminated in points a hand-breadth above the ground. Their hands were the same. The only light in them came from their faces, from long teeth and eyes that reflected cold, icy gleams back at the flickering flame. Malignancy radiated from them in waves, stripping the last of the warmth from the air.

The Swarm.

Again, Seth felt Hadrian's fear. This time, though, it was different. Instead of freezing him, it gave him strength.

"I've faced you before." His brother's voice came strongly from the mouth of the Homunculus. "Lascowicz couldn't take me, and neither could you. I'm stronger now. How much are you prepared to risk?"

Ghastly mouths widened, but no words emerged. Just more teeth, which Seth could scarcely credit.

"Attack, you fools," screamed the man in Seth's arms. "Don't listen to them. Attack!"

"There are only three of you," Hadrian goaded them. "Where are the other six? Dead, or afraid?"

They came forward with a sound like metal tearing.

Kail's bola spun in his free hand. Seth swung their wriggling captive in front of them, using him as a shield. The creatures parted and came around from behind. Hadrian moved the fastest, one arm coming up to point at the closest black figure.

A stream of shining motes poured from his finger, like electric confetti. Seth felt the cost of them tearing at the roots of his being. He knew that feeling, remembered when Hadrian had last drawn from their combined being to fight off these creatures.

Egrigor, he whispered, dredging the word from Hadrian's memories. Cutting off pieces of oneself and giving them independent life, as messengers, observers, or weapons.

The black figure dodged with a boiling hiss, reaching out with one sharp limb to rake across Kail's chest. Seth warded off another with an upraised fist. The flesh of the Homunculus met the blackness of the vampire with a satisfying thump. The third rose up over them, then came down with a shriek, sending Kail, Izzi, and the twins flying. Vitriol of the deepest, darkest kind filled the night as the flame guttered out, plunging the forest into gloom.

Seth and his brother struggled to their feet, arms outstretched, looking for their captive and ready for anything else to lunge at them out of the forest. First Upuaut. Now the Swarm. Seth wouldn't have been surprised if Gabra'il himself had descended from the sky in orange glass armour and spitted them on his cruel glass sword.

The wind swirled around them, raising up dust and dead leaves, then died away as suddenly as it had come.

They've gone, whispered Hadrian.

Are you sure about that? Seth asked, but his brother wasn't listening. He was dragging them to where Kail lay on the ground, drawn by the sound of the tracker's pain. Their questing hands touched blood beneath Kail's torn shirt, and the ragged edge of a long wound.

"Light," Kail cried. "Light!"

The twins fumbled for the tinderbox and managed to strike a spark. The flame they coaxed into life grew slowly, timorously, and managed to make the darkness around them seem darker, if anything.

Kail's desperate gaze took in the trees around them. His bared teeth were clenched with agony, but he would not rest until certain their attackers were indeed gone.

They were, and so was the man Kail had gone to the trouble of capturing—Pirelius's henchman and Upuaut's latest host. All were on the loose in a night suddenly full of threats.

They took him, said Hadrian, his mental voice full of weariness. *They took Upuaut.*

Why?

I don't know. I don't want *to know.*

Seth kept an eye on the shadows, but it didn't look as if they were going to be attacked again. That was something to be grateful for, even as he realised that he would have to carry both of them back to camp. Hadrian was fading fast, drained by the raising of the egrigor. Kail clutched his chest and winced when he tried to stand.

Seth bent over him.

"You knew we were being followed," he said evenly. "You set a trap for him."

"Yes," the tracker said with pained tones.

"Why didn't you tell us?"

"What would you have done if I had told you?"

Seth hadn't expected that response. "What difference does that make? We had a right to know. If your trap had failed or you'd been caught, we might've had our throat slit."

Kail nodded, but looked unrepentant. "I was afraid you'd run. Not telling seemed the lesser of two evils."

Seth could accept that. "So what's going to happen to you now?" he asked, nodding down at the wound. "Are we going to have to go away so you can use the Change to heal yourself?"

"No. Just get me back to camp and I'll make do with what I have."

"Always prepared, huh?"

"This isn't the first time I've been cut in the line of duty."

Duty? thought Seth as he helped Kail to his feet. *Duty to whom? Or to what?*

Seth didn't feel dutiful. Not in the slightest. He just felt tired. They had so far left to go, and it was all uphill.

He carried their injured guide back to camp one step at a time, the only way he knew how.

THE HEART-NAME

**"All things exist in transit from one state to another.
What is water but molten ice?
What is a sword but artfully frozen iron?"**
THE BOOK OF TOWERS, EXEGESIS 15:3

*"*Y*ou're going after the wraiths too?"* Skender was unable to hide the surprise in his voice, even through the Change.

Sal didn't comment on that. His tone was matter-of-fact, as though the decision had been an easy one. *"While they're in the forest, we're not safe. It seems logical, so last night we agreed to do it. I don't think Griel entirely trusts us yet, despite everything, but he's prepared to take a chance if we help him first, and the Panic are as bothered by the wraiths as your foresters seem to be. The empyricist here calls these wraiths 'the Swarm,' by the way."*

"The Swarm? Seriously?"

"Why? What does that mean?"

"That means they're old—perhaps even as old as the twins. They're men-tioned in the* Book of Towers.*"

"Well, that settles that, I guess. Sounds like Vehofnehu knows what he's talking about."

Skender put aside his mixed wonder and terror at having faced yet another creature he had thought a legend to ask, *"Why have they come back?"*

"I'm afraid your guess is as good as mine."

Skender didn't have a ready response to that. During the brief lull in the conversation, Skender checked to make sure he wasn't dis-turbing Chu, who lay next to him on the thin mattress, curled in a tight ball.

Her face in repose was very different from the one she wore during waking hours. Gone was the wariness, the keen intelligence always on the lookout for a chink in anyone's armour, the faintly mocking smile. In its place was a look of sadness, as though all the losses she had borne could make themselves known while her defences were down. His heart ached to see it.

"*Have you made any specific plans?*" Sal asked.

Skender told himself to concentrate.

"*Uh, not yet. Lidia Delfine—she's the Guardian's daughter, the one whose brother was killed—she had already decided to go on the hunt before we were attacked yesterday. We'd be involved, naturally, because we're outsiders and expendable, and you never know, we just might be helpful. Killing two rabbits with one hammer, I reckon, because it'll give her a way to get us out of Milang without actually expelling us. She and her bodyguard will also be in the party, along with a mage they have living with them at the moment. More covering of bets.*"

"*Milang was attacked?*" asked Sal, picking up on that point with grim interest. "*I had no idea the wraiths would be so bold. I thought they just picked people off in small groups.*"

Skender didn't mention that *he* had been attacked, specifically, not just Milang in general. That memory was still a little too fresh. "*There were at least four: two at the top of the city and two further down.*"

"*Vehofnehu says there are nine of them. So be careful out there.*"

"*You too.*"

"*We'll need to keep an eye out for each other, in order to avoid each other's crossfire.*"

That was a worst-case scenario Skender didn't want to contemplate. "*How's Kemp?*"

Sal's reply came with more than a hint of uncertainty. "*Not good. Vehofnehu says he's never going to recover.*"

The news came like a slow-motion blow to the stomach. "*Sal, I'm sorry.*"

"*You have no reason to apologise. It's just the way things worked out. Life doesn't always go the way we want it to.*"

There was no arguing with that. Neither of them said anything for a long moment, the link open between them but empty of words.

"I suppose I should let you go," Sal eventually said.

Skender glanced at Chu, wondering how it would feel to watch her die, as Kemp might die, with no one able to do anything.

"Just one more thing," Skender said. *"You mentioned something about there being nine of the wraiths. If the thing we pulled out of the forest yesterday is anything to go by, there's now just eight to worry about."*

"Really? That's good news. How did you kill it?"

We didn't, Skender almost said, but things were complicated enough without getting into that. And he was getting a headache from concentrating so long. *"Fire knocks them out. Strong, hot fire. Watch out for the bodies, though. They don't stay still for long."*

Sal sounded puzzled but appreciative. *"Okay, thanks. That's good to know. You'll call us if you learn anything more?"*

"One of us will. Marmion will probably have orders for you when he finds out we've spoken."

"No doubt." There was a hint of a smile in his friend's reply. *"Take care, Skender."*

"Have no doubt of that. And you, well—" He hesitated, struggling to find the right words. *"Just make sure to leave us a couple to deal with, all right? Otherwise we'll feel left out."*

"That's a bit rich, coming from the person with the headstart. Once we make up that lost ground, it's anyone's race."

Skender grinned at that, but the amusement didn't last long. The connection between him and his friend closed. He lay awake in the predawn light, nervous about what the day would bring, and just as uncertain about what had happened the previous night as he had ever been.

"We found this."

Heuve had dumped the crisped, brittle corpse on the living floor of the Guardian's roofless citadel. His beard twitched in revulsion. The darkness of the night above perfectly matched that of the hideous shape displayed for them all to see. Its limbs were stick-thin and flaking into ash where it had been touched. Lacking obvious hands and feet, it looked much smaller than Skender had remembered. Only its head matched his recollection: a hideous mass of canines and eye-sockets that seemed no less fearsome dead than it had alive.

It stank of ash and charred flesh, yet the grass under it turned black with frost.

"Are you sure it's one of them?" the Guardian asked.

"It's definitely not human," the big warrior stated flatly. "Or Panic. We found it three levels down from where Skender and the mage were attacked. It burned through the walkways as easily as a hot blade through cobweb, but set fire to nothing else. We were lucky this was no ordinary flame, otherwise the whole city would be ablaze by now."

Skender couldn't take his eyes off the thing, even though his hands shook to see it and the stink made his stomach roil.

"It—" He swallowed. "We—"

Then Chu was behind him, putting one hand on his shoulder. She didn't say anything. Just having her there was enough.

He straightened and put his treacherous hands under his robes. "Did they attack anyone up here?" he asked.

The Guardian knelt to examine the corpse, answering him as she did so. "Two circled the summit but my guards drove them away. I came out to call them down. They didn't rise to the challenge." From beneath her gown she produced a short stiletto, with which she poked the crumbling remains. "I hadn't expected a physical form behind the apparitions. They are, perhaps, less like us than I had hoped."

"In what way, Mother?" asked Lidia Delfine, standing to one side with her arms folded.

"They hunt purely for the sport of blood and they have no sense of honour. We should not expect to treat with them. We should show them the same mercy they would show us."

"Who said anything about mercy?" asked Chu softly.

"Not me." Skender stared in horrid fascination at the face of the creature that would have torn him to ribbons, given the chance.

With a click, its eyes opened.

"Back!" The Guardian leapt to her feet. Heuve and Lidia Delfine lunged forward. The creature twitched and hissed, gouging furrows in the dirt as it attempted to right itself. Its teeth snapped at Heuve's sword, unafraid of the metal. Clouds of choking black soot rose from its skin.

Skender froze, again. Kelloman was still out cold, drained by the first attack. The mage was recuperating in one of the Guardian's antechambers, watched over by a healer and the bilby. Skender knew *he* didn't have the strength to summon such a powerful flame.

"Out of the way." Marmion's whipcrack command caught the ear of all those retreating from the creature. With his one hand he scratched a charm into the grassy surface of the chamber's floor, a complicated pattern of circles and crosses that Skender didn't recognise. "Lure it over here, quickly."

"I don't think it wants to be lured," said Heuve, jumping back from a sudden snap.

Marmion didn't look up until he had finished the charm with a flourish. Then he turned to face the creature, unwinding the bandage around his truncated wrist.

"Here," he said, thrusting the stump forward. "This is what you like, isn't it?" As though throwing punches with an invisible hand, he caught the attention of the blackened husk. "Smell me. Taste me. Come and get me!" He sidestepped neatly as the creature lunged forward. "That's it."

Marmion dodged again, and again, proffering his injured arm as bait until the creature lurched onto the charm he had drawn. Then he shouted a word that Skender had never heard before, and stepped hurriedly away.

A miniature hurricane sprang into life, defined by and confined to the dimensions of the charm. The column of violent air swept the creature's bitter smoke into a cylinder, and dragged it up as well, so it hung vertically in the air, struggling and snarling. No matter how it squirmed, it couldn't break free. The charmed air coiled up and down around it like a nest of translucent snakes, binding it firmly in place.

"Nice one," said Chu, helping Skender to his feet. He had tripped over his robes and gone sprawling, unable to take his eyes off the unnatural creature's malevolence. The Sky Warden didn't respond. His eyes were fixed firmly on the creature he had captured. He clutched his injured arm tightly to his chest.

"Fire to burn it," said Lidia Delfine, sheathing her blade and walking shakily to her mother's side. "Air to bind it. But how do we kill it?"

"Dismember it," suggested Warden Banner from the small crowd gathered around. "Chop it into pieces."

"And then what?" asked Heuve.

"I don't know. Throw it into a river, let the current disperse it?"

"Sow it into the Earth," suggested the Guardian. "Let the roots dissolve it."

"I wouldn't trust the tree that fed on such a thing," said Marmion softly. "Would you?"

The Guardian looked at him, and shook her head.

"Cast it," suggested Skender, hating the faint tremor he heard in his voice but ploughing on. "Cast it into metal. Burn it, dice it, grind it, whatever; smash it down into a powder; then mix it with molten lead and let it cool. The metal will hold its mind fast—the part of it that will never burn—and if you engrave the metal with binding charms, the deal will be sealed. Then you can drop it down Versegi Chasm and forget about it forever."

Everyone was staring at him by the time he had finished, making him wonder if what had seemed a good idea a second ago was actually the most stupid ever uttered in public.

"Uh, or you could just chop it into pieces like Warden Banner said and leave it at that."

"No," said Marmion, breaking his silent confrontation with the thing in the whirlwind. "That's a good idea. Nearly perfect. The only suggestion I'd make is to cast it in iron, not lead."

"Yes, of course." Skender nodded, feeling himself beginning to babble with relief. "Iron is stronger, and even if it took hundreds of years for that thing to get out of lead—"

"It won't. It attacked us, and it will pay the price. It and all its kind. That's a mistake they will not make again."

Skender's mouth snapped shut at the fierceness of Marmion's tone. He had never heard the warden speak like that before. The dark anger in every line of the warden's face was echoed in the foresters around him, and he knew that this promise was being taken very seriously indeed.

Later, when the Guardian's citadel was cleared so Marmion and Lidia Delfine could begin the chopping-up process—which Skender preferred not to think about, although he felt no pity for the captured creature—he and Chu were given the opportunity to eat and freshen up in temporary quarters set aside for the visitors. Skender had become conscious of a smell emanating from himself that had something to do with the mud of the previous day and a lot to do with fear. The foresters showed him to a bath filled with warm water and left him alone. He soaked and soaped until his skin tingled, and then he just lay back and relaxed. For once, no one was pressing him for information or trying to eat him. All he could hear was the dripping of water, a low murmur of voices in the distance, and from still further away an enigmatic moaning that he eventually identified as the stone faces the locals called moai. He pictured them leaning out of the cliff, staring fixedly into the mist and singing their strange, fearful song. Their combined chorus was peaceful, but in an unsettling way, as though at any moment it could rise up and explode into an angry crescendo.

Flashes of the day's events—teeth and fire and blood—came and went. There was nothing he could do about them. Neither time nor effort could erase them from his perfect memory, but at least he had a patina of good memories between them and the present moment. If he breathed deeply, he smelled sweet perfume instead of a reminder of his recent travails.

When he clambered out of the bath, he found that his robes had been taken away. In their place lay an entirely new outfit: ochre pants and a baggy black shirt. He groaned on seeing them, but had little option but to put them on. He struggled into the pants and slipped the shirt over his head. A green thong went around his waist when he was done.

"Fresh as a daisy," Chu commented as he walked into the common area given to the visitors. She was sprawled comfortably on a broad cushion, dressed in a yellow-and-white robe and picking at a platter of fruit and nuts. The space was elegant in its simplicity, with sliding doors separating the many bathrooms from the common area. The floor was neither stone nor wood, being covered with delicately woven mats that gave slightly underfoot. Each cushion possessed a different colour and arboreal pattern, yet they complemented each other perfectly. Warden Banner lay sound asleep in the far corner on three cushions laid end to end. From another room came the sound of Warden Eitzen humming as he continued to bathe.

"Do you have daisies in Laure?" Skender chose a cushion facing Chu and leaned on one elbow, leaving the other hand free to sample the food. He wasn't particularly hungry, but he knew he should eat. The sight of Chu in what amounted to a dress definitely made up for not having a robe of his own. "I thought it was all dead rats and dust."

"We hear stories," she said. "I saw a picture of one, once."

Skender couldn't tell if she was being serious or not. *He* wasn't, not entirely, but his impressions of Laure had for the most part been grim and unhappy. A city where the rulers drained the blood of the populace to draw water up from the depths of the Earth was by nature a desperate one. But that didn't mean that joy couldn't exist there. People could get used to anything—even a sudden excess of water.

They exchanged easy, free-flowing banter for a while. He had thought Chu knew nothing about his home, but it quickly became clear that she had been making inquiries. The Keep wasn't well known beyond the borders of the Interior—not being as famous as the Nine Stars where mages met every full moon to apply the laws of the land, or as essential to trade as such cities as Ulum and Mayr—but it had a certain notoriety. Some of the Interior's finest mages had studied there, and the name Van Haasteren was closely associated with it. Nine consecutive generations had overseen the school, earning the privilege by virtue of their remarkable memory and—Skender admitted in the face of Chu's suggestion—a profound disinterest in doing anything else.

"Maybe you're the one to break the chain," she said, smiling as she popped a dried fig into her mouth. "Isn't it about time you lot let someone else have a go?"

Skender dreaded what his father would say if he even suggested such a thing—then berated himself for letting his father's feelings rule what should be his own decision. Perhaps that decision would be easy to make: his mind was full of images of murdered old women, malicious golems, rampaging man'kin, and now bloodthirsty wraiths . . . He didn't know how much more it could hold before he would never sleep again.

To change the subject, he asked her what she had done that afternoon, while he had been with Stone Mage Kelloman. Nothing much, she told him, beyond more talking and arguing. Marmion and the Guardian had done most of it while she had stood around, waiting. Two guards had come to take her wing away, and that had caused a lively argument. In the end she had relented, having no real choice but to accept the word of the locals that her means of flight would not be damaged. They only wanted to move it to keep the Guardian's open-air hall tidy. The Outcast's baggage messed up the place.

By that time, they had been seated in a close triangle on delicately carved wooden seats brought in by underlings, with Lidia Delfine and Heuve standing apart but watching closely. As the cloud-obscured sun moved slowly across the framed sky, the discussion finally came to focus on what to do with the visitors, rather than what the visitors were doing in the forest.

"That's when the Guardian sent for you," she said. "I think she already knew what we'd decided, but needed to go through the motions for the people around her. They're sad and angry people. They've lost loved ones and friends. They need an outlet. Hunting the wraiths will give them that."

Skender still couldn't quite accept the decision, although he could understand it. Putting all their problems in one basket made sense, especially when a small chance existed that the problems might actually cancel each other out.

The hunting party would be led by Lidia Delfine and include the visitors to the forest, Mage Kelloman being one of those. Skender didn't know what he himself could offer, except to be someone to trip over and to have panic on demand.

"Don't be so hard on yourself," Chu told him. "You have your moments."

"Like when?"

"Well, when we crash-landed and everyone was giving us—*me*—a hard time, for instance. I could only stare at them, but you took them on. I was quite impressed. It makes a change to step back and let someone else fight for you, every now and again. I could get used to it."

"Well, that's *my* usual modus operandi. Did you see me earlier, with the wraith?"

"And I was right there beside you, rooting Marmion on." She tilted her head to one side. "I'm not going to agree with you when you say you're hopeless or a coward. You wouldn't be here if you were either."

Wouldn't I? he asked himself, unable to face the intensity of her brown eyes. *What if I didn't have a choice about it? What if I'm just too stupid to know when something is more trouble than it's worth?*

"I'm lucky to be here at all," he said, "after the snake-thing and the wraith almost got me."

"Exactly. That's twice this week I've thought I was going to have to take you home to your parents in a box."

"Three times, if you count the crash in the mud."

She threw an almond at him. He responded in kind, and that resulted in the sort of play fight he had occasionally had at the Keep with members of the opposite sex. Close physical contact with girls was something he never quite got the hang of. He either flushed and went quiet or overcompensated, becoming boisterous and belligerent. He could hear it in his voice and see himself as though standing outside his body, but there was nothing he could do about it. He had once been too scared to approach a girl he had had a serious crush on. The thought of being close to her had made him preempt the possibility by fleeing before anything happened.

Not so with Chu. They were all over each other before he had time to become nervous of the possibility, scrabbling for grip and flinging their centres of gravity backwards and forwards, looking for leverage. Mindful of Banner, who slept through it all, they kept their battle as quiet as they could, but cries of outrage and victory still filled the room. Of about the same height and weight, both with short hair and trimmed fingernails, neither of them possessed a clear physical advantage over the other. But Chu was nastier than any schoolgirl Skender had fought, and Skender, unaccustomed to trousers, found his usual tricks didn't work quite as well. Barely had he had time to work up a serious sweat when he found himself pinned beneath her, her hips pressing down on his waist and her hands forcing his wrists onto the floor.

"Now what?" she asked.

"Shouldn't I be saying that?"

"Says who?" She grinned wolfishly. "Tell me you're sorry for forgetting that night in Laure."

"Tell me what happened and I'll tell you if I'm sorry or not."

"What do you *think* happened?"

"I don't know."

"Do you think we had sex?"

He bucked and twisted but couldn't get her off him. "Why are you doing this to me?"

"Because it's fun."

"You might think so."

"Oh, I do." She laughed at another attempt to free himself. "I could keep this up for hours."

"Please," he begged, giving in to his helplessness. "You got me. I give in. Let's go back to talking about why I'm a loser. That seems to be the theme for the evening."

"You're not a loser," she said, her face turning serious but her grip not letting up one iota. "Don't say that, or I might start to believe it."

She leaned down to kiss him and he arched up to meet her halfway, struck by the fresh fragrance of her skin and the heat of her lips. All other thought and sensation vanished. The universe consisted of her and nothing else. Even time stopped, and he didn't quite notice when it started up again.

She leaned back and studied him with half-lidded eyes. "I know your heart-name, Skender Van Haasteren the Tenth."

"How?" Of all the things he had expected her to say at that moment, that wasn't one of them. "Who told you?"

"Can't you guess?"

"Sal or Shilly? Highson Sparre?"

"Not even close."

"They shouldn't give out things like that, whoever it is. My heart-name is private." An uneasy indignation rose up in him. Enough people already knew his heart-name: the golem that Sal and Shilly had fought in the Haunted City; the Homunculus; everyone who had been locked up with him in the Aad, including Mawson, Shom Behenna, and Kemp. Too many by half. "It's supposed to be a gift!"

"Oh, I agree."

"I bet you don't really know," he said. "You're just making it up to taunt me."

"Why would I do that?" Her fingers tightened around his wrists. "Is it really that big a deal to you?"

"Of course it is! What if I knew yours and you didn't want me to. How would that make you feel?"

"Much like you seem to feel at the moment, I guess." All sense of play had vanished from the conversation. "I'd only tell mine to someone I really liked. Someone who liked me back. And even then, I'm not very trusting. You know that. I've been betrayed by men before. He'd have to give me his first, before I'd consider reciprocating. It'd have to *mean* something. Or I'd have to think so, anyway."

"You mean I—" His mind tripped over the revelation. "But surely I'd remember!"

Her weight came off him. "Surely, yes. I would've thought you'd remember *thinking* about doing it, too. Or were you so drunk at the time you weren't thinking at all? Was it just a spur-of-the-moment joke to you, something you didn't mean?"

"No, I—that is, I don't know." He stared up at her in despair. "Are you *sure* you're not having me on?"

She towered over him, impossibly distant.

"If you really want me to believe you're a loser, Galeus," she said, "you're doing a bloody good job of it."

She was gone before he could sit up. He didn't call after her, knowing it would be useless. Knowing, at last, that it would be the wrong name.

The cushioned chamber turned out to be a communal sleeping area. Banner slept on, undisturbed either by Skender and Chu, or by the others coming in, one by one, to rest. Marmion looked exhausted, and immediately collapsed in the nearest available spot, his wounded arm stretched before him as though appealing to someone in his dreams. His stump had been bandaged with fresh linen, but that was the only concession he had made to cleanliness.

Not long after Chu ran off, Skender had found a selection of robes in one of the other rooms and swapped them for his ridiculous pants. He didn't care if they were meant for women or men, as long as he was comfortable. There was nothing in traditional Stone Mage colours, so he made do with black.

Chu hadn't returned by the time the delicately carved brands dimmed. He considered going to look for her, but figured she would have come back had she wanted to see him. He had no doubt that she would be safe, wherever she was. Heuve wasn't going to let her roam unchecked through the city, no matter how badly she might want to. He tried to put her out of his mind as best he could.

You're not a loser. Don't say that, or I might start to believe it.

Skender didn't need to say anything. There was no hiding the truth of him. It shone through every clumsy attempt to be . . . what? A Stone Mage? A hero? Himself?

Somehow, he managed to fall asleep.

His dreams were full of Rattails—stalking him, mocking him, leering at him—but there was nothing he could do to make himself wake up. He was trapped.

Then, when Sal had woken him up by calling from the Panic city, Chu had been beside him. Not touching, but there, facing him, dressed in her old clothes and with a frown line between her eyebrows. Her eyelids were red.

Galeus. He had given her his heart-name at some point during the missing night in Laure. She in turn had given him hers. And he had completely forgotten the transaction. No wonder she was angry with him. This was much more important than *sex*.

But even as he saw her side of it, he wondered if she wasn't being unfair. He had made the gift, even if he couldn't remember it. Didn't that count for something? She still knew his heart-name. He couldn't —and wouldn't—take that back.

If only he could remember *hers*, then perhaps everything would be all right.

Mute daylight, filtering through the clouds and the translucent paper screens that substituted for windows in that section of the city, painted patterns across the people sharing the room with him. The syncopated rhythms of their breathing marked time as implacably as the ticking of a roomful of clocks. He didn't know even roughly what hour it was, or when they were expected to begin preparations for the hunt. He could only assume that someone would come for them when the foresters were ready.

Screw that, he thought, getting up as quietly as he could and cleaning his teeth.

When he stuck his head out the common room door, he found two guards keeping watch.

"Am I confined to quarters?" he asked them. "No? Well, I need to see the Guardian about the hunt. It's important."

One of them took him through the accommodations of the Guardian and her staff. The citadel possessed a lean, elegant simplicity, even as it rambled up and down through the forest canopy, linked by ramp and platform from tree to tree. He couldn't estimate the number of rooms in the building, since, like the city itself, its structure was determinedly organic. If the people who lived in it wanted a new wing, they would have to plant a tree and wait two hundred years for it to grow tall enough. So what space they had they used well.

He came at last to a smaller version of the Guardian's citadel, a rectangular space defined by woven bamboo screens and open to the sky above. Instead of the dawnlit clouds, however, Skender saw only leaves. From elsewhere in the citadel came a harsh, constant ringing of metal hammering against metal. It contrasted sharply with the liquid nighttime susurrus of the forest and he tried not to think about what the blacksmiths responsible were making.

The Guardian sat on a low, backless chair, dressed in a grey gown that stopped short of her bare feet. She looked as though she had been woken from sleep by her daughter, and Heuve, who stood opposite her stiffly at attention. A circular pendant, too large to be a bracelet but too small to be a crown, hung on a silver chain from her neck.

"Where is he?" she asked, continuing the conversation Skender had interrupted.

"Changing into a fresh uniform," said Lidia Delfine. "He insisted."

"He would." The Guardian turned her tired gaze to Skender. "Yes? You said you wanted to see me?"

"I—uh." His resolve faltered momentarily now that he was in front of her. "I've received a message from the others."

"So have we."

"You know, then?" He didn't know whether to be relieved or disappointed.

"The hunt will go ahead. They won't intimidate us so easily."

Intimidate? he wondered as another man entered the room. That wasn't the reaction he had expected.

"Guardian." The new arrival knelt before the seated woman and inclined his head in deep respect. "Forgive me for being the bearer of such tidings."

"You don't need my forgiveness, dear friend, and you should know better than to ask for it." The Guardian leaned forward and reached out a hand as though to touch him. It hung in the air for a moment, then returned, trembling, to her lap. "That you are alive is cause for celebration in my heart."

"I'm honoured."

"You're welcome, you old fool. Now stand up and look at me."

The man raised his head and stood, and Skender was astonished to recognise him as Seneschal Schuet.

"But you're—" he stammered. "I thought—"

Schuet turned and frowned slightly. "Skender, isn't it? Sal and Shilly's friend?"

"Yes, but—how did you get *here*?"

"He brought the message from the Panic," said Lidia Delfine. "They dropped him on the outskirts of Milang under cover of darkness. With his hands tied, he couldn't climb. It took him three hours to attract attention."

Schuet shifted uncomfortably on his feet. "There's no denying it was a calculated insult," he said, "but let's not dwell on the details. My pride is the least thing at stake here."

"What *is* at stake?" asked Skender, becoming thoroughly confused.

"War," said the Guardian. "Seneschal Schuet returned to us with a warning from Kingsman Oriel of the Panic Heptarchy. I know how events transpired in the Pass two nights ago. I know that the Seneschal and my daughter were not the aggressors. Oriel, however, sees it differently. He views the arrival of more humans as a hostile act: the calling of reinforcements. He uses the conflict to press for open hostilities."

"Should our peoples cross paths again," said Schuet, his voice solemn, "more blood will be spilled."

Skender just stared at him, thinking: *Two hunting parties, both seeking the same thing. If they meet, it'll start a war. This isn't going to end well.*

"I think," he said, "with respect, that we should wake the others and have a bit of a talk."

THE HUNTERS

"Prayer is all that separates the hunter from the hunted. When a rabbit feels the jaws of the wolf close around its throat, what other option is there but to pray? The ability to bring death, not life, is what inspires worship."
THE BOOK OF TOWERS, EXEGESIS 8:15

A powerful stink of blood and offal made Shilly gag as she climbed aboard the balloon's sleek gondola. Seeing her reaction, Griel explained with one word: "Bait."

The gondola was narrow, barely wide enough for one person to squeeze past the single row of seats down the left-hand side. She took a seat at random and leaned over the edge to see what made the smell. Below, hanging from a sturdy rope, was the skinned carcass of a large, four-legged beast. Probably a pig or a boar; Shilly couldn't tell, and she didn't particularly want to know.

She was sure that, even if it failed to attract the Swarm, it wouldn't go unnoticed by the forest's insect population.

Sal took the seat behind her, looking as though he had finished his conversation with Skender at last. His attention was back on the world again, no longer fixed an unknown distance deeper into the forest.

"What did he say?" she asked him.

"They're hunting too," he said. "They've dealt with one of them already, apparently. He says they're hard to kill, but flame hurts them. I think he's speaking from experience."

"We should be grateful, then, that he's still speaking at all." Shilly remembered with terrible clarity the body that had been left on the boneship, rent and drained by the creatures she was now trying to find.

The gondola rocked beneath her as the rest of the party climbed aboard: hollow-faced Highson Sparre, looking as though he needed an extra night's sleep; Warden Rosevear with a bagful of medical supplies topped up by Vehofnehu; Tom, who took the rearmost seat by the balloon's chimerical engine without uttering a word; dour Griel, in full leather armour and lugging a heavy bag that Shilly assumed was full of weapons; and Mawson last of all, looking even less animated than usual. With each person, the tapering lozenge keeping them airborne dipped a little lower. Shilly was relieved that the gondola would still have empty seats.

Then the Panic soldier that Griel had called Erged jogged up trailing an upset-looking forester: the young woman, Mikia, with a bandage tied tightly around her wounded head.

"Sir, forgive me." Erged executed a breathless bow. Her hair was shaved very close to her rounded scalp but still glowed visibly red in the morning light. "I was not the first to visit the cells this morning. Oriel has taken the other one away."

"The *other one* has a name," said Mikia, pushing forward. "If Seneschal Schuet has been harmed—"

"That's out of our hands for now," said Griel. "Get aboard, both of you. Time is even shorter than I thought."

"And you have one seat empty, by the look of it," came a voice from the dock. "Perfect."

Shilly looked up to see the Panic woman Jao hurrying towards the gondola, dressed in green cotton overalls and toting a bow and quiver.

"Jao, no—" Griel raised both hands to ward her away.

"I'm not hearing it," she said. "And you're not going off without me again."

"I'm not saying I don't want you to come. I just need you here, where you can do the most good."

"Precious little that is." Jao tipped her head to one side, making her beads rattle. "Why do you think I want to come with you? The bough has finally broken. Those who can are jumping off—and those who can't are being thrown. Leave me behind and I might not be here when you get back. Not if Oriel has his way."

A great weariness swept over Griel's face as he nodded and waved her aboard. She brushed a hand across his goatee and lips as she went, taking the seat two back from the front of the gondola.

"What happened to Schuet?" Shilly asked, expecting Mikia to answer.

It was Jao who explained that the Seneschal had been sent back to Milang to offer his Guardian an ultimatum: stop attacking the Panic or there would be trouble. The trouble *was*, though, that the wraiths were neither human nor of human origin. Oriel was giving the humans a test they couldn't possibly pass.

Shilly wondered what, exactly, that might mean. It certainly wouldn't make conditions in the forest any easier—especially for a group of nonaligned humans caught in the crossfire.

Fail in this instance and all will fall, Vehofnehu had said, and Tom hadn't disagreed with him. She couldn't afford to gainsay both of them. If hunting the wraiths would help them solve the mystery of the flood, then she would take that risk.

Griel barked an order to the sole remaining Panic on the dock, who untied the last stay. Griel sat in the foremost seat and gripped the balloon's controls. With a whir, they edged away from the deck.

"This Oriel," called Highson from the rear. "What does he want, exactly?"

"Nothing to do with humans," grunted Griel, wrenching the balloon down and to port. Shilly clutched the back of the seat in front of her, surprised by the sudden acceleration. The balloon's sleekness was clearly for more than aesthetic reasons.

"Why not?" bellowed Highson, not easily put off.

Jao fielded the question as Griel flew the balloon away from the floating city and into impenetrable fog. Her voice, more musical than

Griel's but still rough-edged compared to a human's, carried clearly through the misty air.

"In the days following the Cataclysm," she said, twisting in her seat and hollering loud enough to be heard, "our ancestors had nothing to do with humans. The forests were empty; we lived here alone, under the rule of the King. Then humans came down from the top of the mountains, and the peace of the forest was forever shattered. The line of the King was broken. Some of our people—Oriel included, and now the Heptarchs that rule in the King's place—wish to restore by any means available the peace we lost. War is, unfortunately, their preferred option."

"Sounds to me like this Oriel wants to be King," said Mikia.

"Or the next best thing. He has the Heptarchs tightly between his teeth. They won't stand up to him. We've lost too many people in recent weeks, and who else is there to blame but the humans?"

"You do believe us," said Highson, "when we say that we have nothing to do with any of this. Don't you?"

"Of course." Jao's smile was fleeting. "But the Quorum has acknowledged you and that means you're involved—for good or ill, whether you want to be or not. The Heptarchs would never ignore such a ruling, although who knows how far Oriel might go in such times?"

"At least the Seneschal got to go home," said Mikia sourly.

"If we track down the Swarm and stop the attacks on the kings-folk," said Highson, "we might be able to prevent Oriel from getting his way."

Shilly didn't dare assume it would be so simple. The Panic political system was complicated and ambiguous. The Quorum existed to "advise" the Heptarchs who made the actual rulings, but what happened if Heptarchs and Quorum disagreed? Who made the final call? It couldn't rest on the back of one person, no matter how qualified Oriel thought he might be. Not even the Alcaide had supreme power over the Strand; he ultimately answered to a Conclave of high-ranking Sky Wardens and could be deposed if he ever went astray.

She said none of this, not wanting to sound critical of a system she didn't entirely understand. Panic and human were different in many subtle ways; maybe the murmuring of rebellion she heard in Griel and Jao was part of the system's natural checks and balances. Maybe it would somehow work out all right in the long run.

"I bet Vehofnehu saw this coming," she said. "I bet that's another reason why he sent us on this hunt."

Jao shrugged. "Perhaps. He sees much from his perch."

Shilly clung tight again as Griel brought the balloon out of its steep descent and took them on a steady eastern heading. A wall of trees loomed out of the mist to their left, seeming close enough to touch. Shilly kept her hands carefully where they were as the green wall swept by.

"You said that humans came down from the top of the mountains," she said, to keep her mind off their wild trajectory. "You mean there are people even further up than here?"

"Yes," said Tom, attracting the attention of everyone in the balloon, then looking as though he wished he hadn't. He had been very quiet since his nightmare about the Swarm, and Shilly felt bad about being snappy with him earlier. Between worrying about Sal and the Swarm and what was happening to Skender and the others, and trying to work out the Panic, she didn't have room in her head for his issues, whatever they were. She swore to make it up to him later.

Griel turned sharply to port, following the contours of a steep, heavily wooded cliff. Another cliff appeared out of the mist to Shilly's right. They had flown into a ravine barely five metres wide but many more deep. The balloon struggled against a strong headwind that rocked it from side to side. Griel kept a firm, long-fingered hand on the controls and let them gradually shed speed.

They came to a halt within a stone's throw of the end of the ravine, where the two walls came together in a narrow cleft, choked with vines and tumbling flowers.

"Great," said Shilly. "A dead end. What happened? Did you take a wrong turn?"

Griel fiddled with the controls, but didn't retreat. "This is exactly where we need to be. We're a long way from the human settlements; there's only one way in; and the breeze will carry the scent of blood a great distance. The only question is: what do we do when the wraiths come calling?"

The balloon hung in space, swaying slightly, as Shilly considered the answer.

It was obvious, really. So Sal told himself as Griel dropped off the last of his passengers. The balloon responded more quickly the less weight it carried, and the fewer eggs they had in one basket the better. But he still felt exposed alongside Shilly and Griel as the Panic took the balloon back up to its midair station, where he planned for the three of them to wait for the wraiths to come.

Shilly took his hand, either sensing his nervousness or seeking comfort for her own. Perhaps both.

They had it worse than the others. Mikia, Rosevear, and Jao crouched in a tree on the right side of the ravine, armed with bows and slingshots, opposite Highson and Erged on the other side. Tom and Mawson sat in a small cave in the cleft itself, well out of harm's way. Griel had offered the young seer a hook to defend himself with, should the worst occur, but Tom had initially waved it away.

"I won't need it," he said, "and what good would it do against the Swarm?"

Griel insisted. "The wraiths aren't the only predators in the forest. There are wild cats, snakes, and worse. Best take it, just to be sure."

Tom had shrugged and accepted the weapon. Mawson, impervious to all animal life, had expressed no opinion.

From the beginning, Griel had insisted on Sal being in the balloon with him. Griel hadn't seen Sal in action, but knew what a wild talent was and wanted one at his side. Sal was happy enough to go along with it, but agreed with Shilly that she should be with them too, not crouching in a cave with Tom and Mawson, sitting out the real work.

"We work best as a team," she had told Griel. "My brains and his brawn. It's worth the extra weight. Believe me."

With a grunt, Griel had let her stay. And Sal was glad. They had spent entirely too much time apart in recent weeks. If something were to go wrong, he wanted her nearby.

"No offence to Tom or Mawson," she said as they settled back to wait, "but if you're so worried about deadwood, why did you bring them?"

"Because they're safer with us than back at the city," Griel explained, his dark inset eyes scanning the fog for any sign of the wraiths. "Oriel will come down hard on foreigners and troublemakers. Even Vehofnehu won't be safe for a while, until the glast is dealt with. This seemed the safest of our options."

The moaning of moai echoed down the ravine, an ululating, incessant call that made Sal's flesh crawl in response. Sometimes the sound faded into the background, filtered out by his mind when there were other things to think about. Other times, it sounded as though the Earth itself was humming, killing time before the next tumultuous upset.

"Talk to me about the Change," he said to Griel. "The Panic obviously use it, but I've yet to see anything like a mage or a warden—unless you count Vehofnehu. But he's something else, isn't he?"

Griel's gaze flicked at him, then returned to sweeping the mist. "You're right. He's not a Change-worker as you're used to them. We don't really have them. We have Engineers who maintain the machines built centuries ago, machines designed to tap the mist, to turn it into water and to store the energy released for future use. Next time you see the city, look for the vanes hanging from the balloon supports. Each one is perfectly aligned with respect to its neighbours to maximise its potential. They are literally the city's lifelines. If you cut them, it would die as surely as if you'd cut my throat. We rely on chimerical energy for everything—from something as small as heating to as big as moving the city."

"Are you serious?" asked Sal. "Move the whole city?"

"Of course," said Griel. "It's not fixed to the ground. In theory, it can go anywhere in the mist forest, if the motivators are fully charged."

Sal pondered the things Griel had told him for several minutes, wondering at what it said about the Change and the people who used it. Sky Wardens and Stone Mages had long argued that there were only two major reservoirs in the world—those of sea and stone—but even they acknowledged such secondary sources as fire and air and Ruins. Lodo's heresy had been to claim the existence of a third major source, the beach, and to believe it superior to the others. Now Sal could add trees and mist to the list, along with blood.

The Change was everywhere: *that*, Lodo had definitely taught him. Wild talents were supposed to be dangerous because they didn't worry about reservoirs or sources; they just tapped right into the raw energy and used it as they willed.

It seemed to Sal sometimes that the only difference between him and every other Change-worker on Earth was that they had been trained to use the Change in certain ways, and he hadn't. Perhaps everyone could be like him, if left alone to develop their own way.

But what would that mean? He had trouble controlling his wild talent. If everyone *was* like him, the world would be a chaotic, dangerous place, as it had been immediately after the Cataclysm.

And therein, according to the Weavers, lay the reason for all the various schools and disciplines in the world. The Weavers believed that change was good only up to a certain point—and that *they* should be in charge of what changes came, and when they came. Without them, there would be no order, no certainty, no safety. Sal wondered what the ancient order was up to during these times of flood and disaster. If the Weavers hadn't heard about the Homunculus from Highson, they might not even be aware of the crisis taking shape in the mountains . . .

The balloon murmured to itself as its propeller spun to keep it in position. With the wind blowing constantly down the ravine, it had to accelerate just to stay in one place. The wind, fortunately, also carried the stink of meat away, and soon Sal was able to forget the bait hanging metres from his feet. Time passed in a daze of anticipation and dread as he waited for the wraiths to come—which they could, at any moment, without warning. The mist gave everything a blurry, mystical atmosphere. If he squinted, he could have been rocking in a boat on the surface of a very clear lake, surrounded by steep canyon walls. The creaking of the balloon's stays sounded somewhat like oars.

He half-smiled at the thought that they were indeed fishing—fishing in the air for a creature much more dangerous than a shark. When or if they caught it, he hoped Griel knew how to reel it in. Just in case Griel didn't, Sal kept the Change ready to call into service.

The mist-shrouded sun appeared at the top of the narrow canyon, making the air thick and soupy and marginally less heat-sapping. Griel communicated with hand signals to Jao and Erged, and at one point drifted close enough to each to toss over supplies for lunch. When he approached Tom, the young seer was asleep again, catching up on that rest he had lost after the previous night's nightmares. Mawson stared back at them as inscrutably as a miniature moai.

Blood and fire. Death in the mist.

The memory of the thing that had attacked him and Marmion in the Divide was bad enough to give Sal nightmares, too.

The strangler, the blood-red, the screecher, the black-hearted . . .

Late in the afternoon, with the sun beginning to lose its brilliance through the eternal mist, a strange silence fell. It took Sal a moment to notice, but when he did it bothered him more with every passing second. No bird called; no creature stirred in the trees. Apart from the wind and the ever-present moaning of the moai, the ravine was suddenly, utterly still.

He looked at Griel. The Panic had noticed too, and crouched forward on his seat, hands ready at the controls. Sal nudged Shilly, who had slumped against the gondola's lip. She jerked awake.

"What—?"

"Shhh."

The air felt as heavy as wool. Nothing disturbed its closeness. The longer the silence lasted, the more nervous Sal became. He leaned over the edge and saw the bait hanging untouched, but he half-expected something to rush out of the fog and snatch it away at any second.

Griel waved to catch their attention and mouthed: *Listen.*

The sound of something moving through the trees reached them from below. Something large, judging by the cracking and splintering of wood that gradually became audible. Sal glanced over the edge of the gondola again, but could see nothing below the bait but fog.

He moved within arm's reach of Griel, and sent to him through the Change: "*We need to go down.*"

Griel nodded, but still didn't move. Sal could understand his unwillingness. In the air, they had bows and slingshots poised to take down anything they couldn't deal with themselves. Lower, perhaps as low as the very bottom of the ravine, they would be entirely on their own, and less able to manoeuvre. The decision wasn't an easy one.

The crunching sounds grew louder.

Shilly's hand touched his, and he felt her Taking from him.

"*It's not cold,*" she said.

Griel looked at her, hearing her words through Sal. Her meaning was obvious. The wraiths brought cold and fog with them when they came near. Since the air was neither colder nor obviously foggier, maybe it wasn't a wraith crashing through the forest below, after all.

With a nod, Griel touched the balloon's controls. Slowly, in near-silence, they began to descend.

Sal didn't drop his guard. The obvious explanation was all very well, but if Shilly was wrong, the consequences could be terrible. They were, after all, hunting hunters.

He leaned over the edge of the gondola while at the same time trying to keep as much of himself aboard as possible. Shilly did the same on the other side. The Change flowed around and through them in many different forms. Sal could tap into it in a moment and burn anything that dared approach.

The crushing of trees continued. Below the bait, the canopy was impenetrable. Sal had only just come to terms with the size of the individual trees, so could barely imagine something large enough to smash through them. But something was definitely doing so. He could see the uppermost boughs swaying in response to the violence taking place further down. Clouds of leaves and flying insects rose up in outrage. The path the thing had carved through the forest was therefore easily discernible: a meandering line of broken branches and collapsed foliage stretching downhill into the mist.

Griel halted their descent when the bait brushed the top of the canopy. It had provoked no obvious response from the thing below.

"Remember to look up," said Shilly, Talking from him again.

He nodded. If this *was* a trap, it would spring from anywhere but the distraction below.

That provoked an ugly thought. If the thing were to grab the bait and pull the balloon down . . .

Griel was ahead of him. Tugging a lever sharply backwards, he disconnected the cable connecting the carcass to the balloon. The bait dropped into the trees, trailing the cable behind it. When both disappeared, the thundering crashes ceased.

Sal held his breath. Directly below them, where the bait had dropped, was a creature large enough to make treetops sway and to smash a path through the forest. How would it react to the fleshy missile from the sky?

After a second, the sound of its thunderous passage resumed.

"I get the feeling we're being ignored," said Shilly aloud.

Sal agreed. "One of us is going to have to go down there and attract its attention."

"*Both* of us."

"No, Shilly." Griel spoke without taking his eyes off the controls. "Just Sal. I want you here, with me."

Her lips narrowed. "If you're saying that because of my leg—"

"Partly, yes. Partly because I want to be certain Sal comes back."

"I'm your hostage now?"

Griel did look up at that, and regarded her for a full second as the balloon turned a half-circle beneath them. His eyes were unsympathetic, but not threatening either. "I prefer to think of it as giving Sal extra incentive to be careful."

Sal didn't see the point in arguing. "I'll be okay, Shilly. At the slightest sign of trouble, I'll either blow something up or run away. You can rely on me for that."

She wasn't so easily mollified. "I'm tired of sitting around while you do all the dangerous stuff."

"Don't worry," said Griel. "I'm sure you'll get your turn."

Sal kissed Shilly quickly as the Panic tossed a rope ladder over the side.

"Bring me back a flower," she said.

"Anything for the lady." Sal swung his legs out of the gondola and tried not to think about the drop or what might be waiting at the bottom of it. The balloon had descended a considerable distance, but the top of the canopy could have been dozens of metres from the actual forest floor, for all he could tell.

He descended rapidly, then slowed when he met the level of the foliage. Shadows reined below that point, and he took a moment to let his eyes adjust. The crashing of the thing was moving away from him at a steady pace, but was still fearsomely loud. The leaves shook.

Pausing only to reactivate the camouflage charms he had inscribed into his skin, he climbed rung by rung down into the gloom, feeling as though he was slipping underwater. The air grew still. Leathery plants crowded him on all sides, sticky with sap and cobwebs. A tiny brown lizard clinging to a branch caught his eye. Instead of jumping away at the sight of him, it stayed frozen, bulging eyes watching him, unmoving.

When he reached the bottom, he dropped onto a dense mat of rotting vegetation and fungus that might have been undisturbed for centuries. Nothing molested him, so he tugged the ladder three times and waited until it snaked up through the branches. He would call Shilly through the Change when he needed to ascend.

The crashing sounds came from his left. Crouching, he proceeded to track its source, confident that the racket would cover his footsteps. Within moments, he found the broad swathe of destruction the creature had left behind. Splintered tree stumps, snapped branches, and crushed ferns lay in its wake. Vines hung limp like severed streamers. He checked for tracks, but found only broad, circular indentations that he didn't recognise. Each was wide enough for four of his feet, and lacked any sign of toe, hoof, or claw. Whatever made them was heavy enough to punch right through the undergrowth to the soil beneath and to crush rocks to powder. The pattern of footprints puzzled him in other ways, too; there seemed to be too many of them on one side, as though it had more than two legs.

The trail led uphill, occasionally switching back on itself, avoiding the steeper areas. Sal couldn't see far ahead, so went carefully, mindful not to twist an ankle in the pothole-prints or to spear himself on a jagged splinter.

"*I'm following it*," he told Shilly, to allay any worries she might have felt. "*Don't know what it is, yet, or where it's going. I'll call again when I do.*" He wanted to ask her if she recalled the name of a giant creature spoken of only in stories about the Cataclysm. *Elephand? Elevant?* He couldn't quite remember it. There was no way she could reply, so he kept the question to himself.

The creature, whatever it was, had a considerably greater stride than he did, and it didn't have to walk around pitfalls or stumps either.

Although Sal started cautiously at first, soon he found himself scrambling just to keep up, hands and shins bloodied from fresh scratches. His breath came heavily in the thick, pungent air. The sound of thunderous footsteps reverberated in his head, drowning out any other thought.

When it stopped, the silence crashed down like a lid over the world, and he froze in place, fearing he'd been discovered.

Nothing jumped at him out of the undergrowth. He slowly let free the breath he had been holding and realised that he could still hear movement ahead, albeit not on the previous scale. He resumed the climb, sticking to the edges of the path rather than blundering right up its centre, and keeping his eyes fixed firmly forward.

The trail turned at a sharp angle to avoid a stony outcrop painted green with moss. Sal brushed against it as he went by, distantly noting its coolness against his skin. Ahead, around the corner, he saw a giant moai jutting out of the steep hillside like a crooked tooth, surrounded on all sides by overlapping, cagelike tree trunks. Its wide eyes stared out through the trees at nothing he could discern. Its mouth hung open but uttered no sound.

He didn't know he had seen the thing he hunted until it moved. And when he *did* see it, he dropped flat to the ground and didn't dare look up for at least a full ten breaths as he waited for the heavy footfalls to come his way, for its massive, alien shadow to creep over him . . .

Nothing happened. He had, somehow, not been spotted. Raising his head slowly, he peered over a fallen log and gazed in wonder at the creature he had followed.

The first thing he did was put all thought of animals out of his mind, legendary or otherwise. Flesh and blood had nothing to do with it, something he should have guessed much earlier. At least five metres tall, it stood on three thick legs, one at the front and two at the back. They supported a lean, cylindrical body that was barely thicker than one of the legs. From one end sprouted a rounded, stubby tail, almost crude in its bluntness. From the other, a straight, proud neck led to a triangular, tapering head that appeared to have no eyes, mouth, ears, or nostrils.

Had it been an animal, Sal would have wondered how it sensed the world around it. He would have assumed it to be stumbling at random through the forest, lost in its own private misery.

That it moved with the jerky, powerful grace of a man'kin, however—and the way it stood face to face with the moai, as though communicating with it—strongly suggested otherwise.

Sal stared it for an unknown length of time, hypnotised by its size and strange form. Its grey skin was pitted and worn by age. Even in the shadowy depths of the forest he could see faint colourful markings that might once have been charms painted down its flanks. On the right-hand side of its single front leg was a crack wide enough to put an arm through. Through the crack, he saw only darkness, as though the creature was hollow.

As he watched, it lowered its arrow shaped head and began clearing the vegetation away from the moai. The giant head's eyes slowly closed. Its mouth sealed shut in a straight line.

When the ground was clear around it, the massive, three-legged man'kin inserted the tip of its head into the earth at the moai's back, and pushed. There came a grinding, splitting sound. The great stone head tipped forward, further and further, until it overbalanced. With a mighty series of crashes, it tumbled down the side of the hill, all the way to the bottom of the ravine.

Sal lay stunned into immobility as the echoes faded. The giant man'kin stood, braced firmly on its three legs, and peered down the slope where the moai had gone. Checking to see if the moai had been smashed to pieces, Sal assumed.

Then its head tipped upwards, at the sky. Through the misty foliage, Sal glimpsed the underside of the balloon drifting above the treetops, and he sent a hasty message to Shilly, warning her to stay clear.

"Whatever this thing is," he said, *"it's big and mean. Stay away until I tell you otherwise!"*

A faint whine came from the balloon's chimerical engine as it lifted up and out of sight. The man'kin's eyeless head swivelled to where Sal lay in the dirt, exactly as though it had heard his warning. He ducked his head down, hoping against hope that he hadn't been seen.

A heavy crunching came from behind him. Footsteps, coming up the creature's path. With a sinking heart, he rolled over and saw two grotesque man'kin lumbering towards him. There was nothing he could do to avoid them. He lay in full view.

One—a long-necked, short-winged gargoyle with a square face and pointed ears—thudded up to him. Its broad, lipless mouth opened.

"Angel says run," it grated past fangs longer than Sal's thumb.

He prepared to do just that.

Shilly hung half out of the gondola, trying desperately to see through the dense canopy what was happening below. Since the almighty crash of something falling down the ravine wall and Sal's warning to stay away, there had been no sound at all. She half-glimpsed shapes moving in the shadowy undergrowth, but she couldn't make them out.

"We have to go down," she told Griel. "I have to find out what's going on!"

The Panic bared his teeth. "First up. Now down. What is this, Shilly? What are you playing at?"

She wanted to tear her hair out. She pulled herself back into the gondola and limped forward. Grabbing his leather jerkin she pulled him close. "Does it look like I'm joking?"

Griel's nostrils flared. "You're a human. Your face is small and flat. I can't read it half the time." He brushed her aside. "All right. We go down, but not alone. I'm getting the others first. If Sal's in trouble, I'm not throwing you in too. I want Jao with you, at least."

Shilly couldn't argue with that, although the thought of abandoning Sal ached inside her. She went back to her seat as Griel twisted the controls, lifting the balloon upward so fast her body felt heavy. Streamers of fog whipped by them, thrown into disarray by their sudden ascent. She wished there was something more concrete she could do than wait.

As they reached the level they had started at, she sought the hiding places of those stationed to catch the wraiths. The Panic were invisible in their brown-black armour. Where Tom and Mawson crouched in the tiny cave, she thought she glimpsed a flash of blue—Tom's robe, she presumed—and a patch of glowing green.

Her eyes narrowed, struck by this detail. Griel angled the balloon in towards Jao, Rosevear, and Mikia's perch. As their perspective changed, she confirmed that it was Tom she could see, and a second figure that wasn't Mawson. That figure matched the one she had seen by the waterfall, and Sal's descriptions of the Quorum. But why would one of them be out in the forest, talking to Tom?

Then she remembered Sal telling her about Mawson speaking the Quorum's strange backward language. Maybe Tom wasn't the reason for the Quorum member's visit, but the man'kin.

There was no time to ponder the mystery. Jao was waving at her with one long arm, calling for a rope. Shilly tossed one to the Panic female and helped her climb aboard, her beaded hair flailing like whips. Mikia and Rosevear followed, full of questions. Why had they dropped down to the bottom of the ravine? What had they seen? Where was Sal?

Shilly felt too exhausted and full of questions herself to reply. Had *they* seen the glowing person sitting with Tom? Did they know what was going on inside that tiny cave?

Barely were they aboard when Griel sent the balloon plummeting downwards again. Shilly clutched the side of the gondola, afraid of falling out. Only minutes had passed since they had left Sal, but it felt like hours. The day was darkening. It wouldn't be long before night fell.

Finally, as the bottom of the ravine appeared through the mist, word came from Sal.

"Shilly, I'm okay. I'm sorry if I gave you a fright. I've had a bit of a one myself. There's something down here you need to meet. It's not the Swarm. I don't think it means us harm." He paused for a second, as though he couldn't quite bring himself to believe what he was about to say. *"It's the Angel, Shilly. We've found the Angel."*

In the excitement over the Swarm, Sal had quite forgotten the *other* mystery creature they were supposed to be looking for in the Hanging Mountains.

Angel says run.

The words, uttered by a voice as rough and grating as a tombstone dragged along a road, triggered a cascade of memories from his brief journey along the bottom of the Divide, before it had been flooded. Several of the man'kin that he had asked about the Angel had each given him a different answer. The Angel was necessary, Mawson said. It was a gathering point of some kind, a focus; it drew many towards it; it told man'kin they must be free; it said that humans were nothing, not worthy even of anger. No one would survive without the Angel.

The last statement was the most peculiar of all. Sal had been unable to determine if Mawson had been referring to man'kin only, or every living thing. Either way, the Angel was clearly important. Its word alone had triggered the migration down from the mountains that had saved thousands of man'kin from the flood, apart from those who hadn't moved fast enough.

Angel says run, the gargoyle man'kin had said.

At first he had thought the words constituted an order, perhaps a threat. Then he guessed that the man'kin was using the words as a

mantra or a mnemonic, similar to those used by Sky Wardens and
Stone Mages. To it, he was an alien, peculiar creature, just as it was to
him. It might even have offered the words to him as advice, the only
form of verbal communication it had to give.

He rose slowly to his feet, holding his hands up and palm forward,
indicating that he was unarmed. That was true enough, although the
Change was ready to do his bidding, should he need to defend himself.

The man'kin repeated its simple mantra, while the second, a muscular, bat-winged beast that walked on four clawed feet, watched in
silence. Their blank, granite eyes didn't blink.

"My name is Sal," he said, conscious of the creature behind him.
Wood and Earth complained as it shifted position. That was the only
sound it made. For the first time, he became aware of how eerie it was
that man'kin didn't breathe.

"I set a man'kin free, once," he said, hoping to avoid a repeat of
that particular dispute. He glanced over his shoulder, and found the
tip of the arrowhead snout directly behind him. He hadn't imagined it
could move so fast.

"*Angel knows*," said the gargoyle.

Sal took a deep breath and forced himself to face the worn, feature-
less head. Its surface was lined with cracks that crossed and recrossed
like a crocodile's back.

"Are *you* the Angel?" he asked.

"*Yes*," said the gargoyle from behind him.

"Why don't you talk to me directly?"

"*You don't have the right ears.*"

"What ears should I have?"

"*Ones that hear.*"

The Angel's head didn't move, which he took as a positive sign. It
could have killed him easily, had it wanted to. He wasn't planning on
giving it a reason to change its mind.

The balloon had obediently flown away when he had thought that the man'kin might grow angry at its presence. Taking advantage of the frozen stillness, he quickly called Shilly. She simply had to see this; she would understand it better than him. After a moment he heard the humming of the chimerical engine returning.

"What are you doing here?" he asked the Angel to cover the sound.

"Liberating the 'kin."

"Which 'kin?" Then he realised. "Oh, the moai. What are you liberating them from?"

"That which comes."

"What which comes?"

"Angel says that which comes."

"We want to help you," Sal said, slowly and clearly, emphasising the plural. "Many man'kin died in the flood. We want to find out why that happened and prevent it ever happening again. Will you help us? Will you help us understand what's going on?"

"Angel says 'kin do not die. We are not born. We just are."

"Drowned, then. Buried in mud. Whatever. You'd have to agree that this isn't a good thing."

"All things are as they are. Angel says—"

"The Angel says a lot of things." Sal thought of Mawson, far above. Now more than ever he needed a man'kin interpreter, a voice he could trust among these strange, confounding minds.

Three stone heads swivelled as a rope ladder slithered down the trees nearby. Sal hastened to reassure them.

"It's just Shilly. I want you to meet her."

"We have met her," said the gargoyle.

"You have?" His puzzlement couldn't have been more complete.

"She raised us."

"She *raised* you? I don't understand."

"She knows us."

The bottom of the rope ladder danced as someone descended. It was moving too quickly to be Shilly, though, with her weakened leg.

Sal assumed it wouldn't be Griel, since Shilly didn't know how to operate the balloon's controls. They must have ascended and brought someone else down with them.

"This isn't Shilly," he told the man'kin as Jao climbed warily into view, moving with swinging, loose-jointed grace. "This is Jao. She's a friend."

"Let me judge that for myself, will you?" said the Panic female, dropping to the ground with one hand on the pommel of her hook. "Griel sent me to check on things before letting Shilly down." Her dark eyes took in the tableau before her: two roughly human-sized and human-shaped man'kin, plus another considerably more alien, surrounding Sal near the clod-filled hole where a moai had once sat. Seeing that Sal wasn't obviously harmed, she waved vigorously at the balloon, barely visible through the foliage.

"I wouldn't have called Shilly down if it wasn't safe," said Sal, resentful at having his judgment questioned.

"Griel wouldn't let her go until he knew what else was down here." Calm black eyes regarded him, then flicked to the Angel. The tip of its nose didn't shift to acknowledge her. "Another friend of yours?"

"I don't know," he admitted. "Are we friends?" he asked it, then corrected himself, remembering what Tarnava had said about man'kin not knowing the meaning of friendship. *They will charm your mind into knots.* "Are we on the same side?"

"*We are not your enemies,*" ground out the gargoyle.

"That's something, I guess." Jao walked around the giant man'kin while Shilly descended one awkward step at a time. The balloon dipped lower, saving her some degree of effort. When its underside bent the topmost boughs, she was within a metre of the undergrowth.

Sal gripped her hips and lifted her the rest of the way.

"Where's my flower?" she asked.

"I got you this instead."

She leaned on him, missing her walking stick, and looked at the man'kin in wonder.

"I know you," she said, pointing at the two facing the Angel.

"That's what they say." Sal turned to study her, mystified. "How is that possible? I didn't think man'kin ever came as far south as Fundelry."

"They don't. I fished these two out of the lake by the waterfall, while the Panic were attacking us."

"We weren't attacking you," said Jao in a defensive tone. "Griel thought you were human reinforcements from the west, come to fight alongside the Guardian. Then the wraith attacked, and he assumed you had summoned it."

"However it happened, you were boarding the boat and I couldn't just sit back and *let* you." Shilly turned back to Sal. "The bottom of the lake is full of man'kin. These two looked the most desperate. But when I pulled them up, they ran away."

"*Angel says run.*"

"Yes, so you keep repeating." Sal couldn't keep a lid on his exasperation. It would soon be dark, and he didn't want to be stuck on the ground with three unpredictable man'kin any longer than he had to. "Will you talk to them, find out what they're up to? They say they came here to liberate a moai—" he pointed at the hole where the stone had previously sat "—but they won't say why. Maybe you can make sense of this."

The great stone head swung silently, as though on massive, internal gimbals, to face Shilly.

"*Angel says the sense is this: there is no sense. There is only what is.*"

"What's that supposed to mean?" asked Jao.

"My question exactly."

Shilly waved them both silent. "I raised you from the bottom of the lake," she said to the gargoyle, "but you didn't stick around. You ran here to meet the Angel."

"*We ran here to meet you.*"

She blinked. "Why?"

"*You know us.*"

"I don't know you. I picked you at random."

"*Angel says there is no random.*"

"Then what is there? Some grand design?"

"*Angel says there is no design or sense or random. There is only what is. You know us. That is, Shilly of Gooron, and so it is—like the things you dream.*"

Her dark skin went a shade paler. "How do you know that I dream? How do you know my name?"

"*It is, so we know.*"

"But how?" Sal could see Shilly struggling for a way around the break in comprehension. "Is it like a memory? A memory of the future?"

"*Angel says there is no future. There is only now.*"

"Yes, that's right. All times are one to you. Does that mean you know me in the future?"

"*You know. You dream.*"

"Can you tell me what my dream's about?"

"*You know. You dream,*" the gargoyle repeated. "*Angel says run.*"

"Why do you keep saying that?" She flexed her stiff leg irritably. "And anyway, I *can't* run."

"*Angel says—*"

"Don't you dare."

"*Angel says there are ways of running that don't require legs, just as there are ways of hearing that don't involve ears.*"

The surprisingly long sentence was followed by an odd moment in which all three man'kin turned their heads to the east, as though at a noise Sal couldn't detect. They held that pose for a heartbeat, then began to move. The two smaller man'kin turned and lumbered down the hill, along the Angel's ragged path. The Angel man'kin took three giant, lopsided steps around Shilly, Sal, and Jao, then began to lope after them.

"Wait!" Shilly called. "You can't just leave!"

"Looks to me like they're doing just that," said Jao dryly as the giant form vanished into the shadows at the very bottom of the ravine.

The sound of its progress—less noisy than it had been on the way up, since it had already flattened most of the trees in its path—faded into the distance.

When it had gone, the Panic female turned to her two human companions. "Are you going to fill me in on what just happened?"

"As soon as we work it out," Sal promised, "you'll be the first to know."

Shilly cursed herself for not thinking quickly enough as the balloon ascended through the mist. The sun had long vanished from sight, plunging the ravine into utter darkness. How Griel navigated, she didn't know, but he did it much more carefully than earlier. The fog was cool and clammy against her cheeks and ears. Sal's hands on her shoulders reassured her somewhat, but didn't touch a deeper core of dissatisfaction.

They had learned next to nothing from the Angel. Instead of blathering on about memory and the future—always a fruitless task with man'kin—she should have pinned it down to specific issues, or tried at least. What else did it know about the Homunculus and the twins, which other man'kin called "the One from the Void"? What was it trying to save the moai from? What did it mean by *that which comes*?

The balloon slowed and drifted to port. At Griel's command, Jao flashed a shuttered mist globe at Erged and Highson. An answering flash indicated that they had been noticed. Griel swung the balloon in close to the treetops.

When the two of them had settled into their seats, Sal outlined what had happened below.

"The Angel?" Highson's expression was invisible in the gloom, but his incredulous tone allowed her to picture it perfectly. "Here? Remarkable! And you don't think it was a coincidence?"

As Sal repeated what the man'kin had said about the Angel liberating the moai, she told herself that, mystery or not, the incident hadn't been a complete waste of time. They may not have found the Swarm, but they had found *something*.

The knot she felt tightening around her would unravel in time, if only she kept picking at it.

"What now?" asked Mikia. "We've got no bait, and it's as dark as a crabbler's armpit out here."

"Let's get the others," said Jao. "Then we'll decide."

Jao flashed the light at the cave containing Tom and Mawson and waited for an answer. Receiving none, she tried again.

"He was asleep before," said Sal. "Maybe he's nodded off again."

"Try calling him," Jao ordered.

Sal hollered Tom's name three times, sending echoes dancing around them. No answer came.

Shilly's gut felt tight. She had completely forgotten what she had seen earlier: a green figure sitting with Tom and Mawson in the cramped cave.

When she told the others, they were as mystified as she.

"What would the Quorum be doing out here?" asked Jao, her prominent brow dropping even lower.

"Get ready to find out," Griel barked. "I'll move us closer."

Jao and Erged moved forward, preparing to leap across to the cliff face the moment Griel negotiated his way through the trees. They kept the light unshuttered and their hooks drawn. Shilly clutched the back of the seat in front of her, fearing the worst.

Jao jumped first, landing nimbly on all fours on the rocks. She disappeared into the cave, trailed closely by Erged.

The five seconds that followed were the longest in Shilly's life.

Jao emerged, grim-faced, shaking her head. In her hand she held the hook Griel had given Tom.

Shilly barely breathed. *Dead?* First Kemp, and now Tom. It was too awful.

"They're gone!" Jao shouted across the gap. "Both of them!"

"Where?" called Griel.

"Hard to say. There's no blood. No sign of a struggle. Maybe they went willingly."

"With the Quorum?"

Jao just shrugged.

Shilly rested her head on her hands as the two Panic climbed back aboard. Sometimes she despaired of ever understanding anything.

"So what do we do now?" asked Sal.

"We keep hunting," Griel ground out from the darkness. "That's what we do. Wherever your friends have got to and however they got there, I'm not going to rest tonight until they're found."

"Out of the goodness of your heart or because you think they're up to something?"

Griel didn't answer. With a whir of its propeller, the balloon lifted up and away, into the night.

THE WOUNDED

**"Of all our senses, the heart is the least reliable.
It blinds us when we need most to see. It stops up
our ears when we need most to hear. But we grant it
influence out of all proportion and beyond all need,
because it never lies."**
THE BOOK OF TOWERS, EXEGESIS 4:22

The knoll stood out from the surrounding forest like a bald man's head, with a fringe of palms resembling a crown in which a colony of tiny flying insects had made a home. Getting there had taken half a day's walk along winding, increasingly overgrown paths, up and down the hilly terrain. All of them in the expedition—bar one—did their share of lugging equipment, from stuffed packs to heavy cases slung between two people and filled with arcane paraphernalia.

Their arrival at dusk either accompanied or triggered a major swarming event, resulting in the inadvertent swallowing of more than a few hapless bugs. Skender pulled the neck of his black robe up over his nose and blinked furiously to keep his eyes clear. Even so, he was not immune. When a bug went up his nose, he coughed and spluttered and tried not to think of it wriggling down into his lungs. At least, he told himself, they weren't biting.

When the sun faded and the sky turned dark, the swarm of insects died down. The party set about preparing the camp for both night and a wraith attack.

Skender could think of a thousand places he would rather be, but it was Mage Kelloman who voiced the concern he didn't dare put into words.

"Why are we getting involved?" Kelloman asked Marmion when the journey was still in its planning stages. "The Swarm is the Guardian's problem. What possible difference does it make to *us?*"

"It makes a difference because people are dying," Marmion had said, not hiding his scornful tone. "Because standing by and letting it happen would make us as bad as the things doing it."

"And because you need the Guardian's help, I suppose. Let's not forget that."

"Of course not. If we want them to help us, we have to earn it. That's perfectly reasonable to me."

"Perfectly venal, I would've thought. You're talking about the end of the world, aren't you? A civilised person would willingly help, not have to be badgered into it."

"A person such as yourself, for instance."

Kelloman pursed his lips and looked away. He had no comeback, having been carried to the site on a litter, complaining of weakness after his encounter with the wraith. Skender had been appointed his attendant and was forced to walk beside his litter, listening to an endless spiel of discontent. If there was one thing the mage liked less than a forester, it seemed, it was a Sky Warden, and being forced to co-operate with Marmion and the others rankled at every turn.

But Kelloman had no choice now. He had proved his worth and would not be allowed to back out of the hunt, no matter how much he tried. The Guardian had appealed to his vanity in the end, painting him as a force to be reckoned with against evildoers and monsters. He had puffed up at that, and been reluctant to open himself up to charges of cowardice if he chose not to join the hunting party.

Once the insects settled down, the camp rapidly took shape. A ring of tents surrounded the knoll, under cover of the ferns. All those not participating directly in the experiment would sleep in light armour, and all would be armed. No one knew quite what to expect, so they prepared as a matter of course for anything.

Skender took the opportunity to escape Kelloman by helping unload the carts and backpacks. Not only did the foresters excel at growing trees rich in the Change, but they had developed an impressive array of biological tools with which to apply it. A crate of skull-sized growths as hard and dry as almonds and as black as ebony hummed with stored energy, grown and harvested from a species of tree particularly strong in the Change. A dozen tall poles, each composed of three branches coiled around each other, stood in for the crystals or stones used by wardens and mages. The potential each stored in the dense fibres and cells of the still-living wood was as powerful as a fully charged light-sink and had to be moved carefully. If one were to explode, it could easily kill the person handling it.

While the foresters had no distinct Change-working caste—much like the Panic Heptarchy, Skender had learned—two practitioners of chimerical plant husbandry had been allocated to the group. They explained how the poles and other grown artefacts could be utilised to channel and focus the Change around the knoll. Marmion paced out the knoll and its leafy surrounds, indicating where holes should be dug and charms laid. The perimeter formed by the poles would protect everything—tents and all—from the forest outside.

Skender kept himself busy sweeping the ground around Mage Kelloman's chosen site of any loose dirt or stone. As he worked, he kept his eyes down, telling himself to keep his mind on the job. It didn't matter what other people thought of him. He was doing the best he could. No one could ask for more than that.

When everything was in place, Lidia Delfine called the group together. Under the light of glowstones provided by Kelloman and mirror lights improvised by Marmion, Banner, and Eitzen, twenty people met to discuss how best to deal with the wraiths.

"The perimeter is in place," she said, coming to the point directly. "Once it's activated, nothing will get in or out without our knowledge, so the chances of being taken by surprise are minimal. Still, I want lookouts at eight points within the perimeter, watching in three-hour shifts. At the slightest sign, raise the alarm. The same goes for everyone. Don't be afraid to shout. I'd rather have a dozen false alarms than be taken off-guard once."

She handed over to Marmion, who stood in the centre of the cleared area on a very solid heavy box and spoke loudly to everyone gathered.

"I want to remind everyone of our objectives tonight. They're twofold: firstly, to attract the Swarm, so we can confront them, and secondly, to do what damage we can while we have the chance. We can try to talk to them, try to warn them away from the forest if we can, but in the end force is likely to speak louder than words."

Skender listened with the rest of them, unable to avoid filling in what Marmion wasn't saying. Only a quarter of those on the knoll had been present that morning, during the planning session with the Guardian. Only a quarter knew just how many uncertainties they had to negotiate.

How do we know they'll come? Marmion had said in response to criticism of his plan. *Well, we know the Swarm likes blood. We can use that to our advantage. But blood is everywhere. How can we be sure they'll want* ours?

Skender had glanced around the group, from Lidia Delfine's pale, tight-lipped expression to Kelloman's studiously maintained air of nonchalance. He wondered what he himself looked like, and decided *terrified* was most likely.

As well as blood, I propose we offer them something more substantial. In the last twenty-four hours, in an environment lacking specialised Change-workers, they've attacked me, Sal, Skender, and Mage Kelloman. That suggests quite strongly to me that we have something else they want, apart from blood. Those who know us will agree that we have little in common but the Change. That, I think, will draw them in.

A trap, said the Guardian, *baited with the Change.*

Exactly. Marmion had met her gaze unflinchingly. *And we will be at the centre of it. Well away from the city, of course, so innocent people won't be hurt.*

Of course.

And in the event that nothing happens at all, that our best efforts produce no response whatsoever . . . Marmion had shrugged. *Well, we still have something up our sleeve.*

To the group assembled on the knoll, with the dark sky above and whispering forest on every side, Marmion was brisk and businesslike, discouraging speculation.

"In a moment, Mage Kelloman and I will begin the work that we hope will draw the Swarm to this location. Wardens Banner and Eitzen will assist me. Skender, you will assist Mage Kelloman. I advise everyone else to stand well clear, as far back as the perimeter will allow, and to keep distractions to a minimum. We'll call if we need anything. The only circumstance in which we're to be interrupted is if you see the enemy coming."

"What about the Panic?" asked the woman called Navi, who had first named Chu an "Outcast." "What if we see them?"

An awkward silence fell. Marmion glanced at Lidia Delfine, who shook her head slightly. The Guardian had made it clear before they left that Seneschal Schuet's return to Milang and the message he carried was not to be made public unless absolutely necessary. Preempting hostilities would be the worst possible outcome.

Reinforcing that message, Schuet himself had remained behind at Milang. He would have come but for an order from the Guardian herself, insisting he recover his strength before throwing himself into danger again. The Seneschal had wanted to argue—Skender had seen it written in every sinew, every pore—but loyalty had won out, and perhaps a small amount of exhaustion too. Schuet's time with the Panic had drained him. He looked older than he had the night he'd fished Skender and Chu from the mud.

"If the Panic come instead of the Swarm, at least we'll know our charms aren't completely worthless," said Marmion. If it was an attempt to relieve the tension, it wasn't entirely successful. "Let's not make problems for ourselves before then. That's all I have left to say. I suggest we press on before we run out of nighttime to do it in."

Lidia Delfine broke up the gathering with a string of snapped orders. People moved off to follow them, dispersing to the shadowy fringes of the knoll. Marmion climbed down from the box and ran his hand through his thinning hair. He looked tired but determined as he examined the paraphernalia laid out before him.

"Well, my boy." Kelloman managed to sound both bored and put-upon. "We'd best get started. Do you want to darken those "stones down for me?"

Skender crossed to each of the glowstones in order to reduce the light they cast. Eventually, the knoll would be lit by three natural bonfires, stoked by Lidia and Heuve. The flames would release a noisy chimerical ambience, as well as provide light and warmth. As Skender went to adjust the last glowstone, a tiny, dark shape scampered across the ground and ran up his arm.

He squawked in alarm. Tiny claws gripped the skin of his neck. Two of the foresters ran over, asking him what was wrong.

"Goddess. It's nothing." He felt like an idiot. "It's just Warden Kelloman's pet."

"Not mine, lad," came the immediate protest. "Filthy vermin."

"It must've hitched a ride on the litter." He managed to disentangle the bilby from the collar of his black robe and placed it more securely on his shoulder. "Sorry to give you a fright," he announced to the group in general and to the two who had run over to help in particular. "I'll try to keep it down from now on."

As he returned to his duties, he caught sight of Chu watching him from further around the perimeter, frozen in the act of pulling a coil of rope out of a crate. When she saw that he had noticed, she brushed the hair out of her eyes with an irritated flick and went back to work.

The wardens dimmed their mirrorlights, plunging the heart of the knoll into a deep gloom, but not for long. Sparks flared as, with a crackle and a flicker of flame, the first of the bonfires caught. Skender hurried to Kelloman's side and helped him arrange a series of small jars next to where he sat cross-legged on the naked stone. The jars contained sand of numerous different colours, from pure white to deep red. Each had to be uncorked—carefully, so not even a single grain spilled—and placed within arm's reach of the mage. Skender tried to put all thoughts of the wardens and their activities from his mind, even though out of the corner of his eye he could see them making their own preparations on the far side of the knoll. He also tried not to keep looking over his shoulder at the dark sky and forest. If the Swarm came, others would raise the alarm.

And if she's *worried about me*, he told himself, *then she can find a better way of showing it.*

Finally they were ready and Skender completely extinguished the glowstones. Flames cast towering shadows all around the knoll, dancing and writhing like demented spirits. His skin crawled as Kelloman closed his eyes and began a simple deep-breathing exercise, focusing his concentration on the task ahead. Already the Change was gathering around the knoll, building up an invisible thunderhead as the Change-workers looked inside themselves to the source of their power.

Kelloman reached out with his left hand and picked up a pot of yellow sand. With eyes still tightly closed, he tipped the pot onto its side and traced out a single curving line across the bare stone. Switching to his right hand, he repeated the process on that side of his body. Then he selected another pot and another colour in order to create two more lines. He repeated the process nine times, until a complex charm lay completed around him, humming with potential. Even the partially empty pots became part of the design, signifying points of focus where energy gathered.

The night was growing unnaturally warm. Despite this, the bilby quivered on Skender's shoulder as though freezing cold. He reached up and stroked its ears in an attempt to reassure it. Tiny teeth nipped his fingers, and he hastily withdrew the hand.

Kelloman's breathing slowed to the brink of stopping entirely. Skender stood well back, wary of disturbing the mage's intense concentration. The charm was one he had read about, but had not seen practised before. Requiring advanced proficiency in a number of meditation techniques, it stood far beyond the abilities of most students—and masters—at the Keep.

As Kelloman's concentration deepened, his appearance seemed to change shape. The slight young woman whose body he inhabited became blurry and a glimpse of his true self came through. Skender detected more than just his tattoos this time: a new roundness to his cheeks; large hands with square fingernails; a long nose, hooked like an eagle's. His skin paled to white and he seemed to swell, as though holding his breath, but the exhalation didn't come.

Then he began to glow, faintly at first and only around the edges, but becoming stronger by the minute. Skender was reminded of the times he had held a glowstone in his hand and watched the light shining through the flesh of his fingers. The mage took on the same sense of translucent pinkness, as though at any moment he could become fully transparent and disappear into sunlight. The light grew brighter, self-contained, self-defining. Skender could see it, but it didn't touch him or anything else outside the limits of the charm. It simply *was*.

The mage's efforts reached equilibrium. Filled with the Change, at one with the deeper energies and patterns of life, he hung poised on the brink of the world, experiencing neither time nor thought. He could, theoretically, stay that way for a thousand years if undisturbed. Past mages had sought immortality through such suspended modes of being, but all had failed. No one on record had maintained the state for longer than a month at a time, and always at great cost. Some had never woken.

Kelloman had only to hold it for a few hours—or until the Swarm noticed him, at least. If Marmion was right and they were attracted to the Change as well as blood, then the mage would shine out like a beacon, brighter than the three bonfires to the right kind of eyes.

The bilby leapt off Skender's shoulder and curled up by Kelloman's charm on the side facing the nearest fire and appeared to go to sleep. Every now and then, its black eyes opened, as though checking on the mage.

Skender's attention wandered. There was little for him to do since Kelloman had achieved the concentration required except wait for sharp-toothed death to descend from the sky. Over in the Sky Warden camp, Marmion was staring into a wide, shallow bowl of water watching ripples form and intersect. The patterns they cast constantly shifted but never descended into chaos. These were the equivalent of Kelloman's static, sand-painted charm.

Skender thought about calling Sal, but decided that conserving his strength was more important, and he didn't want to distract his friends from whatever hunt they were pursuing.

It seemed like months since they had all been on the boneship and the Hanging Mountains had been a vague objective, growing only gradually closer . . .

A light wind sprang up, sweeping sparks from the bonfires high up into the sky. Skender tracked them with his eyes, picking sparks at random and following them as long as he could. In the absence of stars, they were the only lights in the sky. He wondered what it would be like to fly in such a dark void with only the three bonfires below, and was reminded of the first time he and Chu had glided together over the Divide at night.

Forcing the memory down, he kept watching the sparks, wishing he could float aloft as easily as them. His legs were aching from the long walk that day. Unable to rest properly, and with the fear of the Swarm dropping out of the sky at any moment constantly hovering, he sat on a crate and rested his chin on both hands.

Lamia . . .

The voice came from nowhere. Out of the wind and the crackling fires; out of the rustling foliage and the whispering of the foresters; out of the pulsing of Skender's heartbeat and the air in his lungs.

Lamia, come for me.

He looked around, wondering if anyone else had noticed. No cry went up. No one looked around questioningly. Only he heard it, like a whisper in his bones.

Come, Striga. Come, Lemu. Come, Camunda. Come, Phix!

As insidious as a cold breeze down the back of his neck, the recitation continued.

Come, Kukuth. Come, Kiskil-lilla. Come, Kalar-iti. Come, my sisters. Come!

He looked around again, expecting a reply although he didn't know where from. He wasn't even sure the voice was real.

I, Giltine, await you!

Silence greeted the cry. Skender held his breath, mentally and physically. A log fell in the nearest bonfire, sending a spray of sparks up into the air. He jumped as though a light-sink had explosively discharged behind him.

"Are you all right there?" asked a forester doing the rounds of the perimeter.

"Yes, yes," he said, hastily standing and brushing down his robe. "Fine, thanks."

"Are you sure?"

Only on second glance did he realise that the woman addressing him was Chu, not a stranger at all.

He shook his head, wondering what was wrong with him.

"I could hear someone," he said. "Someone whispering."

"Voices in your head, eh?" She looked at him thoughtfully. "I thought you'd be used to them by now."

She went to walk off, swinging a glowing barbed staff over her shoulder.

"Chu, wait." He took a step towards her, stopped when she turned to look over her shoulder.

"Yes, Skender?"

"I—" He found himself at a loss for words. *I don't know how to undo what I've done. All I know is that I don't know* anything. *Except . . .*

He couldn't say that.

"Nothing."

Expressionless, she turned and continued on her way.

Utterly dispirited, he went to sit down on the crate again—and consciously noted exactly *where* he had been sitting. The crate was unmarked in any way. Nothing distinguished it from the others, which was how Marmion wanted it, but Skender could tell which one it was because it alone had not been opened. It alone was still locked.

The heaviest crate.

Skender lay his left hand flat on the top, unsure what exactly he feared most: hearing the voice again, or *not* hearing it.

Come, my sisters. Come!

He flinched, but kept his hand in place.

I, Giltine, await you!

The wraith Kelloman had nearly killed and which Marmion had entrapped was calling for the rest of the Swarm.

In the event that nothing happens at all, the warden had said, *well, we still have something up our sleeve.*

"Warden Banner." His voice emerged as little more than a whisper. The night was suddenly dreamlike, a nightmare in which certain disaster approached, but he could neither move nor speak. "Warden Banner!"

"What, Skender?" She was at his side instantly, shushing him. "Has Mage Kelloman asked you to open the box? He should know that only Marmion has the authority to do that, and I'm not likely to disturb him at the moment."

Her wide, friendly face, framed with thick greying curls, was reassurance personified. How could he tell her a thing that shrieked and ate foresters for dinner was calling through a solid box?

There was only one good way . . .

"Here," he said, taking her hand and putting it firmly on the crate. "Listen to this."

"What—?" She stopped, frowning. "Yes, I hear it."

"What should we do?"

"Do?" Her wide brown eyes looked at him sharply. "Why, nothing. Let it call. If the others come in response, it'll be doing us a favour."

"But—" He stopped, accepting the truth in her words. That was indeed what they wanted. It just felt wrong that the wraith should get its own way. "What if it breaks free?"

She smiled. "Don't worry about that. If it could have broken free, it would have done so already. Isn't that right, Skender?"

"I suppose."

"You can do better than that. You can accept that you're still alive and talking to me now, not eaten by our friend here. That's proof enough for me."

She patted him on the shoulder and went back to assisting Marmion. Skender looked restlessly around. Kelloman still glowed, pink and radiant, with eyes peacefully closed at the centre of the elaborate charm. The mage wouldn't need his assistance until waking at dawn, or when the alarm was sounded.

"If I can hear you," he told the crate, "you can probably hear me."

He put both hands on the wooden lid.

"Hello?"

Lamia, Lamia, come for me!

"I'm not Lamia. My name is Skender."

Come, Striga. Come, Lemu.

"There's no one out here by that name."

Come, Camunda. Come, Phix!

"You might as well quit now, for all the good it's going to do you."

Come, my sisters. Come! I, Giltine, await you!

He sighed. *"Do you have anything else to say? Anything at all?"* Silence. *"Are you really in there, Giltine? Whoever you are?"*

When the voice returned, it sent ice through every nerve in his body.

I am the one who stings.

He sat with his tongue frozen in his mouth for a terrified, timeless moment.

Then: *Lamia*, the wraith moaned. *Lamia, come for me!*

Skender fell away, knowing the cycle was about to begin again. The wraith would call for its sisters by name, pleading for rescue. Skender wondered if it could say anything more than that. He sensed cunning and hunger in that voice, but little intelligence. It reminded him of a wild hound: smart in its own way, but at the mercy of its nature. He could talk to it all night and it might tell him nothing more than he had already heard.

Maybe they were the only words it knew. Maybe it knew nothing else except the hunt for blood and the Change and its companions in that hunt. Maybe they couldn't be reasoned with or warned away, and the only way to deter them was to capture them and bind them to iron.

So be it, he thought, quashing any faint feelings of pity he might have felt for the creature. That pity wouldn't be returned were their situations reversed. Of that he was completely certain.

Giving the crate one last nervous pat, he went to sit elsewhere.

The night air was clammy and cold. To stop himself shivering, Skender took a bracing walk around the perimeter, clapping his arms about his chest and stamping his feet. His back was stiff and his jaw ached. His feet made the only sound on the quiet knoll, even though some other people were awake—including Kelloman, still glowing, and Marmion, still concentrating on the ripples in his bowl. All but Skender sat quietly facing outwards, waiting. The fires had burned down to coals, and the twisted brands of the foresters glowed with a faint reddish light. The boundary, protected by charms and lookouts, was impossible to mistake.

Aimless, but needing to move, he circled the knoll over and over while his thoughts went in a similar fashion.

What was he to do about Chu? The distance between them ate at him, distracting him from what he should be thinking about. At any time that night, if Marmion's plan panned out, they would battle up to eight of the voracious wraiths. Wasn't it time to put their misunderstandings behind them?

Chu obviously didn't think so. Whereas before her irritation with him hadn't been sufficient to stop them interacting, now she studiously avoided even looking at him. He, on the other hand, had to exert the utmost willpower to keep his eyes off her. She had added a leather chest guard and gloves to her flyer's outfit, just in case anything with teeth made it past the knoll's more esoteric defences. That was something of an accomplishment—an Outcast wearing official garments—and one that had to be in defiance of every possible forester convention, but he did note that the uniform was scuffed and worn and lacked the circular insignia worn by even the lowliest soldier—marking it as the scrappiest Heuve could find.

Skender noticed the bodyguard keeping a suspicious eye on Chu too. Every time her duties took her close to Lidia Delfine, Heuve made certain to keep between them. If Chu noticed and was bothered by the constant scrutiny, it didn't change the way she behaved: she and Heuve still argued constantly.

Skender would have been happy to argue, to do anything other than maintain the simmering silence that was currently the sum of their relationship. If she would just let him talk to her . . . If he could just make himself try . . .

He reached his starting point and commenced his seventh circuit of the knoll. Dawn was still a good two or three hours away. If something was going to happen, he told himself, it would have happened already. The wraiths must have found better hunting elsewhere, or had enough in their bellies from the previous attacks. He would be better off saving his energy for the long walk home. So he reasoned as he walked past a glowing pole and realised that someone was standing in the bushes, watching him.

He stumbled in midstep, not immediately sure he wasn't seeing things. The figure was perhaps five metres away and shrouded in shadow. Not a large person, but definitely male, with hands hanging at his sides and face turned towards Skender.

"I thought I'd find you here," came a soft voice.

"Who—?" His voice cracked slightly. He swallowed, tried again. "Who are you?"

The figure's head tilted to one side. "Don't you know me, rabbit? You look much better in black. Funereal."

"No—no—you can't be . . ."

All breath left him as Rattails stepped out of the shadows and into the light.

"—you can't—"

"Oh, but I can and I am." The spectre of the jailer grinned at him, exposing blackened teeth. Shadowed eyes regarded him with menacing intensity. "You left me for dead. Do you remember that?"

Skender nodded. There was no denying it. "You deserved it," he hissed, remembering what Rattails had done to his mother and Shom Behenna, and the Goddess only knew how many other captives down the years.

Rattails came right up to the boundary line. "Probably," the man said with an uncaring shrug, "and maybe far worse. Does that make you feel any better about what you did, rabbit?"

Skender backed away, wondering where everyone else was. Didn't they see? Didn't they hear? The night had congealed around him like gelatine. *Am I dreaming this time?*

"Don't worry," said Rattails, "I'm not here for revenge. That can wait. Instead, I have a message for your new friends. Tell them to go home, where they're wanted."

"Marmion won't listen to me—"

"Not those blue-robed idiots. The tree-lovers, the leaf-fanciers. That's who I'm talking about. They're wasting their time out here in the woods. They'll see that soon enough—but I'd rather sooner than later."

"Why would I do anything you tell me to?"

"Because I frighten you. I see it on your face, in the way you tremble. I've been haunting your dreams since you left me to die. Isn't that right, Skender? I come to you at night, trying to wrap my skinny hands around your throat and hurt you as you hurt me. That's what *I* dream of."

Rattails's hands came up and squeezed empty air.

"You can't get me in here," said Skender, feeling as though he was suffocating. "You can't touch me."

"But I *am* in there, Skender. In your head. I can hurt you any time I want."

"No."

"Oh, yes. Go on, call for help. I'm right here, right now. You know who I was, and you're beginning to suspect what I've become. Why don't you raise the alarm, try to catch me? Why not, Skender? Could it be that I'm right, and you *know* that I'm right? That no amount of shouting will get rid of me? That you're stuck with me forever?"

Skender took another step back. The shadowy depths of Rattails's eyes radiated a malignancy Skender had experienced only once before: in the Haunted City, in the body of Lodo, Shilly's former teacher. Skender had watched that hateful intelligence strangle the life out of Sal's grandmother, and had been powerless to stop it from using him and his friends in any way it chose.

Something soft tangled in his heels. With a cry he tripped over and landed on an empty bedroll.

Rattails laughed mockingly.

"Ladybird, ladybird, fly away home," the creature said, retreating into the shadows as the camp came alive behind Skender. "Go back to

Milang, where *my* new friends have been busy. We'll talk again soon, I'm sure."

Skender lost sight of the dark figure just as hands gripped his shoulders. Legs surrounded him. Faces pressed forward, worried, well-meaning.

"What is it?" Curly hair surrounding a round face: Warden Banner again.

"A golem!" He felt himself lifted upright. His right arm stabbed into the darkness. "It was right there, talking to me."

"Voices again?" That came from Chu. Her familiar form approached the perimeter at a cautious lope. "I can't see anything. Perhaps it was another bad dream."

Skender felt like tearing his hair out. Trust *her* to be there when he looked like an idiot again. "I wasn't imagining things before, and I'm not imagining them now." He turned to the woman at his side. "Warden Banner, you heard the wraith; you heard Giltine. Tell her I'm not making things up. This is real. *I saw it.*"

Half the camp milled around him at that point. The brands defining the perimeter grew brighter at Lidia Delfine's command. Heuve approached the nearest with his blade drawn, inspecting the area Skender had pointed out.

"There are footprints," he said. "Human, one set."

"Don't follow them," Skender cried. Relieved though he was to have his vision validated, he feared what might happen to anyone hard on the golem's heels. There would be traps awaiting them. Of that he was certain.

The foresters ignored him. Delfine snapped her fingers: three of the sentries hurried out into the trees with brands held low to the ground, Navi among them. Warden Eitzen followed, a flash of blue against the green.

"Be careful!" he yelled after them, knowing it was useless. They would be, and it might make no difference in the world.

By then everyone had gathered. The commotion had shattered all concentration on the charms. Skender could hear Kelloman muttering in irritation behind him. He wasn't surprised at all when Marmion came to stand next to him, his expression weary and haunted.

"What did the golem say?" the warden asked.

Skender repeated the message, word for word, but only the relevant parts: *Go back to Milang, where my new friends have been busy.*

"Why did it talk to you?"

He stumbled through an answer that Marmion might have seen right through. It sounded flimsy enough to him. "The golem was in the body of someone I met in the Aad. One of Pirelius's bandits. I thought—I thought he was dead." *I thought the Homunculus had killed him.*

"What did it mean?" asked Lidia Delfine. "Is it trying to get rid of us? Is there something near here it doesn't want us to find?"

Marmion and Skender shook their heads at the same time. He let the warden speak.

"Golems are complex, devious creatures. If it *did* want us out of here, you can be sure it wouldn't do something so obvious as ask us to go. And you can bet it wouldn't give advice out of the goodness of its heart. It doesn't *have* a heart." Marmion's face was deeply etched with shadows. "No. There's something in Milang it wants us to see. Something that will hurt us, one way or another. I can't say that leaving now will make our situation any worse or better. I put that difficult decision into your hands, Eminence."

Lidia Delfine walked off into the darkness, her young face looking as old as Marmion's. Her right hand rested heavily on her sword's pommel while her left worried the back of her neck. Skender felt a rush of pity for her, lifted out of his own concerns by her uncharacteristic display of emotion. In a short time, she had lost her brother to a mysterious creature and had been attacked herself. She had had to deal with foreigners with mysterious motives and an Outcast who simply wouldn't obey the rules. On top of that, the latest plan to trap the wraiths wasn't going at all well. Skender felt nothing but relief that he didn't have to decide what to do next.

She turned, standing noticeably straighter. "The golem wants us gone, and I am disinclined to give it what it wants. We'll stay for the rest of the night at least, and see what the day brings."

Heuve bowed his head in acceptance of the decision. He clapped his hands to draw attention to him and began shouting orders. The perimeter was in tatters. Wide sections of it hadn't been under surveillance for minutes while everyone gathered around Skender. During that time, all manner of creature could have crept onto the knoll.

A jolt of fear went through Skender's exhausted frame as he thought of the crate containing the captured wraith. His relief at seeing it undisturbed was decidedly mixed.

"You should get some rest, Skender," said Warden Banner as Marmion headed back to his bowl.

He shook his head, knowing that if he closed his eyes he'd only see Rattails's face grimacing back at him.

"I should make sure Mage Kelloman is okay," he said, conscious of a torrent of complaints going unnoticed by anyone else.

Banner, perhaps guessing the truth, didn't push the point. She patted Skender on the shoulder and followed Marmion.

That left just Chu.

"Listen, Skender—"

The sound of Heuve's voice calling her name from the far side of the knoll cut her off.

"Ignore him," Skender said. "What were you going to say?"

"We'll talk later. I promise." She turned and jogged over to where the bodyguard waited, glaring. Skender watched her go with an uncomfortable, full feeling in his chest, as though a bubble growing there for days was about to pop.

The feeling subsided. With a deep breath, he gathered his black robe about him and went to tend to the mage.

The knoll never quite returned to the same state of poised expectancy as before. Heuve replaced the lookouts with patrols pacing up and down the perimeter, lit from above by the golden brands. Only the most hardened or exhausted managed to sleep; everyone else sat up working or whispering, whiling away the remaining hours until dawn.

Skender paced on, tired of feeling damp and half-frozen all the time, and wishing the fog would give him just a few minutes respite. No matter how he tried to distract himself, his attention constantly returned to where the golem had come from. Neither the golem nor the four people who had been sent to search for it had been seen or heard from since. He told himself not to read too much into their absence. Any number of explanations could account for it; but he didn't like the sick churning feeling in his gut, and the way he couldn't help but think the worst.

When the sky lightened, that feeling didn't go away.

"That's it," muttered Kelloman, breaking the trance he had resumed with difficulty after the interruption and letting the Change he had harnessed drain away. "I've had quite enough of this farce. Wake me when someone decides to do something sensible, will you?"

The mage stretched out flat on the ground with his hands behind his head, no longer caring if the charm he had so painstakingly drawn was disturbed. The bilby tried to sleep next to him, but he brushed it away with an irritable swipe of one hand. It circled him once, then curled up at his feet.

Skender cleaned up the jars of sand and put them away. Marmion was doing the same in his section of the knoll, a puzzled and frustrated expression on his face. The plan hadn't been a bad one and it should have worked. The fact that they had lured a golem out of hiding, instead of the wraiths, wasn't much of a consolation.

The morning could have got off to a worse start, though, Skender told himself. The wraiths hadn't attacked; no one had died. The worst thing he had to look forward to was the long walk back to Milang.

From the south came a loud bang, as of a light-sink exploding. A second and a third struck echoes off the mountainsides.

"What is it?" Chu asked Heuve.

"A bad sign." The bodyguard shaded his eyes with one hand, as though trying to penetrate the mist. "Eminence?"

Lidia Delfine's jaw worked as the sequence of three explosions was repeated. "The Guardian has recalled us. We must break camp without delay."

"What about those who went after the golem?" Skender asked.

Heuve pointed at two people, one of them Chu, and jerked his thumb in the direction the search party had gone. "They'll have heard the signal. Do your best to find them, but don't take too long. If you're not back by the time we're ready to leave, we're not waiting."

Chu and the other guard dropped what they were doing and hurried into the forest. Skender watched her go with concern, wondering if he should follow.

"What's happened?" asked Marmion. "Why have you been recalled?"

"I don't know," Delfine said. "It could only be something important. Mother—the Guardian—wouldn't disturb us for anything trivial."

"Could the Panic have attacked?" asked a forester.

"Perhaps the war started while we were away," said another.

"*What* war?" said Skender, wondering how rumours like this got started. "The Panic Heptarchy isn't our enemy. The Swarm is."

Some of the foresters looked less than convinced, and Lidia Delfine had more on her mind than countering anti-Panic rumblings. She had the camp to pack up and get back to Milang, and she had their failure to report to her mother.

The foresters hastily gathered their gear in orderly piles. Skender helped Kelloman prepare his litter and made sure all his accoutrements were safely stowed. As he was strapping down the cases, he saw the man who had left with Chu to look for the search party run onto the knoll and talk in hushed, urgent tones to Heuve.

The bodyguard nodded, then whispered in turn to Lidia Delfine, his face pale. When the three of them hurried into the forest, Skender wasn't far behind and was able therefore to overhear part of their conversation.

". . . not far from the camp. We would have come for you straight-away, but we had to see to them first. See if anything could be done."

"And?" prompted Heuve.

"They had been there at least an hour, sir. We think they were taken elsewhere and brought here . . . afterwards."

"Why?" asked Delfine, her tone aghast.

"To taunt us, Eminence. I can think of no other reason."

They came to a shadowy clearing and stopped so suddenly in their tracks that Skender almost ran into them. The first thing he saw was Chu standing in the middle of the clearing, her face streaked with tear tracks. Not thinking, just seeing her upset and responding with his heart rather than his head, he pushed past Heuve and Delfine and went to her.

She grabbed the front of his robe and buried her face in his neck. His arms automatically went around her. He felt her shaking against him and held her as tightly as he dared.

Only then did he look around and realise what she had found.

Blood—on the ground at his feet, on the undergrowth where the bodies had been laid out, and on the four trees around the clearing where they had been discovered. The bodies themselves were barely recognis-able as human. Their throats had been torn out and bellies opened. Eyes and tongues were gone, leaving sockets and mouths horribly empty. Naked, scored back to flesh, they looked butchered, not merely killed.

"Who did this?" he heard Lidia Delfine say as though through kilometres of fog. "*Who did this?*"

"We think—we assume it was the golem." The man who had accompanied Chu into the forest sounded shaken. *And no wonder*, Skender thought.

"Alone?"

"Well, it wasn't the wraiths," said Heuve. "We've seen what the Swarm can do. Look here." Skender did the exact opposite. "Teeth marks. Tear wounds."

"The Swarm have teeth," said Delfine.

"Not like these. And the Swarm don't eat the flesh of what they kill. They just take the blood." Heuve circled the clearing, inspecting the bodies one by one. "If I didn't know better, I'd guess a large dog or a wolf had done this."

"The golem." Lidia Delfine's normally deep voice had risen a fifth. "It knew we'd send someone. It waited until they were far away from camp, so we wouldn't hear them screaming. Then it attacked them, maybe picked them off one by one. It killed them, then brought the bodies back here for us to find. While we thought they were tracking it, it was long gone and laughing at us."

"You didn't see anything?" Heuve asked Chu.

"No, but—"

"What about tracks? It must have left some trace, after doing this."

"There *are* tracks, Eminence." The pinched, pale look on the face of the man who had found the site with Chu said more clearly than words what he thought of following them, after what had happened to the last group.

"Eminence—"

"If you're going to say that I shouldn't blame myself, Heuve—"

"No, Eminence. I was simply going to point out that the golem might not be long gone at all. It might still be in the area, waiting to see what we do next."

A dreadful stillness filled the clearing as that thought settled in.

"I can live with that," said Delfine. "Our first priority is to get the bodies back to camp and prepare them for transport. I'm not leaving them here for scavengers, or worse. We're taking them home with us. Skender?"

He stirred from shock at the mention of his name and looked directly at the woman. Not left, not right, and definitely not down. Keeping the red a blur at the corners of his eyes, he grated, "Mage Kelloman will be glad to volunteer his litter for this duty." And if he wasn't, bad luck.

Chu's shaking had eased. She stepped away and stood at arm's length. "We need to tell Marmion," she said. "Warden Eitzen—" She stopped, swallowed, and pointed at one of the bodies. "I think that's him."

"Okay," he said, trying not to think about who they had been. One of the bodies belonged to Navi, too. "Let's go do that." He took her hand and held it in both of his. "Is that okay?" he asked Heuve. "Can we go back?"

The bodyguard nodded and waved them up the trail. As Skender passed by, he thought he saw a glimpse of something new in Heuve's black stare. Guilt, perhaps?

Skender had more important things to worry about. There was blood on his shoes and on his black robes where Chu had clutched him. Her hands were stained red-brown, and her clothes, too. The two of them looked fresh from a slaughterhouse.

He felt Chu's need to talk: it radiated from her like heat. But her lips were sealed so tight it looked like she was trying not to vomit, and he didn't break the silence.

The knoll was abuzz when they arrived. That threw him for a second. How could they possibly have known? No one had said anything.

But the reason for the excitement wasn't the discovery in the forest. It was a messenger who had arrived during their absence and who immediately sought directions from Skender and Chu on how to reach Lidia Delfine. Skender gave them, and the messenger—a red-faced, breathless teenage girl—hurried off.

"Who was that?" he asked Warden Banner.

"Ymani, a runner from Milang. It was she who sounded the warning signals before."

"It can't have taken her that long to get here, surely."

"She was held up on the way, apparently, by someone needing help on the road."

"Did you hear her message?"

"No, but Marmion did."

As a group they confronted the warden. His expression was grim.

"Milang was attacked last night while we were away. At least twenty people are dead and many more have been wounded."

"Who?" asked Skender. "Who did this?"

"The Swarm," Marmion said bluntly.

Skender felt awful for adding to the man's worries. "You need to follow the runner to the others. You need to see what happened."

Immediate concerns replaced those more distant. Marmion noticed the blood on their clothes for the first time. "Are you all right? Is anyone hurt?"

"Don't waste time talking about it," Chu said. "Just go."

Marmion did, with Banner close behind. Skender and Chu were suddenly alone again. The knoll had fallen restlessly silent, as preparations to move out ground to a halt. Too much was happening to concentrate on ordinary chores. People clumped in curious groups, speculating worriedly about what was going on.

"I—I need to be alone for a bit," said Chu to him.

"Are you sure?"

"Yes."

"Okay." He looked down at the ground. She wasn't meeting his gaze. "Don't go anywhere. Don't go off on your own."

"I won't. I'll stay right here. Just give me a minute or two, and I'll try to be all right."

The rawness in her voice matched the redness of her eyes. "You don't have to be okay," he said. "Not for my sake."

"I know. It's not for you, or me. It's—" She stopped and turned away, shoulders shaking.

He understood, then, and let her be. She was not just trying to be stalwart in the face of death. The uniform she was wearing; the work she was doing; leaving her wing behind in Milang . . . everything fell into place. The people of the forest were the closest thing to family that she had. She was trying to fit in. She was trying to be *worthy*.

His mind full of death and foreboding, he went to give Mage Kelloman the bad news about his litter.

For the next two days, Kail woke up certain he would have to set the camel free.

After bathing and gingerly changing the dressing on his wound, replacing the sticky brown bandages with ones he had boiled the previous night and hung out to dry, he ate breakfast and contemplated which supplies he could most afford to lose. Without knowing how great a distance stretched ahead of them, it was impossible to calculate how much food they would need. Similarly with clothes—if their destination lay high in the mountains, he would need protective garb to avoid freezing—and medicine. The extra precautions he had taken had already proved invaluable. A wound such as the one he had received from the Swarm would have killed him had he not had the camel to supplement what he and the Homunculus could carry on their own backs.

The exercise in logistics sustained him on their journey until midday—such as it was, with the sun stifled behind dense layers of fog and gloom-shrouded forest—when they paused to rest. Kail was acutely conscious of his slow pace, but he knew better than to push himself. The twins' impatience was evident but contained. They made no move to strike off on their own, and probably wouldn't do so while their fear of Upuaut and the Swarm remained strong. That they had not been attacked since the ill-fated trap Kail had set for their pursuer was of little reassurance. *A wolf knows how to wait.*

The afternoon was spent walking again, waiting for the camel to slip or to baulk at a particularly steep slope. The overgrown path they followed led steadily uphill, following a series of long switchbacks up the side of the mountains. Under the constant cover of fog, it was hard to tell whether the slope they climbed was one side of a valley or an exposed face of the extensive range. Either way, the trunks around them grew taller and the undergrowth more variegated. If not for the path, they would have had trouble finding a safe route through the vegetation.

The air was cold, but unexpectedly still and close at the same time. Kail's clothes were soon drenched from his sweat and the moisture in the air. He took great pains to keep his wound clean, although he worried that the damage had already been done.

The camel plodded on, managing surprisingly well on its wide-padded feet. What it thought of their journey, Kail couldn't tell, but he was grateful for its perseverance. He walked when he could, and when he couldn't he rode, ducking branches and constantly brushing webs and insects from his hair. The richness of the animal and vegetable kingdoms of the forest delighted and confounded him. For every species he recognised, there were dozens he had never seen before. Hunting for medicinal herbs became difficult, not through scarcity, but because they were among such a large crowd.

On the second day he felt a strange twitching in the small pouch of valuables he carried around his neck. Assuming that an animal had crawled into it—although how that could be possible he didn't know, given that he kept it carefully tied at all times—he tugged it from its well-worn thong and looked inside. Several small, familiar trinkets greeted him, including his mother's bond-ring, tarnished and worn; an ancient metal spring he had found in a previously unknown Ruin; two square coins from distant Ulum, carved with signs for prosperity; a brief note on a folded square of parchment from a woman he had once cared for, whose name he now couldn't remember. And safely stored with these things, the source of the twitching: an opalescent fragment as large as the first joint of his thumb, plucked from a stone deep under the ruined city of the Aad.

He smiled to himself. Abi Van Haasteren was looking for the missing piece of the Caduceus, it seemed. Surveyors had ways and means of finding lost things, so it didn't surprise him that she had negotiated the waters of the flood and, on reaching the resting place of the powerful relic, realised that part of it was gone. The tiny stone gleamed and shivered in his palm as though eager to be reunited with the rest of itself—a unique artefact older than humanity, older than the Change, perhaps even older than the mountains he climbed.

He put it back in the pouch and placed it once more around his neck. Then he dozed as the camel plodded onward along the path, taking one careful step at a time ever upward, mindful of the swaying passenger perched on its back . . .

He dreamed of the vast, stony plains of his adolescence, where, free of the stuffiness of his family and the Haunted City, he had been able, finally, to find himself. The open spaces had simultaneously liberated and defined him. In the strange dancing of dust devils, in the shivering mysteries of the horizon, he saw a reflection of Habryn Kail that looked like a stranger; when he lost himself in the sky and the stars, he returned renewed, more sure of who he was than ever before.

The swaying of the camel's back stirred memories of boundary riding—his first paid work—prowling the edges of the Strand for man'kin; and well-reading, when he sought signs and messages in the reflections of boreholes. But moisture in the forest air subverted the dreams, changed them into something very different from reality. Water bubbled up from the bores and flooded the land. His camel was swept from under him, and the flood carried him away.

"Kail, you're dreaming." Seth's voice woke him from restless slumber.

"Goddess," he muttered, feeling the flush on his skin. "I'm not well."

"We should've left you sleeping. I knew it." That was Hadrian, disagreeing with his brother again. They might have been arguing about him for hours inside their shared head.

"No, you did the right thing. I need to be awake to tell you what to do at the next stop. There's a herb I need, a particular plant called harpweed. It'll be difficult to find so you'll have to look hard for it, then grind the leaves into a paste so I can apply it to the skin around the cut. I have a fever, and it's worsening fast. I might not be able to help much."

He could feel the sickness rising in him, fogging his mind and sapping his strength. The wound was festering, despite his best efforts. He didn't think the problem was poison in the wound. Just the air, ripe and heavy with moisture, a breeding ground for disease.

"Tell us what to do," said the twins. "We'll look after you." He wondered if that might be cause for argument between them, but didn't ask. He didn't want to know.

"What will happen if you die?"

The question took him by surprise. He hadn't seriously considered the possibility, although he knew it to be one. Far from medical help, in an environment he knew little about, with unknown enemies possibly closing in and his health fading by the hour . . .

"What do you mean, what will happen? You'll leave me behind and keep going. There's nothing else you can do."

"No, I mean what happens to *you*?"

"What happens?"

"Where will you go?"

He pondered the question, struggling to think clearly through waves of sleepiness. The proper answer was "into the air," since he, like most Sky Wardens, expected to be cremated on death and scattered to the winds. If he died in the forest, though, he was unlikely to be burned—he could hardly expect the twins to backtrack many hundreds of kilometres to the Haunted City just to ensure the proper respect was accorded him—so he supposed he would go the way of Stone Mages, and be buried in the soil.

When he tried to explain all that, he soon realised that it wasn't what the twins were asking at all.

"No, your self, your soul—where does that go?"

"My what?"

"Your essence, the part of you that survives death. Who you *are*, behind everything."

"Who else could I be but who I am right now, right here?"

This puzzled the twins, and prompted a swap of legends and stories. Most of his were about the Cataclysm and the early days of the Change, when the world was fluid and humanity struggled to survive. Theirs were about quests for secret lands, higher beings, or life after death—an obsession that struck Kail as deeply peculiar.

"Why worry about things you can't see or touch when the world itself is already complicated?" he asked. "Aren't there enough questions waiting to be answered without inventing new ones?"

"In the world we came from," the twins began, speaking in one voice as they did less and less these days, "humans lived in three Realms. The cycle starts in the Realm of flesh, the First Realm, where the physical body is born and lives. When it dies, the people we have become wake in the Second Realm, the Realm of the mind, where will determines the way life is lived. The First and Second Realms are very different, but they are connected, for humans anyway, by our lives in them. One follows the other as naturally as day follows night."

Kail had heard this before, but understood it no more than the first time. "Where was this Second Realm? Underground? In the sky?"

"Neither. It wasn't part of the physical world. That's the whole point. The Realms were separate; they didn't touch. To get there humans and other beings had to cross through Bardo and the Underworld, which kept everything apart."

"Until you brought the two Realms together," he said, remembering that much.

"Yes, but the important thing is the Third Realm, which connected birth and death by creating a circle. Reincarnation. We're born in the flesh; grown in the spirit; made whole by . . . destiny, I suppose you'd say. In the Third Realm, you can look at your life as though it was a tree, seeing every decision you made or might have made, and all the different consequences that flow from each. In the Third Realm, we get to see how things could have been, and choose a point from which to start over."

"Like a moth," said just one of the twins, perhaps Seth. "It starts off as an egg, then becomes a caterpillar. The caterpillar goes into a cocoon and wakes in an entirely new state. It flies around, looking for a mate, then lays an egg, which starts the cycle again. We're not exactly the same—there aren't as many transformations for a moth as humans have—but the metaphor is sound. In the Third Realm, humans are like moths trying to work out where to lay the egg. We get to try again, to live our lives over and over any way we want—the same again and again, or in new ways each time. In sadness, in happiness, in terror, in peace. The choice is ours."

"But now that choice is gone?" asked Kail, struggling to stay upright on the camel let alone grapple with the metaphysics of a lost world. "You brought the Realms together. You broke the cycle."

"I don't think so," said Hadrian. "The First and Second Realms were one in a time before we were born. Someone cut that Realm in half like we would slice an apple in two. Humans adapted, took the change in their stride. Then we came along and mashed the two halves back together. But doing that doesn't make the apple whole again. It just makes a mess."

"I think," said Seth, "that you live your First and Second Realm lives at the same time. That's why you have the Change—some of you, anyway—and why you don't seem to have any knowledge of the afterlife. We, in our days, had legends of heavens and hells inspired by memories of the Second Realm. Here, you don't have anything like that—but you do have Second Realm creatures all around you, like ghosts and golems."

"And the Third Realm is still out there," concluded Hadrian. "Humans must still end up there, otherwise you wouldn't be human. The signs might be hard to see, but they must exist, somewhere. Its existence will make itself felt."

"How?"

"The same way it did in our world, I guess. Prophetic dreams; people who move the wrong way through time; déjà vu."

Kail thought of seers and the man'kin, two types of being he found equally puzzling. "So if I died," he said, "I would go to this Third Realm and choose where to start again?"

"Yes. I'm sure of it." Hadrian didn't sound certain, just emphatic. "I can't imagine how else it could be."

Kail wondered what he would possibly do differently, and was immediately swamped with choice. "What if I don't want to come back?"

"I don't think it works like that. Does the caterpillar have any choice about becoming the moth?"

Kail supposed that was a reasonable question, even if it didn't truly answer his. He thought of the seer in Laure and her fear of the darkness: *Your shadow stretches before you, blacker than night.* The blackness of his own death, perhaps? But why would that have frightened her so badly?

"I'm not planning on dying," he told the twins as they plodded on through the trees and the thickening mist. "Just in case you were wondering."

"Good," they replied. "So tell us about that plant you need, and leave the rest to us."

Kail had quite forgotten about the harpweed in all the discussion about death and what came afterwards. That was a bad sign—one that would've hastened his end if he'd fallen into a feverish coma and been unable to finish instructing the twins. He told the twins everything they needed to know, and more besides, before allowing his heavy eyelids to fall.

The desert of his dreams awaited him. He strode forward, unafraid and heartily glad to see the sun again.

They camped that night near the intersection of the path they were following with another path, which crossed at right angles and led steeply uphill on the left and equally steeply down on the right. What lay at either end, the twins didn't know, but they saw no harm in halting nearby. Although Kail had slept most of the afternoon, his skin was flushed and sticky, his breathing as ragged as his pulse. Being bounced around on the back of the camel probably wasn't doing him any good.

They laid him flat and started a fire—a skill they had picked up by watching the tracker over the previous nights, just as they had learned to care for the camel without his help. Then they went in search of harpweed before the light failed completely. Fine, feathery strands dangled from a single, threadlike stalk, Kail had said, and the plant would be protruding from the trunk of unfortunate trees; unfortunate because harpweed was a parasite, one that reached deep into the heartwood and sucked it dry. It was also a powerful curative—the local version of aspirin, Hadrian assumed. It might make all the difference to Kail.

The forest was full of parasitic plants. They found several handfuls of the weed competing for space among giant fungi, lichen, and things they didn't have words for. Taking it back to camp, they became aware that certain trees visibly reacted to their presence, shaking their limbs as though in a heavy wind and dropping all manner of litter on them. The phenomenon seemed neither deliberate nor directed specifically at them. Not unlike a sea anemone reacting to the touch of a passing fish, Hadrian thought. A reflex.

But what did that say about the trees? That they were alive in a different way than normal trees? He thought of the creatures called man'kin and the way they reacted in the presence of the Homunculus. Stripped of the Change, they froze solid. Perhaps something similar was happening here.

Living trees? asked Seth, almost mockingly. *It'll be gingerbread men next.*

Kail was moaning and stirring restlessly when they returned. Nursing was new to the twins, an uncomfortable task they nevertheless felt they owed the man who had helped them since the flood. If harpweed didn't break Kail's fever, they were out of ideas. Watching him die wasn't an attractive option—for Kail as well, they were sure.

They crushed the harpweed fronds between two flat stones and added a small amount of water. The resulting paste had a sharp chemical smell that reminded them of eucalyptus oil. They scraped it onto the blade of Kail's hunting knife and set about removing his bandage.

Hadrian didn't want to look, but forced himself to. The sight was as bad as he had imagined. The long, ragged gash stood out against the tracker's skin: bright red around the edges and yellow in the wound itself. Pockets of pus were building up at two points deep within his flesh, and the twins paid particular attention to these areas. Seth wanted to prick the wound with the tip of the blade to relieve the pressure, but Hadrian feared that might start the bleeding again.

They had made barely enough paste for one application. It stained Kail's skin green but had no other immediate effect. They reapplied the bandage and put a wet flannel on the man's head.

Perhaps none of their efforts would make a difference, but Hadrian refused to worry. Instead he urged Seth back out into the forest in search of more harpweed.

With no moon or stars to see by, even their superhuman eyes had trouble telling the plants apart, and the night passed slowly. When they had gathered enough for two more full doses, they changed Kail's cool flannel and lay down next to the fire to rest. They would need all their strength in the coming days. If the camel could go no further up the steep inclines, they would have to carry the injured man to get help, just as they had carried Highson Sparre.

Seems our lot, doesn't it? said Seth. *When we're not saving people we barely know, we have saving the world to look forward to.*

Hadrian didn't sleep, kept awake by Kail's worsening breathing, but his brother did. Seth's dreams cut across his thoughts like intrusive daydreams, full of uncertainties and glimpses of their old life. Skyscrapers, freeways full of cars, television, blood, a knife through the heart . . .

An hour before dawn, Hadrian heard the sound of booted feet hurrying down the other path. He sat up, dragging his brother with him and shaking him awake.

Someone's coming!

So?

So it could be Upuaut.

Seth struggled to shake the sleep from his mind. *If it is, what do we do?*

Protect Kail.

What about us?

We're not running without him.

Making a stand, huh?

Looks like it.

They crouched by the side of the path, confident they couldn't be seen. Kail was more problematic. He was hidden effectively in the bushes, but he might stir at the sound or cry out in his sleep. Hadrian tried to ready himself for anything.

A glimmer of orange light appeared through the vines and forest trunks: a torch of some kind, held upright like a burning brand, but there was no sign of flame. As it drew closer, Hadrian could make out the figure holding it aloft. A slightly built Asian-looking girl of fifteen or so was following the path with grim determination through the night.

Something about the set of her face made it clear she was running *to* somewhere, not from.

As she neared the intersection, Hadrian stood up.

What are you doing? Seth hissed.

"Please," Hadrian called to her. "Please don't be frightened."

The runner's concentration was shattered in that instant. She skidded to a halt, and backed away, holding up the brand. "Who's there?" she called, breathing heavily. "What do you want?"

"We need your help. My friend is injured—"

"I can't stop for anyone." Her determination didn't completely hide her nervousness. "I have an urgent message for the Eminent Delfine."

Hadrian didn't know who or what that was and he didn't care. "Just for a moment. Please, at least look at him. I'm afraid he's dying and there's nothing I can do." He put every scrap of helplessness he could muster into the plea. It wasn't hard. That Kail hadn't woken at the sound of their voices was proof he was deathly ill.

The runner vacillated, peering at the shadowy shape in the bushes and clearly wondering if she was about to be ambushed. "All right," she eventually said, "but I want you to stand back, well back."

That suited him. If he and his brother came too close, the light she carried would stop working. He retreated four steps deeper into the forest. "Is that far enough?"

She nodded, sending a black ponytail dancing. "Where's your friend?"

"Straight ahead of you, lying down by the fire." What was left of it, anyway. Hadrian had let it die down during the night, not wanting to attract attention.

The camel snorted, and the girl jumped, raising the brand high.

"It won't hurt you," Hadrian reassured her, "unless you try to get it moving too early in the morning."

She crossed to Kail and bent low over him. The twins couldn't see what she did, but he did hear the breath hiss between her teeth.

"Can you do anything for him?" the twins called in unison.

She rocked back on her heels. "We need to lance the wound, get the pus out of him."

I told you so, said Seth.

Hadrian shushed him. "How do I do that?"

"You don't know?" She glanced at the paraphernalia scattered around the campfire. "You've got a knife, and I see you've been using harpweed. That's good."

"He told us to do that before he passed out."

She peered into the shadows, to where the twins stood. "What did this to him? Was it you?"

"No." How to explain? "We were attacked by terrible creatures that have tried to kill us before. Kail was hurt before I could drive them away."

She stood. "Are you talking about the wraiths?"

That was as good a description as any. "Yes."

"And you said you drove them away?"

"Yes."

"Are you a Stone Mage?"

"No, but my friend is a Sky Warden. Will you help him?"

The messenger looked thoroughly confused. Her sense of duty clearly ran deep, but Hadrian's talk of driving off the Swarm had impressed her. That much was obvious. She had reacted, too, to the news that Kail wasn't just any traveller.

"All right," she said, "but I have to do something first."

The twins watched, puzzled, as she produced three fist-sized seeds, like giant acorns, from the miniature backpack she wore, and fired them into the sky using a powerful slingshot. They exploded in midair with a trio of deafening bangs.

Fireworks? thought Seth. *I didn't think they had gunpowder here.*

They don't, said Hadrian. *But they have the Change, and it's powerful stuff.*

"What was all that about?" they asked the girl.

"A contingency in case I can't get through. The signal tells her Eminence to send a runner of her own. Three bangs for Milang, they say. But I still can't stay long. That alone isn't enough. She needs to hear the rest of my message as a matter of urgency."

"Do what you can," Hadrian said. "I'm grateful to you for this much."

She busied herself with the harpweed, the knife, and the embers, stirring the latter back into flame and carefully heating the metal blade. The twins inched closer by degrees, wanting to see what she was doing, but the foliage constantly got in the way. Her face in profile, elegantly boned and youthful, was all they could see clearly.

"Why won't you come out of there?" she asked while she worked, clearly having decided to trust them. "If you're so worried about your friend, why don't you help me save him?"

Hadrian recoiled, unsure how to answer. It was Seth who said, "Because I don't know how you'll react."

"Why? Are you Panic?"

"No." He didn't know what that was either, but judging by her tone it was something to be frightened of.

"Not a man'kin. You don't sound like one of them to me, and I come across them often enough in the forest."

"No. I'm not a man'kin."

"What, then?"

"I'm something different. Have you always done this—run messages from one place to another?"

She accepted their evasion without comment. "Since I was twelve. I may not have the longest legs in the world, but I am quick, and I can run all day if I have to." Her right hand worked the knife while her left applied the harpweed. "My name is Ymani," she said. "So you know who to tell your friend to be thankful to, when he recovers."

"Thank you, Ymani," said Seth. "We both owe you."

"Your job isn't done yet. Tear up some cloth to make new bandages. Boil the ones you've been using to make them clean. Wake him in a little while and make him drink. I wouldn't move him at all, if you have that option."

"I'm not sure we do," said Hadrian, feeling the shadow of Yod looming longer over the land every day.

Seth was, as always, less eager to run headlong into that waiting maw. "If it means the difference between Kail living and dying, I don't think we have any choice."

Ymani looked up like a startled meerkat. "Okay. Are you talking to yourself, or are there two of you out there?"

"It's complicated," Hadrian said, mentally cursing his brother. "Best you don't know."

Her eyebrows knitted together. Then she moved so quickly both twins were taken by surprise. Pulling the brand out of the ground and holding it like a spear, she launched herself into the undergrowth, following the sound of their voice. Hadrian and Seth stumbled backwards, flailing for balance. Roots tangled their feet as they did their best to get away.

Wait! Seth's command cut through Hadrian's instinctive panic. *Stop running. Crouch down.*

Hadrian did so, unable to resist the imperative of his brother's will.

Ymani crashed through the trees. "Where are you? I know you're in here somewhere."

The brand died the moment she came too close. A reddish tracery remained just for a moment, hanging in the darkness like a sketch of veins through a human arm, then even that vanished.

Ymani stopped in her tracks as darkness fell around her. Hadrian heard her breathing, heard the undergrowth crackle underfoot as she tensed to run away. He could smell her fear, her certainty that she was about to be attacked, even though it was she who had come after them.

"We don't mean you any harm," he said, knowing she could see next to nothing in the shadows before her. A hunched shape, perhaps, with too many limbs to be truly human. "It would be best if you left, Ymani. We're sorry for delaying you."

She backed away, holding the brand uselessly before her. It flickered into life the moment she was far enough from them. That only unsettled her further as she hurried back to the campsite.

"Don't move him," she said, picking up her backpack and slinging it over her narrow shoulders. "If you move him, he'll die."

Then she was running again along the path she had originally been following. Hadrian watched the tip of the brand bobbing through the trees. Her footsteps were fast and sure even as they faded into the distance. Ymani was making good speed.

And who could blame her? Seth asked. *We'd run too if we bumped into us in a dark alley.*

The thought was a dismaying one, but it possessed more than a grain of truth. Of all the people they had met in this strange new world, at least half had run from them or tried to kill them.

He rubbed the shoulder where the bandit Pirelius had stabbed them, outside Laure's steep, forbidding wall. The wound had healed perfectly, but a mental scar remained.

Come on, said Seth. *No point moping about it. We were never going to ask her out. Besides, we have to get moving.*

That's not why—but she said—

I know what she said, but what do you think she meant? She's carrying a message to someone that way from someone that way. How long do you think it'll be before they all come marching back and find us sitting here, twiddling our thumbs?

The twins stepped out of the bushes and looked down at Kail. He seemed to be breathing more easily, and the pressure on the wound had definitely eased.

Hadrian nodded, seeing the sense in his brother's words.

You think we can move him?

I think we have to.

Not before we've boiled the bandages. I don't think she was lying about that.

Seth didn't argue, and they set about filling the kettle with water from the camel's saddlebags. The fog around them was beginning to lighten, signalling the strange dawning of another new day.

What about the camel? asked Hadrian.

It can come with us if it wants. Besides, we can't carry everything.

The long-faced animal blinked uncannily at them as the water boiled and they made preparations for breaking camp. When Kail's wound was clean and the bandages sterilised, they picked him up in their arms. He was heavy but not unbearable for their Homunculus body.

There they froze, just for a moment.

What do you think is going on? Hadrian asked, unable to put the encounter with the runner out of his mind. *In the forest, I mean. Ymani knew about the Swarm, that much was obvious. Yet still she was out in the forest at night, on her own. Why? What could possibly have been so important?*

It's not our problem, brother.

I fear it might be.

Well, if it is, we'll deal with it when we have to. I don't think anyone can ask more than that from us. Do you?

Hadrian supposed not.

Kail stirred in his sleep.

"Easy, big guy," Seth said to him. "You get to sit this one out."

Leading the camel on a short length of rope, they headed off along the path uphill, and the mist grew tight around them.

THE CROWN

"The Goddess ascended in a vessel of pure gold. Together, she and the Sun-King vanished behind a cloud and were never seen again."
THE BOOK OF TOWERS, FRAGMENT 146

ttacked?"

The single word hung in the predawn air like a curse. Sal heard the disbelieving tone in his own voice and saw it echoed on the faces—human and Panic—of those sharing the balloon with him. They waited with tense anticipation for Griel to reread the message that had arrived with a flutter of feathers out of the night, strapped to the leg of a wild-plumaged bird.

When he was finished, he folded the paper and put it carefully back into the tube.

"Two hours after midnight," he said, with no discernible emotion, "the wraiths struck the city. Four of them in total, from two directions, under the cover of dense fog. They hit before the alarm could be raised."

Sal imagined them shrieking and slaying through the walkways and ladders of the airborne city. It wasn't a pretty picture. "Was anyone hurt?"

"They cut three stays of a dormitory vessel. We take precautions against accidents, but this was too much. Forty-five people fell to their deaths before the wraiths were repelled."

By the light of Highson's pocket mirrorlight, Jao's face visibly aged. "We have to go back," she said. "This is more than just a hunt, picking people off one at a time. This is war."

"What about Tom and Mawson?" asked Shilly.

"We've been looking all night and haven't found them. While we were looking, my home was attacked. People died. This is more important."

Shilly nodded, even though her friends were still missing. It wasn't about the dead; nothing could be done for them. Jao needed to go back to tend to the living, to help organise a counterattack, to search for *reasons* . . .

"We have to go back," Highson agreed. Rosevear nodded, curls bouncing, adding his support.

Griel chewed the inside of his full lower lip. "There's something else," he said. "In the wake of the attacks, Oriel has disbanded the Heptarchy and placed the city under his rule."

"Of course," sneered Jao. "Expect him to use this as an excuse to further his own ambition. He probably says it's only temporary, but a fool knows better."

"It gets worse still. There's evidence that humans were involved in the attack."

An awkward silence greeted the news. Sal glanced at Mikia, who raised her chin defiantly.

"I don't know anything about this," she said, "but I can tell you one thing. We'd never work with the Swarm. They kill us too."

"I believe you," said Griel. "Oriel won't, though. Most won't, while fevers are up. That means we can't come into the city the usual way."

"Is there another?" Mikia asked.

Griel nodded.

"Through the observatory," Shilly said.

"Yes."

Sal remembered the open skies and cloudy expanses visible from the empyricist's aerie. If they could get there, it would be a relatively simple matter to climb down the Way connecting it to the city and get past the guards at the bottom.

"How long will it take?" he asked.

"The rest of the night."

"Are you going to last that long?" They were all exhausted. The encounter with the Angel had been draining enough, but combined with the fruitless search for Tom and Mawson, and the ever-present fear that the Swarm might strike at any moment, all of their reserves had run low. Griel seemed particularly haggard. His hair and goatee hung limp; his broad lips drooped.

"I'll last as long as I'm needed," said the Panic soldier with grim certainty. "And I will offer you this much. My duty takes me to the city, but yours may not. By coming with me, you place yourselves in danger. I do not believe that you are responsible for this attack, so I will leave behind those who don't wish to come with me. Where you go from here will be your problem, not mine."

Sal and Shilly exchanged a glance. She looked torn, but he wasn't. Being stranded in a forest, kilometres from anywhere, solved nothing. He would rather be hard on the heels of the Swarm, even if doing so put him at risk from reprisals.

"I think we should go," said Highson.

Sal nodded. "Me too."

"All right," said Shilly. "And me."

Mikia pulled a face. "I'm going to take my chances on the ground. No offence."

"None taken," said Griel. "In your position, I would do the same."

The balloon descended until it brushed the treetops. A soft rustling came from the sea of leaves as the branches below swayed in a cool predawn breeze.

Mikia climbed over the side, then paused.

"Thanks," she said to Griel. "When I reach Milang, I'll make sure your side of the story is heard."

"I would be grateful for that."

She briefly placed a clenched fist across her heart and then dropped out of sight. When the ladder stopped moving, Jao drew it up, arm over long arm, and placed it in a bundle on the gondola floor.

Whirring, the balloon rose through the clouds. Sal silently wished Tom farewell, for now. Whether they would meet again, only the seer himself could possibly know.

Shilly drowsed as the balloon ascended through the clouds. Dimly she overheard a conversation between Highson and Griel about how high the balloon could go. There was a limit, apparently, which it would strain to achieve with so many people aboard. As the air thinned, its buoyancy dropped. At extreme altitudes, breathing itself became difficult. Eventually, the charms helping the balloon stay aloft would fail, and a return to the Earth would become unavoidable.

Shilly couldn't see why anyone would want to fly that high. It sounded boring and dangerous. She had had enough flying for one lifetime, and would trade the solid ground beneath her feet for even the highest view ever obtained.

"She's asleep," she heard Sal say to someone, and she wanted to correct him. Not asleep; just resting. Then the world faded away entirely, and she *was* asleep. And the dream came almost instantly.

Tom and Mawson featured in the beginning. Sand had buried them and she tried with all her strength to uncover them, but with every armful she swept away another wave rolled down the dunes and filled in the hole. The miniature avalanches came with greater frequency and severity until she began to fear for herself as much as her friends. She staggered backwards, feeling feathery tendrils of sand creeping over her ankles.

"Take my hand." The woman's voice came out of the sun. Her face was hidden in shadow. Shilly took the offered hand and immediately found herself at the top of a large dune, overlooking a petrified forest. Blunt stone stumps lay on the ground beneath the heel of a wide blue sky. The woman holding her hand was chocolate brown, with long, straight hair that made a streamer in the wind. Lithe and straight-backed, she had a proud nose and blue-flecked eyes.

"Who are you?"

"Do you really not know me?"

There *was* something familiar about her, but Shilly couldn't put her finger on it.

"We have something in common, you and I." A fleeting sadness crossed the woman's face. "We both came to the attention of ghosts in the Haunted City."

Realisation struck her then. "You're Sal's mother?"

"I was." Years of age and time took their toll in moments. Hair greyed and hands bent into claws. Mere moments passed as she turned from a beautiful young woman, not much older than Shilly, to a beldam old enough to be her great-grandmother. "I am no longer."

The woman's face changed again. Beneath wrinkles and age spots, she became someone else entirely, a woman with round cheeks, piercing green eyes and a slight squint. Wiry grey hair hung in a thick ponytail down her back.

"Come with me, girl. You have work to do."

The hand holding hers clutched painfully tight. Shilly resisted. "Who are you? What do you want?"

"I want what you want. You just don't know it yet."

"What does that mean?" Shilly found it surprisingly hard to resist the woman dragging her across the dunes. Her feet made furrows in the sand. Her wrist bones grated against each other. "Where are you taking me?"

"Look up," said the beldam. "See what I see. Know what I know. Stand still if you can."

Shilly looked up. A wave of giddiness swept through her. The sky was blue no longer. Night had taken its place, deep and profound. Stars turned in that blackness, wheeling and spinning around a central point. The longer she watched, the faster they moved, faster and faster until the horizon contracted around her and she was swept up into the hurricane of light.

"Now look down," came the voice of the old woman, clear and

gravelly through the scintillating brilliance of the stars. "Do what you need to do. Don't delay any longer. There's almost no time left."

Shilly stared down between her feet at a depression forming in the sand. The sand blew back to expose bedrock carved with a pattern too complex for her to bear.

She cried out in protest, "I can't do this! Why won't you leave me alone?"

"Just look," said the voice. "Stop complaining and really look. I won't leave you alone until you try."

Despairing, Shilly did look. The lines and whorls were as complex as ever, crisscrossing as though carved over and over down thousands of years. She could never remember it, never copy it down, not if she stared at it for the rest of her life.

Then a new presence moved into the dream, one she hadn't felt before. Male and calm, it too prompted a strong sense of recognition.

"Lodo?"

"No, but look here." Shilly's gaze moved across the face of the pattern as though following a pointed finger. "Doesn't that remind you of something?"

Shilly opened her mouth in denial, then froze. It *did* look familiar. She had seen something very much like it the previous night, in the stars above Vehofnehu's observatory.

"What does it mean?" she asked. "Who are you?"

"So many questions. Who do you think you're asking them of?"

"Kail—you're Habryn Kail! What are *you* doing here?"

"I'm not, Shilly." The tracker's long, lean face leaned towards hers. The way he appeared reminded her of someone coming out of the sea or emerging from a very deep bath. "I'm not here at all. There's only you. Only you . . ."

He faded back into the dancing lights surrounding her. Though she clutched at him, she couldn't pull him back. "Kail, wait! Don't leave me here!"

With a hissing roar, the sand rushed back in, swallowing the pattern and her and the stars, all at once.

Shilly woke in darkness, the echo of her cry ringing in her ears. Or so it seemed to her. The dream had been so vivid, so convincing—and yet, on waking, so nonsensical and frustrating it made her want to scream.

She sat up and adjusted the shawl Sal had draped over her shoulders. The air was bitterly cold and damp, as it always seemed to be higher in the mountains, sapping the warmth from her bones. Everyone was asleep apart from her and Griel. The Panic soldier hunched over the controls like a man tending a fire, occasionally adjusting a lever or turning a handle by minuscule amounts.

Shilly tried to go back to sleep, but her tiredness had evaporated. The dream disturbed her, confounded her. She tried not to think about it, but it kept returning to her thoughts. What did it mean that Sal's mother and Lodo's nephew had appeared to her? Were they ghosts haunting her, taking shapes she knew in order to taunt her? Or was she losing her mind?

And that brief moment of recognition, when she had glimpsed something comprehensible in the terrible pattern, where there had never been anything comprehensible before—what did *that* mean? Was it a genuine insight, or was her sleeping mind manufacturing insight where none truly existed? Once, she had dreamed that a talking, three-eyed crab had told her the meaning of life. On waking, she had been convinced that seaweed possessed a special significance. The feeling had persisted all morning, unshakeable despite its absurdity. Could this new feeling be nothing more than that?

She despaired of ever knowing. Insight or illusion, it was gone now, vanished into half-memory and confusion, where imaginary solutions to imaginary problems arguably belonged. She scolded herself for mourning its passing. Like it would make any difference at all . . .

The fog seemed to be getting lighter. She sat up and looked around, wondering what was happening.

"Despite everything that brought me here, to this moment," said

Griel softly, barely audible over the sound of the engine, "I'm glad of it. Watch."

The command woke new echoes of the dream—*Just look*—as with a soundless rush the balloon cleared the top of the clouds and launched into a sky freshly painted with the colours of dawn.

Shilly sat up straight, all sleepiness forgotten. The sight overwhelmed her, so wonderful and removed was it from her usual experience. Clouds stretched into the distance in ripples and dunes of pure white, like and yet utterly unlike a desert. The illusion of solidity was disarmingly convincing, leading her to wonder, just for a moment, if she was still dreaming. Or if this was the greater reality and her life up to that moment had been nothing but a dream.

"It's so beautiful," she whispered.

"Yes. I'd live up here, given the chance. Some say the King did just that, before the Cataclysm."

"Why would he ever come down?" she asked, speaking rhetorically rather than literally. She could think of plenty of reasons: fresh fruit and vegetables, coffee, the sound of the sea . . .

"It's said by some that the King was driven out of the sky by his own people; that they took control of the vessel he commanded and took it down, into the clouds. Another version of the story has it that the sky changed so much after the Cataclysm that it could no longer sustain my people. Rather than see them fade and die, the King ordered his vessel down as far as it would go, and relinquished command, for voluntary immobility was not something he enjoyed. His people founded the city and selected new leaders. A generation grew to adulthood that had never known the open skies. The memory of the King faded, became legend."

Griel spoke with longing and wonder—so much so that Shilly could barely credit it. His attention had shifted from the controls before him to the ancient memories he spoke of, and with it his posture had changed. He sat erect and twisted halfway in his seat to look at her. Light gleamed off the beads in his goatee.

"Where did you hear these stories?" she asked.

"Vehofnehu told me when I was a child. I used to climb to his observatory instead of going to school. He tried to get rid of me, but I wouldn't go away. I insisted on staying and watching what he did. When my parents found out, they were angry with him, tried to bring him before the Heptarchs for punishment. I had been earmarked for early service to the city, you see. My career lay before me, even then, and every day of missed study worsened my chances of advancement." He patted the stitched chest of his leather armour. "The Heptarchy was kinder then, more tolerant of Vehofnehu and his ways. I received special dispensation in exchange for a commitment to make up the study in my own time. That seemed reasonable to me. I worked hard and received a better education for it. Nothing I learned in school came close to that which Vehofnehu taught me. He said—" Griel paused for a second, as though reconsidering what he had been about to say, then continued. "Vehofnehu told me that I should become his apprentice. The offer honoured me, but I knew my family wouldn't approve. I chose the path they had laid out for me instead. Vehofnehu tried to change my mind. He said that age had taught him the wisdom of keeping a low profile, that more gets done in the shadows than in the light. We argued many, many times—and still do, when the mood takes us. Sometimes I like to stray from the traditional routes, as he taught me to do, but overall I feel I made the right decision. Vehofnehu, you see, can be wise and knowledgeable without always being right."

Shilly nodded, reminded of Lodo. Although she had trouble picturing Griel as a child, his story was enough to make him feel more human to her. Or if not human, then at least comprehensible.

"There it is." Griel looked over the side, indicating a valley of clouds that pointed away from the strengthening sun. A long, skinny shadow ran up the centre of the valley: a shadow cast by the top of Vehofnehu's observatory tower. The Panic adjusted the balloon's course and headed straight for it.

Amidst her relief they would soon be at their journey's end, Shilly was glad she had some time remaining to take in the view. The clouds approached infinity in all directions, but shied away from the brink; to the south and west, they petered out into empty air. Beyond that point lay the barren plains of the Eastern Interior. To the north and east, vast grey shapes loomed: mountains, jagged and forbidding, topped with ice. Compared to them, the mountains shrouded by the eternal cloud cover were just foothills.

Griel brought the balloon around the observatory in an unhurried circuit. He seemed to be waiting for something—a signal from Vehofnehu, perhaps, that it was safe to land, but it either didn't come or was too subtle for her to see. When he had gone around once, he came in closer, clearly intending to settle on the roof.

Shilly nudged Sal and reached further along the gondola to wake Highson.

"We're here."

Sal blinked in the dawn light and looked blearily around him. A freshening breeze caught his hair and draped it across his face. He didn't seem to notice.

"Cold," he said, indicating the view.

Shilly thought of Tom and his dreams of ice, but did not pursue the worry that prompted.

"How do we get in?" Highson asked Griel.

The Panic's attention was firmly back on the controls of the balloon.

Jao, stretching with arms that seemed to reach forever, answered: "There's a hatch. I haven't come this way before, but I have gone up on the roof from the inside. It needs to be deiced, sometimes, to prevent the windows becoming coated. It's a very dangerous job given only to the lowest-ranking novices."

"A girl died here, once," said Erged through a yawn. "She slipped and knocked herself out. Vehofnehu had been sleeping and didn't hear; he didn't know she hadn't come down. Only when her father came looking for her was she discovered, still on the roof, frozen solid with a pick in her hand. They say sometimes you can still hear her, when you're out on the roof, hammering away to get Vehofnehu's attention. And he always closes the windows on the warmest day of the year, just in case her spirit melts and comes to get him."

Jao laughed. "They're still telling that old yarn to novices? I thought it had died out when I was a kid. Mention it to Vehofnehu and he'll tie your ears in knots."

Erged flushed and ducked her red-frosted head in embarrassment, but Griel's serious expression didn't change.

"It's true," said Griel, as he brought the balloon around preparatory to landing. "The girl dying, I mean, not the rest."

Jao sobered, studying Griel with a curious expression. "How could you possibly know this?"

"Get Vehofnehu drunk and he'll tell you all manner of things."

Then the balloon was landing, and the time for talk was over.

Sal climbed carefully over the edge of the gondola and placed his feet one at a time on the roof. Although Griel had tied the balloon down and assured everyone they were perfectly safe, he still didn't entirely trust his footing. The wind seemed much more powerful here than it had been when travelling in the gondola, and much colder, too. The thought of slippery ice underfoot made him take every step carefully.

The hatch hung invitingly open on the other side of the slightly domed roof. Shilly already stood by it, waving him on, and he chided himself for being nervous. Clutching himself to keep the heat of his body in, he followed her as quickly as he dared and breathed deeply and gratefully of the warm air rising from the space below.

A collapsible ladder led down to floor level. The familiar space was in even greater disarray than he remembered, and contained no sign of either the empyricist or Kemp. A possible reason why became apparent when all of them were inside with the hatch firmly shut behind them.

"I knew you'd come back here," said a voice from the stairwell. A large female Panic with her face set in a scowl stepped into view. Her weapon wasn't drawn, but her right hand hung at the ready. Sal recognised her stormy mien, and the metal-clad ponytails.

"Ramal." Griel didn't sound especially surprised. "What did you do with him?"

"The old fool? Nothing. He was gone when I arrived. I thought he'd gone with you."

Griel shook his head. "He stayed behind to look after the injured visitor."

"Kemp," said Shilly. "His name was Kemp."

"He's gone too," said the soldier.

"Vehofnehu couldn't have taken him on his own," said Highson. "He must've had help lifting him, at least."

"If not you, then who?" asked Ramal.

"Why are *you* here?" asked Jao. "Have you come to arrest us on Oriel's orders?"

Ramal snorted. "Naive and foolish I might consider you, but not dangerous, and my line still owes yours a debt of honour, Kingsman Griel." She bowed in grudging respect. Griel didn't react in any visible way. "I'm here to warn you that Oriel is preparing a full offensive against the humans in retaliation for last night's attack. The dead demand it, he says. Until the humans have suffered as we have suffered, we will not rest. Oriel has, therefore, ordered the city moved to a new location where it won't be so easily found. Anyone who disagrees is being taken away as traitors. That's what you're strolling into. Are you sure you want to stay?"

Griel looked undecided. He glanced at Jao, who said, "We need to talk sense into *someone*. If we just walk away, we're as bad as Oriel."

"Hardly," Griel snarled. Then he nodded. "Yes, you're right. And where would we go, anyway? To Milang? The humans would have us arrested as spies, or worse."

Ramal looked at them as though they were dangerously mad. "It's your decision. But you won't get far with these in tow." She flared her broad nostrils at Sal, Shilly, and Highson.

"Don't worry about us," said Highson. "We're not exactly helpless."

Sal nodded. His reserves of the Change were fully recovered. It would feel good to be *doing* something. "What have you got in mind?"

"Charm our way past the guards. Shilly can help design something for the three of us."

"Of course," Shilly said, "but to what end? Oriel won't listen, and shouting on street corners is only going to get us arrested for sure."

"The Quorum," said Sal. "We'll talk to them, see what they can do for us. They've come from the future. They must know *something*."

She looked at him, wide-eyed. "Yes. Yes, of course. And we can see if they know anything about Tom while we're at it."

"All right," said Griel. "That's what we'll do. Ramal, are you going to stand in our way?"

The big female raised her hands. "I will let you get yourselves killed, if that's what you plan to do."

"Thank you. You're dismissed, then."

Ramal bowed with the minimum of deference and headed back down the stairwell.

"Right," said Griel. "You three get started on your charms while we try to work out where Vehofnehu might have gone."

Sal, Shilly, Rosevear, and Highson went into a huddle while the three Panic set about searching the observatory. Aiming for complete invisibility would be too draining, they quickly decided. Better to deceive an observer's eye into thinking they were Panic than to cloud it completely.

While Shilly sketched the charm required on a scrap of paper, Sal crossed the room to talk to Griel. "We need clothing or armour—as much as you can find that'll fit us. The fewer holes the charm has to patch, the longer we'll be able to maintain it."

Griel took him to a large chest near the entrance to the stairwell. It was full of clothes, redolent with the musty smell of the empyricist. "There might be something in here."

"Thanks." Sal began the slightly distasteful task of picking through an old man's wardrobe. Gloves that looked like they might fit Highson, even with their short thumbs; a brown robe for Shilly decorated in gold thread with the tree motif of the Panic; a broad leather belt that barely went around his waist. There was nowhere near enough to act as an ordinary disguise, but sufficient, he hoped, to shore up the charm Shilly was designing. He tossed aside a pair of broad, open-toed sandals that would never accommodate human feet and an endless series of faded long-armed smocks.

At the very bottom of the box he found a battered iron circlet as wide across as his outstretched fingers. Although obviously very old, it showed no sign of rust and was surprisingly heavy. He weighed it in his hands for a moment, then, feeling no telltale tingle of the Change, slipped it onto his head, wondering if it would fit.

As soon as the cold metal touched his temples, a strange sensation swept through him. He felt suddenly hollow, like an empty bottle— and as soon as that feeling registered, something rushed into him, filling him up like water, right up to the brim. Every nerve tingled, from his fingertips to the depths of his stomach. Every sense thrilled. He wanted to leap to his feet and shout for the joy of it. Never before had he known such vitality, such inspiration, such *completion*.

The voice that roared through him nearly knocked him off his feet. // YOU COULD BE THIS POTENTIAL SUCH GREATNESS INSIDE YOU WAITING TO BE FREED SUCH STRENGTH //

He reeled from the sound of it, although he heard nothing at all with his ears. The stream of words dropped directly into his mind with the force of weights. They didn't seem so much directed at him as granted him, as though a window had opened on the mind of something much larger than him, giving a glimpse into its incredible workings.

// YOUR POTENTIAL YOUR GREATNESS WHAT COULD BE I GIVE YOU I OFFER YOU YOUR STRENGTH AND SURETY //

Another window, another blast of pure, powerful thought. He understood then, that he was being offered something—a gift, perhaps, of power. He saw himself at the head of a mighty order, great and luminous, uniting the many disciplines of the Change across the Earth. Wild talent would no longer be feared or forgotten, an aberration left alone in the hope that it would burn itself out quickly. Instead it would become the norm to which everyone aspired. An era in which wildness was, if not tamed, then at least *used*—for wildness had its place in the world, and was dangerous only when misunderstood.

Beside him, Sal saw Shilly dressed in the finery of a queen, brilliant and insightful, the mind behind the power. The two of them would transform the Earth and its people into something wonderful and irresistible. Together, they would rule forever.

"That's not who I want to be," he said, hearing the words as though they came from the bottom of a well. "I know who I am. I don't want all that stuff. I have everything I need already."

The window remained shut, but the seductive vitality remained.

"I'm serious. I had this choice years ago. I would've taken it then if I was ever going to. Don't you think?"

// RELEASED //

The hole in his mind closed with a slam, and this time he *was* thrown off his feet, away from the crate and across the observatory, scattering chairs and maps and ornaments as he went. He skidded to a halt on his back, ears ringing. The crown flew from his head and skittered away, out of sight under a daybed.

Shilly was instantly at his side. "What is it? What happened? Are you all right?"

He looked up into her worried face, and felt himself break out into an inappropriate smile. He cupped her cheek, relishing the warmth of her, the feelings she evoked in him.

"I'm all right. I touched something I wasn't supposed to, I guess, and turned down an offer most people would kill for."

She frowned and looked to Highson, as though wondering if he also thought Sal had lost his mind. Rosevear pressed forward to examine him, but Sal brushed the healer's hands away. Physically, he was fine.

"What did you touch?" asked Griel, his face alien and unreadable.

"An iron circlet. It went—" He sat up and peered past Shilly in the direction he thought it had gone. There was nothing under the daybed. "I don't know where it went."

Griel and the others searched the observatory for any sign of the circlet, but it had disappeared.

"Do you know what it was?" he asked Griel. His legs wobbled underneath him as he climbed to his feet, but an echo of the unnatural vitality he had felt lingered still. The touch of Shilly's hand thrilled through him like an electric shock.

"If you were anyone else, I'd say you must be lying or mad." Griel spoke with his usual frankness. "But you're not Panic; you can't possibly know the legend of the King's crown. He may be gone but it remains, appearing in times of crisis to those with great potential. I always thought it was just one of those stories designed to teach kids proper ways to behave—like don't boast or you'll do badly; accept your strengths quietly and you'll succeed. But if you've seen it, received the offer right in front of us . . ."

Sal didn't know how to respond. Shilly was still staring at him. Jao looked more annoyed than surprised. He dusted himself down with shaking hands. The last dregs of euphoria hadn't faded, and he repressed an urge to laugh uproariously.

"How's that charm coming along?" he asked Shilly and Highson. "Can we get out of here soon, before I stumble across something else?"

"Just about done," she said. "Give us a minute and we'll be ready."

Sal had more than a minute. He had a whole lifetime ahead of him. He didn't need to be king of the world to enjoy his place in it, and at that moment, more than any other, it seemed as though nothing could harm him or those he loved. As he gathered up the accoutrements he had deemed useful from the empyricist's wardrobe, he hummed a tune his adopted father had once sung. Even that memory of past loss couldn't touch him.

Griel uncovered no notes left by the empyricist, no clues as to his whereabouts, and no indication that he and Kemp had been taken by force. The lack of evidence gave little reason for them to linger. As soon as Shilly was ready, they left the observatory and headed into the city. The cage made three trips up and down the Way, bringing two or three people at a time down to its lowest level. There they found that the guards had been dismissed by Ramal.

Charmed to resemble Panic citizens with long arms and jutting faces, the humans hurried along the floating city's complicated byways once more. Shilly avoided looking at Sal, unnerved by his altered appearance even though she knew it was still him, beneath the illusion. They encountered no resistance and few Panic; those they did see barely glanced at them. The mood of the city was tense and distracted by anger and grief. Children were kept indoors for fear of another wraith attack; windows were shuttered and doors locked; the only songs breaking the silence were in mourning to the dead. Griel didn't take them anywhere near the section of the city that had been destroyed, but the pain of it permeated everywhere.

Sal didn't seem to notice. Amongst Lodo's notes were descriptions of tinctures used by some Change-workers to keep people awake longer or to make them feel temporarily stronger. Sal's behaviour reminded Shilly of those descriptions. Immediately after the incident in the observatory, he had been restless, confident, unable to rest, and now he scaled the city's ladders and ramps like he was genuinely one of the kingsfolk. His thoughts seemed half a second behind his actions.

They met the first signs of resistance at the entrance to the place where the Quorum lived. There, beneath three golden balloons, each as large as the Alcaide's boneship, four guards tried to arrest them. Griel and Jao's names were on a list of dissidents circulated by Oriel, it seemed. People on that list were to be apprehended and taken for interrogation, or killed if they resisted. Griel, of course, resisted. Once hooks were drawn, events happened very quickly.

It ended with one Panic soldier bleeding from a wound inflicted by Griel, and another gutted by Erged. The guard who had tried to lunge at Shilly had caught the full force of her charmed walking stick right between the eyes and he lay sprawled, stunned, at her feet. The fourth had gone for Highson. Sal, stepping in to defend his father, had exerted his wild talent in response.

The shock of it still echoed off the hanging buildings around them. Ties and stays vibrated, humming notes too low for her to hear. Even Sal seemed surprised in the aftermath, and that surprise finally erased the odd look that had been in his eyes since trying on the iron crown. Now he was himself again, and she was relieved on that point, if few others. His exertion had disrupted the charm camouflaging them. Anyone looking would see them for what they were.

They discarded their makeshift disguises, useless now the charm was broken. Griel opened the doors and hustled them inside. They hurried along a spiralling corridor that led to the heart of the building, passing a series of interesting artefacts Shilly would have liked to examine more closely. They sparkled with the Change, clearly relics of the times before the Cataclysm. Two tall doors stood ajar at the end of the corridor. A terrible wailing came from the other side of them, piercing in its volume and distress.

"Srosha, why?" wailed a Panic female's voice. "Avesta, Armaiti, Mannah—how could you do this to us? Have we not been dutiful? Are we unworthy?"

A series of loud crashes followed. Griel burst through the doors, exposing a startling scene.

Shilly recognised the room instantly—the black-walled octagonal chamber lined with bookshelves that Sal had described—only now the books had been hurled around the room and the font at its centre had been tipped over. The fluid within now lay in a puddle across the floor, still casting a green light, so that shadows danced crazily on the walls. Shilly felt as though she had been plunged underwater. Her chest tightened instinctively.

Nowhere in the room was the Quorum to be seen.

"You too, Bahman? And you, Horva? Why do you abandon us? What have we done to deserve it?"

The cry came from a dishevelled Panic female of middle years on the far side of the room. Her grey hair, once long and straight, now hung in wild disarray, as though repeatedly yanked at in despair. Her lined face was disfigured by deep scratches. Hollow eyes gleamed in the light. She didn't react to Griel's entrance, except to exclaim "Why? *Why?*" at him, as though he possessed the answer.

"Tarnava!" He took her by the sloping shoulders and shook her. "Tarnava, what happened? What's wrong?"

"They've gone. Can't you see?"

"I see, but I don't understand. Was it Oriel?"

"No. Oh, no." Tarnava wept openly, tears smudging the kohl painted around her eyes. "It was them *themselves*. They left us in the night. No word, no thanks, no signs at all. Just gone—gone, and nothing left for us who cared for them all these years. What are we to do now? Why would they have done this to us?"

"You're a fool, cousin," said a low voice from the shadows. A second Panic female—Elomia, Shilly presumed—stepped forward. She looked as wild as Tarnava, but radiated potent fury rather than desperate loss. Just looking at her, Shilly knew she was the one responsible for the chaos wreaked on the bookshelves. "You're asking the wrong questions. They haven't left us. They haven't even arrived yet. In your madness you forget everything we ever learned about them.

"They seemed restless to us all week, forgetful and incommunicative," she told Griel. "We didn't realise they were settling in, that from their point of view they had only just arrived. They didn't know who we were, and yet we knew *them* . . ."

Elomia bent down and picked a book up off the floor. She weighed it in her hand then threw it at the wall. Her long right arm exerted surprising force. The book's spine split and pages flew everywhere.

Tarnava collapsed to the floor in a torrent of tears, wailing. Griel softened her fall, then let her go.

Elomia glowered at Sal. The incident with Mawson was clearly neither forgotten nor forgiven. "We should have recognised the signs," she said. "The day had to come eventually. But why now? Where *are* they now? Who sent them here? Will we ever see them again?"

Shilly thought of the strange trio she had glimpsed in the cave: Tom, Mawson, and one of the Quorum. Three beings who lived, partly or wholly, outside the usual flow of time. Three who had, along with the rest of the Quorum, disappeared.

"There's something going on," Shilly said. "Something bigger than all of us."

"There is indeed," said a male voice from the entrance. Shilly turned to see a Panic male standing with a retinue of guards behind him, splendidly armoured in black and gold. His broad face was twisted into a snarl beneath a shining bald pate. A slick black beard coiled down to two elegant points that looked as though they had been waxed. "It's called history, and we are all part of it. Some of us ride the winds of change willingly; others fight it and are swept away. The time has come to choose which path you want to follow."

"All this talk of wind is just that, Oriel." Jao loped forward, her anger a match for Elomia's. "The only wind you're riding is your own hot air."

"Is that so?" Oriel gestured and guards rushed into the room with hooks in hand. "You defy the orders of the Heptarchs. You help prisoners escape from the holding cells. You bring the enemy to the very heart of our city. You murder your own. It seems to me you've already made a choice. No matter how your lips may phrase it, your actions speak volumes."

Griel, Jao, and Erged were herded with Sal, Shilly, and Highson into the centre of the room. Shilly raised her cane and knocked the nearest hook aside, but another immediately took its place.

"You can't kill us," protested Jao.

"On the contrary, I can, and may yet, when you've faced trial. For now, though, you live. The humans are a different story."

"They're innocent!"

"Like the ones who attacked us last night, I suppose?" Oriel said, beard quivering. "A misunderstanding, you'd say. A mistake. I say otherwise. They have misled you. Their intent is and always has been murderous. They are spies and conspirators and guilty of crimes against the kingsfolk. I will not suffer them to live."

Shilly didn't waste time protesting. She took Sal's hand and spoke to him through the Change.

"*I'm ready,*" he said. "*Which one should I hit first? Oriel? The guard in front of you?*"

"*No. We need to disable all of them at once.*" Panic soldiers shoved her, Sal, and Highson together and raised their hooks. Green light gleamed off their sharp points. She fought to think clearly through rising terror, imagining herself gutted as the guard had been outside the entrance. "*Take Highson's hand. Use this charm, as hard as you can.*"

"*What will it do?*"

"*Don't ask questions! Just use it!*"

She felt Highson join the momentary gestalt and Sal's unease at bonding so intimately with his father. She felt her own fear at the consequences of what she was about to do. She felt the Change flex as the Panic soldiers drew their hooks back to strike.

"I accept!" cried Griel in a loud voice. At the same moment, a bright light flashed and the floor literally fell out from underneath them.

THE QUAKE

"We know for a fact that the firmament is
decidedly infirm. That it moved cataclysmically
in the past we take as axiomatic; that it might move
again is a possibility we cannot ignore.
Therefore two of the most important responsibilities of
a Sky Warden are to look for signs of such a recurrence
and to take all steps necessary to prevent it. These
transcend all other duties. The world is still recovering
from the last Cataclysm. It might not survive the next."

MASTER WARDEN RISA ATILDE: NOTES TOWARD A UNIFIED CURRICULUM

"It was here!"

Skender stayed well back as Marmion raged about the campsite,
clutching his injured hand to his chest and kicking at the evidence:
rapidly cooling ashes; the remains of a small meal; numerous footprints, human and camel; harpweed fronds and the remains of a herbal
paste; a patch of dried blood.

A Change-dead circle ringed the campsite, confirming what could
merely have been supposition.

"We suspected as much," said Banner soothingly. "The description
matched perfectly."

"But to have been so close—" Marmion stopped and stared at her,
wild-eyed. "To know for certain that it lives—"

"What is this creature?" asked Lidia Delfine, a suspicious look on
her face. "You made no mention of it when addressing the Guardian."

"I told your mother what she needed to know—as much as *we* knew, in fact. Anything else would've been pure speculation." He went back to pacing, unrepentant. "It was with Kail. That runner of yours named him, healed him, said he was travelling with one or two people who stayed hidden from her in the bushes. What in the Goddess's name is that fool up to?"

Skender piped up at that. "Sounds to me like he's helping the twins. I mean, think about it," he went on, although daunted by the angry look Marmion shot him. "They were together when the flood hit. The twins must have saved him, earned a favour or two. He's bound by that even now, as they continue on their way. Northeast, the same as before."

He glanced up the path the Homunculus had followed. It wound and twisted up the side of a mountain, but its heading was clear.

"Kail might be hoping to learn more about what the Homunculus wants," added Banner. "When he knows for sure, he'll make a break for it and let us know in turn."

"Or maybe he already knows," said Chu, "and he's helping out of the goodness of his heart. You may not like that possibility, but you do need to consider it."

"What lies in that direction?" Marmion asked Lidia Delfine, pointing with his one hand along the uphill path.

"A pass leading to the deeper ranges," she said. "There are mining villages up there. We trade with them for metal."

"Is that all?"

"*I* have no reason to lie."

"It's going to be hard for them to travel quickly, if Kail is injured," Marmion thought aloud, ignoring her dig at him. "They can't have gone far."

"What does it matter if they *do* go far?" said Skender, feeling a flash of irritation at the man's doggedness. "We have work to do right here. It's personal now. The Swarm attacked Milang while we were out hunting for them. Eitzen is dead. We can't take on every problem at once. If we don't finish what we started, we'll have the Swarm breathing down our necks every step we take into the bloody mountains."

Marmion looked down at the ground. The mood of the group became quiet at the reminder of their recent losses. Skender couldn't close his eyes without seeing flashes of red. Kelloman's litter was a sombre and very heavy presence behind them.

"I hear you, Skender Van Haasteren," Marmion said. "I hear you, and I know you are right. Yet I would chase this thing to the end of the world if I thought it would divert what's coming. A few lives will make no difference."

"A few lives?" spat Lidia Delfine. "The end of the world? You will speak plainly with us, warden, or I'll send you back to your Alcaide in six pieces."

Marmion's balding head bobbed in a nod. "I'll tell you all, if we keep moving while I do so. I'm anxious to deal with these wraiths so my real quest can resume. We have been held up too long already."

The party of foresters and sundry other people resumed their march for Milang, leaving the brief resting place of Kail and the Homunculus behind. Wondering at this unexpected turn of events, Skender attempted to raise Sal through the Change, but he received no response. That gave him even more reason to worry, and he wished he hadn't tried.

The path snaked at a constant height along the rippling side of the mountain range, so they walked with tree trunks crowding on their left and the canopy sloping steeply downward to their right. Kelloman and Chu brought up the rear of the column—the mage because he constantly dragged his heels, and Chu because she had been assigned there by Heuve. She didn't look happy about it, either. In the rush to break camp, there had been no time for her and Skender to have the talk that she had promised. Skender, walking a little ahead of them and listening in to their conversation without trying to make it too obvious, could feel the tension boiling inside her. He wasn't surprised at all when she tried to pick a fight.

"Is this your pet?" she innocently asked the mage, stroking the ears of the bilby perched on her shoulder.

"Certainly not. The filthy thing is covered with fleas."

"It seems perfectly healthy to me. What about the girl?"

"Which girl? What about her?"

"The girl whose body you're inhabiting, of course."

"There's nothing to know."

"Who was she? What happened to her? Why was she given to you?"

"That is of no relevance to me. Why would I care?"

"It just seems odd to me, that's all—being in someone else's body. I can't imagine what it must be like."

"Uncomfortable, if you must know."

"Would you prefer to be in a man's body?"

"Bee's whiskers, girl, you ask the most impertinent questions!"

"That's the best way to learn. Or so I'm told."

Kelloman blustered for a moment, then answered her question. "Of course I'd prefer a man's body. But this is what I was given. I've tried to change it, and they won't let me. It's a concerted campaign, you know—a deliberate attempt to break my will. My so-called friends back home punish me by sending me here. The people here do their utmost to make me go home. Well, I won't give in to either of them. Do you hear me? I won't!"

"The whole forest can probably hear you."

"And who are you to question me? Outcast and bloodletter—"

"Hey—I have nothing to do with the yadachi, and it's not my fault my family left the forest. I wasn't even born when that happened."

"And it's not *my* fault this poor child ate moonflower that hadn't been cured properly and lost her mind as a result!"

"So you *do* know."

"Of course. I'm not a complete ass. She did it on a dare to impress some boy. But that doesn't change anything. Her stupidity has become my prison."

"How is it your prison, really? She's young and healthy."

"Well, there's the family to think of, and the people she knew. I'm obviously keen to spare them further distress—but how can I do that? It's impossible to avoid all of them all of the time."

"What about you? Does it cause *you* distress?"

Kelloman said nothing for a long while, and that silence was more eloquent than anything the mage could ever have said.

Some of the tension left Chu, then. "Do you know what I think?" she prompted.

"No, and I'm not entirely certain I care to hear it."

"I think this little fellow was her pet."

"Preposterous. The girl's mind is dead."

"But her body is still alive. That's what the bilby recognises. No matter how much you might care to ignore it, part of her is still here, and you should honour it."

A strange thing happened then that brought the entire party to a halt. With an explosive release of colour and noise, every bird in every tree surrounding them took to the air and flew off into the fog. Birds from further afield joined the throng, flying overhead with a deafening clapping of wings.

Skender stood stock still, gaping up at the riotous mayhem. From the front of the column, he heard Marmion exclaim, "What the Goddess . . . ?"

Then the ground kicked beneath them and Skender fell to his knees. The trees shook as though in a heavy wind. Trunks swayed; dead branches fell. Skender dived forward and clutched the treacherous Earth, seeking stability it didn't provide.

The tremor lasted a dozen breaths but felt like a lifetime. Even as the deep rumble eased, the danger didn't pass. Over cries of relief came a new sound, this time from above: a growing roar that could only be one thing.

"Avalanche!" cried Lidia Delfine, waving people to her. What good *that* would do, Skender couldn't imagine, but he went along with them on shaky legs. He found himself pressed between Chu, Kelloman, and a large man whose eyes were slitted, almost closed. The roar became louder but he could see nothing through the fog. It sounded like half the mountain was coming down on them.

Skender felt the ground kick again—then the roaring was all around them. The air swirled as though stirred by a giant hand. Chu's mouth was open but he couldn't hear her screaming, the noise was so loud.

Incredibly, it passed. Dust rolled over them, thick and cloying in the humid air. He coughed and heard others doing likewise as his hearing returned. The day turned yellow and dark.

"Is everyone all right?" Heuve and Lidia Delfine moved through the party one at a time, checking to make sure no one had been hurt. Skender and Chu nodded dumbly when their turn came, not realising until then just how tightly they were clinging to each other. They stepped apart, avoiding each other's gaze.

"That was close," said Banner. Her hair and face were coated with dust. "Does that happen here often?"

"The occasional tremor, yes," said Lidia Delfine, "but rarely like this. The last one was just before the flood."

Kelloman interrupted them. "That was no ordinary quake."

All eyes turned to him. "What do you mean?" asked Marmion.

"Earthquakes are natural occurrences. The Earth flexes, changes—just like us, only on a much longer timescale. Sometimes it shrugs to make itself sit more comfortably, to relieve a growing tension, or in response to pressure elsewhere."

"Yes, yes. But you're saying this wasn't like that?"

"It didn't feel so to me." Kelloman bristled at being rushed. "There was no warning, no natural trigger. Whatever caused this earthquake, it wasn't the Earth."

Lidia Delfine exchanged a quick glance with Heuve. "Thank you,

Stone Mage Kelloman," she said. "We'll talk about this more when we return to Milang. Until then, checking that the path is still passable is the most important thing."

She called out instructions and the tight huddle began to break up. Chu stepped in close to Kelloman to whisper, "Nice one. What did you go and mention that for?"

"Why wouldn't I?"

"Because this lot's already half-expecting another flood, another village to be wiped out. And now you've suggested that the Panic might be behind it."

"I didn't say that. I just said it wasn't natural."

"Which means something apart from nature is behind it. And that means some*one*. Who else do they have to point their fingers at apart from the Panic?"

"The wraiths, the golem—"

"And us, sure. There are lots of possibilities. But I think their traditional enemies will be assumed guilty first, don't you?"

Kelloman looked somewhat abashed, but still irritated. "These people—I mean, *really*—"

"We're no different," said Marmion. "Let's not be guilty of the same assumptions they make, eh?"

A series of shouts and whistles saw the column moving again. Marmion hurried off into the mist, heading for the lead. Word spread back that the path was intact and that all should make the utmost haste or be left behind. Kelloman scowled but stepped up the pace.

Chu came to walk with Skender, but didn't make any overtures to talk. Skender honoured that silence. Just moments ago he had been certain they were both about to die. It wasn't the first time he had felt that way around her, and he was certain the feeling was mutual. Words couldn't do it justice.

Silence was enough, for now.

A trio of blasts sent the birds—only recently returned after the shock of the quake—scattering up into the air again. Three more came soon after, prompting Lidia Delfine to split the party in two. She and the fastest runners would go ahead while the rest followed on. Heuve chose Chu to be one of the runners, but not Skender.

"Don't worry," she said, giving him the bilby. "I'm sure it's nothing personal. You've just got stumpy legs."

"I don't see why you're so keen to go running anywhere. It sounds like hard work to me."

"Hey, yeah." Her face fell. "Maybe it *is* personal. That son of a bitch . . ."

She went off to argue with Heuve, and didn't return. Lidia Delfine and her honour guard disappeared into the mist with a rattling of armour and rapid tramping of feet.

Marmion had stayed behind in the slower-moving group along with Skender, Banner, and Kelloman. Four guards escorted them.

"Any idea what's going on?" Skender asked Marmion.

"Another messenger arrived from Milang. I didn't catch all of it, but he said something about the Panic being on the move."

"That could mean anything."

"It could, yes, but it will most likely be taken one way. After the message Seneschal Schuet brought, and rising tensions between the two parties . . ." Marmion looked grim. "I fear this will not end well."

They passed within sight of a moai, perched above the path on a natural shelf where it might have sat for centuries for all Skender could tell. It had tilted to its right, giving it a slightly dangerous air. Its wide eyes and shadowed brow revealed nothing of its inner thoughts. The ghostly moan issuing from its wide mouth was equally uninformative.

"Why do they do that?" asked Banner, looking pained at the sound.

"We don't know," said one of their escorts. "They don't normally. It started three weeks ago, out of nowhere."

"Is it getting worse?"

"Much worse today."

Skender performed a quick mental calculation. "Three weeks is about the time that Highson Sparre made the Homunculus."

Marmion nodded. "I think they're afraid."

Skender looked up at the strange face peering out from the undergrowth. *Afraid?* he wondered. "Of what?"

The warden shrugged. "Perhaps nothing more than another flood. The first one must have swept a few of them away down the Divide, maybe smashed them to pieces. They're not really capable of running away, no matter how much warning the Angel gives."

Skender thought of the man'kin he had met in Laure and the Divide repeating "*Angel says run*" and the many hundreds of them who had run to Laure and taken shelter behind the city's charmed wall. He shuddered to think of being trapped in the face of that terrible deluge, able to do nothing but watch it bearing down and sweeping him away. He had come quite close enough to that as it was.

"There have been reports," their escort said, "of moai being stolen by other man'kin. You wouldn't know anything about that, would you?"

Before Skender could hazard a guess, a shadow passed over the path. The guards immediately pulled them off the path and under the cover of the trees, practically dragging Kelloman off his feet.

"Was that really necessary?" the mage blustered.

"Balloon," explained the escort with the beaded hair.

"Does that mean the Panic?" asked Marmion.

"Yes." The shadow slipped silently into the forest but still the guards kept them motionless. "There could be more. Combat blimps sometimes travel in pairs."

"Is that what the messenger meant by them being on the move?"

Skender asked. He had pictured the Panic crossing the forest much as they were, in single file through the trees.

"They always travel by air," said the guard, "sneaking around in the clouds and dropping things on people, only coming down to steal our crops and livestock. Get them on the ground where we can fight them face to face and they won't last long. Trust me."

"They live in a floating city, you know," said Kelloman to Skender. "Never seen it myself, but one hears rumours. As big as the Haunted City, apparently, and strung about with the skulls of their enemies."

Marmion looked at the guard. "Do you believe that?"

"I believe they're overhead right now and heading for my home," she responded defensively. "Are you trying to claim otherwise?"

"No, no." The warden peered up at the sky. "There's no sign of a second one, though. Perhaps we should keep moving."

They picked up their baggage and hurried along the path. Not long after, a second earthquake rocked the mountainside, milder than before but no less frightening for it. Skender held his breath and waited for the ominous rumble of another avalanche. None came, and he was profoundly grateful.

A runner overtook them, heading for Milang. Even younger than the first one Skender had met, he stopped to accept their offer of water and gave them part of his message. Word had been sent from an observation post north along the wall of mountains, relayed by any means possible to the Guardian in Milang: spies had seen the Panic city shifting location.

"It's headed for Milang," said the runner, losing some of his bright pink colour and beginning to breathe more easily. "The Panic are going to destroy the Guardian!"

Then the runner was off again, sprinting through the forest bearing the terrible news on his skinny shoulders.

Marmion opened his mouth to speak. The guard glared at him, and he shut it.

As they resumed their journey, Skender glanced backwards over his shoulder, half-expecting a much larger shadow to fall over him—that of an entire city, bristling with murderous warriors. He tried not to believe it, but all he knew of the Panic came secondhand, plus a few frightening minutes of fighting. One had died at his feet. *Pan troglodytes sapiens.* He had only Sal's word that they were peaceful.

When he tried to call Sal, he again received nothing but silence in reply. The thought occurred to him then that maybe his friend's last message had been sent under duress. What if he had been used to make the humans drop their guard and the city of Milang more vulnerable? While Lidia Delfine had been off wraith-hunting, perhaps the Panic Heptarchy had been arming for war.

He hoped not—for Sal and Shilly's sake, as well as for himself and all the citizens of Milang.

THE BLUFF

"Death is not the opposite of life. Death is the opposite of conception. Both can happen in an instant, unplanned and calamitous; both can bring joy and pain in equal measures. But if death is not the opposite of life, what is?"
THE BOOK OF TOWERS, EXEGESIS 13:15

"*Take Highson's hand. Use this charm, as hard as you can.*"
"*What will it do?*"
"*Don't ask questions! Just use it!*"

Sal grasped the charm with his mind, turned it and shaped his will around it, filled every thought with its elegant complexity. Dimly he perceived the Panic guards shoving him, but he couldn't afford the distraction. Griel bellowed something just as he flexed his will and brought the charm to life, but he stayed focused.

Metal tore. Sparks flew. Weightlessness overwhelmed him, sudden and startling.

Then they were falling into smoke and billowing mist, down through the floor of the Quorum chamber, away from the shrieking cousins, Tarnava and Elomia, and away from the furious bellowing of Oriel and the guards. Seven people—Sal, Shilly, Highson, and Rosevear; Griel, Jao, and Erged—suddenly airborne, dropped out of the bottom of the floating building, free but not yet safe, their future suddenly and frighteningly unknown.

And potentially very, very short. As long as it took to drop from the floating city to the ground below. Not far or long enough, Sal suspected.

The Change flared a second time. Fog gathered around them in a dense cloud and turned to frost with a crisp crackling sound. Barely had he time to grip Shilly's hands tighter, to attempt to draw her closer to him, when a broad flat surface came out of nowhere and smacked them apart. The surface flexed like rubber. He literally bounced through the air. Frost turned to ice against his skin as something much more solid loomed out of the mist. This time a metal surface struck him, sending him into a tumble. The ice made it hard to find and keep a purchase. Seams slid by, bruising him, and it was against one of these that he finally scrambled to a halt.

Momentarily winded, it was all he could do just to breathe for a moment and wonder at his survival.

They had fallen. The charm Shilly had given him had blasted a hole in the bottom of the Quorum chamber and they had dropped right through it. Instead of plummeting to the ground, however, they had landed on another part of the Panic city—a fog-collecting vane, perhaps—lower than the one they had been on, and suspended from the upper one by wires and stays, just as every part of the city seemed to support one or more other parts. From there they had bounced onto the next solid structure down. Had that been Shilly's intention all along? Or had she simply taken the only way out she knew, and luck had been on their side?

He didn't care to know, for the moment. Scrambling painfully to his feet—being careful not to slip, for the surface beneath him sloped increasingly downward to a drop shrouded in mist—he sought the others who had fallen with him.

"Shilly! Highson!"

"Over here!" The cry came faintly through the fog: Shilly's voice, some distance away. Sal set off in that direction, wondering what sort of structure they had landed on. The sky around him contained little but the suggestion of shapes: faint outlines of neighbouring habitats and walkways, all connected to balloons invisible above.

A distinctive Panic silhouette loomed out of the mist. "Griel?"

"No." Blood trickled down Erged's face from a gash on his temple. "He fell over there, I think." He pointed in the same direction as Shilly. "What happened?"

Sal briefly outlined the effects of the charm Shilly had made as he helped the Panic across the strange metal surface. "Then Highson condensed the mist around us," he explained, remembering the frost that had formed as they fell and working out for himself where it had come from. "That cushioned the impact."

Erged still looked slightly dazed. "Oriel?"

"Probably still trying to work out where we went." Sal looked upwards, but could see no sign of the structure they had fallen from. He didn't know how long it would be before guards headed their way.

Four figures appeared in the distance, standing and crouching where the metal curve beneath them peaked like a low, time-worn hill. Shilly waved her cane on seeing them. Sal urged Erged to hurry.

"How are you feeling?" Shilly's arms around him were warm and welcome.

"Fine," he said, although his head throbbed and he suspected all his left side was turning into one long bruise. Despite that, he felt vibrantly alive and strong: the aftereffects of wearing the crown, he presumed. "What about you?"

"No major injuries," said Rosevear. "Have you seen Griel?"

Sal noticed then that the Panic standing with her and Highson was a battered-looking Jao, not Griel as he had assumed.

"Over here!" came a cry from his right. "I've found the way in."

Griel's voice. The six of them followed the sound down the sloping hull to where the Panic stood over a large, square hatch.

"I knew it was here somewhere," he explained, beaming proudly and bending down to swing it open. Its hinges complained but his muscular arms were equal to the task. The hatch fell aside with a soft, ringing thud, revealing a ladder descending into darkness.

"Where does that lead?" asked Shilly with a doubtful expression.

"Somewhere safe. That was an inspired idea to drop us down here," he said, clapping her on the shoulder. His eyes held a manic air. On his head he wore the same iron band that Sal had tried on in the observatory.

Sal recognised the look in Griel's eyes. He had felt it from the inside.

"Where did you get that?" he asked, pointing at the crown.

Griel grinned. "I picked it up after you dropped it, thinking it might come in handy. I put it on when Oriel appeared, hoping it might help and not knowing we were about to be ditched outside. As it turns out, though, that has worked out just perfectly."

"What do you mean?" asked Jao, scepticism written across her forward-thrust face. "What has that thing done to you?"

"Nothing I don't welcome. Sal, tell them what you saw when you put on the crown. You didn't tell us everything, did you?"

Sal shook his head. "It showed me Stone Mages and Sky Wardens united under my rule. It showed me a unified system of Change working all across the Earth."

Griel's grin only widened. "Me too, except I see kingsfolk and foresters living together in peace in the forest. That, I think, is not an unworthy dream."

"We all agree on that," said Highson, "but what difference will that thing make? It's just giving you an empty promise."

"I don't think so. Jao, you know where we are. We're in the heart of the city, where it all started. That's why the Quorum gathers nearby, and why Oriel will be furious when he finds out."

Jao nodded. "We're on the skyship."

"And that is . . . ?" prompted Shilly.

"The King's original vessel, where our ancestors lived. The city has grown a hundredfold since then, but this will always be its foundation, its fulcrum."

"And here we are, climbing aboard." Griel swung himself into the hatch. "Come on. Let's see what mischief we can cause down here."

One by one they followed, Shilly grumbling at yet another vertical climb. The way, fortunately, wasn't long. It opened on an attic canted several degrees from horizontal. Dust and debris had slid along the floor to one side. The rubbish was half a metre thick in places.

Light came through round portholes that hadn't been visible on the outside. Everything buzzed and hummed with the Change. Sal felt the skin on his arms and neck creep. Another hatch opened onto the next level down. Griel put his hand on the handle, and hesitated.

"I hear voices. There's someone down there." He stood up. "We'll wait a second, see if they go away."

"So let me get this straight," Shilly said, running her fingers through her sun-bleached curls. "Are you the King now you're wearing the crown?"

"Down the years, many people have worn the crown," said Griel, "but there has only ever been one King."

"And who's that?"

Griel shook his head. "If you don't already know, I'm not going to say."

"Gah." She went to bang her walking stick on the floor, then remembered the people below. "This is getting us nowhere. There will be guards down there for sure, and more on the way. The longer we wait, the less chance we have to get out of here."

"I don't want to get out of here," said Griel.

"No? Well, you have a nice time. I've got better places to be."

He held up a hand as she approached the hatch. "This is the perfect place to be, Shilly. This is the original skyship—"

"The heart of the city. You've already said that."

"Listen to what else I have to say. This is the heart because it's where the motivators are housed. Those people down there, they aren't guards. They're probably Engineers, maybe even pilots. If they are, that means Oriel has already sent word to move the city."

"Why now?"

"To avoid the wraiths or to bring it closer to Milang for an attack on the humans. Take your pick. Either way, it gives us an opportunity we can't ignore."

"If we assume control," Jao said, coming forward to take Griel's arm, "we could go anywhere!"

"That's the idea. But first we have to get down there." Griel touched the hatch again, hearing with his broad fingertips. "Okay, they've moved on. Let's go, but keep it down. We don't want anyone to raise the alarm just yet."

They scurried down the ladder into a room filled with arcane machinery. Giant brass columns turned at constantly varying speeds, slowing down and speeding up with sudden whirring noises. Chimerical energy throbbed through the metal cylinders and made the air itself shiver. Fleeting shapes on the cylinders' polished surfaces painted flickering, powerful charms that came and went in a matter of instants.

Sal watched Griel. With the crown on, he seemed rejuvenated, no longer tired and bitter, but the same person looked out through those eyes. The crown appeared to release an inner strength or capacity—something that had always been there, but might not have had the opportunity to emerge. And if the crown could help make Griel's dream a reality, using all of Griel's resources, so be it.

Another hatch, another ladder. The lower levels were maintained more carefully, but evidence of age lay everywhere Sal looked. Metal scuffed and scratched with time, and even the clearest of glass tarnished. The rumbling of engines grew louder.

Griel led them to a door that opened outward into the main body of the skyship. Sal's eyes boggled at the sight of a vast space crisscrossed with girders and cables through which several Panic workers climbed and swung. The air crackled with the Change; potential flowed back and forth in stately waves. He felt the fingers of his right hand curl tight around the rail he held for balance.

"Back," Griel instructed them, pushing them the way they had come. "We can't go that way. It's too dangerous. We need the activator room."

There was another door on the far side of the room, past a bank of humming machinery. The sound of arguing came through the door. Griel swung it open and surprised two Engineers standing at a complicated series of controls, wearing elaborate red leather uniforms adorned with tool belts and pockets. The sight of humans behind Griel sent the male reaching for a spanner at his waist.

"Who are you? What are you doing here?"

Griel strode forward with hands empty and upraised. Nothing, it seemed, could perturb him now. "You've got two choices. You can try to hit me with that thing, or you can put it down for a moment and hear what I have to say."

"I'll hold it while you tell me what you want. Then I'll make up my mind."

"Fair enough." Griel turned to address both of them. "I've come to take over the skyship. Where has Oriel told you to move it?"

"To the Valley of Glass."

"Why?"

"Do you think he'd tell us that?" asked the female Panic on Griel's right. Her eyes were a surprising dark blue, peering out at him from deep sockets. "We're just Engineers. We don't need to know anything *important*."

Griel smiled at her, recognising a kindred spirit. "How about we take it somewhere else then, eh? Somewhere *we* want to go, not him."

"And where would that be, exactly?" asked Jao from behind him.

Griel glanced over his shoulder. "Any thoughts?

"What is its range?" asked Highson.

"Unlimited," said the female Engineer, "as long as it remains within the mist. That's what powers it, you see."

The male Engineer looked furious at her complicity, but said nothing.

"What about Milang?" asked Griel. "It's time we talked to our neighbours instead of skulking about in the shadows."

Jao shook her head. "They'll think we're attacking. They'll fire on us."

"Not if we tell them in advance that we're coming."

"Why would they believe us?"

"Because we'll send our friends here first, as a gesture of goodwill."

"How?"

"Do you have any maintenance balloons docked at the moment?" Griel asked the Engineers.

"Two," said the female. "They're on the next level down, accessible from the old throne room."

"Perfect. You'll have to go with them, Jao, because they don't know how to fly—"

"I'm rusty myself," she said with a frown.

"It's a simple flight. A child knows how to navigate that section of the forest, even with the compasses playing up."

She put a hand on his shoulder. "What about you?"

"I have nothing to worry about in here. Oriel won't dare storm the skyship with me at the controls. I'll tell him we'll crash the city if he tries."

The Engineer holding the wrench suddenly lunged at him, swinging the tool with all his strength. He moved fast enough to crack Griel's head open like a melon had he managed to connect. Sal had no time to react beyond opening his mouth to shout a warning.

Griel leaned to one side, grabbed his assailant's arm, and twisted. The Engineer went down with a cry and found himself pinned to the floor by Griel's knee.

"Sorry, friend. I'd rather not hurt you. Drop it, please, while we both still have a choice." The tool clattered heavily to the floor. "Thank you. Now, I need some rope or wire to restrain him."

The female Engineer nodded and opened a hatch. "Here."

Griel worked swiftly, binding the male's wrists together. "Good.

Understand that I will do nothing to directly harm the city. No matter what promises I make to Oriel, no matter what threats I make. It's all bluff. Do you believe me?"

The female nodded. Her blue eyes regarded him calmly. "I'll happily trust you over Oriel. His goons beat up my brother for speaking out against him last month."

"What's your name?"

"Del."

"Thank you, Del. Now, how many others out there—" he jerked his head at the door, and by implication the rest of the skyship "—will we have to tie up like this fellow here?"

She thought for a moment. "Four, maybe five."

"Can you call them in here one at a time so we can deal with them?"

"Of course." Del leaned over to talk into a wide funnel. The sound of her voice echoed from the spaces outside the activator room.

Griel turned to face Sal and Shilly. "I suggest the three of you get moving now, before the fun really starts. Tell the Guardian not to be the first to fire. To retaliate if she needs to, but to hold on as long as she can. This is her chance to prove to my people that she doesn't mean us ill."

Sal was far from convinced the plan would work but could see the need for him and the others to be involved if it was to have any chance. He could also see the relief in Shilly's eyes at the thought of being reunited with everyone again. "Are you sure you don't need us here?"

"What?" Griel laughed from deep in his stomach as though at a preposterous joke. "This is the second time I've tried to set you free, Sal. Are you trying to talk me out of it?"

"Griel will have all the help he needs," said Highson. "I'll be staying."

"And me," said Rosevear.

"There's no need for that," said Griel. "We can manage."

"Not without Change-workers, you won't. And especially not if you need to get a message out," Highson insisted. "Should Oriel over-power you, or you decide to alter course for any reason, I can call Sal through the Change and let him know."

"Not in here," said Shilly. "It would be like whispering through a thunderstorm."

"If I can get to the other maintenance balloon, there'd be a chance." Highson looked from Sal to Shilly, then to Griel. "It makes sense. Do you agree?"

"I do, as a matter of fact." Griel's broad callused hand came down on Highson's shoulder, and he nodded at Rosevear. "Your offer is grate-fully accepted. We'll put you to good use, don't worry."

Jao leaned in. "We need to leave now, if we're going to get away safely. The longer we leave it, the more likely Oriel will send patrols after us."

Sal had enough time to shake his father's hand and wish him good luck before being whisked outside and along a short corridor. One final ladder led to a crescent-shaped room that looked as though it had once been open to the skyship's central chamber. A low dais abutted against one wall, home of an unassuming, backless chair.

"Legend says that this was where the King used to sit when the skyship was the home of all our folk," Jao said, a worry line between her eyes indicating that her real concern lay elsewhere. The knuckles of her long arms tapped restlessly at the walls as they went by.

"It doesn't look like much."

"Why should it? We honour the King for his actions, not the things he collected."

She led them through another door. Fresh air greeted them, indi-cating that they were close to the outside. Another door took them to a small docking bay with a single rigid gantry leading to two small balloons. Each was spherical with a tiny gondola, barely big enough for two people, let alone three. Jao took a large toolbox out of one and indicated that they should squeeze in. A moment's fiddling at the controls brought the small propeller at the rear to life. With a spray of sparks, it began to spin.

The ropes fell away, and the balloon dropped out of the dock, into empty air.

Shilly was stunned to see how much of the day had passed in the Panic city. Judging by the position of the blurred sun in the sky, she put the time at roughly three in the afternoon. Tom had been missing almost an entire day. She wondered where he was, and hoped he wasn't as frightened as she had been that morning.

"How long until we reach Milang?" she asked Jao.

"An hour or so. This thing isn't exactly built for speed. Are you comfortable back there?"

Shifting awkwardly in the balloon's second seat, her thighbone still aching from the fall, she couldn't deny that it was going to be a long hour. It didn't seem fair to blame Jao for that.

"We'll manage," she said, reaching behind her to take Sal's hand.

"I hope he'll be okay," Sal said, barely audible over the sound of the wind.

"Who?"

"Highson. And Rosevear, of course."

She twisted to look at him. His expression was brooding.

"I don't understand you two," she said.

"What?"

"You and Highson. He's your father, but you act like you barely know each other."

"Well, we don't."

"Yet when you're apart you worry about him. How does that work?" He didn't answer, so she went on. "If I were you, I'd want to know everything about him: where he grew up, what he likes, how he feels about having you back in his life."

"What difference does it make? I already *had* a father."

"Yes, and he's gone now. Highson won't ever replace him, but he can still be important."

"I have all the family I need right here," he said, squeezing her hand.

"That's very sweet, but we both know it isn't true. What happens if I die? Who will you turn to then?"

"Don't joke about this."

"I'm not joking, Sal. This is too important to joke about—and too important to dismiss."

"Is that why you wanted to get to know Marmion better, when you thought he was Lodo's nephew? So you'd have someone to look after you if I wasn't around?"

She heard it again, that strange edge to his voice when Kail's name came up. Only this time they weren't talking about Kail but Marmion. She wondered then if it wasn't a specific person that Sal was afraid of, but the idea that she might have someone else apart from him in her life. She faced that worry squarely, feeling as though she was finally getting close to understanding him a little better.

"That's not all family is for," she said, "and don't ever think I'm making preparations for you not being here. I'm acting on the assumption that we've got a long time together."

He smiled fleetingly, but the look didn't go away. "Aren't friends enough?"

"Friends *are* family. Don't you see? I'll admit I got a little overexcited about Marmion at first, but that's only natural, I think. I've never had anything like a family before. I've never been able to choose whether or not to like them, as you have. I'd take Kail over Marmion, given the chance. I *like* Kail, whereas Marmion just pisses me off. But there's no possibility of choice if we won't open ourselves up to anything, or anyone."

Sal mulled this over for a while, chewing his bottom lip. She waited him out. "Why doesn't Highson make the first move?" he eventually asked. "Why is it up to me?"

"Highson's waiting for you. He knows he can't force himself on you." She brushed a loose strand of hair out of his eyes. "I know he says he's here because he wants to confront the Homunculus, to find out what happened between them in the Void Beneath, but personally I think that's just an excuse. He wants to be around you. You're all he has left of his marriage to your mother. You're his *child*. Whether you had another father or not is irrelevant to the part of him that's always wondered about you. And if he dies, you'll both have missed out on something important."

Sal shook his head. "I think you're wrong. Not about all of it, just this part. I think he likes the idea of getting to know me better, but he can't until he gets over my mother. It's almost twenty years since she left him, and here he is trying to fish her out of the Void Beneath, screwing things up for everyone. There's no room for me while her ghost lingers."

There was a new edge to his voice.

"Is that why you're cold with him? Because you blame him for what's happened?"

He squirmed. "No. No, not really. It's just—"

The balloon jolted beneath them. An arrow thudded into the gondola from below, making the wooden hull quiver and making Shilly jump. Another missed by a good two metres—but that was still entirely too close for comfort. Jao wrenched the controls to the right and forced them in an entirely new direction.

"A human patrol," she called over her shoulder. Sweat beaded on her furrowed brow. "We must have passed between them and the sun. Luckily they didn't quite have our range."

Shilly swallowed a sudden nausea at the thought of the balloon being punctured. She was becoming heartily sick of heights and the fear of falling.

"I'll try calling Skender," said Sal. "We must be far enough from the skyship to reach him by now."

Shilly kept hold of his hand in order to listen in. Jao took them around a vertical column of rock shrouded with vines as Sal reached out for their friend.

"*Skender?*"

"*Sal?*" came the immediate reply. "*Where are you? I've been trying to call you all day.*"

"*We've been in the city's motivator room. That blocks the Change. Now we're on our way to Milang.*"

"*How?*"

"*By balloon.*"

"*Be careful, then. You're not going to get a friendly reception.*"

"*So I gather. Can you do anything about that?*"

"*You'll need to talk to Marmion. He's in a better position than me to influence the Guardian. We're in transit. There have been . . . complications.*" Shilly detected more than a hint of understatement in his voice. "*Don't waste your strength talking to me. We'll catch up later. Safe flying.*"

"Let me talk to him," said Shilly as Sal sought the mind of the Sky Warden Eisak Marmion.

"Sure, if you want to."

Sal adopted a passive role, and let her Take from him. She could feel his worry for their friend, uneasily suppressed.

"*We have a problem,*" she told Marmion when their minds were connected.

"*Several problems at once, it seems,*" he said, telling them about the sighting of the Homunculus, the attack on Milang by the Swarm, the fruitless stakeout, and the murderous presence of a golem during the night. "*As if that wasn't enough,*" he said, "*there has been another flood. We've just heard from the Guardian. She informs me that the deluge came down a section of the mountainside not far from the first flood, sweeping aside three people assessing the damage already done.*"

Shilly closed her eyes at the news. *Another flood.* What could that possibly mean?

She didn't know, and she had more immediate things to worry about. Their own fruitless stakeout needed to be reported, plus the appearance of the Angel, the disappearance of Tom and Mawson, and Oriel's hostile takeover of the Panic Heptarchy. Lastly, she brought up the imminent appearance of the Panic city in the misty skies of Milang.

"*How long do we have?*" Marmion asked, mental voice suitably grim.

That, she didn't know. Neither she nor Sal had thought to ask Jao before.

"A few hours at least," the Panic told them. "Maybe all night. The city takes a long time to get moving and is a bugger to stop."

Shilly relayed that information.

"*That gives us some time to play with, then.*" Marmion thought for a moment. "*Perhaps we can reason with this Oriel. If your friend Griel is determined to get the two parties talking, someone has to take the first step.*"

The brief glimpse she had had of Oriel didn't fill her with confidence. No one liked being forced to shake hands. And that wasn't the worst of it. "*You say the Swarm attacked Milang last night?*"

"*That's right.*"

"*Four of them attacked the Panic too, planting evidence that humans were responsible. Seems like someone's trying to drive human and Panic apart as hard as we are trying to bring them together.*"

"*Why would that be?*"

"*I don't know. But it's certainly a new pattern of attack. Vehofnehu says the wraiths will get stronger and bolder the longer they're at large.*"

"*Who says that?*"

"*The Panic empyricist. I think he might have been their King once, but can't tell for certain. He's gone missing too.*"

Sal watched her closely during a brief lull in the conversation. They were still connected to Marmion, but the warden seemed to be thinking.

"You think *he* was King?" Sal whispered.

"Just a guess, but I'm pretty sure. He knew the Swarm when no one else did. He had the crown in his possession, even if he didn't wear it. He took Griel under his wing—and look where *he's* ended up." She shrugged, thinking of her strange vision of the young, vital empyricist in his observatory. "If he was here, we could ask him."

"Maybe that's exactly why he's gone away."

"*Shilly? This is a very complex situation. The Guardian is likely to face a revolt if she doesn't defend Milang from a perceived attack, but if she opens fire on the city as it approaches, that will only confirm the Panic's worst fears. We need to find a way to avoid the spark that will trigger a bushfire.*"

"*Agreed.*"

"*We also need more information. I'm therefore going to ask you to do something for me. It's going to take you some way off your current route, if my estimate of your current location is correct.*"

Shilly groaned at the thought of more time in the air. "*I can ask Jao and see what she says.*"

"*I don't think it puts you at any risk. I just need to be sure of something.*"

"*Go on, then. Tell me where you want us to go.*"

"*There's a section of the range called Geraint's Bluff. Your pilot should know it; the Panic use the same landmarks as the people here. It was hit by a landslide after an earthquake a couple of hours ago, so it'll be easy to tell apart from the forest around it.*"

"*Once we get close enough.*"

"*Yes. And therein lies the problem. The Homunculus was last seen in that area. I need to know if it's still alive—and that means risking flying into its wake.*"

She tsked in annoyance. "*Is now really the time to be obsessing about that again? There are more important things, surely.*"

"*Perhaps not, Shilly.*" Marmion hesitated minutely. "*The runner who saw the Homunculus also saw Habryn Kail. They've been travelling together.*"

She sat up straighter, and almost lost her grip on Sal. "*Kail's alive?*"

"*He was. I don't know for how much longer. The runner said that he was gravely wounded. She lent him what assistance she could. He and the Homunculus were gone when we reached their campsite.*"

Sal was looking at her again. "*All right,*" she said. "*We'll do what we can. I'll call you if we encounter any difficulty.*"

She broke the connection. "Do you have a problem with this?" she asked Sal.

"No. If Kail needs our help, we have to offer it."

"Jao?" Shilly twisted around in her seat to face the front. "Ever heard of Geraint's Bluff?"

"Yes."

"We need to go there. Someone's hurt and might need our help."

"But Griel said—"

"Our friends in Milang will look after things while we do this. Please. It's important."

The Panic woman mulled it over, face invisible to Shilly. Eventually she nodded. "All right. But then I drop you off and go back. Understood?"

Shilly did understand. Jao was worried about Griel, although she didn't come right out and say it.

"You sound like a different person when you talk to Marmion," said Sal as the balloon changed course, swinging in a wide arc to starboard.

"Oh? How's that?"

"You're—I don't know. Harder."

"I have to be like that with him, or he gets the upper hand."

"But in a strange way, that makes you more like him." His fleeting smile returned. "You two may not be related but you have more in common than you'd like to admit, I think."

That was a decidedly uncomfortable thought. Shilly pulled a face to show what she thought of it, then tried unsuccessfully not to think of it again.

Kail woke to darkness and a terrible feeling of suffocation. His chest hurt and his right arm was twisted painfully behind his back. When he tried to flex it, he encountered resistance all over. He coughed, provoking more pain. His mouth filled with the taste of dirt.

He couldn't see. He couldn't move. One thought sprang immediately to mind: that he had been buried alive.

An upwelling of panic forced a ragged scream from his throat. Muffled, weak, desperate, he could barely hear it himself, but the exertion took its toll. A fit of coughing brought more dirt into his mouth and made his situation worse, not better. Stars danced before his eyes, cruel visions of a sky he couldn't see. Then darkness swept them away, and he was gone.

He woke again an unknown time later, thinking he'd heard someone calling his name. His heart pounded and he tried to lift his head. Sharp stone dug into his temple, restricting his efforts to a pathetic twitch. Something shifted beneath him and his twisted arm came under even more pressure. He stopped trying to move then, chilled by the realisation that, whatever he was buried in, it wasn't packed down tight and might shift in ways that would only make his situation worse. A trickle of air was somehow getting in; cutting off that supply would be the death of him.

The call wasn't repeated and he eventually convinced himself that he had imagined it.

He tried to stay calm. If he panicked again, he might never awake. The first thing he needed to do was work out what had happened. He remembered rocking on the camel's back, being lulled into unconsciousness by exhaustion and fever. Flashes of dreams were all that remained in his memory after that point. At least he assumed they were dreams: a woman with eyes and skin similar to Skender's friend Chu leaning over him; the Homunculus picking him up and carrying him in its arms; a deafening roar, louder than anything he had ever heard before—louder even than the flood that had swept him and the Homunculus away, two weeks earlier. Then . . . darkness.

Could he really have been left for dead by the twins? It was possible. His condition may have worsened to the point where it was difficult to discriminate between life and death, especially for someone with no experience at it. He had heard tales of people rising from mortuary slabs or sitting up at their own wakes, bewildered but very much alive. It had happened often enough for him to become convinced that it had indeed happened to him.

But what to do about it? He didn't dare move, and doubted he had the capacity to do much, even if he did. What did that leave him?

Only then did he realise that something had been returned to him—something missing for so many days that he had come to take its absence for granted. Although smothered in stone and dirt and weak with fever, he felt the Change acutely, as though standing next to the sea itself. Its return came at a cost—it meant the twins had definitely left him—but the simple fact of his reconnection to the life-flows of the world gave him at least one chance of escape.

He was too weak to move the earth around himself, but he could call for help.

"Can anyone hear me?"

The effort nearly drained him dry. He rested afterwards, conserving his energy and resolving to try again.

"Hello? Hello?"

At the very range of his senses, he thought he detected a response.

"Hello! Please listen! My name is Sky Warden Habryn Kail. I'm underground. You have to dig me out. Hello?"

Stars danced again behind his eyelids, and he feared blacking out.

He needed to remain conscious just in case his call was answered. If he didn't, he would wake up even weaker. Maybe he would never wake at all. He would die in a premature grave, suffocated in a stupid accident.

Fear and anger worked in him. He didn't want to die like this. He had work to do, a mission to fulfil. He had promised to help the twins reach their destination. They had come so far, tried so hard to understand each other's very different worlds, and to see it end now would be galling.

There was more to it than that. His body didn't want to die for its own sake, even if it was fevered and broken. His mind spoke of promises and duties, but his lungs just wanted to breathe, his heart to beat a little longer. His gut was less clear—a loner and wanderer by inclination, he had never let himself become attached to any one person or place for too long. The pit of his stomach hollowed at the thought of leaving it all behind, as though the *possibility* of attachment had somehow been important without him knowing it.

The name of the woman whose parchment he carried came back to him at that moment: Vania, with her deep blue eyes and ability to laugh at anything. He would've handed over the fragment of Caduceus without hesitation in exchange for seeing her again.

"Help me!"

Kail couldn't help but struggle against the soil constraining him. He would shout and curse and tunnel his way out like a worm. It would take more than putting him in a grave to make him lie down for good. The seer in Laure hadn't told him what lay at the end of the path he sought, but Kail swore it wouldn't be this. He would crawl out of darkness into the mist and spit the dirt from his mouth. He would stand up and keep walking. He would find the twins and show them that they had buried him too soon. He would see daylight again.

"Kail?"

The voice was barely audible over the sound of weeping—his own, he realised, as he slowly came back to himself. His cheeks were heavy with mud and his chest hurt. His nose was now completely blocked and he had lost all sensation in his right arm. Instead of fighting for life, he now cursed himself for living. Why not just slip quietly into darkness? Why drag it out any longer? He had had more than enough time to contemplate his sorry, futile fate.

"*Come on, Kail! I know you're in here somewhere!*"

This time the voice was less easy to write off as a figment of his imagination. It was clearly audible through the Change, coming from nearby, and—to his great surprise—familiar.

"*Sal?*"

"*Got you! Now, keep talking and I'll try to home in on your position.*"

"*Where—where are you? How did you get here?*"

"*Two questions we're keen to ask you. You go first.*"

"*I—*" He coughed, bringing a little more dirt into his mouth. "*I think I'm supposed to be dead.*"

"*Nonsense. There was a landslide. You were obviously caught up in it.*"

Kail groggily absorbed that information. A landslide? That would make sense, he supposed. More sense than being buried alive. He was lucky to be alive at all, then. An entirely different story.

But what about the twins? The camel? Had they been swept up in the avalanche as well?

"*Kail? Are you still with us?*"

He forced himself to concentrate, to keep talking. "*Yes, yes, I'm here—thank the Goddess. How did you know where to find me?*"

"*Well, we didn't. Not really. We only heard you when we flew directly overhead, and that was more accident than otherwise. Marmion sent us out here in search of the Homunculus. We didn't think we'd be on a rescue mission.*"

"*Have you found the twins?*"

"*No. A hint of its wake higher up, but that's all.*"

Sal's voice was oddly flat. Either he was lying, or he thought no hope existed for his companions . . . and why would there be, Kail asked himself, when the twins couldn't call out for help as he had?

"*I don't know exactly what they are,*" he said, "*but they're not the enemy. Shilly was right. We need to hear what they have to say.*"

"*Shilly wants to know what they've already told you.*"

"*They say . . .*" His mind wandered. The darkness around him seemed to grow even deeper, if that was possible. "*They say . . .*"

"*They say what, Kail? Don't fade out on us now.*"

In his mind, he heard the voice of the twins echoing from the depths of his memory: *It was our plan to bind the Realms together. There's no point hiding from what we've done . . . We're the source of everything. And the end of everything . . . The Third Realm is still out there. Humans must still end up there, otherwise you wouldn't be human . . . We get to try again, to live our lives over and over . . . In sadness, in happiness, in terror, in peace. The choice is ours . . .*

We're just trying to make sense of the sky.

Kail felt the dirt moving around his face. A heavy pressure came down over his mouth and nose, completely cutting them off. Terror returned and, like a match to alcohol, it consumed his last reserves of energy. He kicked and tried to move his head. *Suffocating*, he tried to say, but the word wouldn't leave his mind. *Suffocating! I'm—*

Then the pressure fell away and light poured across his face. He sobbed with relief, sucking in lungfuls of air even though it made him cough.

"Just lie still," said Sal, no more than a silhouette against a bright background. "We'll have you out soon enough. The more you wriggle, the more likely you are to bury yourself again."

Kail took this advice to heart, remembering his first impression that the rubble around him wasn't tightly packed. That also fit the avalanche scenario. If he squirmed too much, he might start another one.

"Are you thirsty?" asked another voice. Shilly.

"Oh, yes," he croaked.

A hand reached down to him, holding a flask of water. She dribbled a splash or two between his lips, and he swished it around in his mouth before swallowing it. He would be tasting dirt for a week.

The excavation continued, slowly but steadily, as he drifted in and out of consciousness. Two people were working in the hole while Shilly watched over him—but one seemed to be something other than human, with strong arms and hands that made good shovels. Kail felt those hands pulling the dirt away, creating an ever-widening hole through which they could get at the rest of him. He was lying almost horizontally but in a very awkward position with his legs tangled around each other like the roots of a rotten tooth and one arm caught under him.

When he was finally able to move that arm, the circulation returned in a rush, setting fire to his nerves.

"Pain is good," he said in response to Shilly's concerned look. "Pain means I'm not dead."

"Well, hold onto that feeling," she said, looking at the bandages on his chest. "I think you're going to have to live with it for a while yet."

The twins watched from above as Sal and Shilly and their strange companion freed Kail from his premature tomb. The woman helping them was pale-skinned and wearing overalls, but looked like a large ape of some kind. Seth couldn't take his eyes off her.

Simapesial, he said. *It can't be.*

It's me you're talking to, Hadrian said. *Remember?*

Must be a relation. It's the only way.

The twins watched, yearning to help. After hunting for Kail for almost two hours, climbing up and down the ragged, scarred mountainside, calling his name over and over but hearing nothing in return, it now turned out that they had been looking in completely the wrong spot. They would have liked nothing more than to lend their considerable strength to the task of digging Kail out, but they held back, afraid of exposure, still stung by Ymani's suspicion and knowing that Kail would be better off in the hands of those more like him. Besides, the camel was gone and all their supplies with it. They had little choice.

How did they find him? wondered Seth.

Through the Change. Hadrian knew the answer, even if he hadn't heard the exchange himself. *Telepathy, ESP, whatever. That's how you and I communicate. Looks like they can do it too.*

I thought we could talk because we were stuck inside the same head.

That doesn't explain how, *Seth. The Change makes it possible. We inhabit our own little bubble, separate from the rest of the world.*

Maybe one day we'll pop the bubble, eh?

That was a thought Hadrian didn't dare vocalise. Although their physical senses only became keener with every passing day, the two of them still remained at a definite remove from the rest of the world. They were in it, but not yet part of it. What it would take to make the world fully accept them, he didn't know.

"How were you injured?" they heard Shilly ask Kail.

"The Swarm attacked us," the tracker said, explaining what had happened in the lower reaches of the forest two nights earlier. "The wound has festered."

"You need more help than we can give you here." The ape-woman's voice was throaty and expressive, not what Seth had expected. "We'll take you to Milang."

"In that thing?"

Kail indicated the miniature balloon, and Hadrian understood his scepticism. The gasbag was less than three metres across and its basket was barely able to hold the three that had come there. The entire structure looked decidedly less than aerodynamic.

The Change again? asked Seth.

Must be. Hadrian thought about it. *We'd better stay back or they won't get anywhere.*

"One of us will have to remain behind to make room," said Sal. It was clear who he would suggest.

"No, Sal," said Shilly. "You're as bad as your father."

"And making just as much sense. Jao is the pilot and I'm not leaving you here alone."

Shilly looked close to tears. "But what about *you?*"

"Don't worry about me," he said. "Someone can come and get me as soon as you arrive, if Jao isn't willing to backtrack herself. We'll all be back together again soon enough."

The ape-woman looked noncommittal, and that didn't ease Shilly's uncertainty even slightly. "What if there's another earthquake, or the Swarm come for you?"

"I'll be okay." He hugged her and kissed the side of her neck. Hadrian felt a pang of longing at the affection they so openly displayed. "Now, go. The sooner you leave, the sooner you'll come back and get me."

"I'm sorry," said Kail as they helped him to his feet. "Truly, I am sorry. If you left me behind—"

"Don't even think about it," snapped Shilly with more abruptness than perhaps she intended. "You're coming with us whether you like it or not."

They manoeuvred the big man aboard the tiny balloon, and with much wriggling and rearranging Shilly and Jao followed. The ape-woman folded herself into the cramped space with surprising ease. Sal and Shilly held hands while Jao activated some sort of engine that made a broad propeller at the end of the gondola turn. It shimmered, building up speed, and strange patterns swept across the surface of the balloon.

Sal stepped back as, with a faint nasal whine, the unlikely craft lifted into the air.

Definitely the Change, said Hadrian.

These people aren't as hopeless as I thought.

"Hopeless?" *They built this body, remember?*

That's nothing to be proud of, said Seth, flexing his right arm. *It was never meant for us.*

That was the truth of it. They had taken advantage of the opportunity it presented, but Highson Sparre hadn't built it with mirror twins in mind. They were lucky it held them at all.

From their hiding place, they watched Sal waving as his lover and her companions faded into the fog. Hadrian fought the urge to wave also, to farewell the man who had been their companion for the better part of their life in the new world.

What do we do now? asked Seth.

We can't move yet. He'll see us.

So we just sit here?

Got any better ideas?

Sal waited until the whine of the balloon's chimerical engine had faded into silence before turning and looking around him.

"Okay," he called. "You can come out now."

Only the echoes of his voice replied.

"I know you're there," he tried again, louder. "Show yourself."

A shadow moved ten metres up the steep, scarred hillside. Multiple limbs unfolded. The dark shape of the Homunculus separated itself from the boulder it had been hiding behind and stood up straight.

"How did you know we were here?" came the return cry.

"Well, if Kail survived, you were likely to as well. Then I picked up your wake higher up the hill. Were you trying to find him?" He indicated the muddy rubble beneath his feet, the hole Kail had been pulled from.

"Yes. We couldn't call him as you can. We're glad you heard him."

They stared at each other for a dozen heartbeats. There were a million questions Sal wanted to ask, but the black, blurry face of the Homunculus was forbidding. *Brother*, he thought. *My father's creation.*

"Why are you here?" he asked.

A flurry of activity seemed to take place beneath the creature's strange skin. "Here? To save the world and everyone on it."

"Why now?"

"Because it needs saving now. Yod is stirring. All these years it has been trapped, waiting for an opportunity. Now the time is here. Don't you feel the potential rising? Don't you sense the world breaking under your feet?"

Sal frowned, not knowing if the Homunculus meant literally breaking —as in an earthquake or landslide—or something metaphorical.

He shook his head uncertainly. "I don't feel anything."

But that wasn't entirely true. He felt stronger than ever, despite his recent exertions. That feeling, he had assumed, was the result of trying on the King's crown, the exuberant inspiration that had coursed through him during those brief seconds of contact. He still couldn't see any other obvious possibility. How Yod could possibly be connected to his wild talent defied his best efforts at comprehension.

"Maybe you're too close to what's happening," the twins said. "You can't stand outside it, see the way things are changing."

"Does it have anything to do with the Swarm?"

The Homunculus's expression definitely looked surprised at that. "How do you know about them?"

"They've been killing people, trying to start a war."

"The first part sounds very much like them, but not the second. I don't understand."

Then the Homunculus interrupted itself with one word. "Upuaut."

"Yes." Two distinct voices emerged from its strange mouth. "Yes, it must be. They're working together now, like they used to."

With an odd, crablike motion the Homunculus began to descend the rubble. Sal automatically went to retreat, but forced himself to stand firm.

The twins aren't the enemy, Kail had said. *We need to hear what they have to say.*

"Come slowly," Sal called, raising one hand palm out. "I don't want to fall into your wake."

"Understood." The twins descended until the edges of Sal's Change-sensitivity began to blur.

"That's far enough. What were you saying about the Swarm?"

"That something else is behind them, using them as it has used them before. They're the brawn for someone else's brain." The Homunculus shook its head. "But they're not important in the long run. Yod is coming. We've got to be ready for it when it gets here."

"There won't be anyone left to get ready if the Swarm have their way."

"It is a bit of a catch–22. We can see that."

"A what?"

"Never mind. We understand, that's all. And we're as lost as you."

Sal sat down on a rock, feeling unutterably weary.

"Why now?" he asked again—but the meaning of the question was different this time. "Why has this Yod thing chosen this time to attack? What's so special about here and now?"

"That was something Kail never asked."

"Well, *I'm* asking. Do you know the answer?"

The Homunculus's hesitation was hard to interpret. Were the twins talking among themselves again or were they genuinely uncertain?

"I think it's because we're here," said one of them. "Our presence outside Bardo—outside the Void Beneath, as you call it—has disrupted the balance, given it a way out."

"But you're here because *it's* here."

"No. We're here because Highson Sparre showed us the way out."

"Highson?" With a sinking feeling, Sal considered what the twins were saying. He didn't like the direction his thoughts led. "What happened in the Void? When Highson was looking for my mother."

"We were waiting," said the twins, their double stare intense, almost hypnotic. "There was nothing else for us to do. You've been there. You remember the hum, don't you? The drone of infinity, pressing down on you, grinding your mind flat, leaving you nothing."

Sal nodded. He didn't remember anything that had happened to him inside the Void, but he had definitely experienced the hum before when overextending himself through the Change. "Go on."

"We were lost," said the twins. "We only knew vaguely what we were supposed to do, and the Lost Ones were no help. They came; they faded away; they were gone. And so on, forever. We lived nineteen years in our world; in the Void Beneath we spent at least fifty times as long, with no one real to talk to but each other."

Nineteen years, thought Sal with a rush of compassion. That was just over his age. He'd had no idea.

"Then you came, with your friends Skender and Kemp. You jolted us out of the trance we'd fallen into. 'The Oldest One,' the Lost called us, but we were really two fused into something resembling one, like this world. Skender eased us apart by listening to our story. We remembered that we had a job to do. The Void Beneath would never be the death of us, but it could be something worse: an endless non-life. Just because the Ogdoad had protected us from forgetfulness didn't mean we weren't still at risk. We began to look in earnest for a way out, not just to complete our mission but for our own sake too.

"The Void Beneath is very different from Bardo as we knew it. The space between Realms was never a cage. Souls could cross from the First to the Second Realm any time they wanted, if they knew how. Now it's surrounded by walls that can't be broken. It wraps itself in a knot with the Lost Minds, the hum, and—for an eternity—us trapped inside. We couldn't get out, no matter how we tried.

"Finally, a new mind appeared in the Void Beneath. He wasn't Lost, and he didn't stay long. He came and went five times, as though testing the Void, measuring the route to and from it, preparing the way. We watched, distracted from our problems and thinking we might learn something from him.

"This was Highson Sparre, of course, getting ready to rescue your mother. We didn't know that until the attempt itself. Time passed, then he burst into the Void Beneath like a bomb going off, asking all the Lost Ones about your mother, looking everywhere for her."

"Her name was Seirian," Sal said.

"So we learned later, when we emerged, but in the Void you can only use heart-names. Do you know why?"

"No," Sal admitted. He knew neither of his parents' heart-names and felt uncomfortable at the thought of asking. "What happened next?"

"Your mother wasn't there, of course. Maybe she had been, once, but she must have faded away long ago. We introduced ourselves to Highson, wondering if we could help. Barely had we started talking to him when he disappeared. The charm connecting him to the real world had pulled him back. It was programmed to activate after a certain amount of time. He'd taken Skender's warning to heart, you see. Stay in the Void Beneath too long and you might never return; the hum will destroy you. At that point, we're certain, he was determined not to lose himself in there."

"He told Shilly he tried four times that night," Sal said, "and on the last he swore not to return unless he had my mother with him. He must've dismantled the return part of the charm to be sure of that."

The twins nodded. "We talked to him the second time, explained that he'd failed to find your mother the first time. He didn't believe us, of course, and insisted on looking again. The Lost Ones had gathered around him like moths to a flame; none of them was the one he wanted, but they could smell the chance of escape. They learned that he had a body out in the real world ready to take the mind of your mother, so she could live again. They realised immediately that it didn't just have to hold the woman he had loved. It could be anyone, anyone at all.

"His charm pulled him back again. He returned a moment later, his memory wiped once more, but aware this time that something was going wrong in the Void Beneath. If your mother hadn't returned with him, that could be for only one of three reasons: she was dead, she was being held captive, or she didn't want to be saved. All three appalled him, but he was determined to find out which was true. His desperation was awful, his failure inevitable—for no matter what he learned in the Void Beneath, he wouldn't remember it outside.

"The fourth time, we could tell that he had had enough. The uncertainty of not knowing, the futility of it all, was getting to him. If your mother was lost, then he would be lost too. Naturally, the Lost Ones clamoured for him to bring them out instead. They didn't care what happened to him. He would have none of that, but he couldn't stop their pleas, their begging for salvation. They would have hounded him to eternity, crushed him, had we let them.

"We rescued him, and we told him our story from beginning to end. We convinced him to let us take the body—the Homunculus—that he had intended for your mother. We turned his death wish into a sacrifice that might have some meaning to the rest of the world. If he couldn't bring your mother back to you, couldn't he guarantee you a future instead? That was how he came to see it. One love for another. It was a noble decision, at the end.

"You know the rest. Highson didn't remember anything when he awoke. He followed us in our quest, thinking that we had somehow stolen your mother's place in the world. He was too weak to hear the truth when he caught up to us, and perhaps he wouldn't have believed it anyway. In the Void Beneath, our presence had some authority; here we are a monster. But *you* need to believe us, if only to understand that your father did what he did with full access to the facts and nothing but the best intentions. It is we who are responsible, we who are to blame.

"But what other end could there be? We had to emerge. We have to lay Yod permanently to rest or it'll devour the world. We can't sit by and let everyone die."

"No, we can't, none of us." Sal felt drained by the story. He knew, now, what had plagued Highson for weeks: how his intention to save the woman he loved had turned into a monstrous quest taking him and others halfway across the world. But that wasn't the end of it. There was much more left to hear. "I think you'd better fill me in on this Yod thing."

The twins sagged. "Kail said the same, and we've been trying for days to make him understand. How can you understand the end of my world without understanding the world itself?"

"I don't know," said Sal. "But I know one thing. You think Yod will destroy *my* world, given half a chance. Let's start with that and work backwards. Afterwards, when we've stopped it, we can talk about what your world was like. How does that sound?"

To his surprise, one of the twins laughed. "That sounds like a philosophy I can relate to."

"No doubt," said the other, "but we're going to need more than philosophy on our side."

"Still, it's a start. All this skulking around has been getting on my nerves. Let's get moving again, eh, Sal. We have a date with destiny!"

Sal folded his arms and shook his head. "Maybe, but I'm waiting right here for Shilly to come back, just like I promised I would." He thought of Tom's disappearance and how she would react if he wasn't there when she returned. He wasn't going to put her through that. "I'd rather face this Yod thing with everyone behind me, rather than on my own."

The twins froze. How they resolved arguments about when to go and where Sal didn't know. Perhaps until now they had never had any real alternative. He wondered what Kail had told them about wardens like Marmion and the world beyond—or if the tracker, a loner himself, had ever seriously considered bringing the Homunculus into the fold. The idea of an underdog taking on and beating impossible odds had appealed to Sal, too, once, but with the entire world at stake, risking all on such a gambit seemed foolish. He had learned the value of cooperation in the Haunted City five years earlier. There were always alternatives to acting alone.

An echo of the crown's vision of a united world returned to him, this time combined with Griel's grand plan. Sky Wardens and Stone Mages plus kingsfolk and foresters and yadachi—was that too grand a vision? He didn't know—but he *did* know that Yod, whatever it was, would have to think twice if confronted with such an alliance.

"We'll wait," the twins finally said, "one day, and no longer."

Sal nodded. That was something. If, at the end of that day, the situation in the forest wasn't resolved, he doubted it ever would be.

Preferring not to think along those lines, he picked up a stick from the debris and began scratching well-practised signs in the dirt.

THE CHOICE

**"After the Cataclysm, when Babel's curse was finally
lifted, the ills of humanity did not vanish overnight.
To hear is not to understand;
to understand is not to sympathise;
to sympathise is not to obey."**

THE BOOK OF TOWERS, FRAGMENT 333

"War or truce?" declared the Guardian, pacing a well-worn path across the lawn of her open-air citadel. "Truth or lies? This position is untenable. There is no possible course of action that does not put the future of my people and the forest at risk—and that I simply will not allow. Daughter, do you agree?"

Skender waited breathlessly as Lidia Delfine bowed to her mother. The grassy chamber wasn't full, but it contained more people than he had seen in there before. Together with the Guardian and her daughter, Heuve, Seneschal Schuet and three other high-ranking foresters, the Sky Wardens Marmion and Banner, Stone Mage Kelloman, and he were gathered beneath the open sky. Before them stood the Panic female Jao, historian and former assistant to a deposed Heptarch and close ally of the Panic rebel Griel. She faced them with head held high. Her beaded hair tinkled softly when she turned to answer questions fired at her from all quarters. Skender watched her, hypnotised by the way she moved and talked. She was the first Panic he had seen since the explosive attack on the humans in the Divide, three days earlier.

For now Jao was silent, waiting as the Guardian cast judgment on her testimony.

More than a dozen guards blocked the exits from the chamber. The same number of archers crouched above, watching the skies as much as the people below. The atmosphere felt so tense Skender was amazed the fog could move so weightlessly through it.

"Forgive me, Mother," said Lidia Delfine, kneeling, "but I do not agree."

"Explain," said the Guardian without indicating that she should stand.

"When Seneschal Schuet first taught me the art of the sword, many years ago, he bade me remember one thing: that it is much easier to lower a blade in the practice hall than on the battleground. A fight is over not when the enemy is dead, but when all weapons—theirs and ours—are sheathed once more. A wise warrior is therefore determined not to win the battle, but to end it."

The young woman's gaze flicked briefly at Schuet, who stood silently to one side. His expression betrayed neither approval nor disapproval.

"The Seneschal has sent us word of war from the Panic Heptarchy—from one called Oriel, specifically, who styles himself ruler of his people in an ivory tower far from the battlefield. Meanwhile, a seasoned soldier—one prepared to fight his own people in defence of his principles—sends us an offer of peace. I think we would be foolhardy indeed to take the word of the former over the latter."

"Do you?"

"Yes, Mother."

"Even when that word comes via outsiders and a kingswoman of unknown allegiance?"

"One of our own, Mikia, can offer testimony supporting their word when she returns to Milang. She was found not long ago, exactly where our guests indicated she should be. A runner confirmed her safety."

"Stand." It was as hard to read the Guardian's expression as that of the Seneschal. Her hands lay hidden in the folds of her heavy gown, but Skender could see her fingers working. "I've heard Seneschal Schuet's advice many times. Do you think I would not remember it now? I'm no dotard, not yet. But it is good to hear that you agree with my old friend. My heart counsels this too, even if my head rebels.

"How am I to protect my people from the possibility that we are wrong?" she asked the room, sweeping everyone with her gaze. "What can I do to safeguard the city from treachery? I am persuaded that kingsman Griel's intentions are honourable—" Jao bowed slightly at this "—but no guarantee exists that he will not be defeated by this Oriel. What if Oriel takes Griel's tactic and uses it against us? What if the approach of the floating city is turned from a peaceful gesture to one of aggression?"

"I suggest a middle ground, Guardian," said Marmion, stepping forward. "A meeting."

"With whom?" she asked him. "Where?"

"You, Griel, Oriel—and us, if you will grant us that privilege. As to where—perhaps in a place that benefits all parties, and none of them at the same time. Perhaps a dirigible of some kind, in easy range of your archers."

The Guardian eyed him sceptically. "And how would we arrange such a thing?"

"I could carry word to Oriel and Griel," said Jao. "My safe return would prove to both of them that your intentions are honourable."

"It proves no such thing," said the Guardian, "except that I *expect* them to believe that. No. I granted you safe passage. I instructed the archers not to fire when you approached Milang. That was trust enough, I think. You are not a hostage, but you are not free to go either; not yet." She paced for a moment, thinking deeply.

When she came to a halt, she was facing Lidia Delfine. "Daughter, would you carry this message for me?"

"I would, Mother."

At this, one of the three high-ranking foresters spoke up. An elegant, high-cheeked woman of middle height with her hair tied back in a dense bun, Minister Sousoura had been the most outspoken against the presence of Jao in the Guardian's open-air audience chamber. Only a sharp rebuke from the Guardian herself had stayed her tongue. Now, after waiting patiently through the ensuing conversation, she had clearly had enough.

"Please, Guardian, I beg you to reconsider." Her tone belied her submissive posture. "Sending the Eminent Delfine into the heartland of the enemy is madness."

"How so?" The Guardian turned to face her, eyes narrowing even further than their natural state.

"The Panic bear us nothing but ill will. They have never liked us being here, and would spare no effort in getting rid of us forever. What they will do when they have your daughter and heir in their clutches, I dare not think."

"You've heard the testimony of those who tell us otherwise—that the kingsfolk are as much a victim of these evil intelligences as we here in Milang." Skender noted the Guardian's careful use of the respectful term "kingsfolk" over the foresters' usual, more derogatory term.

"The word of outsiders?" Minister Sousoura cast a sneering glance at Marmion and the others, including Skender. "Wouldn't it be better to place one's trust in those who have earned it?"

"That, I suppose, is the question, Minister." The Guardian sighed and turned away. "The flood eating away at our forest continues. Our city is attacked by creatures unknown. Visitors come with news of calamities abroad. Neighbour fights neighbour, and everything we have taken for granted is overturned."

She looked up at the sky. "Warden Marmion, I will take your advice, and you will stand beside me when I meet with my enemy. Should any harm befall me or those dear to me, to this city or the forest, the last thing you feel will be Seneschal Schuet's blade between your ribs. Do you understand?"

Marmion bowed. "I understand. I will stand proudly beside you, and I will earn the trust of your people."

Minister Sousoura sniffed, as unimpressed by the declaration as she was by the Guardian's decision. "All our heads will be on the chopping block, then. We can but hope for a miracle."

"We can do better than that," said the Guardian. "Every able-bodied archer and guard will be at the ready. This city will not fall without a fight, should it come to that. But understand this." Once again, her gaze took in the gathering. Her right hand emerged from her robes to point at each of her ministers in turn. "We will not start that fight. The first person to fire or to shout a battle taunt will be exiled from the forest along with their family. That is my edict. Be certain all hear it. Go now, and see about your duties."

She gestured, and the ministers hurried away, muttering among themselves. The threat of expulsion had shocked them. That much was obvious to Skender, who watched them go with no small sense of misgiving. He knew how serious they were about Outcasts.

The Guardian ran her hand over the greying stubble on her scalp. "There," she said. "It is done. I am committed—and to what? With one hand I throw away my daughter, with the other my home. But that's how it must be, and I will face the consequences. I will . . ."

The Guardian stopped and pressed her palm to her temple.

"You're weary, Mother. You should rest." Lidia Delfine was instantly at her side, followed shortly by Seneschal Schuet.

"I'm all right." She waved them both away. "And I *will* rest, but not until this is finished. Schuet, are the quarters ready for our guests?" The Seneschal bowed. "Good. See they're made comfortable for the night, then sit with me for a while. I will be in my rooms."

She strode off across the grass, a contingent of guards falling in smoothly around her. Skender looked up, noticing for the first time that the day was beginning to darken. Another night in the forest. He was beginning to lose count of how many he had spent here. With the Panic city due to reach Milang around dawn, it was going to be a busy one for most.

Schuet ushered them off the lawn and down the flight of steps outside. There, a mixed group of servitors and guards took charge of them, showing them to the rooms where the rest of their party were waiting.

Jao looked lost and bewildered behind a mask of determined dignity. The corners of her out-thrust lips drooped.

"This is only temporary," Seneschal Schuet assured her. "I swear you'll be returned to your people in due course."

"Your promise I would trust," she replied, "but it's meaningless without the Guardian behind it."

The Seneschal bowed discreetly. "I am not without influence."

Then he left too, and the visitors were alone with the servitors.

"What does *that* mean?" asked Skender.

"Oh, didn't you know?" Kelloman, who had remained silent and bored-looking throughout the proceedings, explained as they walked. "Seneschal Schuet is much more than bodyguard to the Guardian. He is her companion and father of her heir."

"Lidia Delfine is his *daughter*?" Skender saw their interaction in an entirely new light. "He's the Guardian's *husband*?"

"It's complicated. Officially she's wedded to the forest, but in practice, yes, they might as well be married." The mage hesitated. "This means, I suppose, that you don't know about Lidia Delfine and Heuve, either."

"What about them?"

"They've been betrothed since the age of ten."

"What? That's barbaric!"

"I'm hardly going to argue the point." Kelloman shrugged. "But I've never seen either of them complain. Perhaps it's only barbaric if you don't want to be betrothed."

Skender could find no fitting response to that, and allowed himself to be led along the arboreal pathways of Milang without further protest.

"They've been gone so long!"

Shilly looked up from Kail's sleeping form to watch as Chu performed yet another circuit of the common area. The visitors' compound consisted of a series of round-walled rooms teased out of the many branches of two ancient, tangled trees. The rooms were interconnected and entered by a single entrance, at which sentries had been stationed. Bamboo mesh sealed the windows but allowed air to circulate. The common area wasn't an especially large space, and the tracker's cot and Chu's wing consumed a fair slice of that. There was little room left over for Chu's impatience, or Shilly's.

After the drama of the flight to Milang—featuring at least two moments when it had seemed certain the balloon would be shot down, regardless of how many Sky Wardens claimed to be aboard—and a rough landing near the summit of the city, there had been little time for an emotional reunion. Black-clad Skender had hugged her briefly before being led away; Marmion had acknowledged her return with more reserve, but there had been undeniable relief in his eyes; Jao had been whisked off for interrogation while Shilly had supervised Kail's medical examination. The foresters used techniques not dissimilar to those she had read about in Lodo's manuals, although some of the herbs were different. His wound had been cleansed, stitched, salved, and bound, all under her watchful eye. Although satisfied that they had done a good job, she wished Rosevear was around to make sure. She had insisted on keeping the unconscious tracker with her in the visitors' compound rather than seeing him left on his own elsewhere.

"Why don't you ask one of the guards?" Shilly suggested to Chu from her cushion at the head of Kail's cot. The flyer's pent-up energy hadn't changed. "They might be able to tell you how long the meeting will last."

"I tried. They have no idea." The flyer clutched her hair and did another circuit. "It's just not fair."

Shilly could see her point. "Why *is* Skender there and not you?"

"He helped blow up one of the Swarm and spoke to the golem, while I'm still an Outcast no matter what I do."

"Be grateful for small mercies," Shilly said. "All I seem to do is sit around with sick people."

That defused some of Chu's tension. Instead of pacing, she flopped onto a large cushion and her deep brown eyes stared at Shilly.

"Why won't they accept me here?" she said. "What am I doing wrong?"

"You? Probably nothing. Some people are utterly bound by rules and regulations. Once you're labelled something, you just can't change their mind," she said, thinking of *stone-boy*, *deadwood*, and *necromancer*.

"It can't be just that, can it? I mean, if I'd lied and said I was from some outlying village or something, would they have welcomed me with open arms? They can't be that simple."

"They're not simple. It's actually very complex. It takes a lot of effort to be bigoted." Shilly stretched a kink in her back that still plagued her after the long journey with Jao. "You have to really work at it."

"But it doesn't make any *sense*."

"I agree completely." Sensing that her likelihood of getting any peace was minimal unless she offered something more substantial, Shilly tried a different tack. "Look at it this way. You don't know why your ancestors left the forest, but I think we can make a pretty good guess. Your father was a flyer, right? And so are you. Was anyone else in your family?"

Chu's brow furrowed. "My grandmother and great-aunt, and their father before them. Why?"

"Well, we know the people you've met here don't fly, so maybe that's why your family left. To do what they wanted to do."

"Why couldn't they have done it here? Why don't people fly here? It'd make it so much easier to get around."

"Because the Panic are the only ones who fly. And the Panic and humans are rivals. The humans have the trees; the Panic have the mist. Woe betide anyone who tries to cross the line."

Understanding began to dawn. "I see where you're going with this. Tell someone they can't have something and the first thing they do is pretend they never wanted it; the second thing they do is stop anyone else from getting it." Chu nodded thoughtfully. "My family wanted to fly. Neither the Panic nor the foresters would let them. They had no choice but to go somewhere else."

Shilly smiled. "I think you're on the right track. And you being back here now, when things are so tense with the Panic, reopens those old wounds."

Chu looked sombre. "My poor family. Imagine having to make that choice: home or flying."

"They can't have been the first to make it," said Shilly, "and they certainly won't be the last."

Before Chu could respond, voices and footsteps sounded from the entrance to the visitors' compound. The flyer was on her feet in an instant and hurrying to see who had arrived.

Shilly followed at a more sedate pace, taking as much weight as she could on her cane. By the time she caught up, Marmion was halfway through a perfunctory summary of the meeting.

" a summit tomorrow morning, if Lidia Delfine's mission is successful. Skender can fill you in on the details. Now, if you'll excuse me, I need to rest."

The warden did look drawn, but Shilly wasn't going to let him off so easily.

"What about Sal?"

Jao shook her head. "I'm afraid I'm grounded."

"But they're sending someone else, right?"

"He'll have to stay where he is for the night." Marmion's expression softened almost imperceptibly. "I'm sorry, Shilly. If you'd like to talk to him, Warden Banner will help you."

The curly-haired warden nodded, and Shilly swallowed an automatically angry response. She could understand that resources were needed in the city, and that the fate of one young foreigner didn't seem terribly important to anyone but her. But hadn't she and Sal already given enough? When would she finally be able to stop worrying about him?

"Any word from Highson and Rosevear?" she asked, trying to hide her weariness but knowing she would fail.

"No. I'm taking that as a good sign."

"It might not be."

"I know, but I've had enough bad news for one day."

Marmion took his leave, cradling his injured arm as though it pained him. Shilly watched him go, wondering if she should be concerned. If the wound had flared up or become infected, he might be distracted at the wrong moment. Again she wished Rosevear hadn't stayed behind with the Panic.

She went back to the common room to keep an eye on Kail. The tracker was sleeping soundly, oblivious to the furor around him.

Mage Kelloman—who had unnerved her the moment she met him, housed as he was in a completely unsuitable body and trailed everywhere by a large-eared creature that he ignored as best he could—complained loudly and at length at his mistreatment. Why he should be confined with the visitors struck him as exceedingly unfair. Jao, the recipient of a list of wrongs and slights—some of them real, Shilly was sure, but most imagined—looked slightly stunned at the tirade.

Skender and Chu whispered briefly to each other in one corner—about what, she couldn't quite overhear—then went their separate ways.

"Here," said Warden Banner, sitting next to Shilly with a rustle of robes and offering a hand. "Take from me. Call Sal. That'll put your mind at ease—and his too, I'm sure. He's probably wondering where you've got to."

Shilly accepted gratefully. Placing her walking stick in her lap, its heavy solidity a familiar comforting presence on her legs, she gripped the warden's fleshy fingers.

"*Sal?*"

"*Right here,*" came the instant reply. "*Where are you?*"

She explained. He took it well.

"*Don't rush. Nothing's bothering us out here.*"

"'*Us'?*"

"I have company."

Shilly glanced at Banner, who was necessarily a witness to the conversation, since it was taking place courtesy of her talent. The warden nodded and put a finger to her lips.

"Our friend the Homunculus?" Shilly said.

"None other. I presume you told Marmion we found no trace of the twins."

She had, and was glad she had been able to do so with complete truthfulness, as far as she had known at the time. *"Is everything okay?"*

"Fine. We're talking. We've got until tomorrow before the twins will move on."

"What will you do then?"

"I don't intend to be here that long, so it might not be a problem."

She could feel Banner's reserves easing. *"Sleep tight,"* she said. *"I hope it doesn't get too cold out there."*

"We have a fire going." He hesitated momentarily. *"Is Kail all right?"*

"He'll be fine," she said with a faint smile. Whatever his problem with the tracker was, at least he was trying to move past it.

They signed off and Banner let go. The warden stayed where she was, catching her breath. "I don't know how that Kelloman does it," she said softly. "A few sentences wears me out. Imagine sending your whole mind into someone else's body for a year or two."

Shilly nodded. She had seen it done before and it still amazed and unsettled her. It was disturbingly close to what had happened to Lodo, but using a human mind, not a golem.

"Thank you," she said as the warden stood. "Get some rest. You'll need it for tomorrow, as likely as not."

"You too." Banner repeated the finger-to-lips gesture as she walked away. Shilly felt confident that the conversation with Sal wouldn't be reported to Marmion. That, if nothing else, reassured her.

Kail drifted in and out of sleep, registering lights and voices but not taking any of it in. His arrival at Milang had been a blur, and of the flight itself his mind retained nothing. Somehow he had been thoroughly washed and treated and dressed without him knowing. A deep part of him understood that sleep was the most important thing now, and he made sure he pursued it.

The first moment of true clarity came in the dead of night. He rose to full consciousness almost without realising it. Waking with no jolt, no disorientation, no sudden fears, he simply opened his eyes.

Faint, warm light filtered through the room's bamboo shutters, painting crooked shapes across the wooden walls and ceiling. He stared at them dumbly, feeling that if he were to assemble them just the right way, they would form words in another language. From outside came the soft, rhythmic plod of a sentry making his or her rounds. That, at first, was the only sign that anyone else apart from him was awake.

Then a shadow moved in the room, and Eisak Marmion leaned into the light.

"I didn't want to wake you."

"I don't think you did." Kail tried to sit, but the pain in his chest flared from a dull throb to a sharp stab. He fell back with a wince. Sweat sprang up on his forehead.

Marmion moved closer and handed him a ceramic bottle of water. "Drink this. Your fever's broken, but you're bound to be dehydrated. Don't want you dying of thirst now we've got you back."

Kail's moisture-starved lips cracked into a smile. "I'm not sure where I am, yet." He drank slowly, in small sips. His right arm was still stiff from its twisting, under the landslip.

"You're in Milang," Marmion started to say. "Jao and Shilly brought you here after—"

"I guessed that much. What I meant was . . ." He struggled for the right words, knowing that Marmion would take them badly no matter how he phrased them. "I don't know to whom I owe allegiance now. The Alcaide, you, the twins—?"

"The *Homunculus*?" Marmion reared back as though physically struck. "You can't be serious."

"They saved my life at least twice. I owe them something for that."

"Don't you think you've helped them quite enough?"

"I'm not sure I have. That's what I have to work out." Weariness gripped him. Life had been refreshingly simple on the road with the twins. Dangerous and full of misunderstandings without a doubt, but at least their goals had been well defined. They had rarely argued, as Marmion was surely about to, that Kail had a duty to his order and the world he had sworn to protect, to the man whose commands he was supposed to obey, and to the distant authority in the Haunted City who seemed increasingly irrelevant with every passing day.

Marmion surprised him. Anger drained from the balding warden's round face like flour from a leaky sack. "I thought you'd say something like that," he said in resigned tones. "To be honest, I feel it too."

"You do?" Kail stared in frank amazement at his counterpart. "You could down me with a pat if I wasn't already flat on my back."

"Don't be *so* shocked. I'm not an idiot, and I don't have a death wish." He raised the bandaged stump of his right hand. "First me, then Eitzen, then you. We're not faring so well."

"What happened to Eitzen?"

Marmion's gaze dropped. "He was killed by a golem two nights ago."

The news was shocking, but not half as much as the place to which it led Kail's thoughts. "A golem in the body of a scarred man from the Aad?"

"So Skender says."

"Upuaut." It had to be. No wonder he and the twins hadn't been bothered by the creature since Kail's abortive attempt to capture it. Upuaut had been busy elsewhere.

Marmion looked askance at the unfamiliar name. "I think you'd better tell me everything."

"And you."

It took longer than an hour. Kail heard the sentry walk by five times before they finished, and even then there was still much to discuss. His mind proceeded at a furious pace, despite his deep fatigue. Disconnected facts fell into place with disconcerting smoothness.

"So Upuaut and the Swarm are working together to pit humans and Panic against each other." Kail ignored a persistent itch beneath the bandages covering his chest. "To what end?"

"To catch us in the middle, perhaps. Or to hold us up."

"But where are we going? Our stated aim isn't anything to do with Yod. And anyway, the twins say that Yod, the Swarm, and Upuaut aren't really on the same side."

"Not before. Maybe they are now."

"If the world ends, they all go with it."

Marmion nodded, sending the few strands of hair he had left askew. He went to brush them aside with his missing hand, then caught himself with a grimace. "I don't know *where* we're going any more."

"We make a fine pair, then," Kail said without humour. "Have you heard from Highson or Rosevear yet?"

"No." Marmion looked grim. "If they don't call in soon, I'll start to worry."

"Will you let me know?"

"Why?"

Kail ignored a sudden flash of suspicion in the warden's eyes. "I want to be there when everyone meets. Not just because you need the numbers—" Kail wasn't going to mention Eitzen's death; it was clear Marmion felt strongly about it "—but because I'm the only one who can come close to speaking for the twins. That's the central issue here. Not the forest and who fights whom over it. We need to remember what the seers have been telling the Alcaide all this time. Whatever it is they can't see in the future, the Homunculus is critical to it. We have to protect the twins, or at least keep an eye on them."

"If it's still alive," said Marmion, "after the avalanche."

"Oh, I don't doubt it's still out there," Kail responded. "If a wall of water twenty metres high can't kill it, what's a pissy little landslide that couldn't even finish *me* off?"

Marmion managed a small smile. "Quite."

"So that's a yes?"

"It's a 'let's see whether you can stand in the morning, then we'll discuss it.'" On that, Marmion himself stood. "We both need to rest. I suggest we try to get some."

Kail nodded and let himself sink back onto his cot. He was determined to be well enough, but knew that determination alone wasn't enough. A whole raft of factors had to come together before he could take anything like that for granted.

"Just one more thing," Marmion said before he left the common room. "Whatever happens tomorrow, don't go behind my back again. Is that understood? For all our differences of opinion, we're supposed to be on the same side. We're not rivals. Even if you disagree with me, do me the courtesy of keeping me informed."

Kail nodded in the gloom. That appeared to satisfy Marmion, even though it barely qualified as an answer.

When he was alone, Kail closed his eyes and tried to sleep. But his thoughts kept returning to the Homunculus and where it might be at that moment. His promise to the twins had been simple: *I'll guide you across the plains to the mountains and keep you out of trouble.* In that he had failed quite comprehensively. He had been unable to protect them from the forces, old and new, that were stirring in the world, and they had ended up saving him instead. But the fact remained: he had made a promise, one he was unlikely to keep.

We must understand each other, the twins had told him after the flood, or *all will end in disaster.*

With Marmion, at least, he hoped it wasn't too late.

THE CODE

"Following your heart is easier said than done.
First you have to find it, and that can be a long
and fraught journey in itself."
THE BOOK OF TOWERS, EXEGESIS 4:20

S kender woke from a dream of earthquakes to the sensation of someone shaking his shoulders.

"You're snoring. Snap out of it before you wake everyone up."

He stared up into Chu's face, only gradually piecing his thoughts together. "What?"

Satisfied that she had roused him, she stopped shaking. "Come on. We have work to do."

"What work?"

"Real work. Not the boring crap Heuve keeps giving me. Something useful. Something I'm good at."

"Why now?" His head felt as heavy as a boulder when he tried to sit. The room was still dark and the forest outside the windows was redolent with night noises.

"Because it needs to be done. Get *up*." She grabbed his right hand and physically pulled him out of bed. "Why do I always have to bully you into doing things with me? I'm starting to think you're not even interested."

He tugged his black robe over his head to stop himself from saying *The feeling is mutual*, figuring that particular statement was rhetorical. He had tried to talk to her the previous night, but she had begged off again, saying there were too many people around.

"Where are we going? If you're thinking of sneaking past the guards—"

"Not the way you think, although I did consider it. They're too thorough, too suspicious, and everywhere all through the city. If we so much as look out the door, they'll see us."

"So how—?"

She shushed him and led him through the visitors' compound, finding her way with confidence to the common room where Kail slept with his mouth open, breathing deeply. There she directed Skender to take one end of her wing. Silently, they lifted it and carried it out into the corridor.

"Now what?" he started to ask, still not seeing what use it would be if they couldn't get out of the compound.

She shook her head and pointed upwards.

In the ceiling above their heads was a hatch.

He knew, then, *what* she had planned, but he was still none the wiser about *why*.

"Are we running away?" he hissed as she positioned a chair underneath the hatch.

"That wouldn't be very helpful," she said, climbing onto the chair and reaching up to pop the hatch. It opened without a sound, revealing, not a crawl space or attic, but open air and leaves. The foresters didn't need insulation, thanks to the canopy surrounding them. And in a culture that didn't employ flight, why would they consider the possibility of someone escaping *upwards*?

Chu hoisted herself up into the night air, then reached back down for the wing. Skender lifted one end up to her, and she silently hauled it outside. Then he climbed out and shut the hatch behind them.

The foggy night air sucked sensation from his fingertips almost immediately. Together, taking great care to avoid sharp twigs, they unfolded the wing and laid it flat against the roof. Reaching into the pocket of her leather pants, Chu produced her licence, which she plastered to the skin below her throat. Within seconds, the geometric lines of the charm began spreading across her skin. She blinked, and her eyes turned from brown to black.

"Are you going to tell me where we're going?" he whispered.

She shook her head, pointing over the edge of the roof to where the guards paced. He resigned himself to committing completely to her plan without knowing anything at all about it.

Chu strapped in first, then attached him in front of her. His body welcomed the warmth of hers, but he warned himself not to get too comfortable. They weren't about to resolve any issues by jumping from the summit of a heavily wooded cliff face bristling with archers and guards. This was about as far from romantic as they could get.

"Okay," she said, "here's what I think. We jump to get clear of the trees, then we go down to pick up speed. Once we're moving quickly enough, we zip away out of range. From there on, it's easy."

"Let me get this straight," he said, wishing he could see her properly. "We're going to go down as fast as we can through impenetrable fog while worrying about *arrows?*"

"That's right. Good to see you're keeping up."

He took a deep breath. "I'm glad it gets easier after that point. Otherwise I'd be worried."

"What's there to worry about? You've been down there. You've been noticing the landscape, even if you weren't aware of yourself doing it. With the wind on my side plus your memory to back me up, I figure we've got an even chance."

"Of what? Getting out of this alive?"

"Of finding the Panic city, of course. Now shut up and let's do this."

"Why—?" Her hand over his mouth reinforced the order. Giving in for the moment, he helped her manoeuvre the wing into position. They would need a run-up to reach clear space, and the way their legs tangled while merely walking didn't bode well.

"Let me do it," he whispered after one slip almost sent them crashing through the roof. "I'm at the front. It's the only way."

"But you're so *weedy*."

"My legs work fine, thanks, and I only have to carry you for a second or two. It's not as if you're particularly hefty yourself."

"Thanks, I think."

"You want me to give you compliments? Get me out of this alive and I guarantee as many as you want."

She capitulated, lifting her knees and crossing her ankles around his waist. He leaned forward, shifting their combined centre of gravity into a more stable position. They wobbled for a moment, but stayed upright.

He flicked through his memory, seeking camouflage charms that might hide them from view during their launch.

"Now, if we time it just right . . ." Her voice in his ear held him poised and ready. Partially visible over the line of the roof ahead of them was a sentry, going about his usual patrol. When he was well past, she hissed, "Go!"

He gritted his teeth and pushed off with his right leg. Their combined weight, plus that of the wing, was considerable but not immoveable. All he had to do was pick up speed and then fall forward.

One step, two steps. He tried to keep the noise to a minimum. Three steps, four steps. The edge of the roof was before him. Five steps—

With a grunt, he hurled them out into the air.

Chu instantly took over, tipping the right corner of the wing up so the full face of it caught what little breeze there was. With a snap, the fabric filled with air and their downward plummet eased, becoming a downward glide instead. Skender glanced behind him to see if the guard had noticed, but everything had happened so quickly that the visitors' compound was already out of sight.

Leaves and branches flashed by at disturbingly close range. Just one could tear the wing and send them to their deaths. He wanted to close his eyes, but didn't dare.

The steep flank of the ridge on which the city had been built seemed to follow them as the wing's path curved outwards. Chu grunted, exerting all her strength to force the wing away from the vertical. Wind and fog whipped at them, illuminated by the city lights.

Then suddenly all was dark. The sound of leaves rushing by vanished. Skender didn't know what had happened for a heartbeat or two—and then realised that they had flown down past the base of the city and into the Versegi Chasm. He wondered how close they had come to crashing into the rope bridge crossing it—then told himself to be grateful for small mercies. At least now they didn't have to worry about being seen or shot at. There were only the Chasm's walls to watch out for.

"You can see okay?" he asked Chu, knowing that the licence charm saw the wind via means other than light.

"Well enough, but I'm keen to get us out of here."

"How are you going to do that?"

"The air is marginally warmer down here. It'll give us altitude, eventually."

The wing banked and followed a wide spiral upwards. "While we're doing that, you can explain why on Earth we're going after the Panic city. Are you *determined* to get us both killed?"

"No more than usual. It just occurred to me last night that I joined this mission for a reason. I'm the scout, right? So why don't I do my job? Instead of waiting around to hear from Highson or Rosevear—on whose word this entire plan of Marmion's depends—it would be better to know in advance if the city is heading our way."

"That makes sense," he conceded. "Why not tell people what you had in mind? Why all this skulking around?"

"I can't imagine Marmion giving us permission," she said. "Let alone Heuve. The foresters don't like flyers and they certainly don't like me. I bet they won't turn down the intelligence we can offer, though, if we just go ahead and get it."

"So you dragged me along for my memory."

"Partly, but don't sound so disgruntled. It's also for your company."

He took some comfort from that as the wing kept turning clockwise, rising higher with each full circuit. His cheeks were numb with cold, and his eyes could see little in the darkness of the Chasm.

Several distant points of light gleamed in the murky depths. "Do you think the Eminent Delfine was right about people living down here? I think I can see torches. Real torches, not those brand things the foresters use."

Chu shrugged: unimportant. "Let me know if you hear anything from Marmion and co. I don't want our escape to cause a huge fuss."

"Not a thing so far," he said. "We might actually have got away with it."

"I told you they wouldn't think of looking *up* . . ." The smugness in her tone revealed more than just satisfaction at her plan having worked.

"What's going on, Chu? This isn't just about looking for the city, is it?"

"Of course not. Those pompous shits need to be taught a lesson or two. Flying may not be their thing, but that doesn't give them the right to look down on those who love it. It doesn't harm anyone and it's actually rather useful."

"You'd risk an arrow in your back—in our backs—to prove a point?"

"I think it's a pretty important point. Don't you?"

Skender didn't want to disagree. "There might be safer ways to make it."

Chu didn't say anything for a while. He couldn't tell if she was angry at him or just thinking. He decided that the safest course was to wait it out.

"Shilly said something last night," she eventually told him. "Why did my family move to Laure? Because people there have a reason to fly and there's no argument about the point of it. They weren't kicked out of the forest because of something they did; they didn't leave the forest because they didn't like it. They simply didn't fit in. I shouldn't be punished for that."

"So . . . what? You're going to reverse centuries of tradition by proving how useful you are? Is that your plan?"

"No, I'm just going to piss them off even more." He felt her indignation evaporate. "I know this probably isn't going to change anything, but I still need to do it, for my own sake. I'm a flyer. They need to see me as I am, not as an Outcast. If they still won't accept me, then that's their problem, not mine."

Skender knew it wouldn't be so easy. It *was* her problem. She had been dreaming about the Hanging Mountains all her life. To have that dream thrown back at her was a hard thing.

"Is that another reason to go looking for the city—because they're the flyers you've been looking for?"

"Oh, I'm not planning to get so close," she said. "And landing is out. Jao seems nice enough, but I don't think being human is going to count much in my favour at the moment."

"Or mine."

"Well, at least we've still got each other. Eh, Galeus?"

He couldn't see her face, but he could *feel* her smiling. As the wing took one final turn around its imaginary corkscrew and ascended out of Versegi Chasm, he decided that, even though they were back where they had started, that was definitely an improvement.

They flew for an hour, following terrain that he remembered and which she had noted from the ground in the previous three days. They didn't run into any mountains or cities. It was, in fact, rather boring, and Skender had to fight the urge to nod off on several occasions. There was no way to tell the time. Dawn showed no sign of coming, leaving the sky uniformly dull and dark.

"Do you have any idea where this city might be?" . . . after their third traverse of a particular valley.

"Not in the slightest. I expect we'll run into someone who does, soon enough, if the Panic are indeed on the move."

"*That's* your plan? To bump into a Panic patrol and have them lead us home? They're more likely to shoot us out of the sky."

"No way. They're big and slow. We're small and fast. And I bet you anything they're so accustomed to aiming at targets on the ground that they won't look up either."

"I think," he said, "you're already betting everything on that."

"I was being metaphorical."

"I'm not," he said.

"Why are you always so gloomy? You should be glad. Here we are, out getting some fresh air while that stuffy lot back there does nothing but sleep."

"Sleep has its appeal."

"Not as far as I can see." She banked to avoid a landmark he could barely make out through the fog. "When I think about all those hours wasted when I could've been—"

He never found out what she could've been doing, for at that moment a broad, rounded shape appeared out of the mist directly ahead of them.

"Whoa!" Chu wrenched the nose of the wing up, taking them over the balloon with barely centimetres to spare. Skender could have reached out and touched its leathery skin, it was so close.

"Do you think they saw us?"

He didn't know how to answer that. For a moment he couldn't even talk. "I've no idea." He heard no cries of alarm from the vessel they had just flown by. It had already vanished into the mist behind them. "Crashing into them is certainly going to attract someone's attention."

"Don't worry. It's not going to happen again." Skender's limbs grew heavy as she took them upwards. "Here's another bet. They've been flying a long time as a group, and have fixed ways of getting around. Familiar altitudes, usual flight paths, traditional formations. If we steer clear of those routes, we're not going to hit anyone."

"How many other bets are you planning to make tonight?"

"I don't know," she said, "but if you don't take a chance, you'll never get lucky."

She looped back over the Panic ship they had passed, wing slipping smoothly through the cool night air. The balloon—a fat sausage shape that looked like three dark grey spheres squashed together in some kind of net—supported a long, bladelike gondola containing seven Panic soldiers. Skender held his breath as they flew over it, even though he knew any sound quieter than a shout had no chance of being heard through the fog.

Chu took note of which way the balloon was pointing, and changed their course to follow it.

"See?" she said. "Easy."

"We're not there yet. If you can find the city without splatting us like a bug against it, then I'll say you've won the bet."

"What will I win?"

"The chance to live a little longer," he said. "Isn't that enough?"

"There's more to life than just living. I think so, anyway."

"And I'd agree with you. But death is death. There's no way to dress it up as anything else. If things go badly, there goes our chance to live at all, let alone well."

"We're not going to die."

"You saying that doesn't make it any less likely."

"Do you want to go back?"

He thought about it, even though there was no possibility of doing that. She was more likely to undo his harness and let him drop than try to land him back on Milang. "Actually, I don't. I just want you to cut the bullshit and be straight with me—*and* yourself, for that matter. We're taking a risk that could end badly. Pretending otherwise is just . . . well, asking for trouble. Or disappointment."

To his surprise, she chuckled. "You know, Mage Van Haasteren, I think you have something else on your mind than our little night flight."

He flushed. "That knife has two edges."

"True. Too true."

They flew in a straight line for so long that Skender wondered if Chu had fallen asleep. Acutely alert as he was, waiting for any sign at all from her, he could feel her breathing against the back of his neck but nothing more than that. When she wasn't making light of their situation, she was utterly closed to him. Yet he sensed her calling to him, hammering on the doors she had locked around herself. If *she* couldn't open them, how could he?

Don't stop now, he told himself. *Would anyone ever get what they wanted if they turned back at the first obstacle? Would Sal have made it back to Fundelry? Would Shilly have found Lodo? Would those two ever have got together?*

"Did you really give me your heart-name, back in Laure?" he said, hearing his own voice as though through ears blocked by altitude.

Finally, she moved. A quick nudge to tip the wing slightly to port, but it was something.

"Does it make any difference?" she asked.

"Of course it does. I hate myself for not remembering it, and I can understand why you hate me too."

"I don't hate you."

"Do you wish you hadn't told me your name? Do you wish I hadn't told you mine? I can't take that back—but you can. We can pretend it never happened. We can try to be friends, if that's all you want to be. I can live with that."

"Can you?"

"Well . . ." He wanted her to be honest with him, so he supposed he should be honest in return. "I'd be alive, but I might not be *living*."

Her right arm let go of the wing's control surfaces, just for a moment. Not for more than a second or two, but long enough to snake around him and press them together. For one warm, charged moment

their differences were forgotten. Words were unimportant. And neither the past nor the future mattered at all.

By the time he had reached up to take her hand in return, it had
slipped away and resumed control of the wing.

"There's something coming," she said. "I can feel it through the
licence."

"Where?" he asked, taking a deep breath of cold night air to clear
his mind. "Is it the city?"

"I don't know, but it's right ahead of us and getting closer."

She flew on, gripping the controls tightly. He could feel her tension growing as she concentrated on the wind, looking for any sign at
all, any hint that she should pitch the wing left or right, up or down,
to avoid a collision.

Skender noticed three things almost simultaneously: a tremor in the
air, as of a note so low he felt it more than heard it; a smattering of lights
ahead, uncannily like the stars on a cloudy night; and a deadening of the
background potential. The last bore no resemblance to that caused by the
Homunculus or the Caduceus in the Aad. This felt more as though every
last drop of the Change had been sucked out of the world, out of the *fog*.

"I think you're bang on target," he said, staring in a mixture of awe
and curiosity at the clump of fake stars coalescing out of the darkness. His
voice sounded strange in the vibrating air. "The question is: what now?"

"Now we work out where the thing is headed." She tugged the
nose of the wing up. It moved sluggishly but obeyed. "Then we call
the gang back home and let them know."

Skender resigned himself to a closer approach than he would have
preferred. Inexorably, the lights ahead grew brighter, resolving into the
angular shapes of the city. Skender made out dozens of odd-shaped
"buildings" hanging from a dense mass of balloons. There were spheres,
cubes, pyramids, and combinations of all three, all connected by walkways, ladders, and cables. Chimneys, doorways, windows—every aspect
of ordinary architecture was present despite its unusual location, hun-

dreds of metres above the Earth. The structure seemed both rigid and haphazard at the same time, as though it had been cobbled together more or less at random in its early days, but somehow became fixed during its evolution, locked into one particular configuration by necessity or tradition, or some other factor Skender couldn't imagine.

Among the cool, misty globes suspended over walkways and shining through windows, Skender made out flickering yellow patches that looked like nothing so much as fire, and clouds of black smoke rising through the grey mist.

He pointed them out to Chu, who had been concentrating on navigating their way up and over the city.

"Signs of fighting?" she suggested.

"I can't imagine what else it would be." He peered through the intervening fog, trying to absorb as much detail as possible before the mass of balloons got in the way. Black specks—Panic guards—ran back and forth on mysterious errands. None of them, as far as he could see, stopped to gawk at the wing flying by. They were a shadow moving swiftly against a dark sky.

A particularly strong vibration shook the wing. Chu wrenched it from side to side as though wrestling it into submission.

"Is everything okay?" he asked, tightly gripping the harness's leather straps.

"Just some . . . minor turbulence," she said through gritted teeth. "Nothing I . . . can't handle."

The nose of the wing lurched downwards, threatening to dump them headfirst into the conglomeration of balloons. Chu forced it back up, but not before losing altitude. They were now unlikely to clear the top of the city.

"Hang on," she said, dipping the left wing and giving up the fight. "Going over obviously isn't going to work. We'll try under."

"What's the problem?" he asked as his heart leapt into his mouth. Guides and stays rushed by as the wing picked up speed.

"Whatever's moving the city is trying to move us, too. That's all."

That's all? he wondered as a blur of misty lights swept past much closer than they had been before. This time, they were seen. At least one Panic guard looked up when they dropped past, eyes widening before disappearing behind them.

"Shit," he said. "We've been spotted."

"I can live with that," she said. "We'll be gone before they can do anything about us."

Their downward plummet ended with a twirling flourish that saw them swooping parallel to the underside of the city. Skender felt truly exposed there, unable to see directly above them because of the wing and imagining dozens, if not hundreds, of archers lining up for a clear shot. But Chu was experiencing similar difficulties as before; when she tried to peel away from the city, the motivator field resisted, drawing them back in. They were trapped.

He frantically thought through the situation, seeking any possible way out. The city's underside was ugly and not even remotely aerodynamic: pipes and chutes opened into clear air; maintenance ladders and balloon docking points protruded at odd angles. Fewer individual lights marred the sooty blackness, but from one particular structure a strong radiance shone.

"What do you think that is?" he asked, pointing.

"What's what?" she responded, distracted by the recalcitrant wing. "That?"

"What?"

They could have gone on all night if he hadn't realised that she genuinely couldn't see it. That meant the light he saw was coming solely through the Change.

"I think I've found the source of the problem," he said, kicking himself for not thinking of it sooner. An energy source powerful enough to shift an entire city *should* stick out. "That round hull over there, the one that looks like a giant almond shell. That's the motivator."

"Is there anything we can do about it?"

He hadn't thought that far ahead. A quick consideration of their options didn't give him reason to hope. "Not without a dozen Sky Wardens behind us, or maybe Sal."

"Well, I don't see any of them here with us, so we'll just have to ride it out." She put the wing into another nosedive, but it lasted barely five metres before curling around to face the way they had come. The interference didn't feel like wind blowing them off-course. It didn't really feel like *anything*. Instead of flying in the direction they wanted, the world seemed to turn around them, pointing them another way entirely.

As Chu tried once more to orient the wing away from the city, a dartlike arrow hissed past them, missing by barely a metre.

Chu cursed under her breath. Skender twisted to see who had fired at them. The arrow had come from the bottom of the glowing hull. Another quickly followed. Chu wrenched the controls and sent them spinning away.

No more arrows came from that quarter of the city—which surprised Skender, for they were still within both sight and range—but moments later a new salvo came from elsewhere. Three separate archers sent volley after volley at the dodging wing. Some missed by several body-lengths. Others were so close Skender felt they would be hit until the very last second when the wing shifted.

Chu zigzagged as best she could, but her grim silence told him everything he needed to know. She couldn't maintain that sustained effort much longer, any more than she could break the hold of the motivator. It was only a matter of time before one of the archers got lucky.

Glancing at the motivator, he found even more reason to panic. A small balloon had detached from the docks and was angling to intercept them. He pointed it out to Chu, who said, simply, "Fuck."

There was no way out of their predicament. Pinned on two sides, they had zero chance of escaping.

Somehow the balloon managed to move easily against the bubble of energy surrounding the city. It was more cumbersome than the wing, yet flew with surprising agility, slipping out from the glowing hull and swinging smoothly through the air towards them. He looked closely, but could see no obvious countercharms or chimerical mechanisms.

A pinprick of light flashed from the tiny gondola, spelling out letters in code that—much to his surprise—he recognised.

-U-C-H-U-C-H-U-C-H-U-

He stared dumbly for a moment, realising only slowly that one of the passengers in the balloon was wearing blue, not the brown and black of a Panic guard. He twisted around in his harness.

"Do you have that mirror thing Marmion gave us to communicate with?"

Chu reached over her head and slipped a tiny case from a junction of wing struts. "This?"

"Perfect!" He took it from her and opened the metal lid. Stored light flared right into his eyes, and he hurriedly faced it away from him. Snapping the lid open and shut, he rattled off a quick reply.

H-E-L-P-Y-E-S-H-E-L-P

The cycle of letters changed. F-O-L-L-O-W-F-O-L-L-O-W-F-O-L-L-O-W

"Go where they go," he told Chu, pointing. "They're friendly!"

Chu struggled to bring the wing under a semblance of control. Gradually, painfully, it came around on a heading that would take them to the tiny balloon, even now turning to follow a new course.

"Who is it?" she asked. "Highson or Rosevear?"

"Too far to tell." He didn't care either way. "They look like they know what they're doing."

"I certainly hope so." The wing lurched as another glassy arrow came entirely too close. "I'm sorry, Skender. I wasn't planning on us having to be rescued."

"Don't worry. It's better than being killed."

The little balloon led them directly under the glowing hull, where the disturbance was greatest. The wing swayed and shook as though trying to fly through treacle. Skender still wasn't sure they hadn't been lured into a trap. Having all hope snatched away just as he had regained it would be worse than never having had it at all.

"Try flying where they fly," he said. "There might be a particular path to follow."

"Just one? Unlikely, given the way the pilot was zipping around before. But there might be a—" She grunted with satisfaction as the turbulence around them suddenly eased. "Yes. Thank the Goddess. The balloon is protected, and it's leaving a clear path behind."

The going was almost too good, all of a sudden. The wing rushed forward as though set free from a cage. Clear air filled its charmed fabric with a snapping flutter and the little balloon loomed large ahead of them—small compared to the city but broader and more substantial than the wing. Skender saw Rosevear's face clearly illuminated as the warden reared back in alarm and dropped the signalling mirror to the floor of the gondola.

Then Chu lifted the wing half out of the wake. The drag of the motivator partially caught them again and decelerated the wing with a jerk. By dipping in and out of the wake, she was able to keep their speed down to that of the balloon, neither falling completely back under the spell of the motivator nor lunging forward too fast.

Rosevear and the single Panic pilot led them along the underside of the city, then sharply downwards as another brace of archers took a shot at them. As the distance between them and the motivator increased, so too did the turbulence steadily ease. Fog thickened around them; the city lights blurred. The soundless rumble that had rattled Skender's inner ear for entirely too long began to fade.

"Whew," Chu breathed as they finally passed outside the city's powerful influence. "That was too close."

Skender went to reply, but was interrupted by a voice threading through the Change.

"What are you doing here, Skender? I thought you were out hunting."

Skender concentrated to answer Rosevear's faint query. *"We were, but things got complicated. Chu and I came to check on your progress, since we hadn't heard anything."*

"Yes, sorry about that. We saw your wing getting stuck in the motivator field and came out to rescue you before the kingsfolk mistook you for the Swarm. Things have been complicated here, too. We triggered a full-on revolt between Oriel loyalists, the Heptarchists, and old-time monarchists. With the Quorum gone, there's no one left to decide which group to listen to, so they've had to talk to each other—and that's only causing more fighting."

"We saw the fires from the air." Skender glanced behind him, at the glowing smudge of the city fading once more into blackness. *"But at least the city's moving. Does that mean Oriel will talk?"*

"Griel is still working on him. We're hoping he'll cave in, if only to save face. If the city's parked next to Milang and he refuses to show, it'll look bad for him."

Skender hoped the warden was right. *"Well, that's something to tell Marmion, anyway. Do you want to do it or shall I?"*

"I will, but then I'd better get back. This balloon is our only escape route. While it's gone, Griel and Highson are stuck."

Chu circled the balloon while Rosevear called his superior. Skender couldn't hear the conversation, so he used the time to fill Chu in on what he had learned.

"Sounds to me like Oriel has Highson holed up in the motivator room," she said. "If he gets in there, it's all over."

"Don't bet on it," he said. "Highson is Sal's father. He may not be a wild talent, but I bet he can pull a trick or two out of his sleeve when he needs to."

Rosevear returned, sounding weary. His hair looked flat and inert, lacking its usual curly spring. *"Marmion asks that you keep following the city—from a safe distance, of course. If there's any deviation from its course, or any new developments at all, you're to let him know at once."*

Skender resigned himself to spending the rest of the cold night in the air. *"No worries."* The balloon was already swinging around to head back to the city. *"Good luck in there."*

"Thanks. I think we're all going to need it."

THE DELEGATION

"All the ambition in the world counts for nothing when one is isolated from or excluded by those with influence and power."

STONE MAGE ALDO KELLOMAN: ON A PRIMITIVE CULTURE

Shilly woke in the dead of night badly needing to relieve herself. She tried telling herself to ignore it and go back to sleep, but neither her bladder nor her brain would relent. She lay awake for what felt like hours with her legs crossed, worrying about Sal, Kemp, Tom, and Mawson, pondering the maddening patterns in her dreams, and mulling over the words of the Angel. *There are ways of running that don't require legs, just as there are ways of hearing that don't involve ears.* Perhaps there were ways of dreaming that didn't involve being asleep. If so, she had never learned how to do it.

Cursing the deep draught of water she had downed before retiring, she struggled out of bed and onto her feet. The visitors' quarters were very dark. The only sounds were the whirring of insects and the sighing of leaves, and from one of the rooms nearby a gentle, regular snore. Tapping ahead of her with the tip of her cane, she proceeded slowly out of the room she shared with Warden Banner and along the hallway towards the toilet facility: a small cubicle and a hole in the floor that led to a simple but practical system of treated bamboo pipes, flushed by ewers of dew-water refilled by attendants at odd times of the day. Banks of moss and fungus inhabited the sewerage channels, treating the waste so quickly and voraciously that only pure water emerged from the bottom of the pipe network at the base of the city.

As marvellous as the system was, Shilly just wanted to get there quickly and to be back in bed as soon as possible.

Her cane encountered the chair standing in the middle of the hall before her sleep-heavy eyes registered its presence. She stopped, forcing herself to concentrate on the unexpected obstacle. What on Earth was a chair doing in the hall? As she walked around it, her bare feet crunched on a leaf lying next to it on the polished wooden floor.

Slowly, her mind unfogging with glacial momentum, she looked up and saw the hatch.

Putting aside her need for the toilet, she hurried from room to room, performing a quick head count. There were so few people left it didn't take her long. Kail lay as silent as a board, barely breathing, on his cot in the common area. Banner was where Shilly had left her. Mage Kelloman snored softly with the bilby tucked tidily at his side. Jao curled around herself like a child in the room next to the mage's. When she looked into Skender and Chu's room, she found it empty—as she had expected—and so too was Marmion's.

Stranger and stranger.

Shilly found the warden in the kitchen, sitting at the table staring at his unbound arm. She froze in the doorway on seeing him, wondering if she should retreat and leave him to whatever private contemplation gripped him. A wooden brand glowed in one corner of the room, casting a faint yellow light over the awful truncation where his wrist had once been. The wound was puckered and raw-looking, not bleeding but still far from fully healed.

"What is it, Shilly?"

She wrenched her gaze from his arm and realised that he was looking at her.

"Skender and Chu are gone."

"I know. They went off the roof with the wing."

She blinked, startled by his calmness. "So what are we going to do about it?"

"Nothing," he said.

"Nothing?"

He shrugged. "Their beds are cold, so they've been gone a while. No alarm has been raised. If we tell anyone now, our hosts will only cause a fuss—especially on the eve of the summit. I think it's best we keep it under our hat for the moment."

"Just pretend nothing's happened?"

"As difficult as that sounds, yes."

A moment's thought convinced her he was right. What Skender and Chu had in mind she didn't know, but she didn't want to undo anything they might have set in motion. The truth was, she admired their resourcefulness, even if they were running the risk of ending the cautious truce existing with the foresters, should they be caught.

"Join me, if you want," he said softly.

"I don't want to disturb you," she started to say.

"If I'd wanted privacy, I would've locked myself in my room."

"Wait a sec, then." Taking a moment to finish the business she had got up for in the first place, she came back to find him exactly as he had been, staring at the table where his hand should have been as if watching invisible fingers flex.

She put an old black kettle on a bed of coals that glowed brighter as the metal approached, and sat opposite him, not sure where to look. She sensed a need in him to talk that made her uncomfortable even as she couldn't ignore it. "Is it still troubling you?"

"Yes. But my fingers don't itch any more. That's something to be grateful for."

"You don't look grateful to me."

His gaze lifted, met hers. "I'm just tired, Shilly. And maybe imagining things."

"What sort of things?"

"It just seems . . ." He shrugged. "Well, ever since we saw the first wraith, in the Divide, and I warded it off with this . . ." He lifted the stump with a clumsy motion, as though it wasn't part of him. "The yadachi have no idea what they're playing with. Bloodworking is dangerous. It's too close to us, too hard to control. That's what I've always been taught, and tempting though it was to take a disadvantage and turn it into an advantage, I wish now I'd never done it."

"That's what this is about? You used your wound against the Swarm?"

"Blood against blood. I can't say I did it consciously, but I did do it. That it appeared to work is no consolation."

"Appeared?"

"It repelled the wraith, sure enough. But for how long? At what cost?" He looked down at his wound, the lines on his face deeply graven. She studied his features rather than his hand, wondering at how much he seemed to have aged in so short a time. His round cheeks were sagging, the bags under his eyes cavernous.

She thought of Shom Behenna and his broken vows, the way they had eaten at him, darkened him.

"What were you, before this mission?"

"Me?" The question had the desired effect. She had surprised him, distracted him from the matter literally in front of his eyes. "Until a couple of years ago, I was a Selector in Yunda. Nothing special, I'll admit, but not to be dismissed lightly, either. The decisions I made could change lives forever. I like to think I never decided unfairly, or used the small amount of power I had unduly. I was respected by the communities I visited. I was happy."

Shilly tried to picture Marmion "happy," without success. "What went wrong?"

He sighed. "I became ambitious, began to look beyond the world I knew for something I lacked. I'd like to say that I thought myself capable of more, that I was motivated by something other than greed. But I'm afraid that's all it was. And—yes, why not?—there was a woman involved. I went to the Haunted City full of expectations.

None of them warranted, as it turned out. All of them came to nothing."

The mental image of Marmion in love struck her as even less likely than happy. "I'm sorry," she said.

"Don't be. I couldn't go back to Yunda, having burned too many bridges there, and the Haunted City isn't for me. Perhaps the Alcaide understood. He personally assigned me to this mission. You met him, I think. He's no fool."

Shilly nodded. Her memories of Alcaide Braham—a gruff, angry presence, seriously burned by Sal in Fundelry during their first escape attempt—were tied up with those of a time when the entire world had seemed against her. She had learned later that most teenagers felt that way, but she supposed that she had had more reason to think it than many.

"He was probably trying to help me," Marmion said, with no small amount of irony.

"Maybe he has," she said.

Silently, Marmion began binding his arm again.

The kettle whistled softly. She set about making a cup of tea. With her back to him, she asked, "Do you want one?"

Receiving no reply, she turned to see him with his eyes closed, listening to something she couldn't hear. "The city's on its way," he said.

"Was that Highson?"

He opened his eyes and shook his head. "Rosevear. Skender and Chu were with him. They went to find the city, he says, and almost got themselves killed."

Relief and worry combined in her throat. "Have you told them to come back?"

"No. To keep following the city. I don't want any surprises. It's good to have someone I can trust on the front line."

She could see the sense in that. "How long until the city arrives?"

"Two hours. There's an awful lot to arrange before then, and still no certainty as to whether Oriel will play along." He finished binding his wound. "Would you wake Warden Banner and Jao while I alert the guards? I think we should let Kail sleep a little longer."

Shilly poured her tea down the sink and hurried off to do as he asked.

Events unfolded rapidly from there. Although dawn was still more than an hour away, it seemed to Shilly that the Guardian's staff had been poised all night, ready to burst into action at the slightest word. Within minutes of Marmion informing the guards that intelligence had been received, an escort arrived to whisk him off to the Guardian. Shilly remained behind to bring everyone else up to date.

"I still don't see what this meeting can possibly achieve," said Kelloman, sleepily rubbing at his eyes. "The people here are too entrenched in their ways to ever change. The same holds for the Panic. War is inevitable, once they set their minds to it. We'd be better off staying out of the way."

"You do us and the Guardian a great disservice," Jao said. "We have coexisted for centuries. Only now does the relationship between our people turn sour."

"What about you?" Shilly asked the mage, to spare an argument. "What would you be doing if you weren't caught up in this with us?"

"Observing quietly from the fringes, my dear. That is my function, after all. Stand apart and record. Anything else would be interfering."

She held back from stating the obvious: that he carried out his duties safe in the knowledge that he could leave at any time he wanted. All he had to do was break the link between his "real" body and the one he presently inhabited, and he would instantly be thousands of kilometres away.

Word came before long that they were required to join Marmion at the citadel. "Bring the box," came the instruction via the guards. "And Kail."

Shilly knew exactly which box he meant. She told Banner and Kelloman to carry it, one at each end, while she went to wake up the tracker.

He stared bleary-eyed up at her. "It's started?" he said.

She nodded, unable to stop herself trying to find traces of Lodo in his hollow-cheeked, sun-worn face. "You don't have to come if—"

"No." He levered himself upright with one hand pressed firmly to his chest. "I'll be ready. There might be clothes for me, somewhere."

Shilly indicated a blue robe hanging over the back of a nearby chair. "Only this. They threw what you were wearing away, and we never found your pack."

A look of alarm crossed his face. He reached for the robe, and she gave it to him. In its folds lay a small leather pouch on a leather thong. His tension eased once he found it.

"That's safe, then," he said, putting it around his neck with a delicacy belied by his enormous hands, as though it held something infinitely precious. "Give me a moment."

She left him to dress but stayed within earshot in case he needed help. He didn't. When he emerged from the common room, looking awkward and uncomfortable in the traditional garb of a Sky Warden and wincing with the effort required to walk, they were ready to go.

The guards led them in single file up the ramps to the summit. The air was still and cold. Layers of fog hung in fragile sheets across their path; only tatters remained in their wake. A swarm of bats flew overhead, their beating wings and high-pitched cries raucous above the treetops. Shilly looked up, expecting to see the stars and finding only blackness. She would never get used to that—the shock of emptiness and void where there should have been light and wonder. It left the world feeling unbalanced, incomplete.

Both the Guardian and Marmion were waiting for them under the dead sky. The grassy meeting area was worn and scuffed. Servitors, guards, and ministers crowded the fringes, awaiting instructions. Seneschal Schuet occupied a space between both extremes, watching and listening.

"My daughter," said the Guardian, "left to deliver our message two hours ago. We have received a reply from Kingsman Oriel." She produced a curled-up slip of paper, such as might have come from the tube of a carrier bird. "He agrees to the meeting, but under duress. He will arrange for a barge to collect us at dawn, as per our suggestion. He recognises the concession we are making by trusting him—especially we who never fly. We will talk within bowshot of both cities. At the slightest sign of treachery, Lidia will be killed."

She stopped. Her throat moved for a moment, as though trying to swallow something distasteful, then she continued. "We have sent back a reply requesting that Lidia be present on the barge, so we can see with our own eyes that she has not been mistreated. If he accedes to that, all will go ahead as planned."

"And then?" asked Shilly. She gripped her stick tighter as all eyes turned to her. "You'll talk. What if he won't listen?"

"He has no reason to mistrust us," the Guardian said.

"That won't stop him. People can be stupid sometimes and that goes for the Panic too. What if nothing you say makes a difference? What if he insists on blaming you for the Swarm attacks?"

"Then he is a fool, and we will treat him as a fool deserves." The Guardian's expression was grim and determined. "We have no alternative. This is the course of action we will follow. We take it in the hope that those who would call us enemy will accept it for what it is: an expression of trust and respect, unmotivated by anger or fear. We will meet as equals, and talk as fellow victims of the crimes against the forest. I hope we will emerge as allies."

"Have you convinced your ministers of this?" asked Jao, unmoved. "Have you swayed those who wanted to shoot me out of the sky before asking me what I wanted?"

"That is a different battle," the Guardian conceded. "I'll fight it when this one is over."

There were no more questions. Servitors came forward to prepare the party for the meeting. Fresh clothes were offered, along with breakfast. Shilly didn't feel hungry, and she wasn't reassured when she tried to pin Marmion down on who exactly of the visitors would participate in the negotiations.

"I'll be there, of course," he said, "and Kail, representing the Strand. Mage Kelloman will stand for the Interior, since Skender isn't here."

"What about me?" she asked.

"It depends on space. I have no problem with you being present, but the Guardian makes the final decision. She might wonder what you can bring to the discussion, who you represent, why she should put you in the firing line. You understand, don't you?"

Shilly could see his point, but she didn't have to like it. "I understand." It didn't matter that she had met the Angel, or that man'kin seemed to think her and her dreams important. It didn't matter that she and Sal had been caught up in the story of the Homunculus from the start. It didn't matter that Tom seemed to think that she would be critical when the crunch finally arrived. It didn't matter that she hated feeling left out while everyone else got to be important.

She tried to keep her disgruntlement to herself, knowing it to be just that, as dawn approached.

A horn sounded, then another.

"That's the signal from the lookouts." The Guardian clapped her hands for attention. "The city has been sighted. Places, everyone! Set the brands alight."

Shilly watched as servitors ran in all directions raising a dozen massive poles, each no wider than her forearm but many metres tall, around the perimeter of the open area. When they were in place, a bearded man in a yellow-and-brown robe brought them to life. Bright yellow light flared from their uppermost tips, casting pale shadows in all directions.

More horns sounded.

"Remind the archers that the first to fire leaves the forest forever!" The Guardian looked for Seneschal Schuet, and waved him to her.

The humming of a chimerical engine ascended from the background hubbub. As it registered, chatter gradually ceased until it was the only sound to be heard in the citadel. A steady, low-pitched drone, it seemed to be coming from all quarters of the sky at once.

Then a bulbous, multilobed shape appeared, lit from below by the brands. Four balloons bound together in an elongated clover shape suspended a rectangular gondola high above the open area of the summit. Its twin engines glowed like red eyes through the fog as it circled once, then came in to land. Archers followed its movement, ready to loose a volley of arrows at the slightest false move.

The Guardian and her entourage backed away to make room. Shilly stayed as close as she was allowed, craning for a view of the gondola's interior. When their heads finally came into view—one human and a crew of three Panic—she felt a pang of disappointment that Highson wasn't among them. Neither were Oriel or Griel. The only people she recognised were Rosevear and Ramal, the latter standing at the front of the gondola, scowling from under heavy brows at the humans watching her descend.

Rosevear leapt out as soon as the ground came close enough. He ran to Marmion.

"Griel and Oriel sent me to tell you that everything is organised and ready. Everyone intending to come to the barge needs to board this balloon, and it'll take you there."

"Please tell the Guardian." Marmion indicated the woman waiting stiffly to his right.

"Yes, of course. I apologise." The young warden sketched an awkward bow. "It's an honour."

The Guardian waved away the formalities. "Have they acceded to my demands? Will Lidia be present?"

"She will."

"Then I see no reason not to proceed."

"How many can that balloon carry?" Shilly asked.

"Fifteen," Rosevear replied, acknowledging her with a quick nod.

Shilly performed a quick count: the Guardian, Seneschal Schuet, Marmion, Kail, Kelloman, Rosevear and Highson and at least three guards to balance out the Panic crew, and two empty seats for Lidia Delfine and Heuve, after the meeting.

She stepped back as the Guardian picked exactly the people she had expected.

"Don't worry," whispered a voice in her ear. "There's a widow's walk running the entire length of the upper wall."

Shilly turned to see Minister Sousoura standing directly behind her. The woman pointed up at the edge of the open-air roof.

"A what?"

"An observation deck. Somewhere to watch from."

Shilly blushed, feeling decidedly provincial even though she had had no way of knowing what the term meant. "Will you take us up there?" she asked, wondering why Sousoura was suddenly being so friendly.

"When the Guardian has gone, I'll show you the way."

The boarding party filed onto the gondola, one by one, through a gate that opened in the side. Kelloman was puffed up with self-importance and appeared not to notice the tiny creature that followed him aboard. Kail moved stiffly, obviously in some discomfort, while Marmion walked with quiet dignity, as did the Guardian. Seneschal Schuet stayed close to her at all times, accompanied by the three guards. Two of them lugged the wooden box aboard with them. The third carried a black cotton sack over one shoulder.

Ramal boarded last, closing the gate behind her with a firm click. The moment they were all seated, the pitch of the engines increased. With a brisk gust of air, the balloon ascended smoothly into the sky.

The clouds had begun to lighten. Dawn was growing near.

"About that observation deck . . ." Shilly prompted Sousoura, taking some comfort from the possibility that she might be able to see after all.

"Of course. Do you want to ask your companions?"

The minister gathered together a contingent of peers and servitors as Shilly asked Jao and Banner whether they would like to watch from the widow's walk. They agreed, looking equally at a loss as to Sousoura's interest. When the minister pronounced the group ready, they hurried to a stairwell tucked neatly into one corner of the building. The stairs turned in a tight spiral up through the sturdy wooden walls before emerging, as promised, at the very top.

There, the narrow walkway ran the entire circumference of what, in another structure, might have been the roofline, with occasional platforms large enough to hold a group of twenty people or so. The view from the walk was unobstructed by trees. The tall belltower loomed behind them, facing the mountains.

Shilly, when she climbed stiffly to the top, had to force her way through a crowd pointing in amazement and dread at the floating city half-visible as a vast, light-speckled presence within the clouds. The lack of clear detail made it look much larger than the first time Shilly had seen it. Its edges blended with the clouds, borrowing some of their immensity. Even she thought it an ominous, threatening sight.

The balloon carrying the Guardian and the others looked tiny in comparison—and so did the barge where the meeting itself would take place. A broad, square, flat-bottomed vessel supported by two cigar-shaped balloons tied in an X, the barge was stationed exactly midway between the two cities. Shilly could make out several figures standing in the barge, waiting for the Guardian to arrive, but she couldn't tell who they were.

"I don't know whether Panic eyes are any better than human," Shilly said to Jao, who had come to stand next to her, "but if you can tell whether Highson is over there, I'd be immensely relieved."

"So would I," Jao replied. "Alas, I see no better than you. I'm having no luck looking for Griel."

The sight of something moving swiftly and silently through the clouds to one side of the barge sent a momentary pang of fear through Shilly. It came and went, then appeared again some distance away. *The Swarm!* she thought, and readied herself to cry out an alarm. Then she recognised the swept-back lines of Chu's wing, and relief flooded her.

Good luck, she wished them, as the balloon docked with the square barge. The midair manoeuvre was conducted in silence and at a sufficient distance that it would have been easy to feel removed from the events taking place over there. But she felt no such disconnection. Her thoughts were entirely on what happened next.

That explained, she told herself later, why she didn't notice what was happening right beside her—the subtle widening of a gap around Shilly, Banner, and Jao; the lack of conversation when Minister Sousoura glided confidently forward—until the knifepoint pricked her side and a strong, perfectly manicured hand gripped her shoulder.

"If the Guardian dies," said the minister, "you die."

Shilly could only nod, and watch and hope.

THE WRAITH

"Examining the surface of things is the most obvious
and least interesting way of studying the world.
Of greater relevance are the things going on beneath,
between, and behind everything we take for granted."
THE BOOK OF TOWERS, EXEGESIS 25:3

Habryn Kail tried not to wince every time the gondola swayed beneath him. His chest felt taut and hot under his fingers, but the wound only hurt when he moved. Or breathed deeply. Or thought about it.

He concentrated on the spectacle before him: one city clinging to the steep walls of a spur of rock that was a mountain in its own right, by Strand standards; another hanging in the clouds suspended from balloons as large as the city itself.

The barge waited between them, preternaturally still under its cross-shaped balloons, a centre around which powerful forces had gathered. He could see four humans standing with four Panic. Rosevear and Highson he recognised; the two others, he gathered from the conversations around him, were Lidia Delfine, the Guardian's daughter, and her bearded bodyguard, Heuve. The four uniformed Panic figures were harder to identify: he presumed one was Kingsman Oriel, the self-styled leader of the city, and two were obviously guards. But who was the one standing to one side with a crude iron circlet around his head, and why did his eyes seem to gleam brighter than the others in the growing light?

In the exact centre of the platform where the meeting would take

place rested a long, rectangular table on sturdy wooden legs. There
were no chairs, so it wouldn't be a conference as he had initially imagined it. The platform was surrounded by a wall one metre high, and
beyond that was nothing but empty space.

The balloon sidled up to the platform and one of its crew threw
over a rope. Once lashed together, gates on each flying craft were
opened, allowing a gangplank to connect the two. Mage Kelloman
looked at the plank and his white skin paled even further. Guide wires
set at waist height obviously failed to reassure the mage, for the hands
gripping the seat in front of him remained tightly clenched.

Kail could sympathise, but he wouldn't let fear stop him from
attending the meeting. When his turn came to cross, he did so without
hesitation, following Marmion stiffly, trying not to let his infirmity
show and knowing he was probably failing.

Everyone gathered at the table, adopting positions as much by
instinct as by design. The contingent from the Panic Heptarchy stood
on one side; those from Milang stood on the other. Lidia Delfine and her
mother remained apart for the moment, and they acknowledged each
with little more than a slight nod. Highson and Rosevear stood opposite Kail and Marmion. Kail couldn't tell if they were surprised to see
him. He still felt slightly unsettled himself at where fate had led him.

The goateed Panic male with the iron crown took a position at one
end of the table, symbolically standing between the two groups.

"Welcome, friends," he said, encompassing both sides of the table
with outstretched arms. "It's high time we met to discuss our differences. Too long has our true enemy exploited the hostility between us.
The moment has come to put the past behind us and begin building
the future."

"Spare us the rhetoric, Griel," snarled the sour-faced Panic male
standing opposite the Guardian. Oriel's forked beard was an exercise in
vanity. His bald skull shone like polished ivory in the morning light.
"I'm here solely to listen to a confession. It's a bit late for an apology.

Too many of my people have died. When retribution has been made, then and only then will I consider peace."

"Retribution?" the Guardian echoed. "We have committed no wrong."

"No?" Oriel vented his anger directly at her. "You confound our compasses and attack our patrols—"

"As you attack our patrols, without provocation."

"You send your ghouls and wraiths to destroy our homes."

"They have destroyed our homes, too—and killed my own son."

"The kingsfolk have lost entire families!"

"Clearly, both sides have suffered," broke in Griel. "On what grounds do you accuse each other?"

The Guardian turned and reached for the cotton sack carried by one of her soldiers. At the same time, Oriel reached down to his feet.

With a clatter, two bloodstained pieces of armour—one broad leather chestplate patterned with leaves, the other a light chain shirt featuring circular motifs—slammed down on the table.

"The so-called wraith we shot down was wearing this," said Griel, indicating the chain shirt. "The body inside was decidedly human."

"The wraith *we* shot down was a Panic soldier," said the Guardian.

"Both were fakes," said Marmion, stepping up to the table. "Your enemies played on your natural suspicion to divert attention away from them."

"Why should I believe you, human?" sneered Oriel.

"Because I hold no allegiance to either side. Because my people have helped both foresters and kingsfolk in this struggle."

"You've aided traitors and saboteurs. You have kidnapped my entire city!"

"As you have kidnapped the Guardian's daughter and taken prisoner friends of mine." Marmion waved away the objection. "We can stand here all day, trading insults and slights, but that won't get us anywhere. I suggest we open our minds to the possibility that we're being used and do something constructive about it."

"I have no reason to believe you." Oriel folded his long arms. His black beard stuck straight out from his chin, a stance of unmistakeable hostility. "You have no evidence to back up your claims. I see only a plot to undermine my rule and therefore my people."

"*Your* rule?" asked Griel. "*Your* people?"

Oriel puffed out his chest. "I rule by the mandate of the Heptarchs."

"What happened to the King? To the notion that the Heptarchs act in his stead?"

"Times are changing, Griel. Haven't you noticed? The Quorum is gone. The city is under attack. Perhaps it's time for the Heptarchs to step permanently aside for a new King, since the old one obviously isn't coming back."

"Isn't he?" In one smooth motion, Griel took the iron circlet from his head and threw it on the table between them. "Try it on for size. I dare you."

Oriel looked down at the scuffed grey circlet, then back up at Griel. Something passed between the two Panic males that Kail didn't quite fathom. Not an understanding, exactly. Perhaps a recognition, but of what, he couldn't tell.

"I have been granted a vision," Griel said softly, "of a time when foresters and kingsfolk work together. Some say fog and wood shouldn't mix, and traditionally that has always been so. But perhaps the time has come for a change—a change for the better, erasing old suspicions and healing wounds untreated for too long. Fog and wood *do* mix in the forest, to magnificent effect. Why shouldn't we?"

"You're a fool," said Oriel softly, but he made no move to pick up the circlet. "I do not listen to fools."

"Then you'd better listen to reason," said Marmion, forcing his way into the tense standoff between the two Panic males. "You want evidence? I'll give you evidence."

Pushing the crown back towards Griel, he indicated that the guards carrying the wooden box should come forward. They hefted their burden onto the table, where it settled with a thud, then stepped back.

Marmion put his one hand on the box's rough pine lid but did not open it. The barge swayed as though a strong gust of wind had caught its broad underside.

"The creature in this box is one of the nine that has been hunting these forests since three weeks ago. It comes from the time before the Cataclysm, a time we know very little about. I know this, though: it's mindless and rapacious; it would kill us in a frenzy of bloodlust were I to set it free now. It is not the sort to plan and enact elaborate revenge."

"Yet you claim that these are the beings responsible for setting my people against hers?" asked Oriel, indicating the Guardian with a contemptuous flick of a finger. "Your lie is paper-thin."

"It's no lie. Your empyricist recognised the spoor of these creatures. Were he present, he could identify our captive here."

"Do you know where he is, Oriel?" asked Griel, nodding at one of the female soldiers. "Ramal found his observatory empty yesterday."

"That mad old tree frog? Who cares where he gets to when he's not in his nest?"

"Perhaps we all should," said Marmion, "because he might even identify the new player that has joined the game: another creature from the old times, a being called Upuaut that we might describe as a golem. Two of our number have met it: Kail here, and Skender, who is watching this meeting from nearby. The nine hunters, once called the Swarm, have been given purpose and new potential for mischief by Upuaut. This one is your true enemy. The hunters we can kill, one by one, but not if our efforts are divided, not if we set to each other's throats like angry dogs, not if we let Upuaut win before the true battle has really started."

"He's right," said Highson Sparre on the far side of the table. "We have no quarrel with either you or the Guardian, and we have no allegiance, either. That we're human doesn't make us any more likely to cooperate with the foresters. We have our own purpose, our own mission."

"So why are you helping us?" asked Oriel over his armoured shoulder. "Out of the goodness of your hearts, I suppose."

"No," said Kail with utter frankness, "because you're in the way."

Griel barked with laughter. "They have us there, Oriel. Why don't we get a sense of perspective and talk like adults rather than the children we've become?"

Oriel snorted. "You can talk all you want. There's nothing in that box but air, and nothing behind these words but dreams and lies. Minds from before the Cataclysm? I'd rather believe in traitors. Not if we were the last people on Earth would I ally myself with you. And you?" He indicated the outsiders with one sweep of a gloved hand. "You go on your merry way as you wish. I'll not stop you. But if you come near my city again, I'll have you all killed."

"That's a decision you would live to regret," said Marmion softly.

"Is that a threat?" Oriel leaned low over the table so he was eye to eye with Marmion.

"Yes, but I'm not the one making it." Marmion opened the lid of the box and pushed it roughly forward.

Oriel recoiled as though Marmion had thrust a snake into his face. A second later, everyone around the table did the same. Kail felt it too: a wave of icy malignancy and hate radiating outwards from where the wraith lay imprisoned. He forced himself not to look away, darkly curious to see with his own eyes what had only been hinted at since his return.

Within the wooden box, resting on a bale of straw and dried leaves, protected from the outside world by an inner shell of lead, was a cylinder of rough-forged iron. Neither vigorously worked nor completely unfashioned, it looked like no weapon Kail had ever seen before, yet it had a pommel at one end bound up in dark leather thongs and came to a blunt point at the other. Between those two points, the iron resembled a cross between a club and a sword, with blunt charms carved in a straight line down one side. The light skittered sickly off it, as though repulsed.

That wasn't the worst of it. Inside the metal, the being it contained railed against captivity. It hissed through the Change, as if in pain. The sound issued from the metal itself, as though it had been heated and dipped in hot fat.

"Speak," Marmion commanded it.

The hissing continued unchecked.

"I know it can talk," Marmion told Oriel. "I've spoken to it, and so have Skender and Warden Banner. It's a living being, if not very bright, and it has clear preferences. It prefers the night, for one. That's probably why they're here in the Hanging Mountains, where the sun is perpetually shrouded and the hunting is good. Even this morning's weak light pains it. Perhaps it would prefer to be locked up again, safe in the darkness for the rest of eternity."

He reached for the lead-lined lid, and the wraith's voice rang out in the icy morning. *I am Giltine, the one who stings. Come, my sisters, come!*

Oriel stared at the thing with horror on his face. He could clearly hear the voice, although it spoke only through the Change. "What is it? How have you bound it—and why?"

"Its origins are unknown to me," said Marmion. "All I can tell you is that it has been confined to the iron by the charms you see etched in the metal. As to why—"

"We can't kill it," interrupted Kelloman. "Believe me, we've tried. Fire knocks them out but doesn't get rid of them entirely. Not the sort of fire we have access to, anyway."

"This is the thing that killed my brother," said Lidia Delfine, grief and hatred warring openly across her face.

"If it's what you say it is," said Oriel, "then we should throw it into the Versegi Chasm and have done with it forever. Why haven't you?"

"It's only one of them," Marmion said. "Only so long as the metal is intact will the binding remain fast. Should it rust or melt, its efficacy will end, and the creature will escape."

Come, my sisters, come!

Kail raised a hand to his chest, where his wound had begun to itch. He tried to remember everything the twins had said about the creatures called the Swarm.

"There are ways to fight them," he said, a vision burned in his mind of the Homunculus driving the Swarm back with one palm outstretched. "I've seen it done, but the means is beyond my knowledge."

"Where have you seen it?" asked Oriel. Highson, too, glanced at him, lips tightening.

"That's not important," said Marmion. "We can discuss the details later. The important thing to agree on is that *this* is your enemy, not each other—this and eight more creatures exactly like it. Once we cross that hurdle, much that is presently difficult will become simpler."

Oriel nodded warily, indicating that he was listening but not yet fully convinced. "How am I to know that this isn't some elaborate parlour trick?"

Marmion reached out and slammed the lid shut. "If this thing succeeds in bringing its sisters here, you'll be in no position to doubt any longer."

"Is that likely?"

"You now know as much as I do about these creatures. This was a risk I had to take, in order to convince you. *Are* you convinced?"

Oriel looked more shaken than anything else. "You bring me here," he said to Griel, "with threats of death and destruction, only for me to hear more of the same. I am not relieved of any of my fears. They are, in fact, worsened by the fear I see in your eyes." He swept the gathering with his stare. "Are we mice who cower at the shadow of an eagle? We are not. We face this evil the best way we can, and if that means talking—" he put his hands on the table and stared down at the box "—then I will talk. But I make no promises."

"None are required." Marmion stepped back and waved the guards forward. They removed the box from the table and put it to one side. "Guardian? I'll let you negotiate the release of your daughter. When you need my advice regarding the Swarm, I will be here."

Marmion backed away to join the others, leaving the major players to thrash out their differences.

"Clever," whispered Kail.

Marmion feigned a nonchalant shrug. "They would've worked it out eventually."

"I'm not so sure about that—and that's not what I meant, anyway. You did this deliberately. You and Griel, I bet."

"What?"

"Got everyone together in one place. Opened the box." Kail became conscious of Kelloman listening in. "The traps you laid in the forest caught nothing, but what could be a better target than this?"

The mage's eyebrows went up. "A bit of a risk, don't you think? We're not exactly in the best fighting shape."

Marmion shushed him. "We're as able as we'll ever be. And Griel had nothing to do with it. Maybe he guessed, or came to the same conclusion. I don't know. But the result is the same. We're all here and waiting. If the Swarm don't do something now, they never will."

"We're not all here," said Kail.

Marmion looked at him inquiringly.

"The Homunculus is missing. I notice you've been keeping that particular detail very quiet. Are you hoping Upuaut will get rid of that problem for you?"

Marmion leaned in close and spoke with tightly wound restraint. "There's nothing I can do for the Homunculus now. It's beyond my reach—and I'm glad for that, to be honest. I can only deal with one crisis at a time. I'm only human."

Kail raised a calming hand. He believed Marmion, which surprised him, and he resolved likewise to let the matter of the twins go for now. Wherever they were, whatever they were doing, he only hoped they would remain safe.

Silently, feeling the wound in his chest still tingling from the proximity of the wraith, he hoped the same for all of them.

THE SUMMONING

**"Humanity's ability to channel and concentrate the
Change is unparalleled in nature. The only force
capable of such explosive and sweeping energies
is fire, and that is mindless and unfocused.
Conversely, while other minds do exist in the Change,
they don't use it as we do. Humanity therefore stands
at a critical nexus between two worlds—a unique
and sometimes very dangerous position."**
MASTER WARDEN RISA ATILDE: NOTES TOWARD A UNIFIED CURRICULUM

Skender was beginning to feel dizzy. For an hour, he and Chu had been circling the barge, keeping always at a safe distance. Thus far they had avoided any overeager archers while watching people— arguing, gesticulating, pacing back and forth, putting things on the table then taking them off again—but he could no more tell what they were saying than he could have read a book held at that distance.

"Looks like the Eminent Delfine is joining her mother at last." He squinted. "And the Panic soldiers who came with the Guardian are going to stand with Oriel. I think that means our job is done."

"I hope so." Chu sounded tired, and Skender could understand why. Flying was exhausting, even if it had lately been round and round in circles. "If we're going to land, we'll need to signal Rosevear or Highson and get them to talk to the Guardian. She can signal to her people in Milang and tell them not to stick us full of arrows."

"That just leaves the question of where to put down."

"At the bottom of the mountain, where the slope isn't quite so dramatic. There's bound to be a clear patch somewhere."

In the forest? Skender wanted to ask, but didn't. The only clear patch he knew of was the knoll, half a day's march away. "Sounds like a fine idea to me. Got that mirror handy?"

This time he didn't need the starlight it had stored. He was able to reflect the hazy glare of the sun instead. It took him a moment to attract the attention of one of the wardens, but when he did a reply came soon enough.

Fragmented words flashed in rapid code between the barge and the wing. Their plan was quickly approved. The archers of Milang would be told to let the wing land where it chose, provided it posed no threat to the public.

"Yeah, right," said Chu with a snort. "One bad landing and suddenly you're a health hazard."

"You've had more than just the one," he said. "I can think of at least three—and they're only the ones I know about."

"Picky, picky." She tugged the port wingtip down, freeing it from the endless circle. It dropped into fresh air with a sound like a sigh.

The blowing of signal horns accompanied them as they approached the forest city and began to descend. Although they had permission to occupy its airspace, Chu took pains not to alarm anyone—or to stay in range for too long, just in case the order wasn't immediately understood.

Landing first, Skender told himself, beginning to look forward to taking a break from their lookout duties, *then the long climb back up the hill*. That, he wasn't looking forward to. A bath and a change of clothes at the end of it would be very welcome, though. And then, when things quietened down . . . *I don't hate you*, she had said. That could mean *anything*.

The thought trailed off as a hint of smoke hit his nostrils. It made his stomach rumble for breakfast, and that put all other considerations aside.

"I want eggs," he said. "I don't care what kind of eggs they are. Bantam, pigeon, turkey—anything. And I've seen pigs in the forest, so there must be bacon too."

"Thinking with your stomach, eh? That makes a nice change."

"I'm just saying."

"And *I'm* just saying . . ."

They were halfway down the city's southern flank when he realised that the smell of smoke was growing stronger.

"That's some feast," he said, starting to wonder. "There," he said, pointing down at a dark column rising out of the mist below. "Does that look odd to you?"

"Odd," she agreed, "and hot. Hang on."

She put the nose down and headed for the column at speed. Their ride grew turbulent as they flew through dense layers of fog. Skender might have learned to recognise some recurring cloud shapes and the atmospheric currents that caused them, but the lower the wing went, the less familiar the clouds became. What Chu saw through her licence she wasn't revealing just yet.

She levelled out as they approached the top of the column of hot air he had spotted. Distantly he heard the sound of horns blowing—not the calm transmission of orders from above, but a rapid staccato signalling alarm from below.

"There's definitely a fire down there," Chu said, swinging them around the billowing smoke. Strong, erratic gusts shook the wing from side to side. Particles of ash got in Skender's eyes and nose, making him cough.

"We should take a closer look," he said, although his lungs disagreed. "We'll see it better from above—better than those down there, anyway. We might be able to help."

"All right," she said, "but be warned. It's going to get bumpy."

She was true to her word. The closer they flew to the source of the smoke, the rougher the wind became. Great gouts of hot air spewed up from the fire, which appeared to be confined to a vertical strip at the very base of the city. The flames themselves were mostly invisible behind roiling black smoke, but every now and again he glimpsed flashes of orange and yellow licking at branches and leaping from tree to tree, bright and furious.

"You'd think the fog would put it out," he said, his mouth tasting of ashes.

"Not once the wood catches. Full of resins and oils, this lot. Could burn for weeks if it really gets going." She peered over his left shoulder. "There are people fighting it. Look."

He made out figures scurrying through the trees, shovelling dirt or carrying water to the fringes of the blaze.

"There's not much we can do here," he said. She made a noise of agreement. "Seen anywhere flat to land?"

"No, but—" She froze, then groaned. "Over there. More smoke."

She let go briefly to point. On the edge of visibility he made out another column of smoke further around the city's base, not as large as the first but billowing strongly.

"What are the odds of two fires in one day?" he asked.

"Don't even ask." She caught a thermal from the fire below and urged the wing towards the second outbreak. Tongues of fire leapt through the treetops, visible even from a distance. And beyond it, further around the base of the city, a third fire was just getting going.

"Deliberately lit," said Skender, only beginning to think through the ramifications of their discovery. He and Chu had seen torches in the Versegi Chasm just hours before. That would have been a perfect way to get a fire started without being seen.

"But who would do this?" he asked. "Not the Panic. They wouldn't be so stupid."

"Didn't Lidia Delfine mention people living in the Chasm? Perhaps it's them."

"Why would they? They might not even exist." As Chu took the wing along a tight figure eight, uncertain where to fly next, he felt a chill sweep through him despite the warm, ash-heavy air. It would take time for word of the fires to reach the citadel. By then it might be too late to put them out and half the city could be ablaze. The higher it went, the harder it would be for people to escape. He pictured a panicked throng gathering in the Guardian's open-air citadel, with nowhere to run as the fires closed in.

"Over there," he said, pointing along the base of the city at three spiralling trails of cloud. "Those contrails. Can you see them through the licence?"

He felt her nod. "Cold. You don't think—?"

"I *do* think, but we need to be sure."

"Uh, right, but are you sure that's what you want to do? I've seen these things, and they're bloody fast."

"I know. I've seen them too. We'll just have to be faster." A fluttering sensation in his chest greeted that bold announcement. "There isn't time to argue about it. Let's go!"

Chu, perhaps startled by his uncharacteristic decisiveness, stopped arguing and set the wing on a course chasing the source of the contrails.

The Swarm. Skender had no doubt they were behind the fires, but he needed something better than instinct to send the information to the others through the Change. He needed proof, even if it came in the form of an image of a mouthful of teeth closing about his face.

Shilly noticed the flurry of horn-blowing and bell-ringing at the same time as the others around her. Minister Sousoura, who had taken the knife away as the meeting on the barge dragged on without incident, brought the blade back against her ribs.

"What's going on?" Sousoura asked her.

"How should I know? I don't understand that racket."

"Danger," the minister said, listening with one ear cocked for cadences in the rhythmic, atonal calls. "Fire. The city is aflame—and the bridges across the Chasm are cut!"

A ripple of shock and dismay spread through the group of conspirators gathered on the widow's walk. Some of them were guards, and there were at least two other ministers. The rest seemed to be high-ranking citizens who had decided to take the law into their own hands. None had behaved with open aggression to their three captives. Beyond a poke with the tip of a blade and a whispered warning or two, they might have been enjoying a pleasant outing in the misty daylight. Conversation turned around who amongst the Guardian's closest advisers had insulted whom and what would change when Lidia Delfine took the Guardianship. Someone looking from a distance would never have known the truth.

Minister Sousoura was no daydreamer. She had gathered those lackeys around her to use as a camouflage. She was the one Shilly was most concerned about.

"Tell me what you've done," the minister hissed in her ear. "Tell me what new treachery you have planned."

Shilly raised her hands in protest. "No treachery, I swear. You know better than anyone I've been right here the whole time, and I've had no chance to talk to anyone. If something's going on, I'm not a part of it."

Sousoura wasn't so easily appeased. "It was all prearranged," she said, a calculating look in her eyes. "That flyer of yours—I saw it slipping through the clouds. It could set fires while everyone's attention was on the Guardian. Is that what this is? You distract us with promises of peace while you and your Panic allies raze the city to the ground?"

"It doesn't matter what I say. You're not going to believe me." Shilly caught Jao's eye. The Panic female was the oddest note in the conspirator's grand pretence of normality, and the one most likely to attract unwelcome attention. Thus far, she had kept a determinedly low profile, leaning against the wooden wall and watching the meeting on the barge like the crowd surrounding her.

Jao shook her head, saying without words that the Panic had nothing to do with the fire. Shilly believed her.

The minister was thinking while the crowd buzzed restlessly with the news. Shock and alarm were very much the order of the moment, but no one as yet had suggested taking concrete steps.

"Shouldn't we evacuate or something?" Shilly asked, earning herself another poke.

"We're not so easily defeated," the minister said, as though Shilly had suggested a full-scale retreat. "Fires don't frighten us. We're staying right here—so you'd better hope your plan fails, otherwise you'll burn along with us."

Shilly glanced over the wall at a pall of black rising from the base of the city and hoped that, whoever's plan it actually was, someone was doing something about it.

Kail felt Skender's fear a split second before the channel between them truly opened. Every mage and warden on the barge looked up at the same moment, smelling the smoke and feeling their hair singe. Heat blasted their faces. Burning leaves whipped up at them. Powerful waves of hot wind tugged the balloons above them, wrenching them from side to side and making them barely controllable. On the heels of all this, an icy-cold presence came snapping at them.

Then the channel slammed shut and Kail staggered forward, clutching his chest. "Skender!"

"That stupid boy." Kelloman looked as drawn as Kail felt. "Guardian—you must do something. The fire—"

"We know about the fire," the Guardian said, crossing the barge to meet his gaze, forcing him to focus. "What about Skender? What has he seen?"

"The Swarm," said Marmion. "The Swarm is lighting the fires under the direction of Upuaut. They wouldn't have thought of it themselves."

The box to one side of the table caught Kail's attention. Could the Swarm and Upuaut have put such a plan in motion after Marmion had exposed Giltine to the sun, or had this been prepared long in advance? Either way—

"We have to stop them," he said.

Oriel shouted orders instructing the barge to return to the Panic city.

"No!" exclaimed the Guardian. "I'll not watch in safety while my city burns. We'll take the balloon I came here in."

"And I will pilot it," said Griel, picking up the iron crown and tossing it into Oriel's hands. The black-bearded Panic male nearly dropped it, such was his surprise.

"Quickly, now," said Griel, herding the others towards the balloon. The Panic soldier Griel had called Ramal followed them, a suspicious look on her face. Already the barge had begun to move, rocking underfoot like *Os*, the Alcaide's boneship, on the high seas. "Don't forget that accursed thing." Griel pointed at the box. Rosevear and Highson lugged it across the gangplank and into the relatively smaller craft.

"Where to, Guardian?" Griel asked once he was behind the controls.

"Down," she said.

Seneschal Schuet sat firmly at her side, one arm cast protectively around the back of her seat. "Caroi, is this wise?"

"I don't know, but let's deal with the threat first and argue later. Lidia, I can drop you off on the way, if you like."

"Don't even think about it." The Eminent Delfine stood on a seat as the balloon lost altitude, looking overboard with one hand holding onto a guide rope. "Where you go, I go too."

"And I," said Heuve, drawing his blade.

"Put that away," warned Griel, waving. "Cut the wrong stay and you'll send us all plunging to our deaths. There are better weapons to use against these creatures."

Attention shifted to the four wardens and one Stone Mage seated at the rear of the gondola.

Kelloman cleared his throat. "I'll need contact with solid rock if I'm to do what I did last time."

"And I can hold just one, maybe two," said Marmion, a haunted look in his eyes. He kept his injured arm protectively close to his stomach, as though afraid he might bump it.

"Is that all?" Seneschal Schuet asked.

"It may be enough," said Marmion. "We don't know how many there are, and they may run as soon as we confront them, rather than risk losing another of their own."

The balloon rocked beneath them as hot air rose from above. Already the air had turned dark and bitter with ash. Kail thought Marmion's opinion optimistic, but he said nothing. It depended entirely on what Upuaut wanted. If arson was its only intention, the Swarm might run and finish the job later. If Upuaut was tired of playing, however . . .

A shadow fell over them as a dark cloud passed between the balloon and the sky. The gondola lurched violently beneath them. For a second, Kail feared that the Swarm had found them already, but it was just a powerful updraught. He remembered something an old boundary rider had once told him: *storms make their own weather*. He had seen several wildfires burning their way across the plains, whipping up winds and creating clouds out of nothing. If the balloon came too close to the flames, he thought, the Swarm might be the least of their worries.

He felt a touch on his shoulder as they descended. Rosevear had leaned over to make a connection with him, and through that connection came details of the charms Marmion had used to capture the wraith three days earlier. The information was complex, and the link between the four wardens tainted by conflicting emotions carried along with the information. Kail could feel Rosevear's nervousness, Highson's self-blame, and Marmion's doubt. Kail had to concentrate to hold the charm in his mind, fighting complex emotions of his own.

He sensed Kelloman reaching out for Skender and finding nothing.

"There!" cried Lidia Delfine, pointing through a gap in the rising smoke to a complex tangle of trails, ducking and weaving across the forest canopy. Also visible were sheets of flame rising from a nearby firefront. Surges of chimerical energy heralded the burning of trees rich with the Change. Great mushrooms of smoke rose from each such site. Ripples of uncontrolled potential spread in waves through the forest.

Griel pushed the balloon's twin engines to the limit and let gravity pull them downwards. Kail hung on tight as the gondola tilted beneath him and their speed increased. Turbulence increased as well, rattling him from side to side. His teeth bared in a rictus of pain.

The gap in the clouds closed around them. The world turned black. The twins had once talked about the "heaven and hell" of their old world. *Was this hell*, he wondered, *this world of smoke and pain and darkness?*

Then the balloon burst out of the underside of the clouds, trailing black streamers behind it. Kail blinked sooty grit from his eyes and saw that they were much closer to the ground. A tangle of contrails hung directly ahead, already dispersing in the face of turbulent winds rising from the fire nearby. There was no sign of the Swarm themselves.

"Where are they?" The Guardian's voice was barely audible over the rattling and shaking of the balloon. To Kail their flight felt as rough as a fast buggy ride over a rutted old road. "Where *are* they?"

Something cold and black shot out of the nearest cloud. Kail barely had time to acknowledge it before it cut directly across their path, screaming with high-pitched rage. The Change flared as Highson and Marmion tried to snare it. Lines of force rippled through the balloon, throwing people from side to side in their seats. With a shriek, the wraith changed course and darted away.

"Take us even lower," Marmion called out to Griel. "Look for open ground. We—"

He got no further. Three more shrieking wraiths converged on the balloon from three different directions, summoned by the first. Charms flashed and energy flared. The Guardian's bodyguards stood to protect her and Lidia Delfine. The gondola bucked.

Kail, caught in a whirlwind of concentration and distraction, had a momentary impression of tapering midnight limbs and obsidian, inhuman eyes. Coils of air turned to springs around unnatural bodies, pulling tight. Wordless battle cries turned to hisses of alarm and anger.

Slowly, slowly, the three wraiths bowed to the combined will of four Sky Wardens and one Stone Mage.

All might have been well had not another two wraiths burst out of the cover of dense smoke billowing from the forest below. Kail barely had time to see them, let alone muster any kind of counterattack, before the two swept along one side of the balloon, snapping and snarling. The sound of screams and the twanging of stays accompanied a sudden, appalling feeling of weightlessness.

And then, along with everyone else in the balloon, Kail was falling.

Skender felt relatively cold air hit his face and forced his eyes open. They were still flying through smoke, but the flames were thankfully falling behind. He dared to breathe, and triggered a fit of coughing he feared might last forever.

When he looked over his shoulder, Chu's face was black with soot and set in a pattern of lines—slitted eyes, thin lips, furrowed brow— while behind her the wing actually seemed to be smouldering.

"Got any more wonderful plans?" she croaked. "That last one nearly cooked us."

"It shook them off our tail, though, didn't it?" The Swarm appeared to have fallen behind in the face of the fiery heat below. They may have started the fire, but they certainly didn't like coming too close to it. Not with giant trees exploding in every direction, utterly without warning.

"We're lucky we have a tail left." Chu tried to keep the wing steady as it jumped from thermal to thermal, riding the boiling wind upwards. "Can we go, now? Did you send the message to the others?"

Skender had no doubt that his hasty, terrified heads-up had reached everyone halfway Change-sensitive for several kilometres around, even though he had been too distracted since to listen for replies. Keeping the flames away had taken much of his remaining strength and required the use of charms he had only ever read about. Fire-sculpting was a mostly forgotten art, one that looked magnificent when performed correctly but which had severe consequences for audiences and practitioners when things went wrong.

"Yes, it's done," he said. "Let's get out of here."

Chu didn't waste any time. She picked a relatively stable column of hot, smoky air and began to spiral around inside it, trading the steadily rising current against the ability to see well. Or to breathe.

"So," he asked after Chu finished her own protracted coughing fit, "how do you enjoy life in the forest?"

She snorted.

They burst out the top of the column of smoke and rode clear air for only a few seconds before entering another thermal. The smell of burning trees surrounded them. Not just trees, he thought, but fruit and flowers and fungus, and the fauna inhabiting the dense foliage as well. The thought of burning animals—maybe people, too—made him feel abruptly ill, and he begged Chu for a respite.

"It is a bit much, isn't it?" she agreed, tugging the wing out of the column. "We'll take a small breather, and then get going again."

Skender hung limply from the harness as he purged his throat and nose of the smell. His eyes took in the complex topography of clouds around them—bulging ramparts pushing higher layers aside in their urgency to rise—and he wondered distractedly what effect all the smoke and heat would have on the fog. Would it clear the clouds away or make them denser? He didn't know.

He *did* know that the fires were spreading despite the best efforts of those trying to put them out. A wall of smoke now stretched halfway across the base of the city, and the fires ate higher with every passing minute. His vision of the city's frightened population huddled at the summit was becoming horribly real.

"What's that down there?" asked Chu, pointing into the forest city. Treetops were waving from side to side as something massive forced through the undergrowth. Human-made structures crumbled like matchstick houses behind it.

Skender squinted. "I can't quite make it out. Can you go closer?"

"The last time you asked me that, we were almost eaten then burned alive."

"What? Getting cold feet?"

The banter helped insulate them from the reality of their situation as she piloted the wing closer to the steep wall of trees.

"Are they—? No, they couldn't be." Dark grey shapes shouldered trees and habitation aside, half-glimpsed through the canopy but instantly identifiable.

"Man'kin?" asked Chu. "What are *they* doing here?"

Something more pressing still had caught Skender's eye. "Oh, shit. That wasn't supposed to happen."

"What?"

"They came to rescue us—and now look!" He pointed down the side of the mountain to where the Guardian's balloon was under siege from three of the Swarm.

"If you're about to suggest we go down there—" Chu began.

"It's not a suggestion," he said, even as two more wraiths shot out of nearby clouds and raked the balloon from end to end. Cables snapped free like whips. He couldn't see through the balloon to the gondola below, but he imagined people spinning into soft-looking clouds before slamming into fire and Earth far below.

Chu was already moving. His ears popped, they dropped so fast.

More bells and a chorus of hand-wound sirens added to the cacophony on the city's summit. The belltower itself began to chime, deafeningly, with deep, resonant clangs. This time the crowd began to look worried. Watching the Guardian and the others descend out of sight—so soon after getting in the balloon to come home—was bad enough. No one seemed to care that the barge had returned safely to the Panic city. The crowd began to break up as groups of two or three hurried away, anxious about homes and loved ones, and things that needed to be done ahead of this new calamity. Shilly caught one word repeated over and over: *man'kin.*

She, Banner, and Jao exchanged glances. As the number of conspirators decreased, their odds improved. Sousoura, however, only became more edgy.

"Man'kin came to Laure too, you know," said Shilly to the minister. "Only they weren't invading. They were running from the flood. Perhaps that's all that's happening now. The fire has flushed them out of the forest and they're fleeing the only way they can: up."

Sousoura looked unconvinced. Instead of answering, she ordered Shilly to walk along the widow's walk to the far corner. Two of her accomplices did the same with Jao and Banner.

"What are you going to do with us?" asked the Engineer. "There's no point keeping us any longer. You know we have nothing to do with this, and neither do the Panic."

"Down here," Sousoura ordered them, pointing down the stairwell in the corner. Shilly went first, playing up her lameness in order to buy some time. She didn't know where the minister was taking them, but she didn't like what she saw on her face. Sousoura had taken a chance, and it hadn't paid off. Getting rid of the evidence might be simpler than trying to explain herself, especially when any inconvenient details might be most conveniently erased by the confusion of fire and man'kin.

The two minding Jao and Banner were big men, but obviously no more trained for guard duty than Sousoura herself. As they came down the spiral staircase with the guards behind them, Shilly decided that the time to act was now or never.

She feigned a stumble. Crouching over her injured leg, she pulled away from the knife and whipped her stick up into Sousoura's face.

Taken by surprise, the minister fell backwards and dropped the blade with a clatter.

Behind her, Jao didn't waste the opportunity. She dodged aside as Sousoura fell, putting the minister between her and her own minder's blade. Behind him, Banner dived suddenly forward, pushing Jao's minder bodily into Sousoura and tumbling the two of them down the stairs.

Shilly made way for them, already holding Sousoura's dropped knife. She raised it in warning at the third guard, who froze midstep.

"I don't want to use this," she said, "and I'm sure you don't want to use yours. Please, don't prove me wrong on both points."

He backed up the stairs without a word.

Jao had moved past her to disarm her tumbled guard, demonstrating her natural strength when he tried to resist. Her long arms and broad shoulders gave her the leverage he lacked. He went down heavily with one arm twisted behind his back.

"You sure know how to make enemies," said Shilly, hauling Sousoura to her feet. They were still in the stairwell. As far as Shilly could tell, none of the Guardian's staff below had noticed the incident. "Here's your chance to make good. I want you to take us to someone important, someone who knows what they're doing. We need to tell them about the man'kin."

"I'm not afraid of the man'kin." Sousoura's eyes flashed as though Shilly had personally threatened her.

"Well, that's good. I'm not either. And you shouldn't be afraid of us, unless you insist on getting in our way." She waited a second for Sousoura to make a move, but the minister remained stubbornly uninformative. "Okay. Stay here, then. Come and get your pretty knife off me when all this is over."

Shilly turned and walked away, not looking back even when she heard Sousoura spit noisily onto the steps. Shilly ground her teeth and resisted the urge, powerful though it was, to respond in kind.

The grassy area at the bottom of the stairs was a mess of people shouting orders and calling for information. Without the Guardian's calming presence, Milang had devolved into squabbling bureaucracies and fragile egos. Jao kept the blade of her purloined knife carefully out of sight behind her forearm, and Shilly did the same lest sight of the weapons cause even more alarm. Already the guards were watching them suspiciously.

She despaired of learning anything from anyone until she found a servitor she recognised—a lost-looking balding man holding a sheaf of papers—and pulled him to one side.

"What's going on?" she asked him. "Who should we talk to?"

"I don't know," he said. "No one knows."

"Tell us about the fires and the man'kin. We can't decipher what all your bells and whistles are saying."

"The fires are spreading. The man'kin are coming. Nothing we can do is stopping either of them!"

His eyes were frightened. He was beyond reassurances. All she could do was give him orders.

"Find someone in charge and tell them we have information for them. The man'kin aren't attacking. Have you got that? *The man'kin aren't attacking*. We'll be here, waiting to tell what we know."

He nodded rapidly and backed away, still clutching his papers. Shilly watched him push through the crowd, not entirely confident that he would get results but lacking any clear alternative.

"Maybe we should get out of here," said Banner, looking nervously at the restless throng.

"And go where?" Jao asked. "The only way is down, into the fire and the man'kin."

"But if we stay here . . ." Banner nodded at Minister Sousoura, who had slipped down another stairwell and moved into the crowd.

"Off the grate and onto the griddle, as a friend of mine used to say." Shilly looked around and asked herself: *What would Lodo do?* The guards watching them were close enough to see if Sousoura made a move in the open, and they had, as yet, no actual reason to suspect the outsiders of any wrongdoing. "Running will only make us look guilty."

Jao nodded, then looked up at the sky. Her half-human face paled, and Shilly followed her gaze.

Deep black smoke clouds billowed high over the citadel, blocking out the smudge of a sun. A shadow fell over the gathering, ash began to rain down, and Shilly felt real fear set in.

Kail didn't have time to think about pain or falling or who to save. He simply acted, grabbing the back of a seat as the gondola tipped over onto its side and spilled its contents into the air.

He swung giddily from one hand for a moment, watching with a strange detachment as black shapes disappeared into the mist. Two human figures waved and kicked as they fell, unable to slow their descent one iota, no matter how much they screamed. Ramal lost her grip and followed a moment later, tumbling to her death in complete silence, unlike the humans. Maybe Panic soldiers were used to the idea of falling, Kail thought wildly. He certainly wasn't. In Ramal's wake fell an assortment of items: bags, blades, pouches, and the heavy box containing the captured wraith. It tumbled away without a sound, although Kail liked to think the creature inside was screaming too.

He snapped back to himself. People were shouting for help and struggling to hang on as the balloon swayed and tipped. Only one side of the gondola had been freed; the other still dangled from the air bladders above. The engines whined and snarled, turning the entire ungainly arrangement around in an erratic spiral. Shadow and light played maddeningly as Kail brought up his second hand, tightened his grip, and tried to work out what to do.

Most of his fellow passengers had found a solid perch. A couple of people clung to the frame with one hand. Highson had the Guardian tangled in a web of air and was bringing her nearer to a reaching

Seneschal Schuet. Rosevear had another person, and was lowering them to the ground far below. *Sensible*, Kail thought, if the young warden could manage the range.

As Kail adjusted his weight and swung himself closer to the far edge, where help was most needed, movement from the open sky caught his attention. The Swarm were coming around for another pass. Those the wardens and mage had managed to capture earlier were now free also.

The balloon lurched. Griel had managed to reach the controls and sent it dropping downwards as fast as it would go. "Hang on!" the Panic soldier cried. "We'll be on solid ground soon!"

Soon would probably be too late, Kail thought. If the Swarm didn't manage to ditch the entire gondola this time, they would certainly snatch some of the danglers away to their deaths: Kelloman, perhaps, or Heuve, Marmion, the Guardian . . .

As they approached, something golden and black streaked between them and the balloon. It moved too fast for Kail to make it out, but the effect on the Swarm was instantaneous. They changed course to follow, shrieking with anger.

Only as the shape came around did Kail recognise it: Skender and Chu, trailing five angry wraiths in their wake.

"Kail!" The cry drew his attention to much more immediate and urgent matters. Marmion was dangling one-armed from the lower edge of the gondola, making no headway to safety. "I can't hold on!"

Kail checked their altitude. The canopy was visible through the fog, but the fall would still be fatal. He shifted position again, swinging across the protruding back of a seat so he stood directly over where Marmion hung, gripping the side of the gondola with grim desperation.

"Give me your free hand," Kail said, making sure he was securely anchored before reaching out, ignoring the sharp tearing in his chest. "I'll pull you up."

Marmion swung his right arm up and over the edge of the gondola. Only then did Kail realise the stupidity of his request: Marmion had no free hand to reach up with. The only hand he had was busy holding on.

That changed everything. He needed to stretch much further in order to catch Marmion's arm above the elbow. Anything lower than that and Marmion could literally slip through his fingers. But his reach wasn't great enough. He needed to be much closer, and there wasn't time to move.

It looked to him as though Marmion hadn't considered that problem either. He had still not come to terms with his missing hand. In his mind it was still there. Even as their arms swung towards each other, it was clear that Kail would fall short by centimetres.

Yet, as he took what grip he could on Marmion's forearm, a hand gripped *his* forearm in return—a hand where no hand existed. Fingers clutched him, squeezing so tightly they hurt. Cold raced up the bone of his right arm and set the wound in his chest aflame.

His eyes revealed the lie of it, but his body reacted instinctively. He leaned back, shifting his weight to pull Marmion aboard. To his amazement, his grip remained firm, and so did the phantom fingers clutching his arm.

He held on until Marmion was secured and then let go as fast as he could. He gasped with pain and felt his vision grey. The gondola rocked beneath them and fire crackled nearby. He fought a wave of dizziness.

Marmion was trying to tell him something, but the words didn't reach him. The ghost hand had somehow woken the wound in his chest, and he could think no further than that.

Griel hollered and Kail wrenched his eyes open. The balloon had made it to the treetops, but fire was closing fast. The air was thick with smoke and particles of ash, and from nearby came the sound of flames roaring and trees exploding. People were already climbing out, clutching branches and shimmying down them to the solid ground below. Kail forced himself to move when his turn came, keeping his eyes firmly on the bark and leaves before his eyes, not even looking for Marmion.

Griel dropped down last, all arms and toothy grimace, having set the engines on full and letting the balloon roar up into the sky—a distraction for Skender and Chu, should they need it. Kelloman was racing around, drawing some sort of charm in the earth and chanting loudly. To ward off the fire, Kail eventually worked out. His head was ringing loudly and he thought he might throw up.

"It's here somewhere," he heard Marmion saying. "Find it, quickly!"

Kail slumped forward onto his knees. Rosevear caught him barely in time. In the intense heat, the young warden's curling hair was shrivelling. "Are you okay? We need to stand in the charm or it won't protect us."

Kail pushed him away. "The Swarm—got to—"

"Don't worry. Mage Kelloman is going to keep the fire back. Highson will make sure we have air to breathe. Just you worry about moving."

"Got to—" He couldn't get the words out right. Only as Marmion hurried back into his line of sight leading Heuve and Lidia Delfine, who between them carried the splintered box, was he able to finish the sentence.

"Got to *him*."

He pointed at Marmion, but it was already too late. The lid of the box was open and Marmion was bending over it. A ghastly silver light rippled across the warden's face as he reached inside and drew out the imprisoned wraith.

Flames crowded around Kelloman's charm, creating a roaring hurricane of wind that pushed the branches back in a circle overhead. Marmion stood, holding the rough-forged iron weapon upright above him, as one would a sword. Ash and sparks swirled in a furious stream, louder than the hissing of the wraith. Kail wasn't the only one pointing at Marmion by then, at the strange, tortured look on his face and the hand-that-wasn't holding the wraith high. Lidia Delfine was shouting and Heuve lunged forward only to be knocked aside by a mighty whiplash of wind. A funnel of mist spiralled down from the sky, and the roots of the forest writhed at Marmion's feet. In that funnel the Swarm danced—unholy, seductive, and fatal.

A bright, blue-white spark snapped from the stump of Marmion's severed arm to the wraith's iron prison, a palm's-length away. The crack was loud enough to penetrate Kail's stunned state, driving him to his feet. Another spark flashed, then a third, each louder and brighter than the other.

When the fourth came, it lit Marmion up like a sun and drove a wedge between sky and Earth so violently that Kail, just for an instant, felt nothing at all.

Skender twisted his head from side to side, unable to believe they had shaken their pursuers so easily. Not all five of them at once. There *had* to be one left, trailing them in a blind spot, waiting to pounce with claws and teeth as sharp as needles when he and Chu least expected it. But there wasn't. Something had lured them away.

The wing ascended sharply, catching a thermal that lifted its nose almost vertically. Skender saw the stricken balloon careering across the sky. Two Panic combat blimps—sleek, manoeuvrable things that looked like pictures of sharks he had seen once—circled nearby, late but welcome arrivals. Some sort of hurricane seemed to be brewing below them all, whipping up the treetops and stirring the fire into a frenzy. Vast sheets of flame rose up high in the air.

And there, at last—all five of the Swarm, drawn down in a funnel of cloud to meet that rising vortex. Their smaller prey had been completely forgotten in favour of something inside that funnel. Black clouds spread in their wake. Fire and ice. Mist and smoke. The sky clenched like a white-knuckled fist.

Skender gripped the harness. He had never seen clouds behave like that before.

"I think," he said, "that we should get out of here—fast."

"Finally we agree on something," she said, swinging the wing bodily upwards.

Skender looked behind as they ascended. At the centre of the vortex, at the point towards which the Swarm were determinedly closing, a bright point of light flared once, and then again. The third time, it was bright enough to leave a purple spot on his retina.

He turned to say something to Chu. The fourth flash cast shadows all across the sky. He had just enough time to feel surprised at its intensity when the sound hit and shook them like a storm-addled leaf.

Shilly backed into a corner with the others as the sound of the man'kin grew louder. Over sirens and horns, ringing bells and human cries, she could definitely hear heavy footfalls advancing on the citadel. Nothing stood in the man'kin's way. Nothing turned them back. Anyone who tried was pushed aside or physically crushed. Reports of casualties and great swathes of damage preceded the creatures in their thunderous ascent. The whites around Jao's eyes flashed at her as a mass of frightened human flesh crushed them together. Ash fell from the sky like rain. Banner moaned with fear. Shilly didn't understand, and that made her angry as well as frightened. What did the man'kin *want*? Why this tide of destruction if all they needed was sanctuary from the fire? Why fight when the man'kin of Laure hadn't?

She pushed against the people pressing around her, forcing her way forwards to the front of the crowd. Warden Banner called her name, but Shilly only slowed long enough to give the warden Minister Sousoura's knife. Someone had to make a stand, and it might as well be her. She would make the man'kin listen—she who had spoken to the Angel and lived. She would make them listen if it killed her.

She broke free and limped to the centre of the torn and tattered lawn. The crashing and smashing reached a crescendo. Before she could have any second thoughts, the southern wall of the citadel collapsed in a heap, torn down by mighty stone hands. Delicate mosaics went flying in thousands of multicoloured pieces. The belltower dropped with a roar, its giant bell tolling one final time as it fell.

Grey granite shapes burst through the rubble, shrugging it aside as though it was straw. With massive jerking movements they looked at the frightened crowd, then at her, and kept walking.

Two of them, fierce creatures with bat-ears and claws and teeth as long as her hands, thudded to confront her with feet that left deep indentations in the ash-covered grass. Part of her wanted to giggle, despite their ferocious appearance. *Only* two. Judging by the sound they had made, and the reports from below, they should have been hundreds.

She opened her mouth to say something—anything that would make them stop.

A flicker of light registered somewhere at the edge of her vision, and then a clap of thunder so loud it hurt her ears.

And the man'kin did indeed stop right before her, just for a moment.

Lightning.

Kail came back to himself in time to hear the rumbling, rolling echoes of thunder returning from the mountainsides. A jagged violet line stretched vertically down his vision. The air stank of the Change.

Marmion had fallen in a heap at the centre of Kelloman's charm with the lump of crude iron, now glowing red, beside him. Darkness had fallen with him, and a strange kind of silence that spoke of too much noise rather than too little. Kail's senses were overwhelmed. He was having trouble enough standing, let alone keeping up with events.

Kelloman's charm continued to keep the flames at bay, although they danced like fiery dust devils desperate to get in. Kail blinked, registering a change in the wind. The vortex that had gripped them was easing, breaking up into erratic gusts. He looked up, expecting to see the Swarm upon them, with ghastly arms outstretched and mouths open wide, but all he saw were dark clouds looming.

Thunderheads.

What had happened to the Swarm? The last time he had looked, there had been five of them converging on Marmion and the imprisoned wraith. Now they were gone.

Lightning flashed again, but more distantly, and the boom of thunder was less overpowering.

Something new dropped out of the sky, descending in a heavy, shimmering sheet. Kail opened his mouth, feeling hot moisture over his lips and face. His hearing returned, bringing him a loud, vibrant hiss and the sound of relieved cries from his companions.

Rain.

At last he understood. The wraiths were gone, blasted by lightning. The rain would bring the fires into check, perhaps even extinguish them completely. Human and Panic helped each other up and checked each other's injuries. Perhaps, he dared think, all would be well.

Marmion lay unmoving in the mud. Kail went to him, rolled him over. Water splashed the warden's face, and his eyelids fluttered.

"What happened?" he croaked, barely audible over the noise.

"Fires make their own weather," Kail said. "With a little help."

"It worked?"

"Looks that way. I honestly thought you were giving them what they wanted. The Swarm, I mean. I'm sorry."

"Don't be." Marmion struggled to sit, using his one flesh-and-blood hand to grip Kail's shoulder. The mud beneath his feet was a slippery mixture of ash and dirt, but the air smelled clean and cool. "It's not over yet. That was only six of them. There are still three left."

"Three we can handle now we know how to."

"*We* can, yes. But it's not just about us."

Realisation hit him. "The Homunculus. Sal!"

Marmion gripped his arm. "Talk to Griel. See if one of his combat drones can get to Geraint's Bluff at top speed."

"You want to help them?"

"I want to give the twins a chance to prove themselves. We owe them that much."

Kail stood, seeking Griel through the intensifying downpour.

On the ruined hillside known as Geraint's Bluff, a wolf's ululating howl broke the silence. Until recently, Sal had been sitting on a rock waiting for Shilly while the twins prowled restlessly, arguing silently between themselves. His head came up at the sound and he searched the misty forest around him for the source of the call. The sound had a lonely quality to it, as though its owner had come a long way and still had some distance to go.

"Did you hear that?" asked the twins, staring at him with four wide-set eyes.

"Of course I heard it."

"You really did?"

Sal couldn't fathom the incredulity in their combined voice. "Why wouldn't I?"

They didn't answer immediately. Picking their way across the tumbled slope, sending smaller rocks rattling downwards in miniature avalanches, their Homunculus body looked as alien as ever.

When it was standing as close to him as he would let it come, the twins said, "That's Upuaut."

"The golem thing?" Sal had listened for most of the night and the morning to the twins' account of their strange adventures with Kail. "What's it doing here?"

"It's come to kill us, I guess," said the twin called Seth, and Sal could not disagree.

Less than an hour earlier, an echo of distant events had come to him—fire and fright and teeth like broken glass—and he had wondered what was happening with his friends, and with Shilly in particular, elsewhere in the forest.

Then *yadeh-tash*, the ancient stone pendant that the man'kin claimed as one of their own, whispered through the skin of his chest, warning him of a storm nearby. That had surprised and unnerved him, for in the muffled stillness of the mist forest, storms seemed a distant, alien phenomenon.

And finally the warning had come from Highson through the Change: *Be on your guard. The golem is abroad with one-third of the Swarm. We're on our way.*

Sal had kept that warning to himself, not wanting to rattle the twins. The one-day deadline wasn't up yet. He didn't want them to leave before time.

The wolf howled again, louder and longer than before. Instead of loneliness, this cry conveyed eagerness and hunger.

"I want to know why you can hear it," said Seth's brother, Hadrian, "when Kail couldn't."

"Yes, what makes you different? Is it something to do with those signs scratched on you?"

Sal responded defensively to the strange accusation. "They're just ordinary charms, the same as the ones I've drawn to hide us here. Underneath them, I'm the same as anyone else."

"You can't be." The flat assertion defied contradiction. "There must be something about you that's special."

There was no point in denying what he knew to be true, even though he had spent half his life rejecting the assertion that it meant he was special. "I'm a wild talent."

"What does that mean?" asked the twins.

"It means . . . Well, it just means that I was raised away from the wardens and mages who might've taught me how to handle my talent when it came, and because of that I've gone my own way. I do things differently, that's all."

"Must be more to it than that," said Seth, "if you can hear the wolf."

"What if that's all it is—*just* a wolf?" he asked. "You could be jumping at mozzies."

"We could be," the twins agreed. They didn't sound convinced. Their two superimposed faces scanned the tree line for any sign of their ancient enemy.

Sal stood up and shivered. Although it was barely noon, the day seemed to have suddenly chilled.

"It's not just a wolf," said a voice from behind them. "I'm so much more than that."

The Homunculus and Sal whipped around. Above them, stepping out of the trees, was the skinny figure that Sal remembered from the Aad. He had only glimpsed the man's face briefly, but he would never forget its tortured expression. Now, that expression was gone, but the sense of agony, of *wrongness*, remained. There was something entirely new in the man's head now.

"Stay back," said Sal, feeling the Change stir in instinctive response.

"Or what? You know what will happen if you try to attack me. You'll empty yourself and we'll take you over. You'll be lost forever in the Void. You'll die and be no use to anyone."

The man's eyes were awful—black, pain-filled pits—but his mouth was worse. Every word came from a place devoid of hope, waking troubled memories.

"I helped kill one of your kind once," he said. "Or like enough. You're vulnerable inside that body. If I kill it while you're in there, you'll die too."

"But *how* will you kill the body while I'm inside it?" The terrible figure walked down the landslide, following much the same path the twins had before. "There's the rub."

"We could tear your throat out," growled the twins, "as you would tear out ours, given the chance."

"Oh, I'll have the chance. Make no mistake of that." Upuaut showed the yellowed, chipped teeth of its host. "You don't frighten me, even in this puny body I inhabit, with its twisted mind and sordid memories. And you obviously don't frighten Sal. What sort of power do you think you have? If you can't inspire fear, it can't be as great as you imagine."

Sal visualised a series of shapes Shilly had taught him while making repairs on their underground home. As the golem came closer, he shifted the stones beneath it just slightly, enough to make it stagger then freeze with its arms outstretched.

"Easy, boy," it said, "or you'll bring the whole lot down on you."

"And you with it."

"That's not the most stupid thing you could do, but it'd certainly be ill-advised. A wasted opportunity, if nothing else."

"You have nothing I want."

"Oh, no? Don't come to that conclusion too quickly. At least hear what I have to say."

"About what?"

"Your missing friends, for one."

Sal, the Homunculus, and the golem formed an equilateral triangle splayed across the side of the mountain. Sal glanced at the twins, who quivered with suppressed emotions several metres away. Their frames of mind were impossible to read.

"Golems can't lie," Sal said, "but I wouldn't trust you, no matter what you told me."

"Yet you trust this abomination." The golem indicated the twins with one broken-nailed hand. "This freak of unnature. What does it know of this world? What can it possibly tell you about the shadow drawing long across us all? What stake has it in our fates? It doesn't care if we live or die."

"We care," said the twins. "We gave up our lives to be here."

"You made this world as it is by leaving. You fashion its undoing by returning. How does that prove your goodwill?"

"I'm not sure I see the point you're making," said Sal. "Are you suggesting I'd be better off on your side? Because if that's the case, you're wasting your breath."

The ghastly smile faded. "You're being hasty again, boy."

"Empty threats and empty promises. That's all a golem has to bargain with. If I won't bargain, you're nothing. You might as well go back to the Aad and bother someone else."

"My threats aren't empty," growled Upuaut, its guttural tones testing the capacity of the human throat it spoke through. "Look around you. We four are not the only ones abroad this fine afternoon."

A chill wind stirred the hillside. The mist roiled as three tapering midnight shapes glided into view. Sal tensed, but they came no closer than the golem itself. They circled the three-way confrontation making a sound like metal scraping on glass, eyes and open mouths gleaming.

Sal forced himself to speak levelly. "At least you *are* making threats now. That's more in character."

"You aren't the one I'm threatening," it said. "Just your companions."

"What did they ever do to you?"

"They are responsible for the ruin of the world!" The sudden fury on the golem's face was startling and raw. "They will pay!"

"We did what we could to *save* the world," the twins said, eyes roaming across their combined face as they tried to track all three wraiths at once. "We paid the price."

"You saved nothing! Everything I worked for, everything I aspired to, you destroyed. Alongside Mot I could have turned back the tide. Yod would have been repelled. But you got in the way. You denied what was rightfully mine."

"You know nothing about Yod," hissed Seth. "It would've eaten you and your precious Mot and still been hungry."

"You lie!" The golem turned its anger onto Sal. "How can you believe these fools to be your only hope? Your delusion is as great as theirs. Other forces are stirring, other plans. The seers are gathering. The imp is a-wing. I and my kind do not intend to sit idly by and watch."

Sal thought of *yadeh-tash* still whispering at his throat and wished he knew what the other wraiths were up to.

"I see your plan now," said Hadrian. "It's the only one you have open to you. You're going to kill us and return the Realms to their natural state. You know that'll set Yod free, but you think you can fight it better that way. You think you and a handful of tired old energumen can do what the Sisters of the Flame, the Ogdoad, Baal, the Duergar Clans, and the Handsome King could not. You're so fucking wrong it makes me sick."

"Yod is starved and weak," the golem retaliated. "It is as frail as you are. If we control the timing of its emergence, we control its fate. You would rather let it come forth when *it's* good and ready. You'd wait until the jaws of death close tight around the world before doing anything to save it!"

"And meanwhile—what? Your friends in the Swarm cause mayhem in the forest to distract everyone from us?"

"To give me time to find you." The golem looked down at the charms scratched and gouged across the tumbled rock and dirt. "Your friend's skill at hiding is excellent, but insufficient against a hunter such as me."

"So why don't you just do it?" asked the twins. "Why don't you just kill us—or try to? You weren't so talkative the last two times we met."

"Because it's afraid," said Sal. Much of the conversation between the golem and the twins went over his head, but that detail he understood perfectly well. "It's not sure it *can* kill you while I'm around. Maybe if you were alone; maybe if it had caught you in a dark corner somewhere with no one to help you; maybe then it might have succeeded. But not now. I'm too strong for it."

The golem laughed, long and low. The man's face had lengthened and his ears had swept back. He half crouched on bent legs and his hands curled into claws. "You flatter yourself, boy. I was just hoping that you might be convinced to do it for me."

"No chance."

"Not even in exchange for Tom? For Kemp? For Mawson?"

Sal couldn't let himself be tempted. A golem's word was poison. It might know where his lost companions were; it might even have taken them itself. But it was just as likely that it only knew that they were gone, and could be possible bargaining points. He wouldn't commit murder on the off-chance.

"Sorry."

"Then you'll both die, and my pleasure will be doubled."

At no obvious command, the three wraiths stopped circling and rushed in towards Sal and the Homunculus. Sal's first instinct was to close ranks, but he knew that would be suicide. He had to stay out of the Homunculus's Change-sapping aura. Instead he dropped onto one knee and put his hand into the tangled soil. A great deal of potential lay untapped in the jumbled mess of boulders and loose soil. That energy could easily be turned into motion, if tipped the wrong way. If tipped the *right* way, it could mean the difference between life and death for him and the twins.

He knew which way it had to go. Summoning one of the earliest mnemonics he had learned—from Shilly, not Lodo, in a cave filled with bones at the heart of a Ruin—he picked one wraith at random and kindled light in its breast. He pictured a tiny, blossoming point deep within its midnight flesh, growing brighter and brighter with every beat of its dark heart. All his strength went into the attack, and within seconds its effect became clear.

Radiance burst from the wraith's mouth, open and hungry, and flashed suddenly from its eyes. With a screech, it veered violently off-course and careened across the rocky mountainside. Its cries grew increasingly agonised and its movements more erratic until finally, with a soundless pop, it simply burst. For the space of a breath, a tiny sun burned the mist away, and then even that was gone.

Sal staggered forward, pulse pounding in his head. He wanted nothing more than to lie down and close his eyes. Instead, he forced himself to look up. The two remaining creatures wheeled and darted, trying to get at the twins. The Homunculus stood with arms and legs splayed, shooting streams of metallic energy in reply. Sal couldn't make out what exactly the twins were doing, or how, but the Swarm did everything they could to avoid being hit. Where the streams touched, skin peeled back and black blood spurted. Angry, frustrated cries filled the air.

Sal took heart in that, until he saw what a toll the effort was taking on the twins. The Homunculus was losing substance, becoming noticeably translucent as he watched. Each jet of energy robbed it of more and more solidity until Sal could actually make out the shape of tumbled rocks through it. And still the Swarm kept coming, snapping and scratching and getting closer by the second. It was only a matter of time before they came close enough to do real damage or the Homunculus vanished entirely.

The golem howled in triumph. "Kill them! There's no imp to save them this time!"

Sal ground his teeth and dug deeper. Void or no void, he had to try.

"Sal, no. Don't do that."

The voice came through the Change and accompanied a sudden surge in energy. Wisps of mist converged from all directions on one of the wraiths, shrouding it in ever-increasing layers of white. It flailed and struggled, but still the mist thickened. Its flight grew clumsy and slow, its screaming muffled. With one last flex of willpower, the shreds of mist collapsed inward to form a shell of ice, and the wraith fell trapped to the ground.

The one remaining wraith screamed in anger. Sal turned to see a sleek Panic balloon touching down on the far side of the avalanche. Two men—Highson, who had called the warning to Sal, and a mage Sal didn't know—climbed out of the gondola and hurried across the rubble.

The twins had fallen slumped over the rocks. Sal limped forward to defend their body, which looked as watery and fragile as a bubble about to burst. The wraith didn't know who to attack for a moment, and swung from one target to another before making up its mind. It lunged first at Sal, trying to rake him with a flurry of claws and teeth. He fell back, crossed arms blazing with flickering, faltering light, and it skidded blindly away, swinging across the sky in a jagged arc. When its vision cleared, it lunged next at the Stone Mage, who stamped his foot hard on the stone beneath him, just once, and blasted it with blue flame.

The shrieking ceased.

Highson ran over and knelt besides Sal. "Are you all right? We came as fast as we could."

"I'm okay," he said, brushing well-meaning hands away. His thoughts were as turgid and heavy as clotted blood, but he would be all right. "The twins—the golem—"

Highson looked up the slope, then back at Sal. His expression was grim.

Seth?

Hadrian?

The twins floated in blackness so deep they couldn't see each other or even themselves. No light existed to see by, and they had no eyes to see with anyway, even if it had.

We're back, they thought, feeling an awful familiarity wash over them. Bardo—the Void Beneath—was at the same time infinite and claustrophobic. It could stretch forever one moment or collapse as close as a funeral shroud another. This was the one place in the universe they had thought never to revisit.

Are we?

The Void hung silent and empty around them. No Lost Minds clamouring to be heard; no hum, even. Just nothing.

Where else could we be?

I don't know. Maybe we're dead.

I don't think so. There's no world-tree, and we're still together. This can't possibly be the Third Realm.

You don't sound too certain of that.

Are you certain *of anything right now?*

Only that we're talking.

There was a small silence.

How do we get back?

I don't know.

We have to try.

Why?

Not this again, Seth.

I mean it. Why not just stay here, back where we started?

And sulk until the end of the world?

Well, we don't seem to be doing much good at anything else. We're just getting in the way and letting other people do the work. They found out about the Swarm on their own. Sal blew one of them to bits while we dicked around with the egrigor. What's the point of us? What difference can we possibly make?

Upuaut obviously thought we made a difference, otherwise it wouldn't have tried to kill us.

Or it was just wrong. Hunting and killing is its strong point, not long-term planning.

If it was wrong about wanting us dead, doesn't that mean it's better if we stay alive?

This time the silence stretched longer than before.

I don't know what to do.

Neither do I. But I do know that this isn't where we started. We lived in the world once. We can do it again.

I hope you're right.

You have to do better than hope. Pukje said that to me once.

Well, where is he when we need him? Perhaps he'd be able to tell us how to get the hell out of here.

Into the darkness burst a ray of light, carrying with it the voice and thoughts of another.

Seth? Hadrian?

The twins recognised the presence instantly, even though there were no physical features to register. The mind was a familiar one.

We're here, they called.

We thought we'd lost you, said Highson Sparre, who the twins knew better in the Void by his heart-name, Guin. They themselves had no heart-names, just "Seth" and "Hadrian." *What happened?*

It was difficult to explain. The twins remembered Kail describing how golems could take over a Change-worker's body if they extended themselves too far. *We took too much from ourselves. There was nothing left. We ended up here.*

Highson seemed to accept that explanation. It was similar enough, they supposed, to what happened in his world. *You'll recover. Change-workers always recover, or we'd never get anything important done.*

But we're not Change-workers.

We won't know about that until we get you out of here, will we? Whether you want to come or not, I'm here to drag you out again.

So it seems.

I don't remember the last time, but Sal told me about it. He says we made a deal, you and I. You should stick to it. There are things that need to be done.

That's what we told you, *the last time.*

Well, the irony isn't lost on me. You can take that for granted.

In the end, it was the hint of bitterness in Highson's voice that decided the twins on which course of action to take. To come back into the Void Beneath must have been difficult for him—to revisit the place that should, at one time, have been the death of him, and then to rescue the being that had confounded him for so long. Who were they to claim that life was too hard for living?

Highson made no immediate move to leave just yet. *So this is what it's like in here. I wondered.*

It's changed, said the twins. *It's not the same.*

How?

They explained that the Lost Minds were gone, along with the usual mind-numbing hum.

What does that mean?

They didn't know for certain, but a nasty suspicion had formed in their minds. *The hum might not have been part of the Void at all. What if it was something in here with us and we never realised?*

Something like what?

Yod.

But—Highson stopped in confusion. *How can it be just a hum?*

Don't mistake it for anything human, or perhaps even anything we can recognise as alive. In the Second Realm it looked like a giant black pyramid. Why not something just as strange here? A hum that grinds you down, sucks away your memories, saps your will to live . . .

The more they thought about it, the more it made a terrible kind of sense. All that time they had been stuck cheek to jowl, not just with each other, but with their enemy as well. Sandwiched together in Bardo for an eternity, they simply hadn't known—and maybe neither had it. Would a being large enough to eat whole worlds notice two tiny individuals among the many who had passed through its supernatural belly?

Yod had eaten the Lost Minds. There seemed to be no way of denying that probability. It had been absorbing their will, one by one, for centuries, conserving energy until the chance came to get out. And now, after one last meal, it *was* out, somewhere, somehow.

Yod was free.

How long have we been in here?

Hours, Highson said.

They weren't surprised. Time passed strangely in the Void. *What happened to Upuaut?*

While we contained the last of the wraiths, it slipped away.

Of course, the twins thought. *I think it's time we were leaving, too.*

Highson gathered his will about him, processing complicated shapes and patterns in his mind and letting those shapes bleed out into the Void Beneath. The twins were gathered into his mental embrace and bound tightly to him.

How strange to think I won't remember this, Highson said. *It's so clear in my mind now . . .*

Light flared again, blasting through them like a rocket exhaust. The Void flexed and twisted, as though reluctant to give up the last of its inhabitants. The twins felt stretched, compressed, then—

Free. The darkness of nothing became the darkness of closed eyelids. Through their other senses they heard the tinkling of rock, smelled sweat and ash, tasted copper, and felt rough stone beneath their artificial back.

They opened their eyes, and saw the stars.

"What happened to the fog?" Hadrian asked.

"It blew away," said Sal, leaning into view. "There was a fire, then a storm. It's all taking a while to settle down. Maybe the mist and clouds will come back afterwards. Maybe they won't. We'll have to wait and see."

Hands helped them sit upright. Seth felt infinitely weary. "Where's Highson?"

"Right behind you." The warden looked slightly stunned as they turned to face him.

"I remember," he said. "I remember everything we said in there."

"And I can still feel the Change," said Sal, "even though I'm standing right next to you."

Father and son's expressions were perfectly mirrored, just for a moment.

The twins turned away, unable to bear it.

There you go, Hadrian said. *That was our last chance. We gave everything, and it almost finished us off. Then we came back. The world accepts us completely now. Even if we wanted to back out, it's probably too late.*

Even if we wanted to, repeated Seth, thinking of more than just the Change and what Sal had said. *Yod ate the Lost Ones. If we needed proof it meant business, we've got it. We can't walk away from this. We can't run. We have to make a fight of it, or get eaten with everyone else.*

Through eyes perfectly attuned to the nighttime world, they watched as balloons flew in from the southwest, skimming low over mountainsides fully revealed for the first time. Thick columns of smoke towered in the distance, not quite obscuring a city floating in midair beside a jutting tree-covered ridge. And to the northeast, through kilometres of stone and ice, a shadow growing larger, deeper, darker.

We're coming, the twins told it. *We're going to finish you if it kills us.*

The Earth trembled beneath them, as though in reply.

THE SKY

"The pieces of a broken vase are not the opposite of a vase; the clay it came from is not the opposite of a vase. The opposite of a vase is the need that brought it into existence and the absence its departure leaves behind. We too are nothing if we are not desired; we were nothing if we are not missed."
THE BOOK OF TOWERS, EXEGESIS 13:16

Dawn was a special time. Skender sat with his legs dangling over the edge of a platform in the Panic city, waiting for the first rays of the sun to creep over the mountains. He, like everyone in both cities, knew that this could well be the last opportunity, for a long time, to see the day begin. Already the fog was rolling back over the foothills, pressing in from the west like a returning tide. Once the cloud cover closed back overhead, the sky would be hidden again.

A great crowd had gathered to watch with him. The Panic homes had windows but for the most part lacked balconies. The only way to experience the spectacle properly was to stand outside in the streets, on walkways and roofs, and from the gondolas of floating balloons. Bright-eyed, gangly armed children swung bare feet over the edge of horizontal ladders. High-pitched nasal trumpets sounded from every quarter. Judging by the throng, he estimated that perhaps half the city had either got up early, like him, or stayed up all night to take advantage of the strange weather.

And for the locals it was *very* strange. None of them had seen the open sky before, having been born and raised inside the permanent fog. Only those who had flown high enough to rise entirely above the clouds had ever seen further than a dozen metres—and they were few. Panic pilots did indeed learn their routes by memory, as Chu had guessed. Deviations from tradition weren't encouraged. Only a handful dared go beyond the norm to see what lay beyond.

"This is a good omen," said Griel, "and a defining moment for my people."

Skender turned. The Panic soldier had come up unnoticed behind him and stood looking at the sky. His expression was deeply satisfied.

"How so?"

"The sky is where we came from. It's right that we be reminded, once every lifetime."

"Do you think you'll ever go back?"

"Perhaps. Only time will tell—and the success of your venture."

Skender nodded, not quite ready yet to think beyond the moment. "Thanks for letting us land here, and for the beds. Chu wasn't sure what sort of reception she'd get back at Milang."

Griel smiled broadly. When the kingsfolk grinned, Skender thought, their whole faces seemed to light up. With such broad mouths, every expression was exaggerated. That made them bad liars.

"The last I saw of Chu," Griel said, "she was surrounded by balloon-makers, swapping details of fabrics and charms. That wing of hers, even in its present state, is quite a curiosity. Her new friends would keep her busy for weeks if she let them."

"She hasn't decided what she's going to do yet," Skender said, turning back to look at the sky. It was changing from black to blue around the summit of the mountains. Brands still glowed in the city of Milang, as though the stars fading above were finding new homes below. "What about you? There was talk of you being King, wasn't there?"

"Oh, yes, but who wants that?" Griel put a long hand on Skender's shoulder. "Oriel can have the crown, if it'll have him. He's welcome to it. I've got everything I dreamed of in my vision. Kingsfolk and foresters are talking again, and Jao is talking to me—or will be, once we get her back. Beyond that," he added with a wink, "I'm short-sighted anyway."

Just like many of the Panic pilots, Skender now knew. When vision didn't need to extend very far, keen eyesight wasn't a prerequisite. Unlike Chu, who could count the leg hairs of an ant from across the Divide—or so she claimed.

A halo of light blossomed across the top of the mountain. Oohs and aahs of wonder came from the crowd. Fingers pointed.

Griel smiled wider than ever.

Bodyguards followed Skender wherever he went. He didn't let that bother him, as it wasn't entirely a sign of distrust. Since foresters and kingsfolk weren't completely reconciled yet, Griel had insisted that two loyal soldiers remain with Skender in case he needed protection. Their solid, leather-clad forms were a comfort when Panic citizens stared at him with expressions he still found difficult to read sometimes. Skender couldn't tell if they thought him an oddity like the dawn—something to be marvelled at, safe in the knowledge that it would soon go away—or a threat to be vilified and neutralised as quickly as possible. The shocks of recent times still reverberated through the many ups and downs of the city. As often as he heard laughter and joy, he witnessed tears and grief.

Highson Sparre, Mage Kelloman, and the Homunculus had arrived from Geraint's Bluff shortly before dawn. Skender found them in a sealed garden not far from the city's heart. Guards lined the entrance, keeping a watchful eye on the strange creature in their midst—even stranger than a human, and that was saying something, to their eyes. Skender could empathise with their nervousness as he approached the group.

"—what form could it possibly take?" Kelloman was saying,

absently brushing the bilby away from his ear. While he could hardly be described as comfortable with the creature, at least he was beginning to tolerate its presence. "Is it bodiless like a golem, or something stranger, like a ghost?"

"We won't know until we find it," said Highson. "And we'll have to be careful when we do. We know it eats minds."

"Memories and will," said the twins. "For breakfast."

"Speaking of which," said Skender. "Do any of you know where we can get a feed around here?"

"Why don't you just ask the guards, boy?" asked Kelloman.

Skender smiled. "Because I thought you might need a break. You old boys have been worrying at this all night long. It's time you found something new to chew on."

"There's nothing else to do," said the twins, "until we get moving again."

Skender couldn't read their expression, but they radiated restlessness like a well-fuelled fire. Every fibre of their beings yearned to continue their journey, but they had agreed to wait for the others before they did. The events of recent days had demonstrated that they couldn't complete their mission by themselves, or whether those who offered to help could actually be trusted. The Swarm might be gone, but who knew what else had followed them from the old times?

Skender still didn't want to think that far ahead. Just wondering where Rattails and Upuaut might be that second made his stomach turn.

"You know," said Highson, slapping his thighs, "I think I agree with Skender. There's no point running headlong into anything. The Goddess only knows when Marmion's going to want to set off. We should take advantage of the hospitality here before we're on the road again."

"There are few roads where you're going," said Kelloman. "Just long climbs."

"All the more reason to fill our stomachs." Highson stood. "Anyone else?"

Kelloman capitulated, but the twins shook their head. "We'll be all right. We don't need to eat much, anyway."

The mage and warden walked with Skender through a wide doorway indicated by the guards. Within, along a narrow corridor and up a flight of stairs, they found a small but serviceable mess. Skender ate briskly, not realising quite how hungry he was until the plate was put in front of him. Panic food was little different from that eaten by their human counterparts in the forest: lots of nuts and beans, most harvested from the ground, but some grown in rooftop gardens using water collected from the mist. The latter had a smoky flavour that Kelloman assured them was considered quite distasteful in Milang.

"They're a strange mob," expounded the mage as he picked at a wholegrain fritter. "Both of them. Utterly alike in many ways, yet expending so much energy trying to seem apart."

"Just like mages and wardens," said Skender offhandedly.

"Nonsense, boy. *They* are *completely* different."

Highson laughed—a welcome sound, one Skender hadn't heard often from the lips of Sal's father. It didn't last long, but it did lighten the mood somewhat.

"I gather," Skender said when his plate was empty and he had leaned back in his seat to digest, "that you haven't heard from Marmion yet."

Highson shook his head. "Except to say that we're to arrange a transfer back to Milang at midday. He'll announce his decision when we're all together."

"No hints?"

"Not a one. He's going to have to pull something clever out of his hat, though. The boneship isn't much use to us in the mountains, and some of us aren't fit to travel by foot."

"Some of us aren't fit to travel by boneship, either," said Skender, remembering days of water-sickness all too clearly.

"Marmion did say," Highson went on, "that there were things that needed sorting. I'm sure he's right, but what are they and how will they affect us? We can leave Oriel and the Guardian to patch things up here. It isn't really our problem now."

"What *is* our problem?" asked Kelloman gloomily.

"Don't start that again. At least let our food settle."

"What do *you* mean by *us?*" asked Skender. "You're not thinking of coming with us, are you?"

The mage looked aggrieved. "I made the mistake of reporting recent events to the Synod. I say 'mistake' because at the time I thought I was doing the right thing, and that I would be immediately recalled to safety. Unfortunately, they've ordered me to go with you into the mountains, to observe what you find there and report back in due course."

"To spy, in other words."

"Exactly. And alas."

The mage flicked a seed across the table to where the bilby was playing with the corner of a placemat. It pounced delightedly on the small snack.

That's what we are to Yod, Skender thought. *A snack to tide it over.* He thought of all the minds lost in the Void Beneath, all their voices stilled forever. Yod had devoured them and escaped.

He shivered.

"Have you ever thought," he asked Highson, to change the subject, "of separating the twins? I mean, you made the Homunculus. It's designed to adopt the shape of the mind inside it. Couldn't you cut it in two, or make another one?"

Highson looked down at his hands. "I fear," he said, "that some of the ingredients required were very hard to find. That's why I had to steal them from the Novitiate collection. Now they're used up, and there are no more. I doubt Marmion would take the suggestion well, anyway."

"Who cares about what he wants? The twins deserve a break—if you'll pardon the pun."

Mage Kelloman looked at him with eyes narrowed. "What's up with you, my lad? You're entirely too cheerful for someone who almost cooked his hide yesterday."

Skender coughed to hide his embarrassment. He could feel his ears going red. "That was nothing," he said. "My eyebrows will eventually grow back."

"You're stuck here at the end of the Earth with nothing but a bunch of misfits and monsters for company, and you almost seem to be *enjoying* it. I'm beginning to think you're as mad as everyone else around here."

"I just reckon you should think about it," Skender said to Highson, who was also looking at him with a perceptive gleam in his eye. "Separating the twins, I mean. It might do them the world of good."

"Maybe you're right," Sal's father said with a sigh. "They've certainly been asking questions about the Homunculus. Perhaps that's what they've got in mind. There are many things in play that I don't understand, though. If we make the wrong move, it could be a disaster. I wish there was some way of knowing what was coming . . ."

Highson trailed off, leaving the sentence unfinished. Mawson and Tom were still missing, along with the Quorum. Without them, there was no possible way of telling what the future held. They were trapped in the present, like everyone else.

Skender thought of Kemp and the Panic empyricist who had promised to look after him. Neither of them had been seen again, either. The group that had set out from Laure was shrinking fast. They would be lucky, he thought, if just one of them lasted long enough to meet Yod.

That was a thought he kept to himself. When Kelloman and Highson returned to the subject of their distant, mysterious adversary—as he had always known they would—he left them to it and took his bodyguards on a stroll elsewhere.

The fresh air was cool on his burned skin. His hands still stung as though soaked in scalding water. Before going to Milang with Marmion, Rosevear had given Skender a vial of ointment, instructing him to apply it to the sore areas every two hours. The time had come and gone for another application.

As the mist rolled back in, cutting off the view from all but the highest reaches of Milang and the mountains behind it, he returned to his room and did as he was told.

"Your hands are sticky," Chu said when she came back to the room, exhausted from her long discussion with the Panic balloon-makers. Her hair had been braided behind one ear, and beaded like Jao's. He wasn't aware that she had slept at all. He had nodded off before her, and she had been gone when he awoke.

"Yours are dry," he said. "They'll scar if you're not careful."

"So? Adds character." She let go of his hand and sat on the bed next to him. "You can't possibly be tired. Not after last night."

"Are you telling me I snored again?"

"You *always* snore."

"And you always lie." He looked at her, feeling as though he could melt into her brown eyes forever. "You just kissed me, though. That was nice."

"Yes."

"Why?"

"Because I wanted to. I kissed you last night too, if you remember."

"I do remember."

"Well, that makes a change."

He smiled. "Is this something we should talk about?"

"Do *you* want to talk about it?"

"I don't know."

"We talk enough as it is, I sometimes think. Not that I don't like that," she added hastily. "I like talking to you. It always makes me feel better about things."

"Even though we argue?"

"Because we have something to argue about, and because we care enough to argue about it."

"Ah. Clear as fog."

She smiled. "I'm just glad that we didn't die yesterday, or the day before, and I worry that if we die tomorrow *all* we'll have done is talk."

"We're not going to die tomorrow."

"The day after, then, or the day after that."

He brushed a strand of thick, beaded hair from her forehead. "We'll only die if you keep on crashing us into things."

She punched him, then winced at the sting in her hands. "At least we look good in black."

Skender sat up and applied the ointment Rosevear had given him to the affected areas of Chu's hands.

"So, did you get a chance to talk to Heuve?"

"I did." She looked simultaneously smug and sad. "He offered me a position in the citadel guard."

Skender's eyebrows went up. "You impressed him *that* much?"

"It was only a matter of time. He had to give in eventually. They always do."

He didn't rise to the bait. "What did you tell him?"

"I turned him down."

"I thought you might."

"It wasn't easy. Even though I think he was feeling guilty about sending me after Eitzen and the others, it's still a big compliment. I would've killed for it a few days back."

"Was he offended when you said no?"

"You know Heuve. He's *always* offended."

"Did you tell him you're going to change your surname?"

"Hardly. And there's no point making a big deal about that until

I work out what I'm going to change it *to*, so keep that quiet for the time being, okay?"

"I will." He smiled. "You could stay here with the Panic instead, you know."

"Are you likely to?"

"No. I want to see this through, whatever it is."

"Then so do I. If that's okay with you."

"Let me ask you something, first," he said, kneading her slippery hands with his. "Have you noticed how people keep putting us in the same room, wherever we're sleeping? It's like they know something we don't, or they think we're doing something we're not."

It was her turn to flush. "There might be a simpler explanation."

"Such as?"

"I'm one step ahead of you, making sure it stays that way. It just seems simpler," she said, cutting across him. "Would you rather share a room with Marmion? I know I wouldn't. And I'd rather put up with your snoring than Warden Banner's."

He laughed, and pulled her closer. "You're insane."

"Quite probably. And you're forgiven."

"For what?"

They were too close to look at each other. Her breath was hot on his lips. "For forgetting, of course."

He couldn't help teasing her. "Forgetting what?"

"Me." Their lips touched, briefly. "Hana."

Then her arms were around him and she was holding him, nestling her head on his shoulder. He breathed in deeply of her scent and held her back just as tightly.

"Thank you," he said into her hair, meaning every word. "That's a beautiful name."

THE PHANTOM

"The Change is neither good nor evil, but it always comes at a cost. One must let go of something in order to gain something else."
THE BOOK OF TOWERS, FRAGMENT 257

The room had fallen deathly silent. Kail could feel the tension as clearly as if it were wire connecting Sal, Marmion, and Jao with ever-tightening strands.

"What do you mean, she's gone?"

"Just what I said, Sal. She's not here. She was taken when the man'kin attacked."

Sal stared at Marmion, jaw working. The Change stirred restlessly through the room, unfocused, seeking release. For the first time, Kail could see why people feared wild talents. The young man before him contained such incredible potential, and it was building, rising, turning in on itself.

Then—gone. Sal looked down at the ground, exhaled, and looked at Jao.

"I want to know how it happened."

Kail heard a threatening edge to Sal's voice. The anger was not erased, merely buried for the time being.

The Panic female looked shaken and upset. "It wasn't an attack. I keep telling people that, but no one will believe me."

"Then what was it?"

"I think . . ." She hesitated, looking around the room at the people staring at her.

Rosevear sat next to Marmion, and Lidia Delfine sat next to him, a large bruise turning yellow down the side of her face. Heuve stood at the back of the room, looking naked without his beard. The fire had crisped it clean off, along with his eyebrows. Seneschal Schuet stood next to him with his right arm in a sling. The Guardian was elsewhere dealing with a mess of ministers "needing discipline" as she had put it.

Warden Banner was also missing, nursing a broken leg earned while standing in the man'kin's path.

"I think they only came for her," Jao said. "I know that sounds crazy, but that's the way it looked to me. They came bursting through the citadel wall. They could've crushed her and killed everyone else, if that's what they wanted. But they didn't. They stopped in front of her. She spoke to them."

"What did she say?"

"The same thing they kept saying the last time we saw them."

"'Angel says run'?"

She nodded. Her eyes shone. "They didn't say anything in return. The leader, the one in front, just knelt down like a camel and she climbed onto its back. Then they went off the way they had come, carrying her with them."

"Ways of running," Sal said slowly, "that don't require legs . . ."

The way he said it, Kail could tell it was a quote.

"Why would she go with them?" asked Lidia Delfine. "They'd just knocked down half the city."

"She had no reason to be afraid," said Sal. "Man'kin have never hurt anyone we know."

"But without an explanation, without saying *anything* . . ."

Sal looked as though he was grappling with that particular issue too. "Shilly isn't stupid. She wouldn't have gone unless she thought she had to. It might be something to do with Tom and Mawson. Maybe she hoped the man'kin would be able to lead her to them. Or maybe—" He stopped abruptly, and shrugged. "You know as much as I do."

"I'm sorry," said Jao, bowing her head with a tinkling of beads.

"Don't be." Despite Sal's obvious confusion and hurt, he was clear on that point. "It's not your fault."

Kail cleared his throat. "Did they leave a trail?"

"Clear through the city then off into the forest," said Heuve. "A child could follow it."

"Then I suggest I do just that." Kail had become accustomed to hiding the tightness in his chest, and Rosevear's ministrations seemed to be having some effect. "The sooner I leave, the better."

"I'll come with you," said Sal.

"Just hold on a moment," said Marmion, raising his hand for silence. "Let's not dive into anything too hastily."

"I'm going," said Sal, "and you can't talk me out of it."

"Let me finish. Tom spoke to you of a prophecy, did he not? Something concerning him and Shilly and a cave of ice? Doesn't that suggest to you that she's safe for the moment? Or at least that she will be, until that particular prophecy comes true?"

Sal nodded stiffly.

"Well, then. You can go after her with my blessing. I'd do it myself if I didn't have more pressing matters. But at least stop to think, first. We don't want you running into a trap."

"That does make sense," said Kail. "And there's someone else I'd like to have along. If we wait until he arrives, we'll be better off. There's safety in numbers, after all."

"Who?" asked Sal.

"Your father."

Both Sal and Marmion reacted, but neither said anything at first. Marmion, Kail assumed, would want to keep the former fugitive under his watchful eye, while Sal would probably have preferred to go on his own. They both knew it made sense, though. Highson had a stake in Shilly's fate, just as Sal did. And he was no lightweight when it came to the Change.

"All right," Sal said. "We'll ask him. If he wants to come, he can come."

Marmion said nothing, but the wrinkles around his eyes tightened.

Afterwards, while Sal talked with the city suppliers, Kail took Marmion aside. "Are you going to tell anyone what really happened down there, during the fires? Are you going to tell *me?*"

Marmion looked cornered. "It was very confusing. In the heat of the moment—"

"Bullshit. Don't try to play me. The others might not need a detailed explanation, but I do. I saved your life, remember. I *touched* it."

Relenting, Marmion took him to a small antechamber and shut the doors. They sat on two beautifully carved wooden chairs with armrests the colour of bleached bone, not quite facing one another. On a small table next to his seat, Marmion placed a small silver pin Lidia Delfine had presented him with in thanks for saving her and the Guardian during the attack on the city. In the shape of a curled banyan leaf, the pin caught the light and held it, made it flow like liquid across the smooth silver surface.

"I'm still working it out myself. When the wraith attacked us in the Divide, I put up my injured arm to drive it off. It worked, but a piece of the wraith got into me in the process. It burned in me, ate at me, but it took me a long time to work out what it was. It didn't talk, didn't try to take me over. It just made me feel . . . different."

The one-handed warden rubbed his scalp as though at an itch. "The swarm tried to get it back. That's why they attacked the citadel so boldly the very next day. My plan to trap them should have worked, but not for the reasons I thought it would. The thing in me was the bait, not the charms Kelloman and I were working. By then, though, the golem had taken charge of them, and they reined in their baser impulses. The piece in me and the one called Giltine were abandoned for the time being.

"I swear I didn't know about the ghost hand until you saved me. I thought I was just imagining things. But once I knew that the thing in me could manifest, was powerful, I wondered what else it could do.

"The weather was the key. The fire had stirred everything up, made the clouds volatile. It reminded me of spring storms back home, with the horizon alive with lightning. We'd tried air and fire, I thought, and hadn't killed the wraiths. What if I combined the fog and the forest instead? There's a tension between ground and clouds that sparks lightning; it was just a matter of tapping into the roots of the trees and letting nature do the rest. Giltine's cage acted as the lightning rod. The fact that I wasn't actually holding it—my ghost hand had that honour—protected me from the shock."

Kail acknowledged the gambit with no small amount of admiration. "That was quick thinking."

Marmion pulled a faintly irritated face. "I was lucky, and I'll admit it. If it hadn't worked, none of us would be here now."

"It did work." Kail thought of the twisted lump of inert metal found at the epicentre of the first lightning strike. "You killed six wraiths at once. That's something anyone would be proud of."

"Not quite six." Marmion reached out with his injured arm and picked up the silver pin. Invisible fingers held it in midair a palm's-length away from his bandaged stump. "I think I'm stuck with this now. Not as good as the real thing, and certainly not something I'd like to use in public, but better than nothing. Don't you think?"

Kail didn't know what to think. He had guessed part of the truth, but in the heat of the moment had feared Marmion had accepted the ghost hand as a bribe in return for the imprisoned wraith. The fact that it wasn't a powerful charm at work but something more primal, more insidious, wasn't necessarily better . . .

Marmion tossed the pin from his ghost hand to his flesh-and-blood hand.

"Please, don't tell anyone. I don't want people getting jumpy."

"I won't." Kail wasn't sure anyone would believe him.

"No, I suppose you won't. You're very good at not telling people things, like your relationship to Lodo, or that the Homunculus was with Sal on Geraint's Bluff—even when I asked you not to go behind my back again." Kail began to defend himself, but Marmion waved it away and leaned forward in his chair, his expression grim. "I don't like this expedition you have planned with Sal and Highson any more than I like that *thing* walking around among us. I will accept both only under duress, so don't take any more chances with my patience. Please."

"Yes."

"What does that mean? 'Yes' to what?"

"I'm not sure." Kail felt absurdly like laughing, being lectured to by a man he had written off four weeks earlier as a pompous fool, and actually feeling like he deserved the lecture. "Yes, you're right to be angry. I should've told you."

"You should've—but I'm honestly not that angry. Sometimes I surprise myself. We're both trying to bluff our way through this. Maybe it's the only way to cope."

"Maybe." This time Kail *did* laugh, and it felt good, as though it had released something built up in him that he hadn't been aware of. "Shilly would be pleased to see us jumping like this. She's been missing barely a day and everyone's fighting over who gets to go find her."

"I'm not. I can't. I get to fly a balloon up the side of a mountain in search of something that might not exist—and might kill me if it does."

"So that's your plan?"

"Once we've honoured Eitzen and the others, yes. The kingsfolk have returned all the goods stolen from us, so we have no shortage of supplies." Marmion issued a sound that was almost a laugh. "From bonefish to balloon. If you can think of a better way, let me know."

Kail thought of the seer in Laure and what she had told him: *You're walking to the end of the world and do not know it.* He felt he had gained a better idea of what he was doing, but that wasn't the same thing as knowing why. *Blood will run like water . . .*

He leaned forward and held out a hand. "The same goes for you, of course."

They shook, flesh to flesh.

We've both changed, thought Kail as he went off in search of the young runner who had stopped to heal him when she should have been delivering her message to the Guardian. After thanking her, he had an appointment with Rosevear. He would need as much of the local salves and unguents as he could carry if he was going to survive the hunt for Shilly. Unconsciously, his right hand crept up to the pouch around his neck and gripped it tightly. He could feel the Caduceus fragment vibrating through the parchment wrapped tightly around it.

I just hope, he thought, *it's a change for the better . . .*

Sal barely heard a word Marmion spoke as he outlined his plan for a combined expedition of foresters, outsiders, and kingsfolk not long after lunch. Sal hadn't eaten. Inside he felt only tension and worry, as though his intestines were maritime ropes coiled in complicated knots.

Shilly was gone. First Kemp, then Tom and Mawson, then Eitzen, and now her. It seemed that she had gone of her own accord, but that didn't make her absence any easier to accept. Nor was it made any easier by the ache in his gut that told him she was still alive, somewhere. The last time he had seen her, on the jagged slopes of Geraint's Bluff, she had been worried about *him* disappearing. Events since then had taken turns neither of them could have anticipated.

He remembered the confrontation with Upuaut, its taunting of him with knowledge about his missing friends. Had he missed an opportunity to find Shilly without knowing it? Would he have decided any differently then, *had* he known?

Arguments and suggestions filled the meeting room as densely as smoke. He had to get out. Ignoring questioning looks, he stood and slipped quietly out the door.

A guard peeled away from the many watching the entrance and

followed him as he wandered, at random at first, through the citadel. Night had fallen some time ago. The air quivered with the smell of trees and cooking and smoke from spot fires, which hadn't been fully extinguished, drifting up from below. He needed to get higher, away from everything. He needed to think.

As he climbed the steps to the top of the citadel wall, where Jao had said that she, Banner, and Shilly had been held captive, he thought of Marmion's plan to cross the mountains by air and remembered the dream Tom had told them about, seemingly months ago in Fundelry.

Something dark and ancient lived there, under the ice, and it knew we were coming.

Under a starless sky, not far from the hole the man'kin had made, he saw only doom ahead of them all. He leaned on the wall and breathed deeply, as though filling his lungs might somehow clear the pressure mounting in his chest. The citadel's giant bell had been salvaged from the wreckage apparently, but that was very small consolation for other losses.

"We live our lives in shadow."

The woman's voice came from his right, further along the wall. He looked up with a start, wondering who had spoken. Too deep and mature to be Shilly; too smooth and human in inflection to be Jao.

His eyes, still adjusting to the darkness, made out a shadowy shape, head tilted slightly back.

"I saw it, briefly. The sky, I mean. My mother used to talk about it. She went for a ride in a captured balloon once, so high she came out the top of the clouds. I never quite believed what she said. It didn't seem real, that there could be so much beyond the forest, outside our world. Why should there be? It doesn't make sense—yet there it is." The woman sighed. "My grandmother was furious when she found out, and had my father flogged for allowing it. He was, in fact, very nearly dismissed from service. Mother only stopped that by threatening to elope."

Sal knew her, then, as the Guardian, absent from the meeting on the pretext of attending to matters of state. Behind her, standing close but not intrusively so, Sal made out the silhouette of the Seneschal.

"It's hard to imagine," Schuet said, his gravelly voice softened by affection. "Your father made out he'd never put a foot wrong his entire life."

"That's what parents do, isn't it? We paint ourselves in the colours our own parents wore—and we see through our children's disguises as though they were gauze."

Sal felt uncomfortably as though eavesdropping. Neither had commented on his presence, although surely they couldn't have missed his arrival. The fog soaked up all other noise around them. His breathing sounded horribly loud to his ears.

"What do you think, Sal?" the Guardian asked suddenly, startling him. "Is your mind broader for seeing the world? Are your eyes opened wide by travel and exploration?"

He cleared his throat, not sure where the question was leading. "I don't truly know, Guardian. I've been travelling most of my life. My father and I never stopped for long when I was a child. We wandered up and down all along the borderlands between the Interior and the Strand, always on the run from the Sky Wardens. It wasn't until I did finally stop that I had time to think. To learn." *From Shilly*, he added to himself.

"I see." He dimly made out the Guardian nodding, but he couldn't read her expression. "Perhaps change is enough, then. Where it comes from doesn't matter, or how."

"Lidia is brave and resourceful," said the Seneschal, leaning closer. "And she is restless, like your mother."

"Our son is dead." The pitch of the Guardian's voice rose in a threnody. "I would not lose our daughter next, to a world I neither understand nor care for."

"She's no safer here, as recent events have proved. Just because Panic and human are talking doesn't mean all our problems will be solved. It will take more than the mist closing over us again to keep the world out."

"You're thinking of sending Lidia with Marmion," Sal said. "That's what you're talking about."

"Yes." The Guardian sounded incredibly weary. "She wants to go. Maybe I could stop her if I expressly forbade it. Maybe she would go anyway. If I am to lose her, I would do so without harsh words between us. But I wouldn't lose her at all, given the choice."

Sal wondered what he would do in her shoes. Was it better to keep something caged and safe than free and in peril? He thought of Shilly and his jealousy of Kail, and felt bad for wanting to keep them apart. Now their positions were reversed, he wished more than ever that she was still around.

The polished wood under his hands felt as smooth as stone, but he could sense, through the Change, the way it had once been living. Fibres lay twisted in knots like ancient muscles. These planks had once held a tree together, had once been part of the greater creature humans called "the forest." It still remembered life. At his urging, the wood began to glow like a brand, casting a faint reddish glow that seemed bright in the darkness.

"Sometimes we just have to let go of things," he said, "and hope they come back. That's what Highson, my real father, told me once. He gave me away, with my mother, before I was even born. The odds were against him seeing either of us again. When he did, we were both caged, and we didn't want to be there. It went . . . badly." He thought of his mother, tricked by one of the ghosts of the Haunted City into believing its promise of a way out. If Highson's mad plan to rescue her from the Void Beneath had worked, she would have been trapped inside the Homunculus instead. Would that have been better, he wondered, or just another cage? "I escaped, but now I'm back. We're still working things out. He knows, I think, that it wasn't him I was running from."

Even as he said the words, it occurred to him that Highson might not know that at all.

The Guardian's eyes gleamed back at him.

"I'm an optimistic person," she said. "I will try to believe that you'll find Shilly and that my daughter will survive. Marmion will locate the source of the floods, and the evil rising in the mountains can be cast down. I will cling to these things here where I can do little but wait to see what eventuates—reassured by the knowledge that, if the world ends, I will lose no more than anyone else."

The Seneschal put an arm around her shoulders.

"Come back to us, Sal," he said. "Come back to us in peaceful times, and bring Shilly with you. Tell her Minister Sousoura owes her an apology, and that our hospitality will be better then."

"I will."

The pair drew away into the darkness, leaving him alone with his bodyguard, who looked steadfastly out into the night, pretending not to have heard a word. Sal set free the wood beneath his fingertips, and the crimson glow died. The air felt colder than it had before, but he didn't care. Its crispness was bracing, clearing his head of the day's cobwebs and tangles.

Okay, Carah, he sent out into the night. *You've got what you wanted. Highson has had his day with the Homunculus; it's told him everything he needs to know. It'll be just the two of us on your tail, with Lodo's nephew as adjudicator. Wherever you are, whatever you're doing, we'll find you—and each other—along the way.*

He waited a long time for a reply, but nothing came. Not even the use of her heart-name could penetrate whatever hid her from his senses.

Eventually, when the curdling mist had brought ice to every square centimetre of his skin, he went back inside and began packing for the journey ahead.

THE CABAL

"We are beams of white light caught by a prism. At the end of our lives, we look back at the brilliant colours that make us whole: the fiery red of our childhood; the cool yellows and greens of our middle years; the bluish purple of age and decay. Beyond those shades lie colours our ordinary eyes can't discern. We cannot know, except by hearsay, what happened before we were born; we only glimpse in dreams what might come after. A seer, however, is different. A seer perceives the world in all its colours at once, recombined as though through a second prism—and the beam of pure, terrible white they see is a dangerous light indeed."

THE BOOK OF TOWERS, EXEGESIS 5:5

After a full day riding on the man'kin's back, Shilly wished she'd found a new way to run that involved padded chairs and protection from the rain. Since leaving Milang, she had been relentlessly soaked, whipped by branches, pounded by unyielding stone, and ignored. Nothing she said provoked a response, not even when she had threatened to jump off if the man'kin didn't tell her where she was going. They were smarter than they looked, obviously.

She hung on, determined to find out what was going on. The uncertainty of what lay ahead bothered but didn't frighten her. If the man'kin had wanted her dead, they would have killed her as soon as they saw her. The fact they hadn't killed her told her that another fate entirely waited at the end of her journey. What that was, she would only discover when she arrived.

The day grew old and still the man'kin ran: up and down valleys, fording rivers, climbing cliffs, leaping fallen trees, not missing a single step. Birds scattered at the sound of their heavy footfalls. Every bone in her body felt broken. She was afraid to look down at herself for fear of the bruising she would find.

Finally, as the fog turned golden with dusk, the man'kin came to a narrow ravine covered with a dense growth of vines and tree roots. Trickling water echoed from its depths. Her ride made its way almost delicately along a meandering stream, its clawed feet crunching on the hard stone. The air was very still.

Where the ravine should have been darkest and most quiet, a ghostly green glow shone. The burbling of conversation competed with the stream.

Shilly had wondered many times who would be waiting for her at the end of her journey. She never expected to see all of them at once.

Vehofnehu was the first to acknowledge her, rising from a low, knuckled crouch and executing a courtly bow as the man'kin halted in front of the group and stooped for her to dismount. She gingerly did so, feeling as though the bones of her bad leg had been smashed to jelly. Leaning on her stick with greater need than normal, she limped around the broad shoulders of the man'kin to confront the group.

"Hello, Shilly," said Tom around a mouthful of roasted chicken. Her stomach growled at the sight, but her confusion was too great even to contemplate eating.

Behind him sat three of the Quorum, watching her with luminous jade eyes, and Mawson, propped upright by a cloth-covered bundle. Over him loomed the massive, rounded shape of the Angel, blind and expressionless.

"You—" She wanted to say something appropriately outraged, but the right words failed her. Yes, she was angry, but she was also desperately curious. "What in the Goddess's name are you all doing out here?"

The empyricist grinned broadly. "For exactly that reason, Shilly. Please, join us. We'll tell you everything."

The ground shook gently beneath her as she hobbled closer. She looked up nervously, dreading a rockfall, but the tangle of roots and vines above effectively kept such at bay.

"This is Shathra, Bahman, and Armaiti." The three glowing figures didn't react when introduced. Scattered tiles, each displaying a different letter, lay in lines on the loamy ground between them. One line spelt out the cryptic phrase: *world-tree needs pruning.*

"They already know who you are," Vehofnehu went on, reminding her of the time she had seen one of them by the waterfall, and the sense of recognition she had gleaned from that quick glance. "We've been waiting for you. Our numbers are almost complete."

"'Our numbers'?" she echoed, finally finding her tongue. "Who exactly are you, anyway?"

"Sit, Shilly. Eat," he insisted, and she gave in. He squatted opposite her on wiry, flexible legs. Tom's gaze didn't shift from her even as he continued to eat. "We are those who have some knowledge of what's to come—although you must understand that what I mean by 'knowledge' is an ambiguous thing, just like the world itself and the future awaiting it. We know enough to understand that we don't know enough. That's why we have gathered together. To compare notes, if you like. Between all of us, we have a chance of determining what path to take."

"I don't understand," she said. "Don't you already know what's going to happen? You—" she pointed at the Quorum members "—travel backwards in time, so you've seen our future already. You—" Mawson and the Angel "—see all times as one. And you—" Tom didn't react when she singled him out "—have been dreaming about it for weeks. How much more information do you need?"

Vehofnehu was nodding excitedly long before she finished. This was the most animated she had ever seen him. "On the face of it, my dear, you're absolutely right. But the face is just one aspect of a person, and it's also just one aspect of the truth. We see the future from many different angles, and what we see is always incomplete. Tom's dreams are fragments; the man'kin see all possible futures, not just one; the Holy Immortals—as I have known the Quorum for many, many years—are still recovering from that future, and their memories are shaky, traumatised things. And then there's me. Back in my observatory, I studied the movements of the stars, seeing reflected in them the deformations of this Earth. Even there I found only ambiguity and confusion.

"Into this confusion stepped two people. One of them was you, although your significance was not immediately obvious. Only much later, when I had organised the extraction of your friends Tom and Mawson, did the man'kin mention the dreams you've been having. The pattern, the sand, the voice. You've been struggling to understand their meaning, and I believe that I have deciphered them. They're a message, a very important message indeed, and I think our best efforts should be expended in doing as it says—once we work out what that is."

"I thought of that." She stared at him as one slightly concussed, hit by too much information at once. "But who could it be from?"

The Panic empyricist grinned. "I'm pretty certain you wouldn't believe me."

"Why not?"

With a clinking of tiles, the glowing man called Shathra spelt out a new message: *not all golems are evil.*

She stared at the words, unable to decipher them even though their meaning was simple. How did they connect to her question, to her dreams? Was Shathra trying to tell her that the message came from a golem? She couldn't work it out.

Trading one mystery for another, she asked: "So who is the second person?"

The empyricist barked with laughter, and spent a moment spelling out her question with the tiles—so the Holy Immortals could appreciate the joke too, she assumed. She flushed and balled her hands into fists, feeling mocked and left out of some grand conspiracy.

Tom still watched her, as silent as a mouse from his corner of the group. She thought of him, just a handful of days ago, saying *I've dreamed all our deaths* as casually as though talking about eating breakfast or taking a shit, and she wondered what he was thinking about now.

"Listen," she said. "I came here for answers. If you're not going to give me any, I might as well go back to Milang and work it out for myself."

"Let me tell you something you already know." The empyricist calmed her with outstretched palms, patting the air, and she knew she would never get used to the sight of his long fingers and short thumbs like that. "You're here for a reason. We are all here for a reason. What's coming sends shock waves backwards in time, changing the world in ways big and small. More wild talents; restless man'kin; new movements in the stars; and dreams like yours, filled with strange urgencies. Those of us who see the symptoms must band together to do something about the problem. You're part of that now. You can't go back to Milang."

She started to protest, but he hadn't finished. "You're not a prisoner, Shilly. Don't think that. You came of your own free will, as we knew you would. Sal will follow, but we have a good headstart, and that gives us some time. When he catches up, you can go with him. Indeed, it seems important that you do, judging by what Tom has told us. We don't want to stand between the two of you."

Still Tom said nothing, but she heard his words as clear as day: *Kemp is the only one who stands between you . . .* he had said on the bone-ship, *when the end comes.*

"Where's Kemp?" she asked. "What did you do with him?"

"Let's talk about golems, first," said Vehofnehu, shifting on his rump. "Shathra is quite right. They are not all evil, although they seem so to us. You've met a couple and have had good reason to fight them, but there are others with different agendas. They move through the world at an angle to us, finding their own way to their own destinations. When our paths cross, it can be for good or ill, but they have as much right to be there as we do. And some of them can be beneficial.

"There is a crown in my observatory," he started to explain, "a simple circle of iron—"

"I've seen it," she interrupted him. "Sal put it on, then Griel. The last I heard, Oriel was considering wearing it."

That took him off-guard, which pleased her. "Oriel? What on Earth was Griel thinking?" He put the issue aside with an obvious effort. "My point about the crown is this: it's occupied by a creature that has no name, which grants to its wearer a vision of his or her profoundest desire. I've worn it, and I can tell you that the visions are powerfully seductive."

She nodded. "Sal and Griel were very different afterwards. The crown seemed to make them capable of anything."

"That's the charm of the crown. It's not really doing anything but unlocking its wearer's potential. The crown thrives on the achievement of that potential, or at least the striving towards it. It's not harming the wearer, but it is, technically, a parasite, a kind of golem that lives in the crown rather than in a person's mind."

"And that makes it okay?"

"I don't know. That would depend on who is wearing it, I guess, and what they do with their potential."

She could see that, but she still struggled with what it meant. People could be coerced by dreams as well as threats, and coercion of all sorts struck her as being intrinsically wrong.

"This is where you talk about the glast," she guessed. "It's a sort of golem too. Right?"

The empyricist nodded.

"And the glast is the second person?"

With a flick of one long wrist, Vehofnehu peeled back the cloth covering the bundle beside him.

Shilly tried not to react, but her shock was difficult to suppress. Kemp's body lay under the cloth, curled into a fetal ball with knees tight up against his chin. His eyes were open but saw nothing. He could have been dead for all the movement he made; even his breathing appeared to have ceased. But he wasn't dead. He was something else.

In appearance, he had changed utterly. His flesh was black and glassy. His tattoos were white and seemed to hover a fingernail's thickness above his skin. The blacks of his eyes had also turned white and gleamed with a light of their own.

The thing before her was still recognisably *him*. His features were unchanged; the sheer size of his body was unaltered. That it wasn't really him was hard to accept.

"Is he—?" She swallowed. "Is *it* awake?"

"Not yet, but I don't think we'll have long to wait."

"What makes you think it's going to help us? It attacked the boneship, remember?"

"That was no accident, Shilly. It was trying to become one of you, I think, in order to communicate. Sal was probably its first target, but it settled on Kemp when Sal proved too strong. We'll find out what it wants to say when it wakes up—but I can't believe it went to so much trouble without having something to offer."

Shilly nodded distractedly. A cold feeling spread through her at the thought that it might have been Sal lying in front of her, not Kemp. She would have preferred none of her friends to be hurt, had she a choice, but she was acutely aware now of how much worse it could have been, from her point of view.

"And then what?" she asked. "Where is all this leading us?"

"That's the problem," Vehofnehu said. "The future is hidden from us, so we're going to have to make it for ourselves. That's why we're gathering, here and elsewhere, to increase the clarity of our foresight and to muster our full strength. We'll need all we can muster to make sure we *have* a future, to take on Yod and erase it from our world once and for all."

She nodded, thinking: *it had slept for an eternity, but was waking now, and it was hungry.*

"Is this what you dream, Tom?" she asked, remembering his coldness in Vehofnehu's observatory, the sense of increasing distance between him and everyone else.

Tom nodded. Among his new friends he looked perfectly comfortable. *Normal.*

"Have you always known it would end up here?"

He shrugged his bony shoulders. "Dreams are confusing. I see lots of things."

"He does indeed," said Vehofnehu. "Good and bad, bad and good."

"I see Fundelry a lot, but that doesn't mean I'll ever go back there."

The letter-tiles tinkled again, spelling out the word *Goddess.*

Shilly frowned at the tiles, wondering what that interjection could possibly mean. The Holy Immortals were watching her, their glowing eyes creepy and intense. The Angel was watching her too, and so was Mawson. They were all watching her, she realised, and all of a sudden she didn't like it much at all.

"Well, what's your big plan? How are we going to kick Yod out of here, once and for all?"

Vehofnehu indicated the tiles. "My friends here have already answered your question."

"The Goddess? She's just a myth. The weather-worker of the village Tom and I grew up in used to tell me the old stories of the Cataclysm, but that doesn't mean . . ." She trailed off. Vehofnehu was nodding, and she realised that writing off stories about the Cataclysm could be slightly stupid, given the things she'd seen in recent weeks.

"The Goddess is real," said Vehofnehu. "I knew her, and I know where to find her body. We're going to waken her. She's going to show us how to get rid of Yod."

Disorientation swept through her. A goddess and a glast, a conspiracy of seers, glowing green people from the future, a mad not-quite-human—and her, a cripple with bad dreams. What sort of army was this? What hope of success had any plan they concocted?

"You're insane," she said.

"Quite possibly." The empyricist grinned.

"And you, Mawson—I can't believe you're going along with this!"

"The time has come to stop running," said the man'kin.

"Is that what the Angel thinks, too?"

"The Angel says fight."

She felt like putting her head in her hands and either weeping or howling with laughter. *More gets done in the shadows than in the light,* Griel had said, but that reassured her not one jot.

"Why me?"

Vehofnehu barked again. "Where else would you rather be, Shilly, than at the centre of the world? You've already spent too long at the periphery, watching as others excel. Here's your chance to make a difference. Here's your chance to shine. You won't turn us down, not while there is breath in your body."

"You think so?"

"Prove me wrong and I promise that the man'kin will take you back."

She looked at them, all watching her, and knew Vehofnehu was right. At least about that. While there was a chance she could help, she had to stay. She was tired of hobbling along behind everyone else, always feeling left out. Marmion seemed to respect her now, and that was an improvement, but what use was respect when she still had no talent, no official position, no clear role except to boss people around?

"All right," she said. "You've got me. But only if you tell me one thing."

Vehofnehu spread his unusual hands, the picture of reason. "Ask away."

"Who is sending me the dreams? Why have they picked me to be part of your little gang?" *Because I'm going to wring their neck when I eventually catch up with them.*

"There's only one possible person," he said, sobering, "and I don't think she had a lot of choice. It's you, you see. You from the future—or from *a* future, at least—reaching back to give you what you need to defeat Yod. Only time and unlocking the message will reveal what that is. Does that answer the question to your satisfaction?"

She stared at him for a long time, weighing up possible responses. When she did speak again, the single word made birds, not long settled, take to the night sky in a flurry.

To conclude in

The Devoured Earth
Books of the Cataclysm: Four

Author's Note

In a forest, no tree stands alone. Root systems extend for kilometres, linking plant to plant by means invisible to humans and other ground-dwellers. The same applies to writers—this one in particular.

Thanks specifically to: Deborah Halpern for the use of her magnificent creation; Nick Linke and Robin Potanin for much-needed and persistent friendship during the last few months; Seb and Rachel Yeaman, my "other" family; dear friends and respected peers on the Mt. Lawley Mafia, Visions, and Clarion South lists; and Kim Selling who, even while pursuing her own life adventures, still finds time to help with plant names and other important details.

All this, and much more, is deeply appreciated.

Sean Williams
Adelaide/Nagoya, July 2005

ABOUT THE AUTHOR

O ne of Australia's leading speculative fiction writers, Sean Williams is the author of numerous works for adults, young adults, and children, covering new space opera, science fiction thrillers, fantasy, and horror. He has also written for *Star Wars* and *Doctor Who*, two franchises he has loved since a child. A winner of the Writers of the Future Contest, recipient of the "SA Great" Literature Award, and a *New York Times* best seller, he lives with his wife and family in Adelaide, South Australia. You can visit his Web site at www.sean williams.com.